Vampire Game

JUDAL

Vampire Game Vol. 9
Created by Judal

Translation - Patrick Coffman
English Adaptation - Jason Deitrich
Associate Editor - Tim Beedle
Copy Editors - Suzanne Waldman and Neil Rae
Retouch and Lettering - JUNEMOON Studios
Production Artist - John Lo
Cover Design - Anna Kernbaum

Editor - Rob Valois
Digital Imaging Manager - Chris Buford
Pre-Press Manager - Antonio DePietro
Production Managers - Jennifer Miller and Mutsumi Miyazaki
Art Director - Matt Alford
Managing Editor - Jill Freshney
VP of Production - Ron Klamert
President and C.O.O. - John Parker
Publisher and C.E.O. - Stuart Levy

A  Manga

TOKYOPOP Inc.
5900 Wilshire Blvd. Suite 2000
Los Angeles, CA 90036

E-mail: info@TOKYOPOP.com
Come visit us online at www.TOKYOPOP.com

ISBN: 1-59182-561-X

First TOKYOPOP printing: November 2004

10 9 8 7 6 5 4 3 2 1

Printed in the USA

VAMPIRE GAME

Volume 9

by

JUDAL

HAMBURG // LONDON // LOS ANGELES // TOKYO

VAMPIRE GAME

The Story Thus Far...

This is the tale of the Vampire King Duzell and his quest for revenge against the good King Phelios, a valiant warrior who slew the vampire a century ago. Now Duzell has returned, reincarnated as a feline foe to deliver woe to... well, that's the problem. Who is the reincarnation of King Phelios?

For the people of Zi Alda, Prince Yuujel has been missing in action for several years. What they don't know is that he's been alive and well, teaching magic to Princess Ishtar and calling himself Yujinn. The princess, Duzell and Darres are all in the dark as well. So, when Yujinn arrives in Zi Alda and reveals that he's been living a dual life, it's understandable that some people might be a little upset. However, one of those people is the not-so-lovely Lady Leene, and as anyone who values their existence could tell you, you really don't want to make Leene mad.

Ishtar didn't come to Zi Alda looking for trouble, but trouble has a way of catching up with our beloved princess. With Leene mistakenly believing that her beloved Yuujel has fallen in love with Ishtar, trouble has not only caught up with Ishtar, it's wrestled her to the ground and given her a mean set of noogies. Possessing a triptych of poisonous pills, each destructive in its own way, Leene has the ways and means to do away with Ishtar...permanently.

However, as we all know, Ishtar doesn't love Yujinn, she loves Darres. And in a fit of perfect irony, it's been revealed that Yujinn loves Darres as well. Duzell, meanwhile, has been busy contending with a former lover of his own--the Vampire Countess Diaage. And where does Vord fit into this show of amorous antics? You got us.

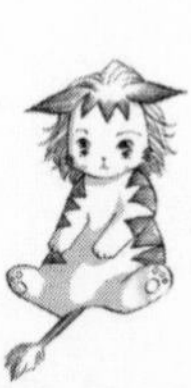

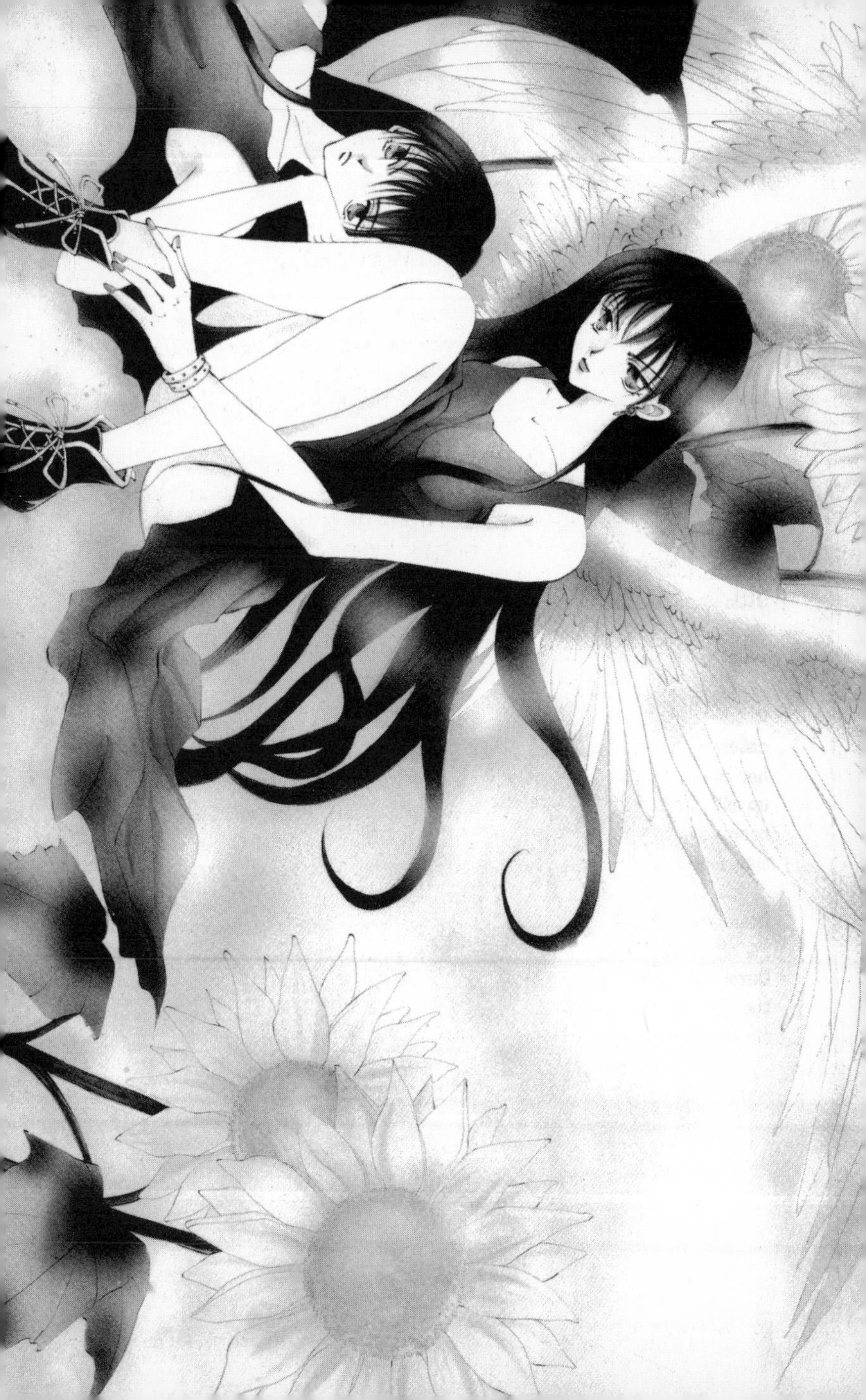

Table of Contents

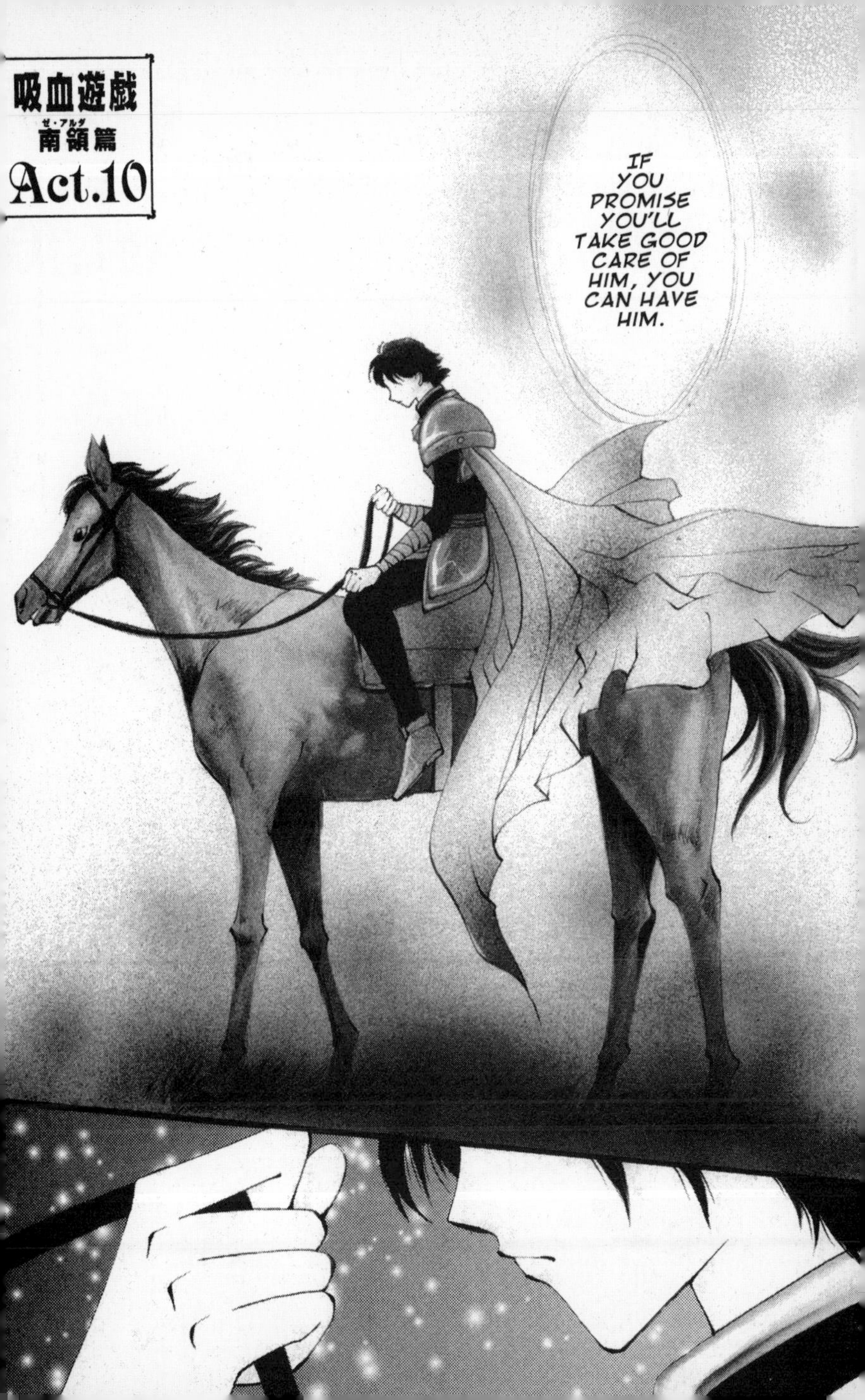
吸血遊戯
ゼ・アルダ
南領篇
Act.10
IF YOU PROMISE YOU'LL TAKE GOOD CARE OF HIM, YOU CAN HAVE HIM.

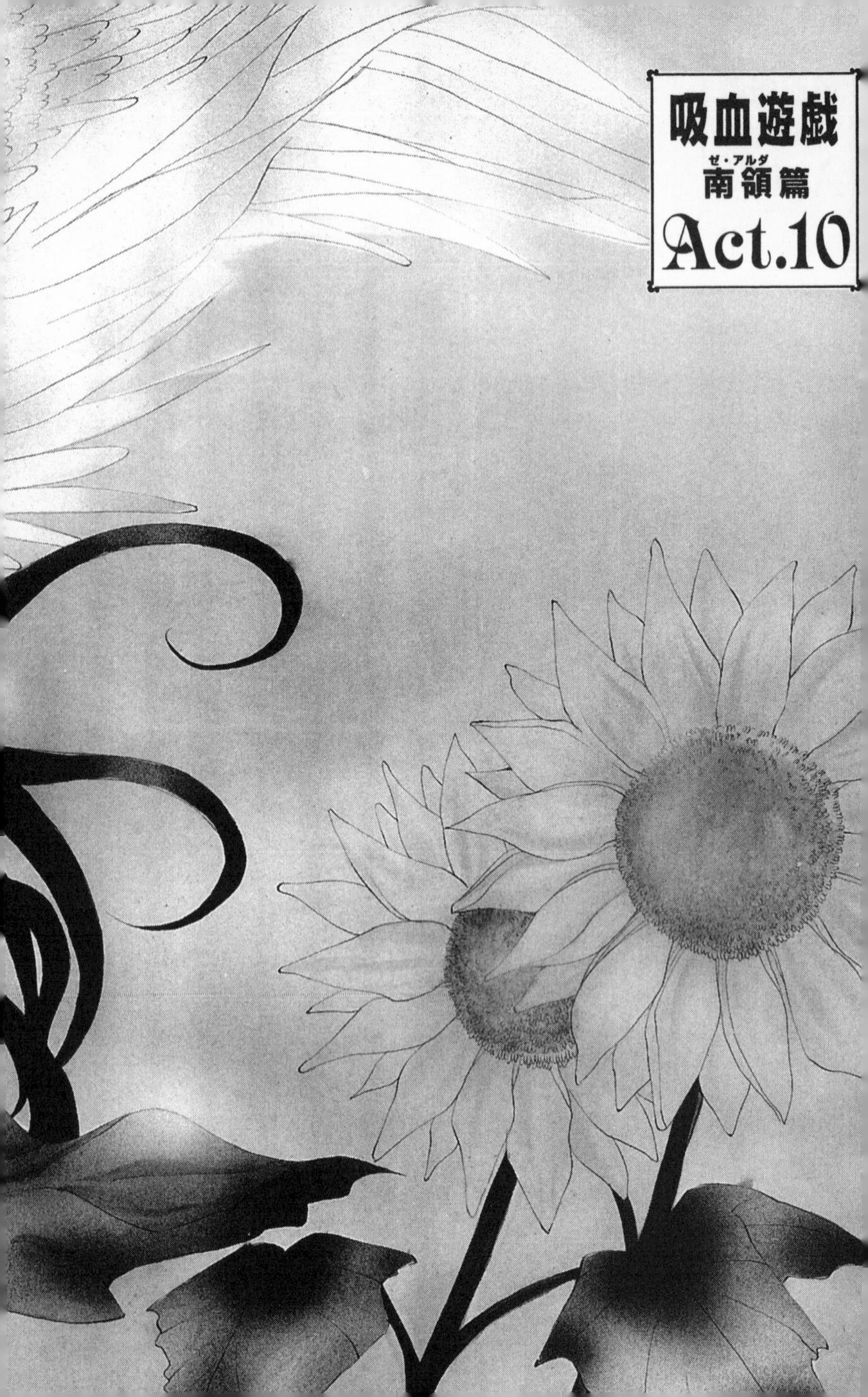
吸血遊戯
ゼ・アルダ
南領篇
Act.10

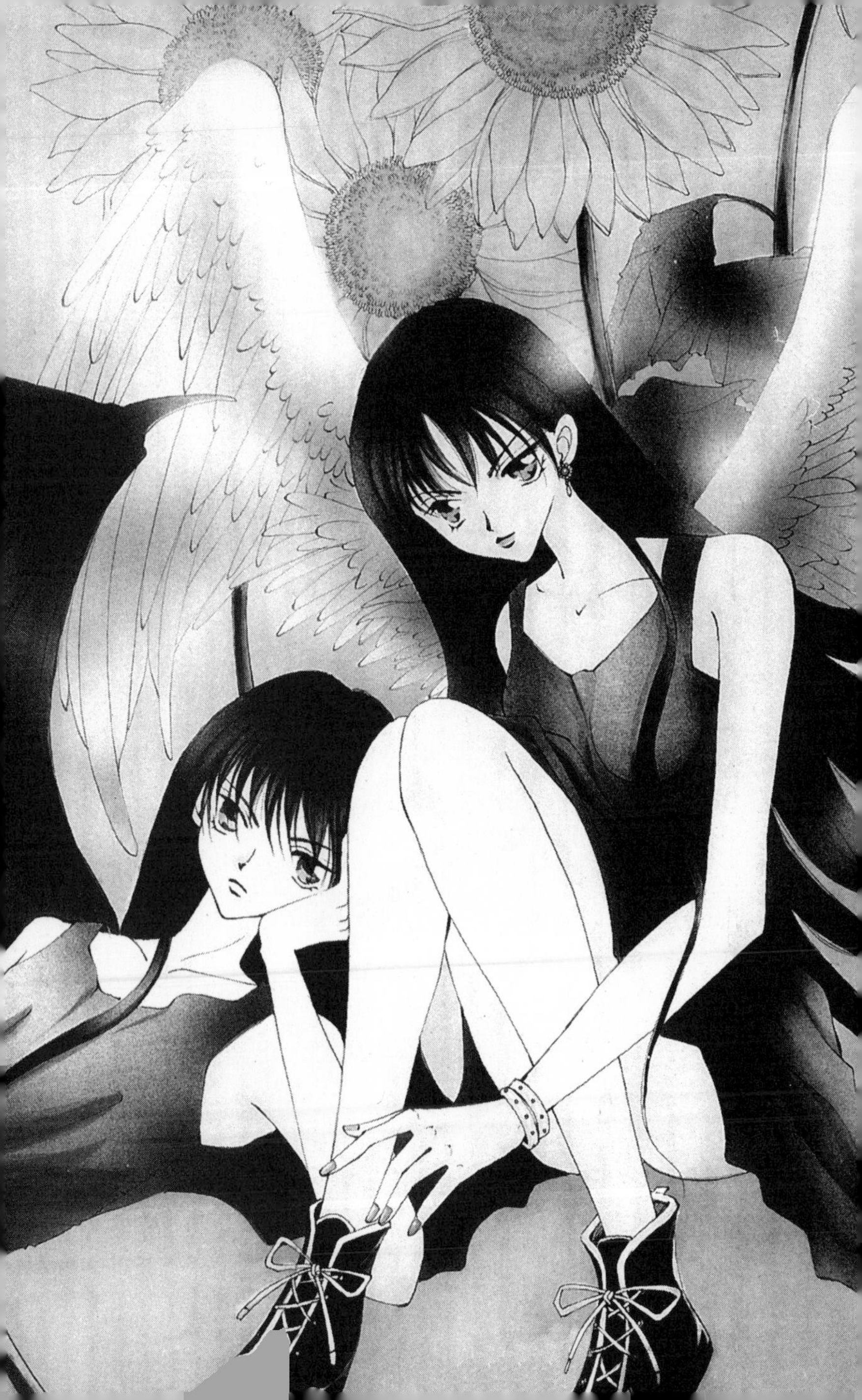

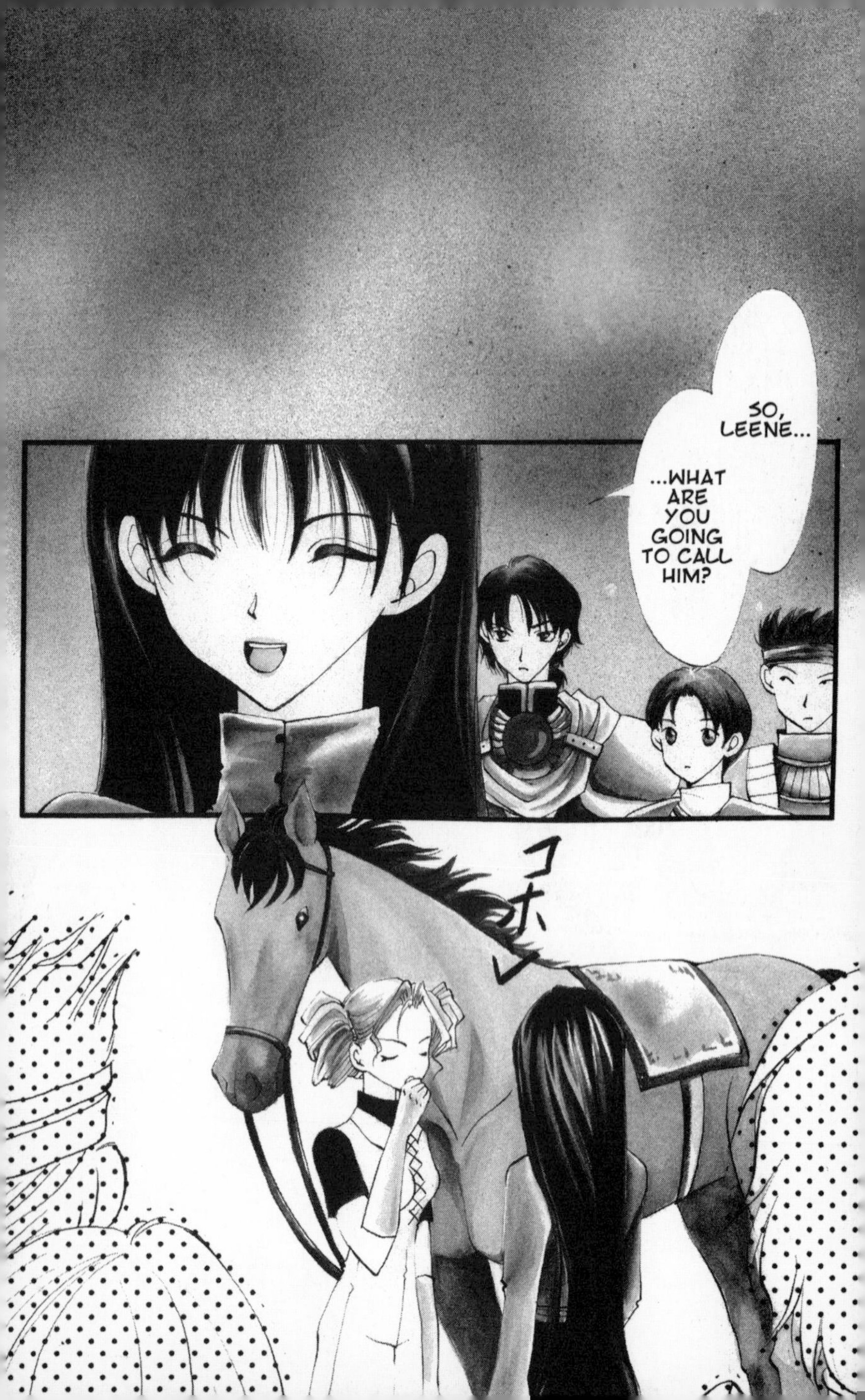
SO, LEENE...
...WHAT ARE YOU GOING TO CALL HIM?
コホン

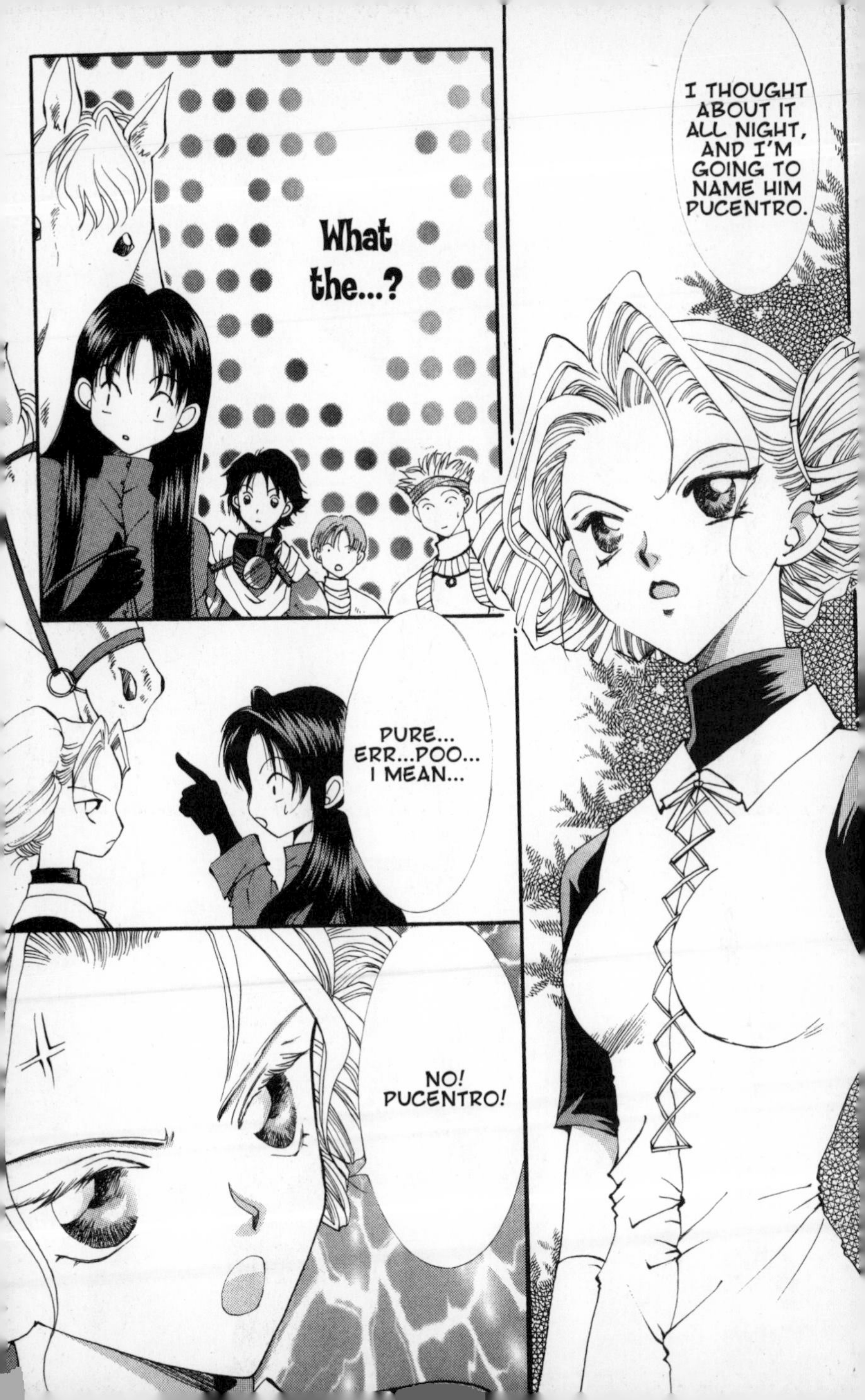
I THOUGHT ABOUT IT ALL NIGHT, AND I'M GOING TO NAME HIM PUCENTRO.
What the...?
PURE... ERR...POO... I MEAN...
NO! PUCENTRO!

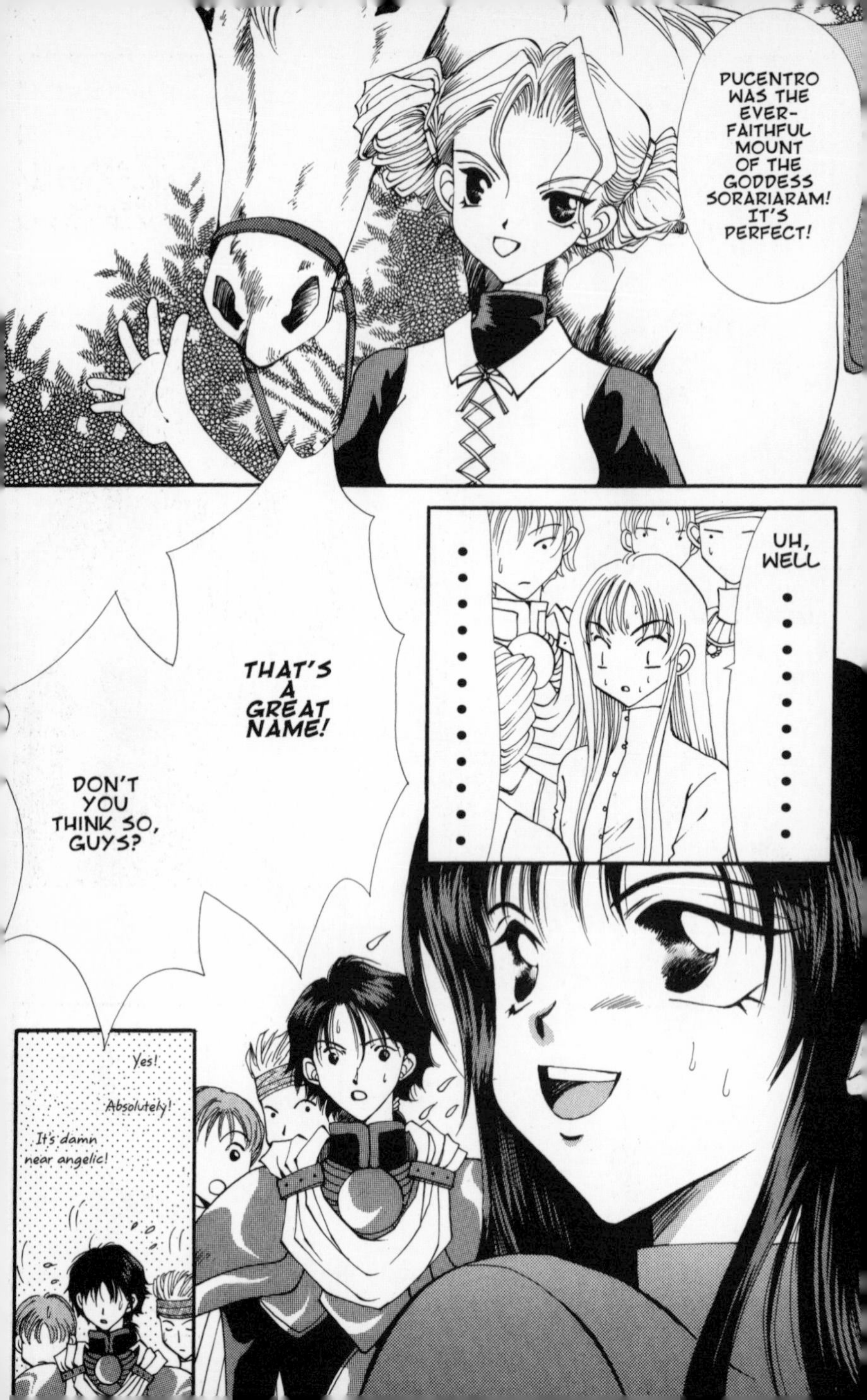
PUCENTRO WAS THE EVER-FAITHFUL MOUNT OF THE GODDESS SORARIARAM! IT'S PERFECT!
UH, WELL ...
...
THAT'S A GREAT NAME!
DON'T YOU THINK SO, GUYS?
Yes!
Absolutely!
It's damn near angelic!

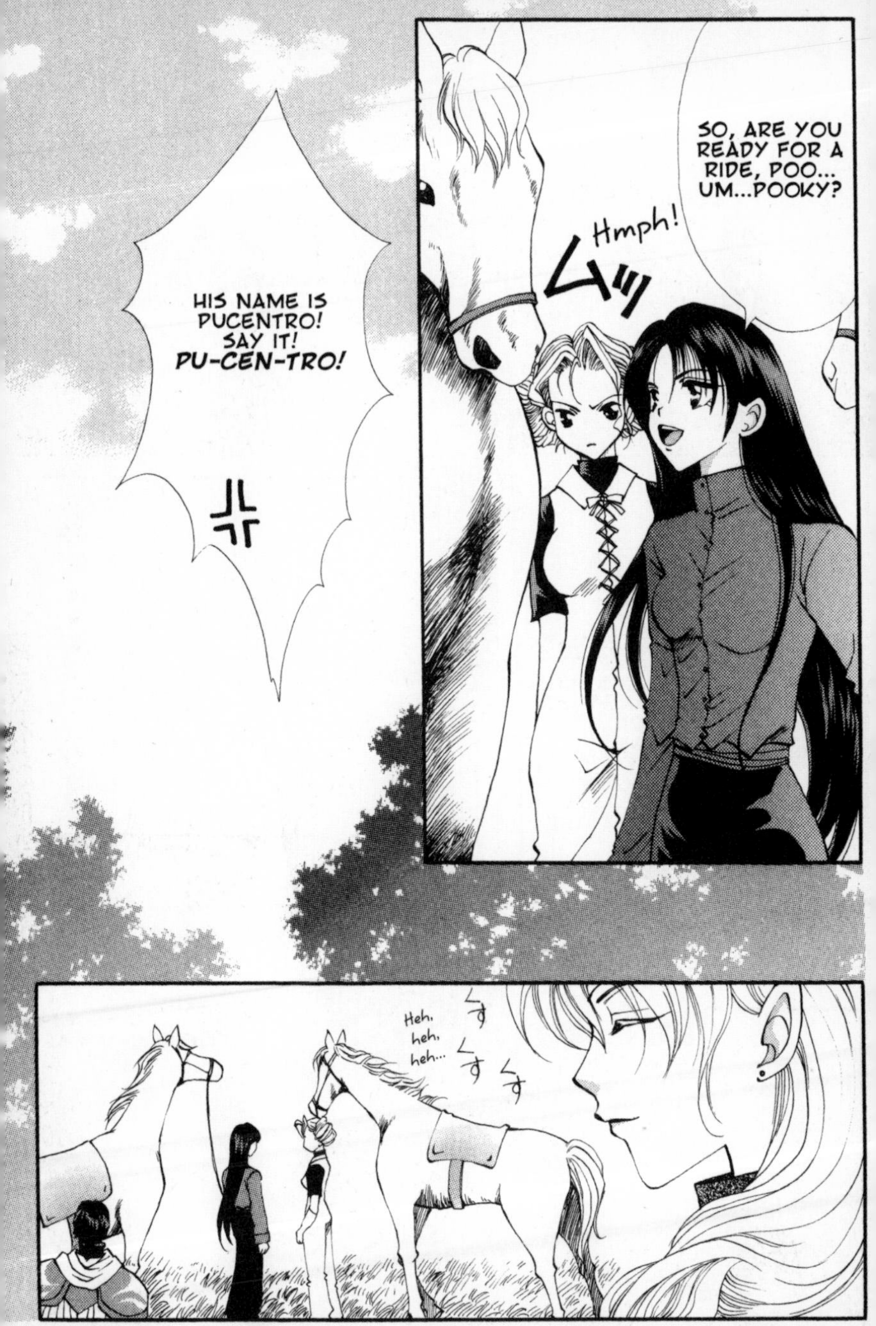
SO, ARE YOU READY FOR A RIDE, POO... UM...POOKY?
Hmph!
ムッ
HIS NAME IS PUCENTRO! SAY IT! **PU-CEN-TRO!**
Heh, heh, heh...
くすくすくす

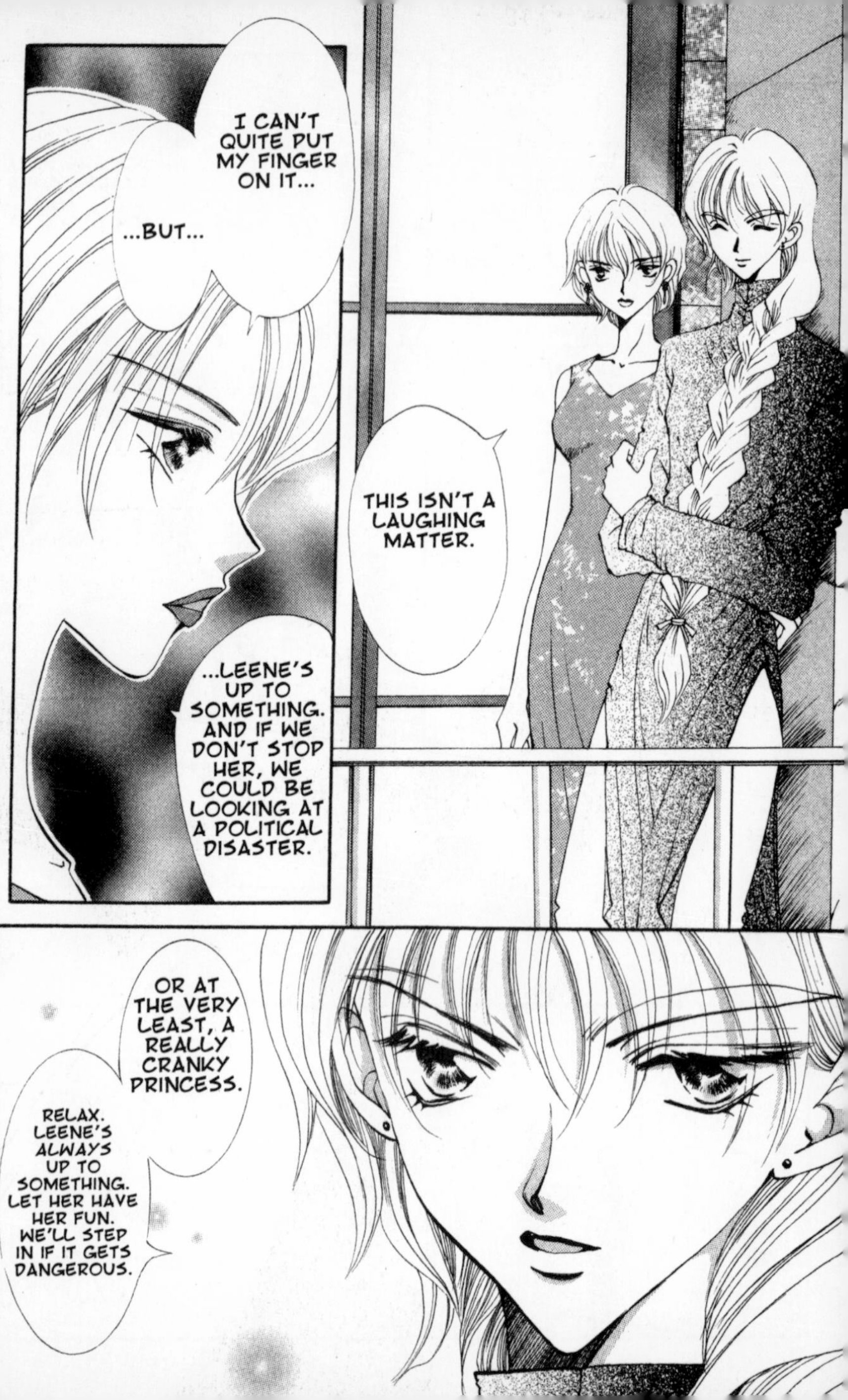
THIS ISN'T A LAUGHING MATTER.
I CAN'T QUITE PUT MY FINGER ON IT...
...BUT...
...LEENE'S UP TO SOMETHING. AND IF WE DON'T STOP HER, WE COULD BE LOOKING AT A POLITICAL DISASTER.
OR AT THE VERY LEAST, A REALLY CRANKY PRINCESS.
RELAX. LEENE'S ALWAYS UP TO SOMETHING. LET HER HAVE HER FUN. WE'LL STEP IN IF IT GETS DANGEROUS.

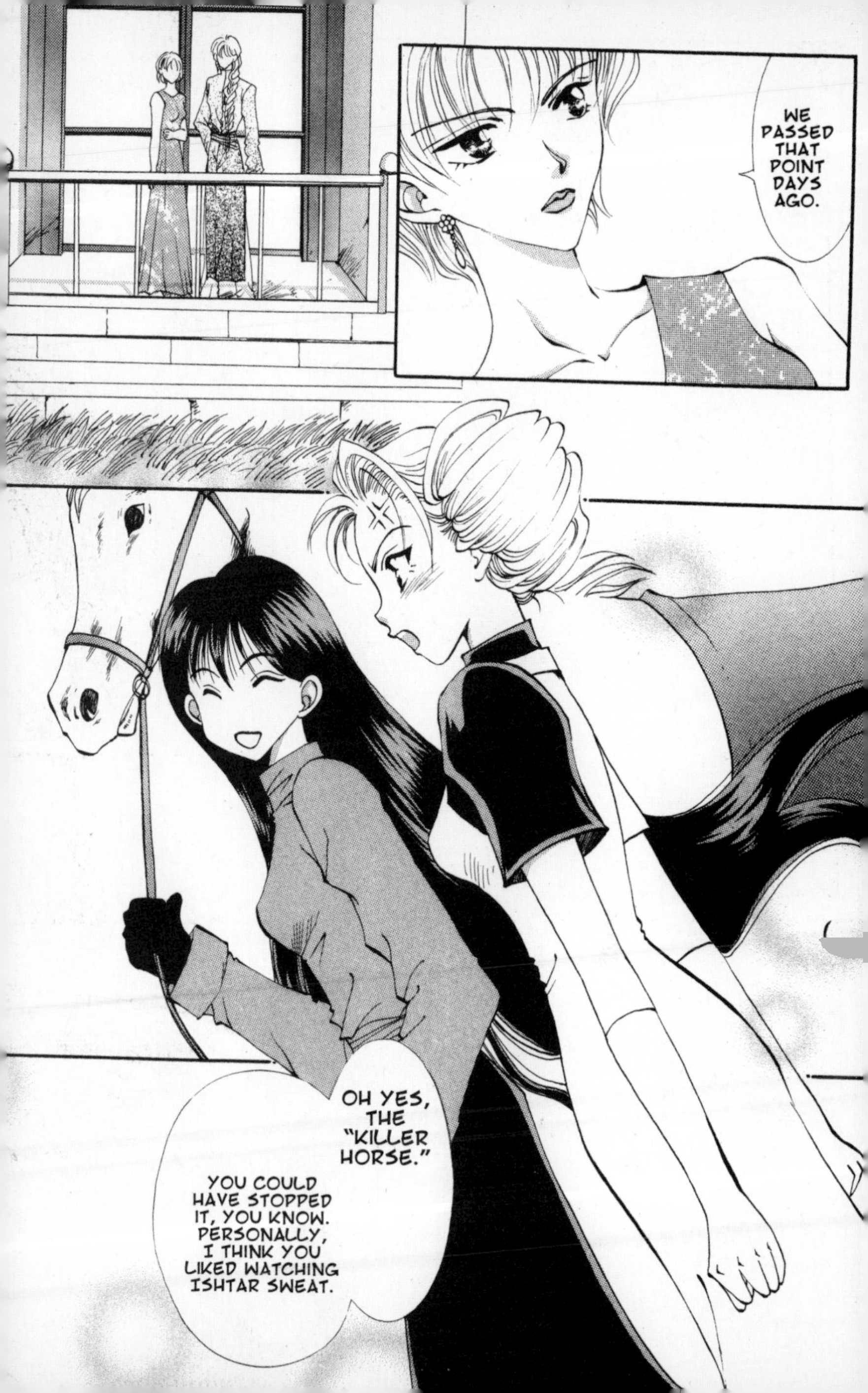
WE PASSED THAT POINT DAYS AGO.
OH YES, THE "KILLER HORSE."
YOU COULD HAVE STOPPED IT, YOU KNOW. PERSONALLY, I THINK YOU LIKED WATCHING ISHTAR SWEAT.

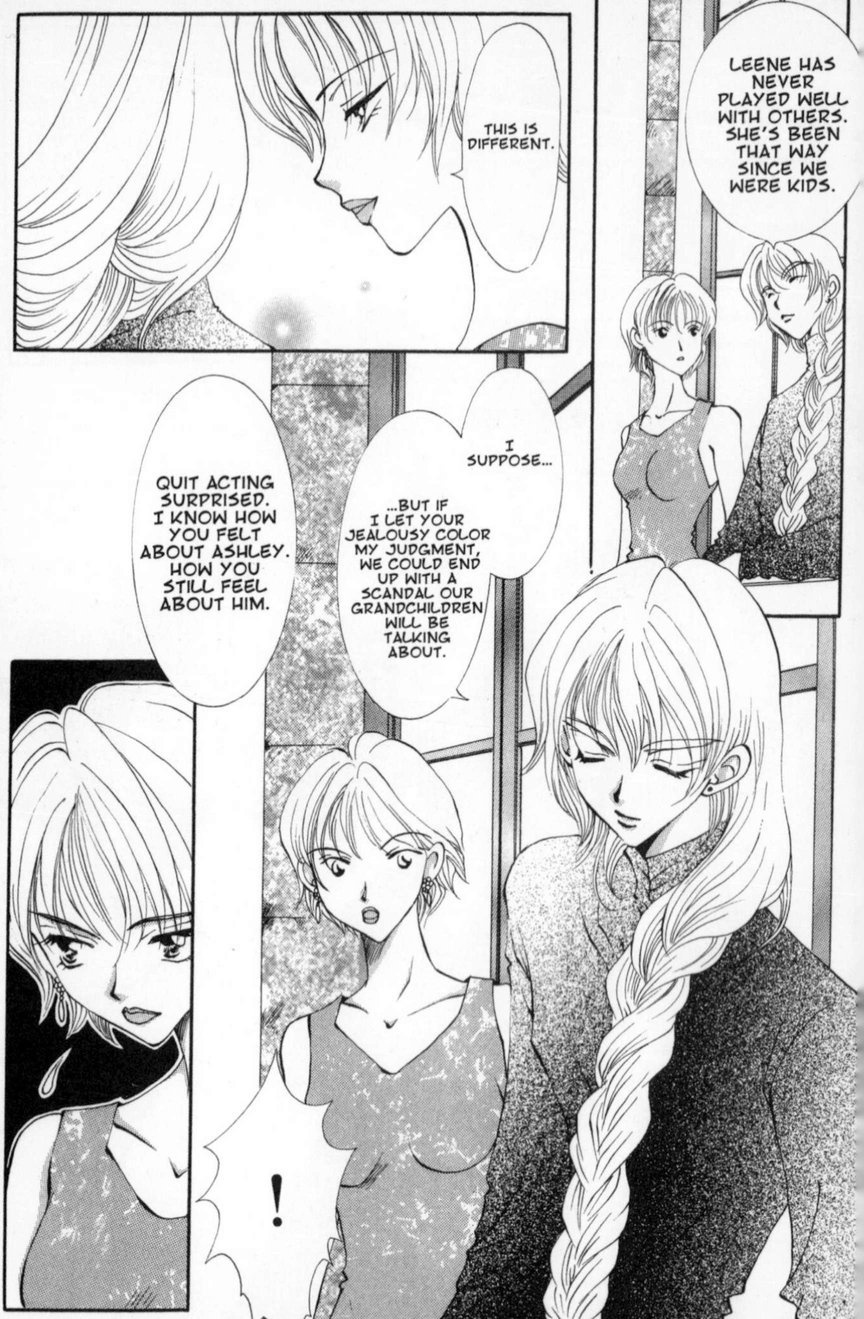
LEENE HAS NEVER PLAYED WELL WITH OTHERS. SHE'S BEEN THAT WAY SINCE WE WERE KIDS.
THIS IS DIFFERENT.
I SUPPOSE...
...BUT IF I LET YOUR JEALOUSY COLOR MY JUDGMENT, WE COULD END UP WITH A SCANDAL OUR GRANDCHILDREN WILL BE TALKING ABOUT.
QUIT ACTING SURPRISED. I KNOW HOW YOU FELT ABOUT ASHLEY. HOW YOU STILL FEEL ABOUT HIM.
!

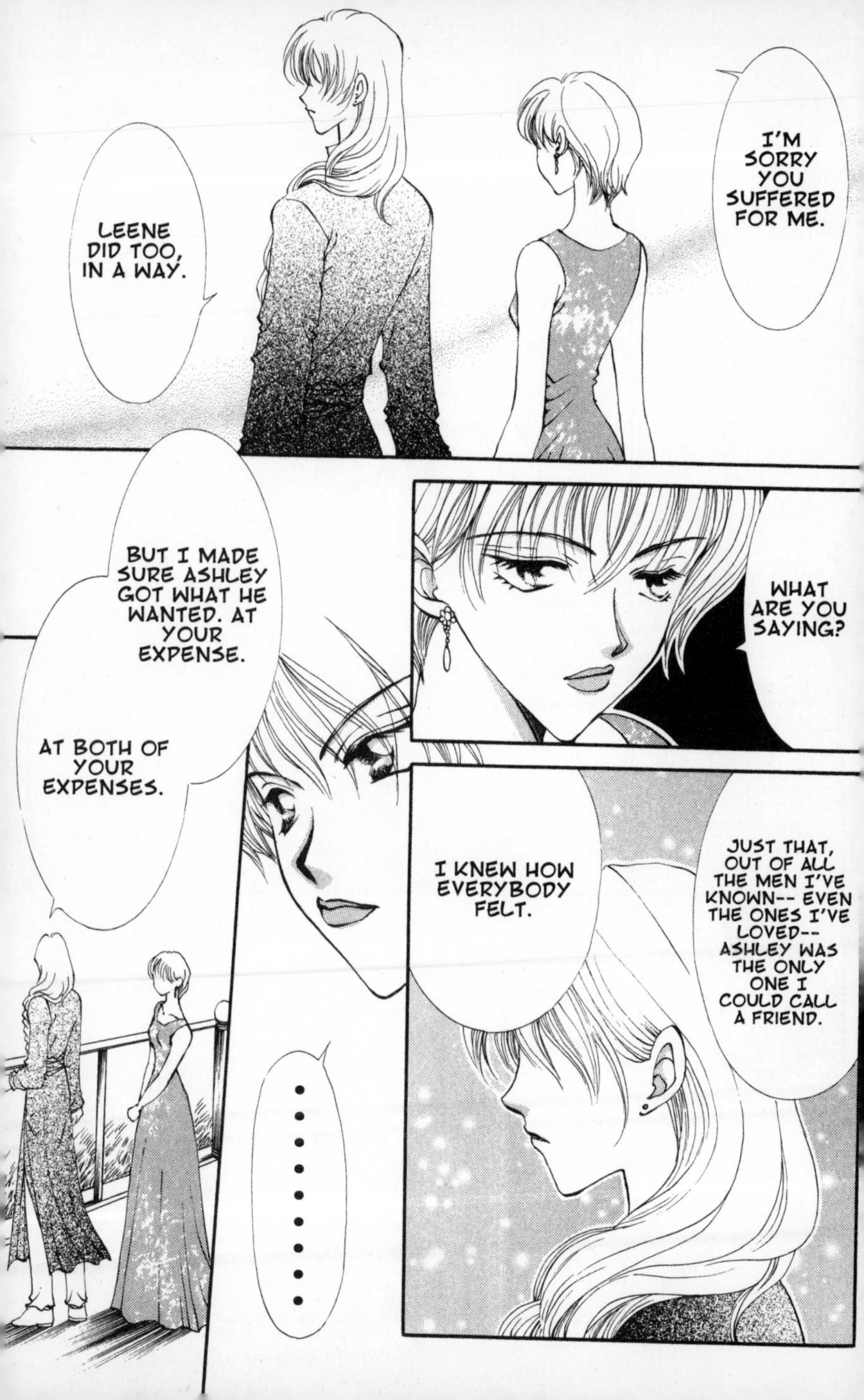
I'M SORRY YOU SUFFERED FOR ME.
LEENE DID TOO, IN A WAY.
WHAT ARE YOU SAYING?
JUST THAT, OUT OF ALL THE MEN I'VE KNOWN-- EVEN THE ONES I'VE LOVED-- ASHLEY WAS THE ONLY ONE I COULD CALL A FRIEND.
I KNEW HOW EVERYBODY FELT.
BUT I MADE SURE ASHLEY GOT WHAT HE WANTED. AT YOUR EXPENSE.
AT BOTH OF YOUR EXPENSES.
....

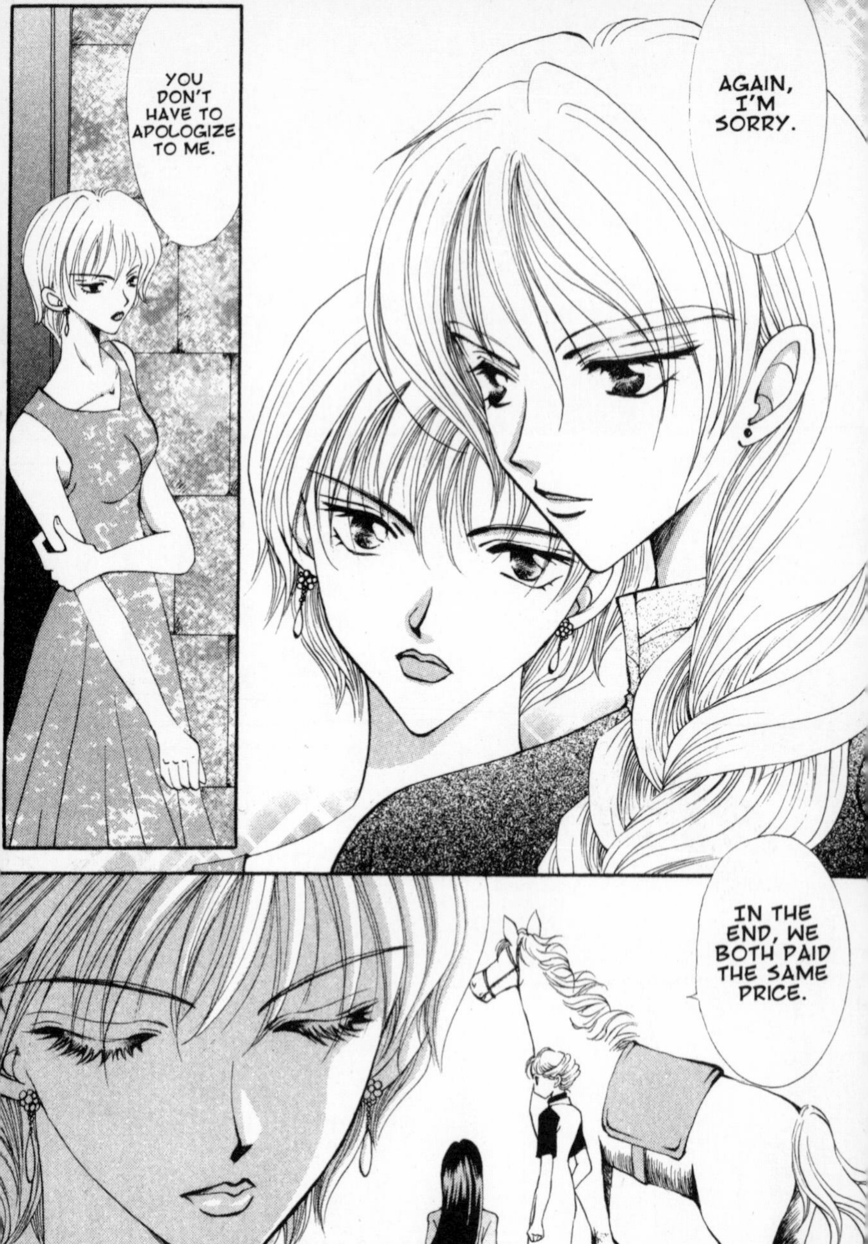
AGAIN, I'M SORRY.
YOU DON'T HAVE TO APOLOGIZE TO ME.
IN THE END, WE BOTH PAID THE SAME PRICE.

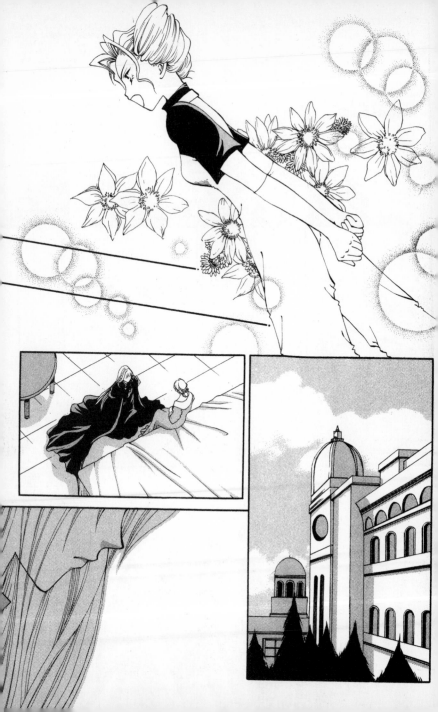

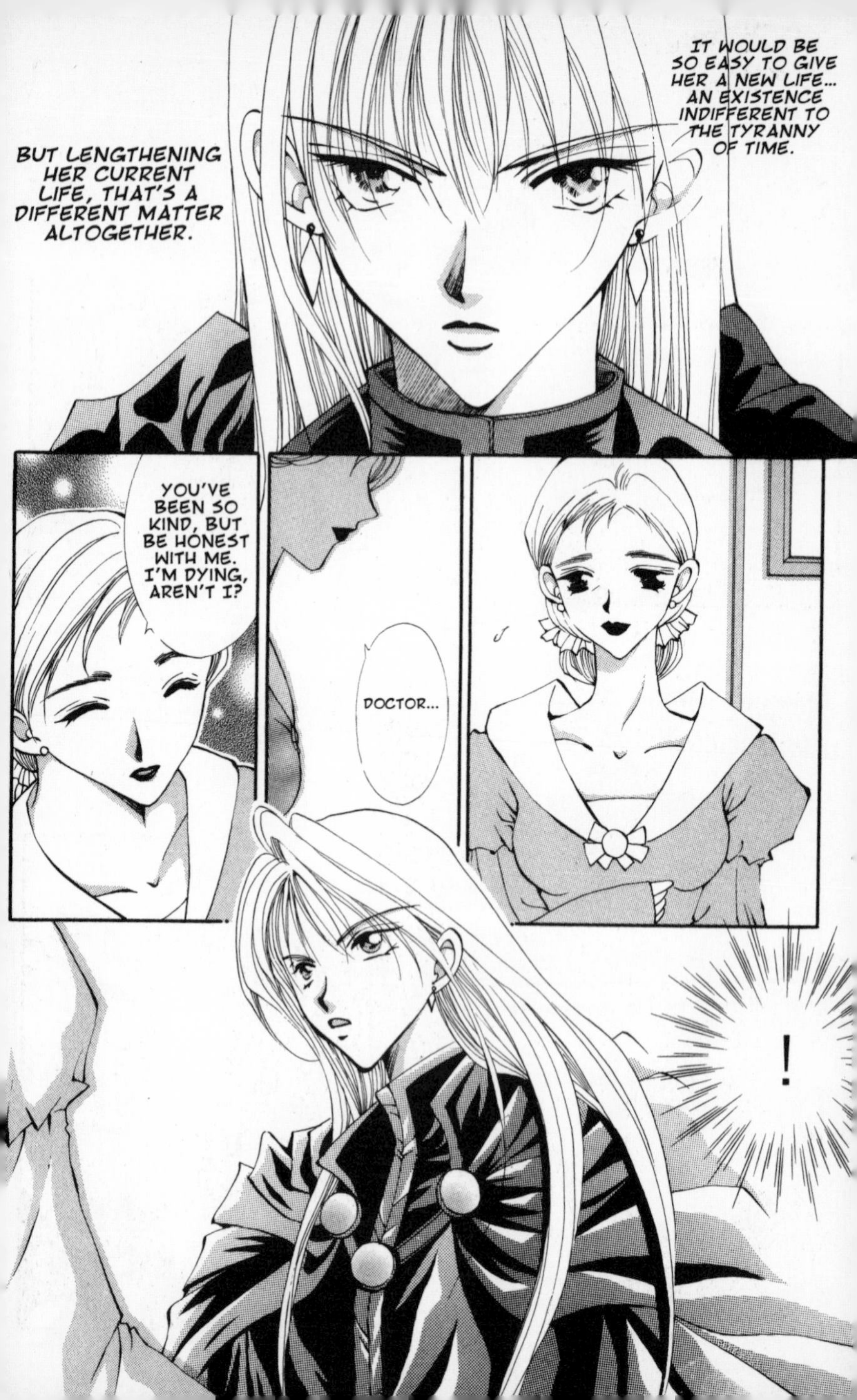
IT WOULD BE SO EASY TO GIVE HER A NEW LIFE... AN EXISTENCE INDIFFERENT TO THE TYRANNY OF TIME.
BUT LENGTHENING HER CURRENT LIFE, THAT'S A DIFFERENT MATTER ALTOGETHER.
DOCTOR...
YOU'VE BEEN SO KIND, BUT BE HONEST WITH ME. I'M DYING, AREN'T I?
!

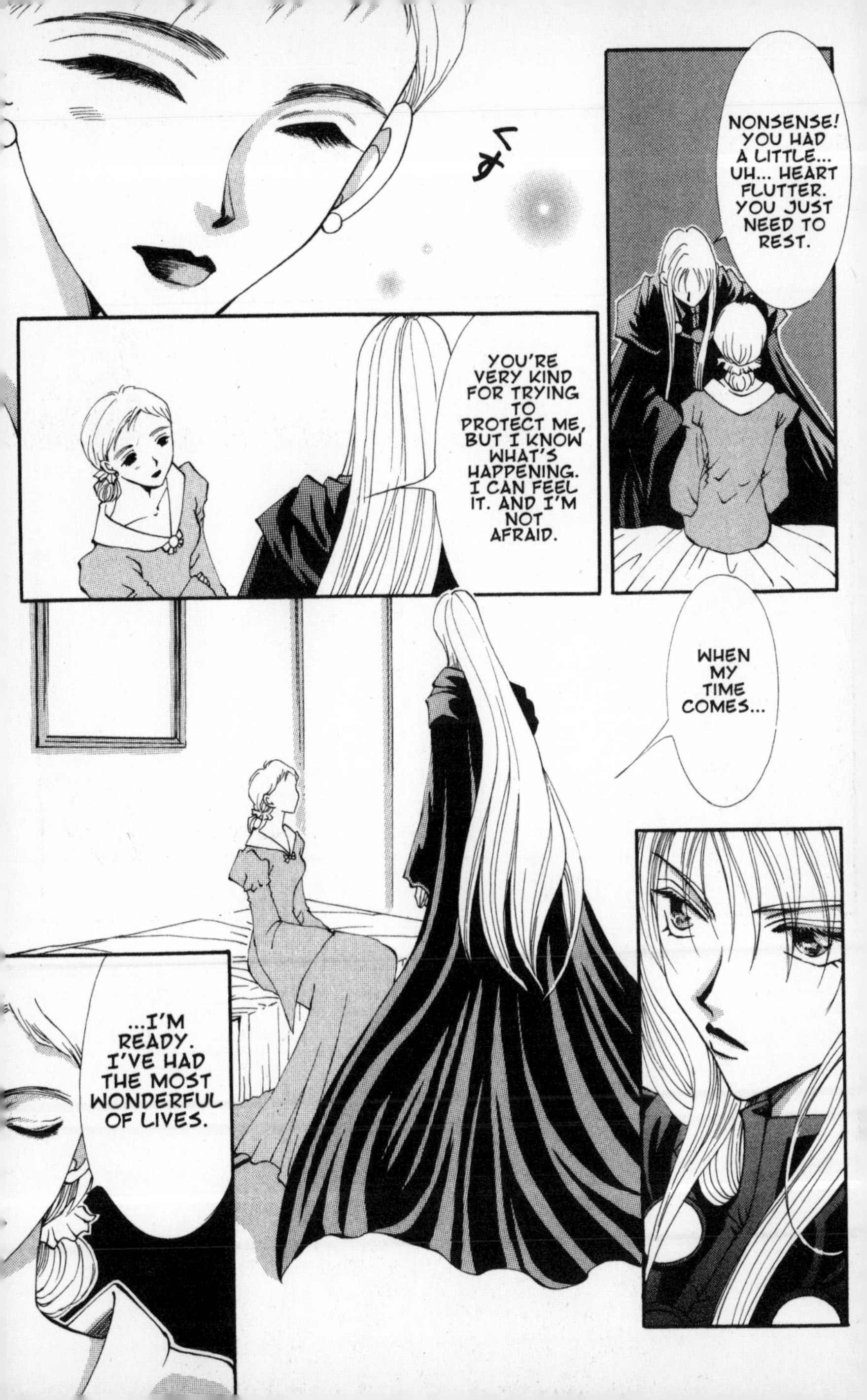
NONSENSE! YOU HAD A LITTLE... UH... HEART FLUTTER. YOU JUST NEED TO REST.
くす
YOU'RE VERY KIND FOR TRYING TO PROTECT ME, BUT I KNOW WHAT'S HAPPENING. I CAN FEEL IT. AND I'M NOT AFRAID.
WHEN MY TIME COMES...
...I'M READY. I'VE HAD THE MOST WONDERFUL OF LIVES.

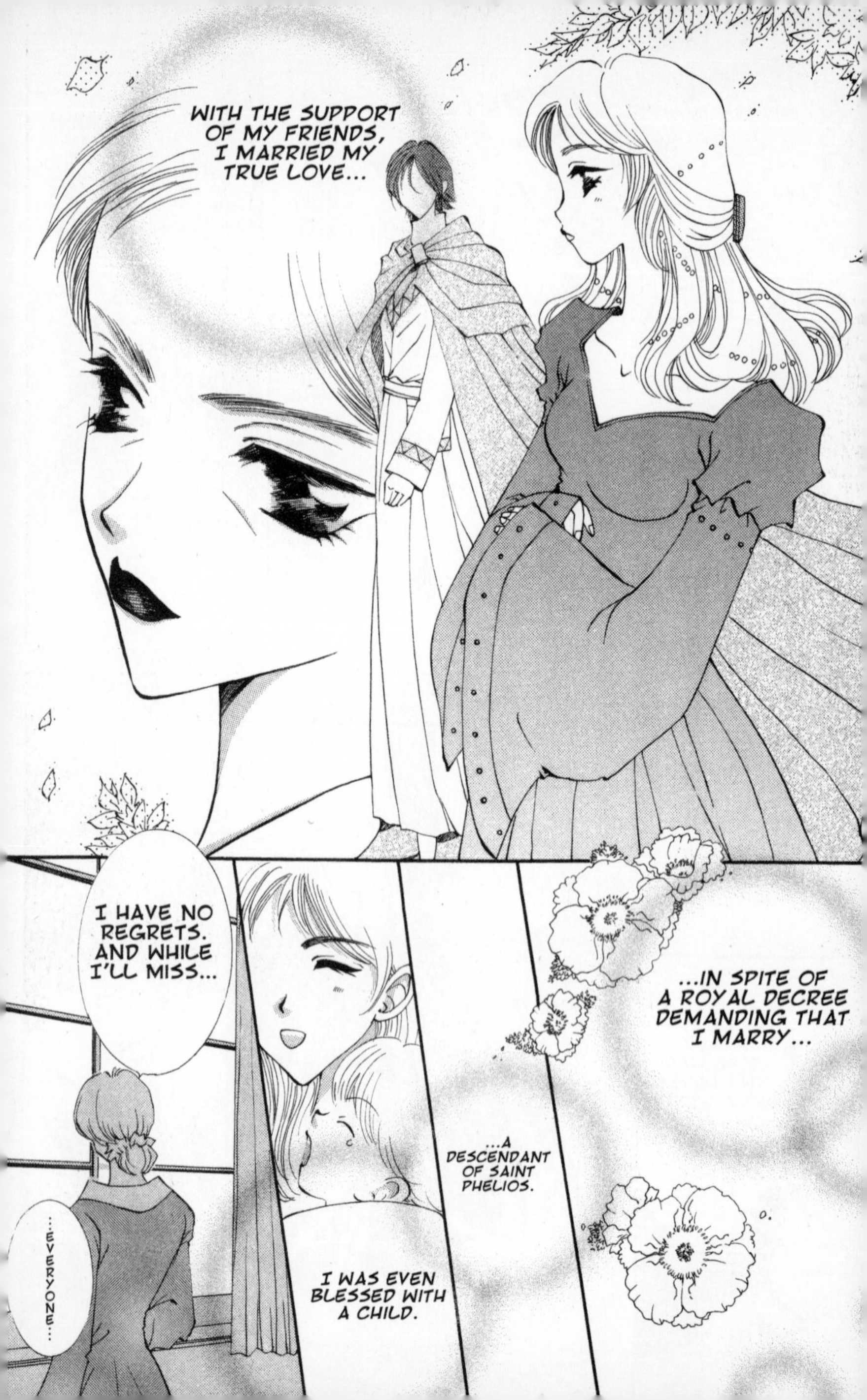
WITH THE SUPPORT OF MY FRIENDS, I MARRIED MY TRUE LOVE...
...IN SPITE OF A ROYAL DECREE DEMANDING THAT I MARRY...
...A DESCENDANT OF SAINT PHELIOS.
I WAS EVEN BLESSED WITH A CHILD.
I HAVE NO REGRETS. AND WHILE I'LL MISS...
...EVERYONE...

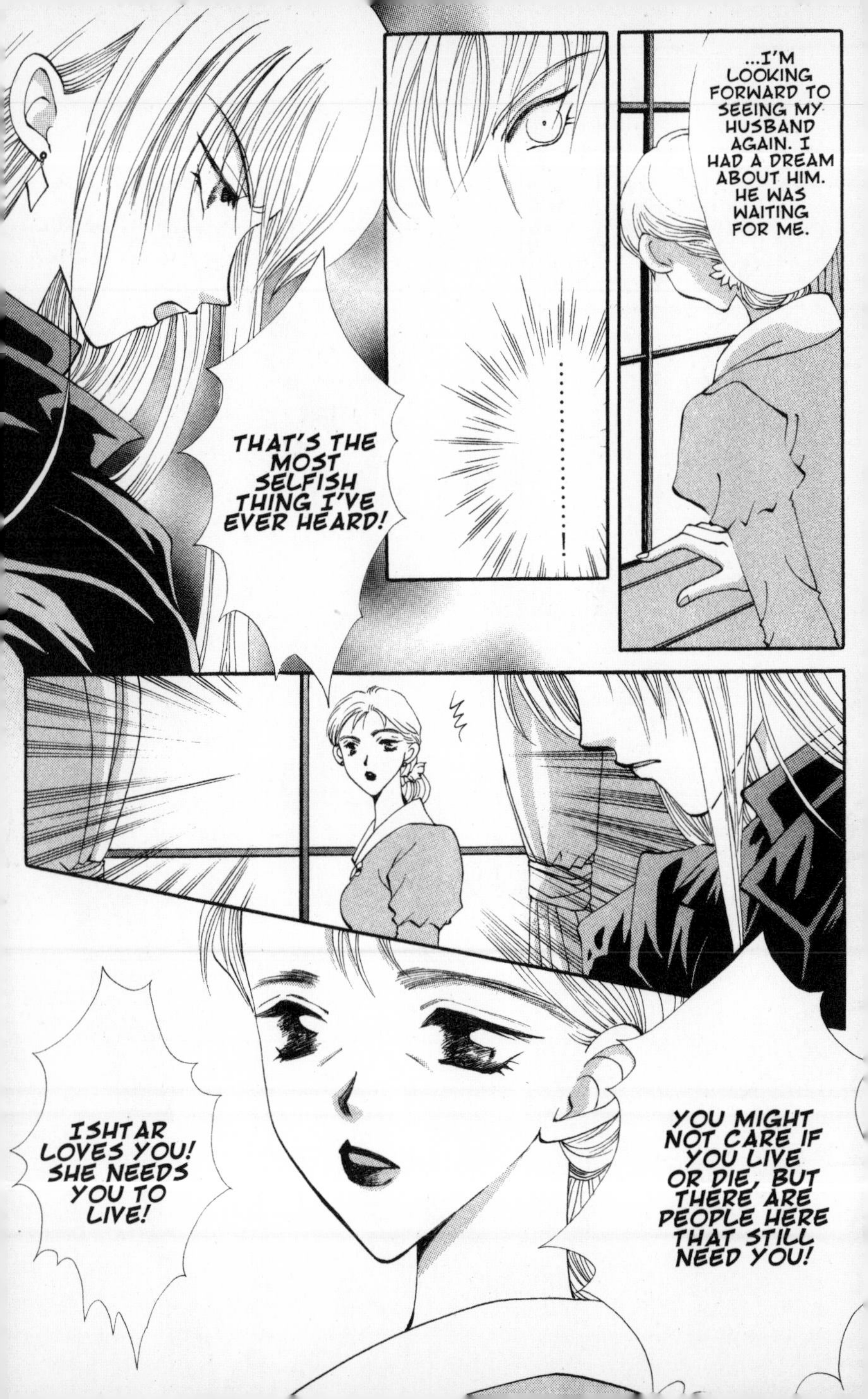
...I'M LOOKING FORWARD TO SEEING MY HUSBAND AGAIN. I HAD A DREAM ABOUT HIM. HE WAS WAITING FOR ME.
THAT'S THE MOST SELFISH THING I'VE EVER HEARD!
YOU MIGHT NOT CARE IF YOU LIVE OR DIE, BUT THERE ARE PEOPLE HERE THAT STILL NEED YOU!
ISHTAR LOVES YOU! SHE NEEDS YOU TO LIVE!

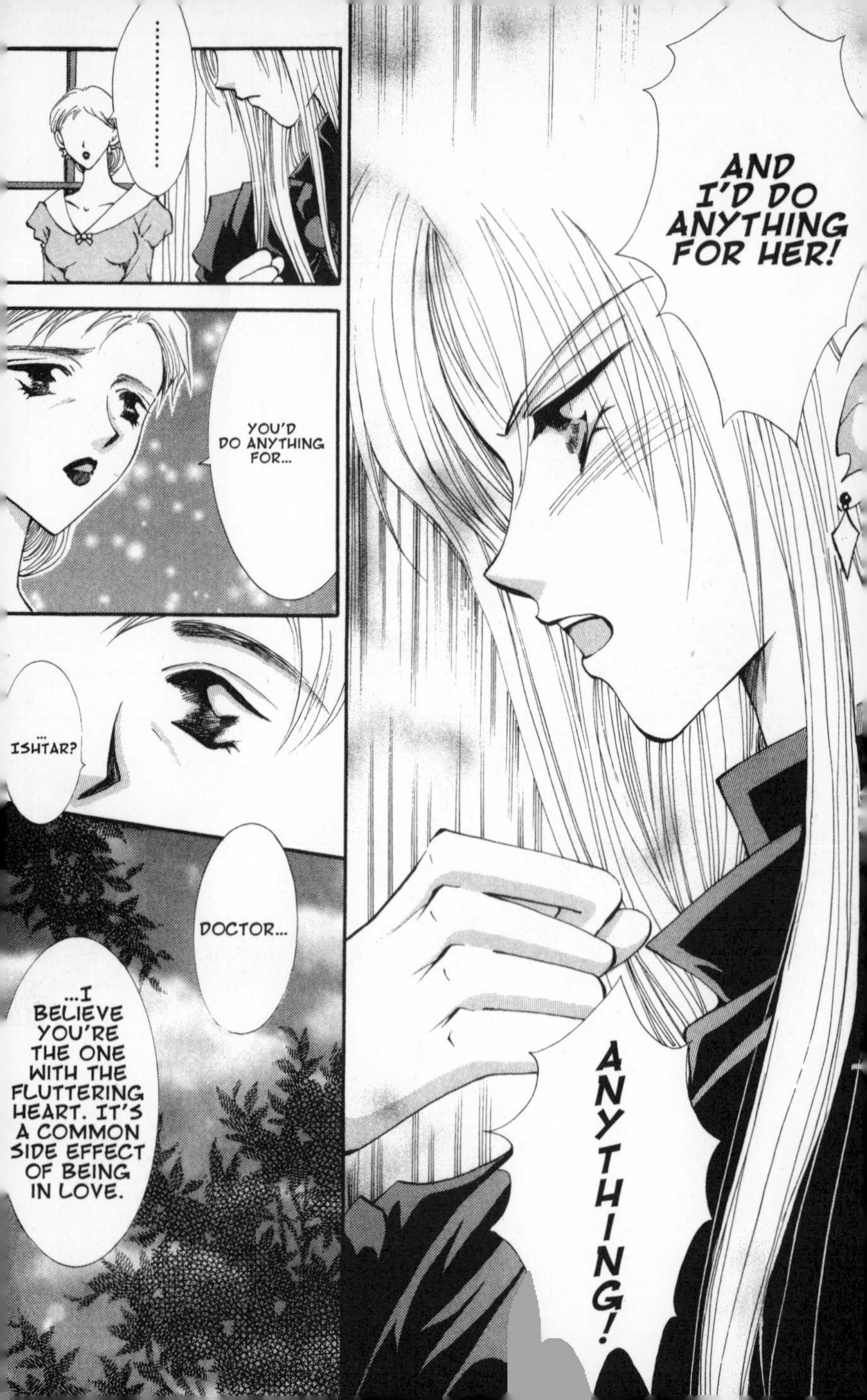
AND I'D DO ANYTHING FOR HER!
ANYTHING!
......
YOU'D DO ANYTHING FOR...
...ISHTAR?
DOCTOR...
...I BELIEVE YOU'RE THE ONE WITH THE FLUTTERING HEART. IT'S A COMMON SIDE EFFECT OF BEING IN LOVE.

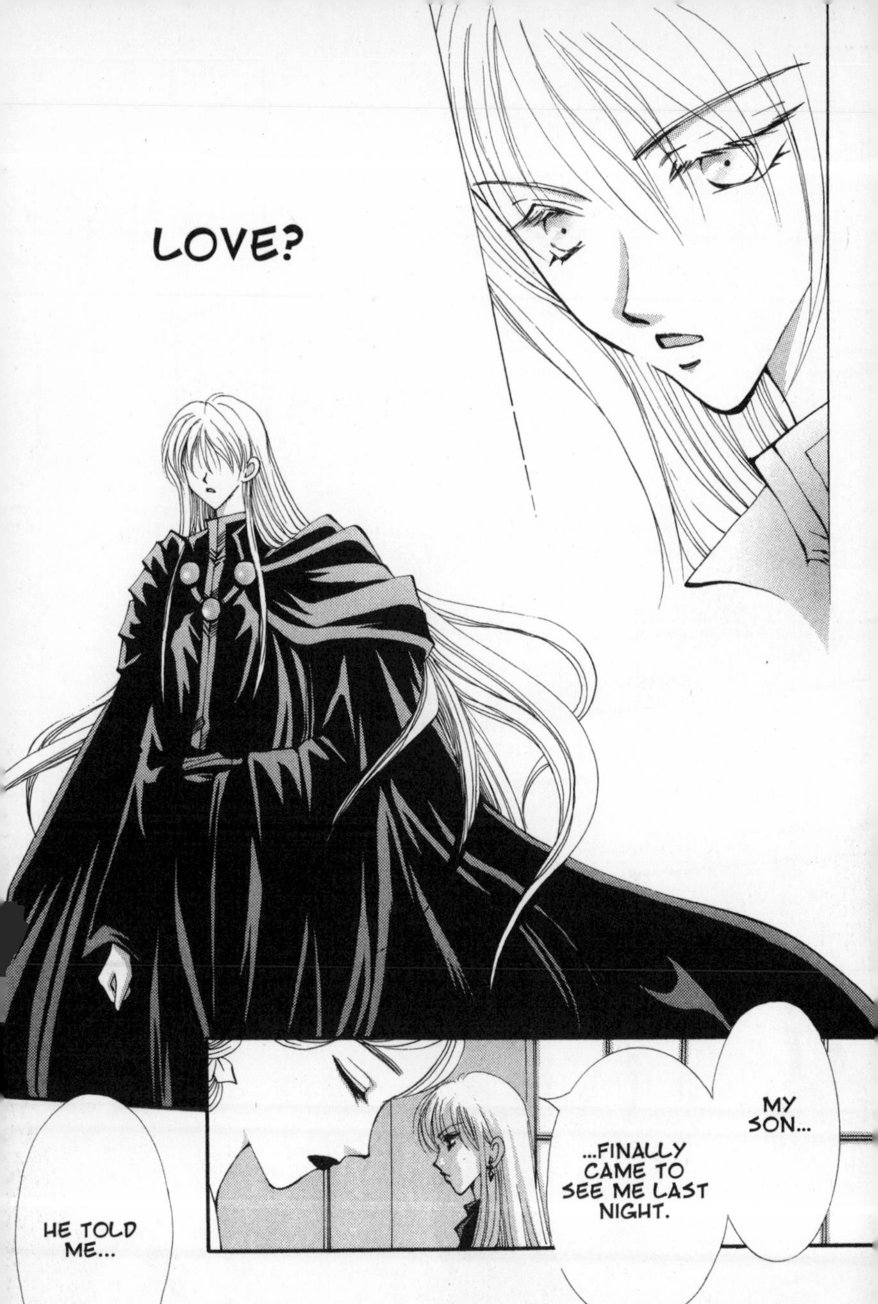
LOVE?
MY SON...
...FINALLY CAME TO SEE ME LAST NIGHT.
HE TOLD ME...

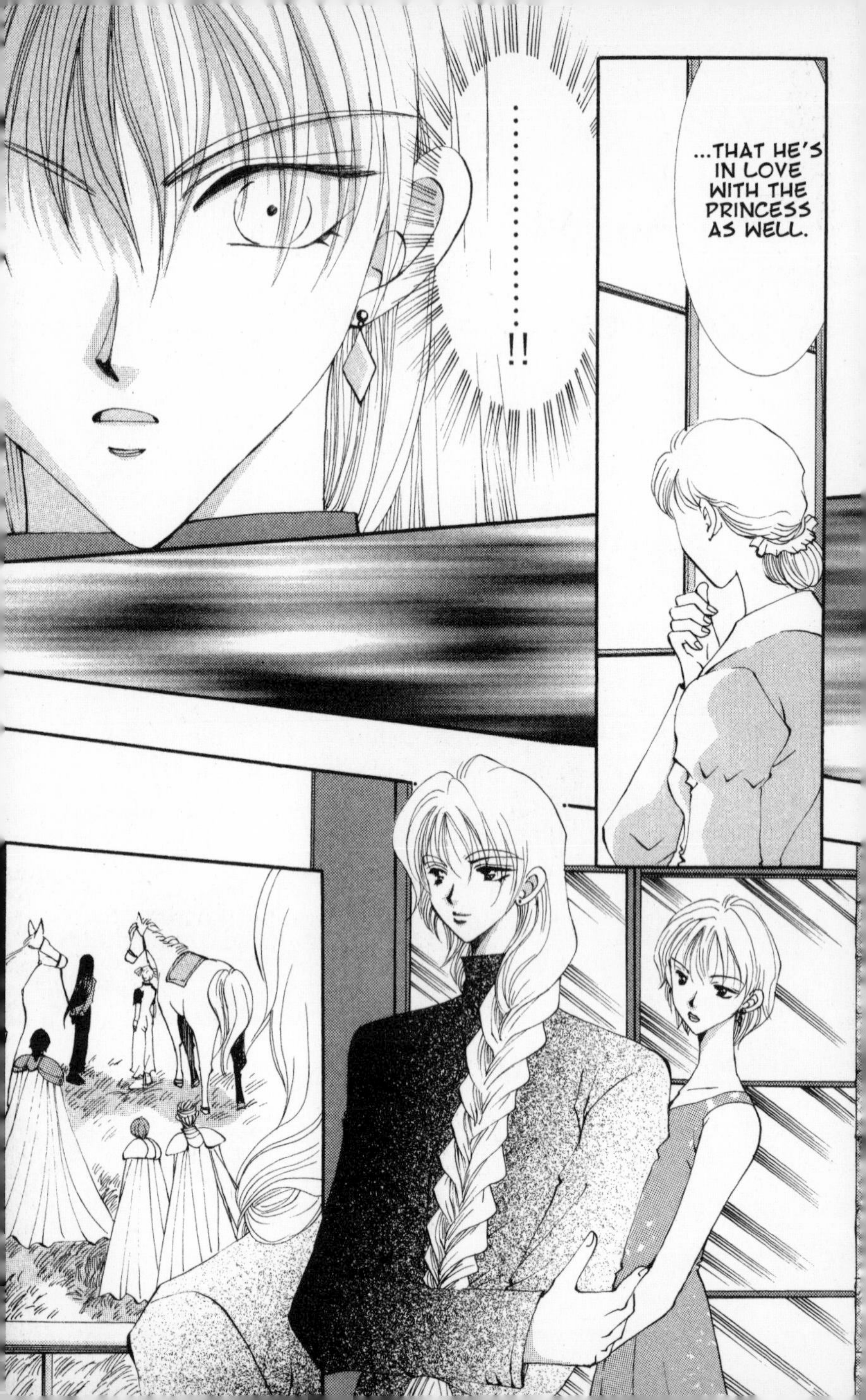
...THAT HE'S IN LOVE WITH THE PRINCESS AS WELL.
......!!

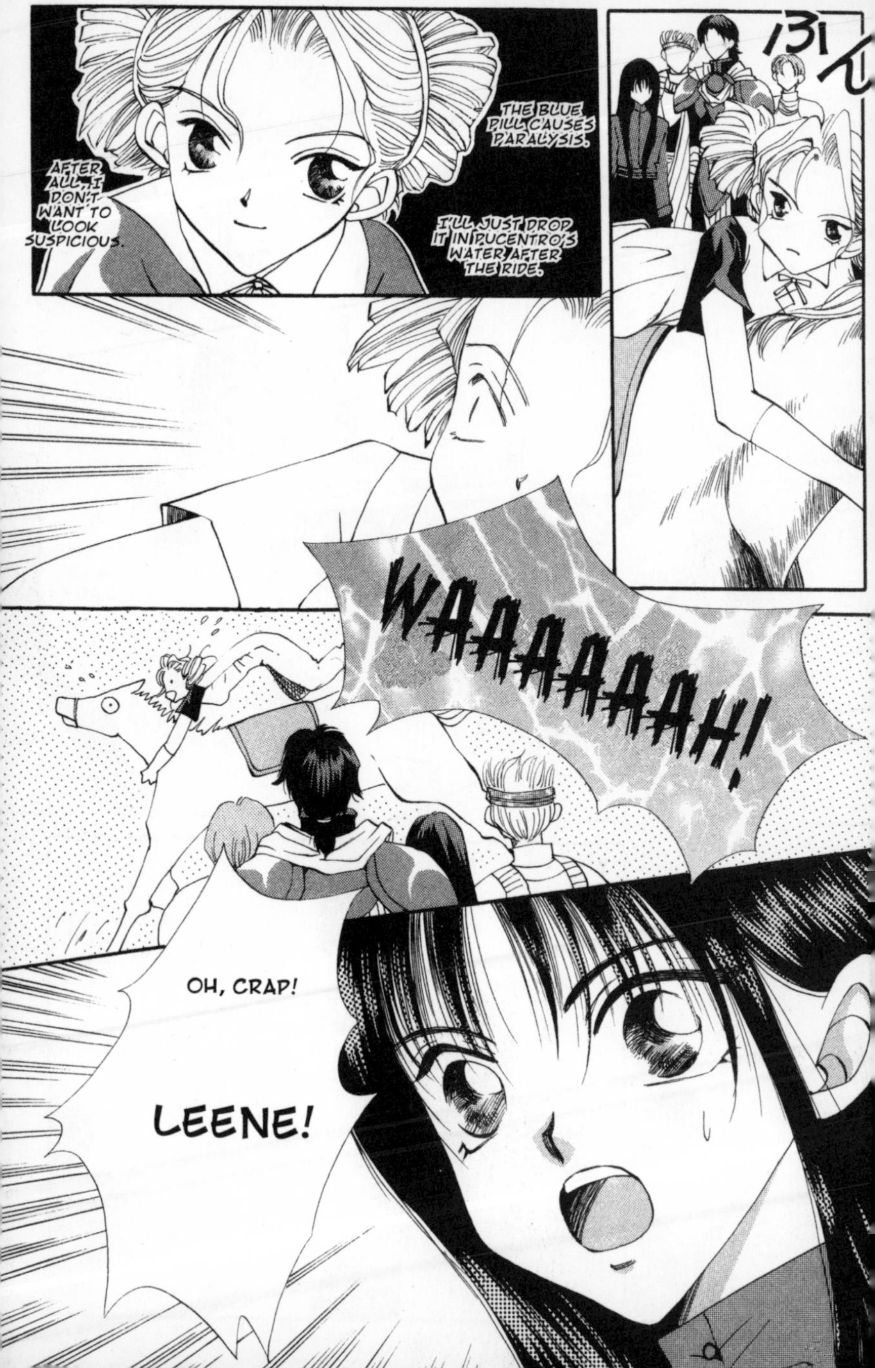
ぷい
THE BLUE PILL CAUSES PARALYSIS.
I'LL JUST DROP IT IN PUCENTRO'S WATER AFTER THE RIDE.
AFTER ALL, I DON'T WANT TO LOOK SUSPICIOUS.
WAAAAAAAAH!
OH, CRAP!
LEENE!

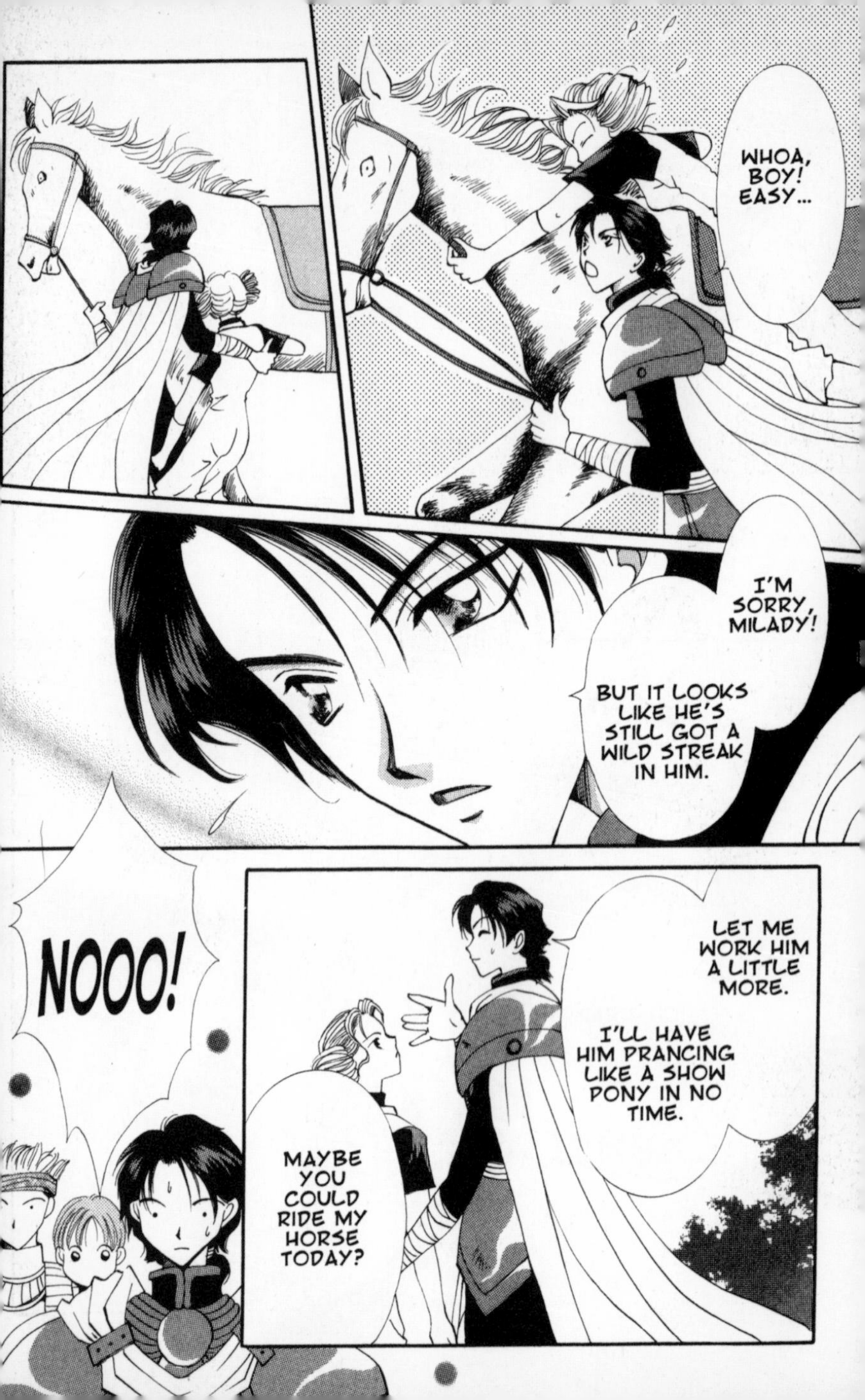

WHOA, BOY! EASY...
I'M SORRY, MILADY!
BUT IT LOOKS LIKE HE'S STILL GOT A WILD STREAK IN HIM.
LET ME WORK HIM A LITTLE MORE.
I'LL HAVE HIM PRANCING LIKE A SHOW PONY IN NO TIME.
MAYBE YOU COULD RIDE MY HORSE TODAY?
NOOO!

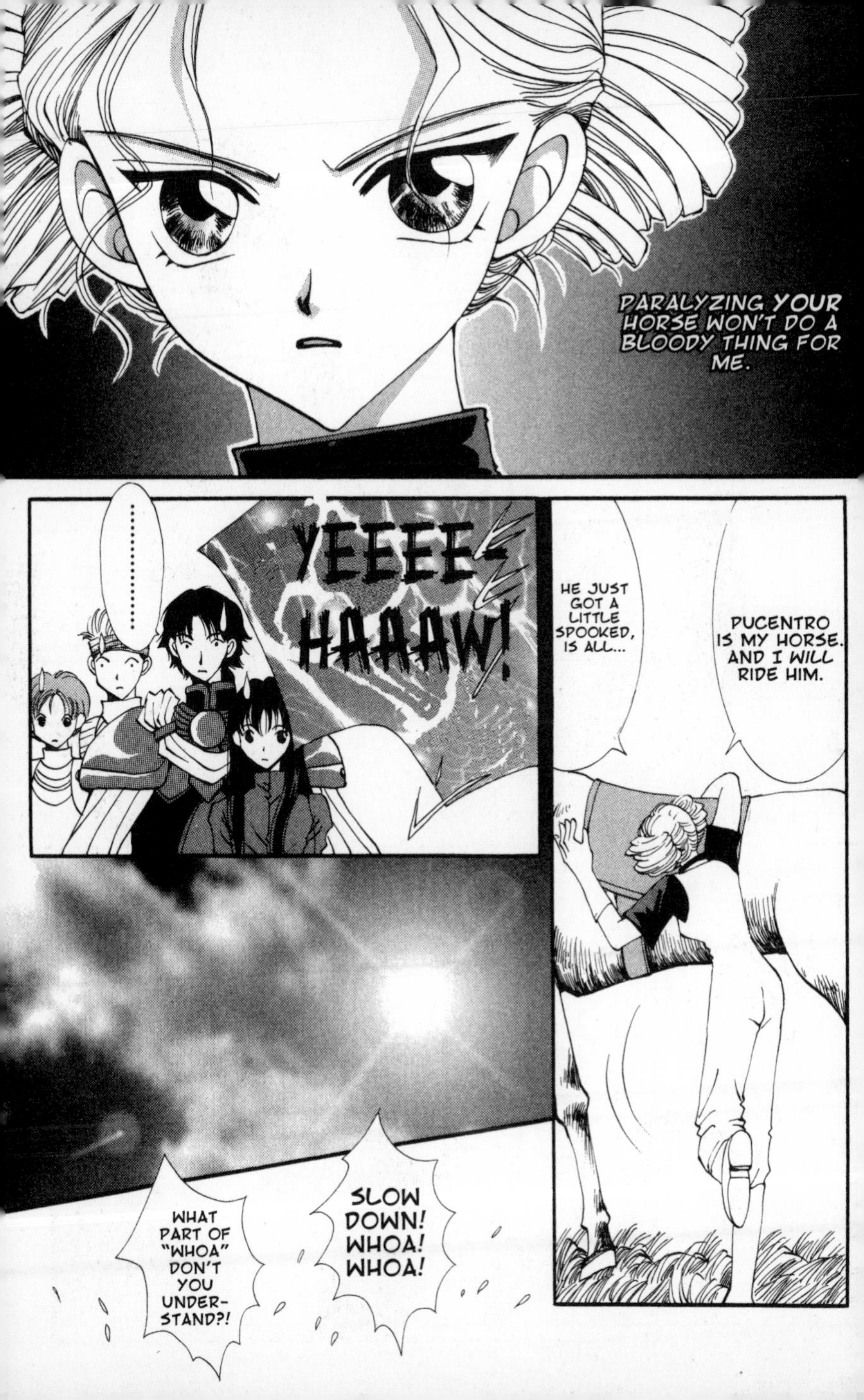
PARALYZING YOUR HORSE WON'T DO A BLOODY THING FOR ME.
PUCENTRO IS MY HORSE. AND I WILL RIDE HIM.
HE JUST GOT A LITTLE SPOOKED, IS ALL...
YEEEE-HAAAW!
......
SLOW DOWN! WHOA! WHOA!
WHAT PART OF "WHOA" DON'T YOU UNDER-STAND?!

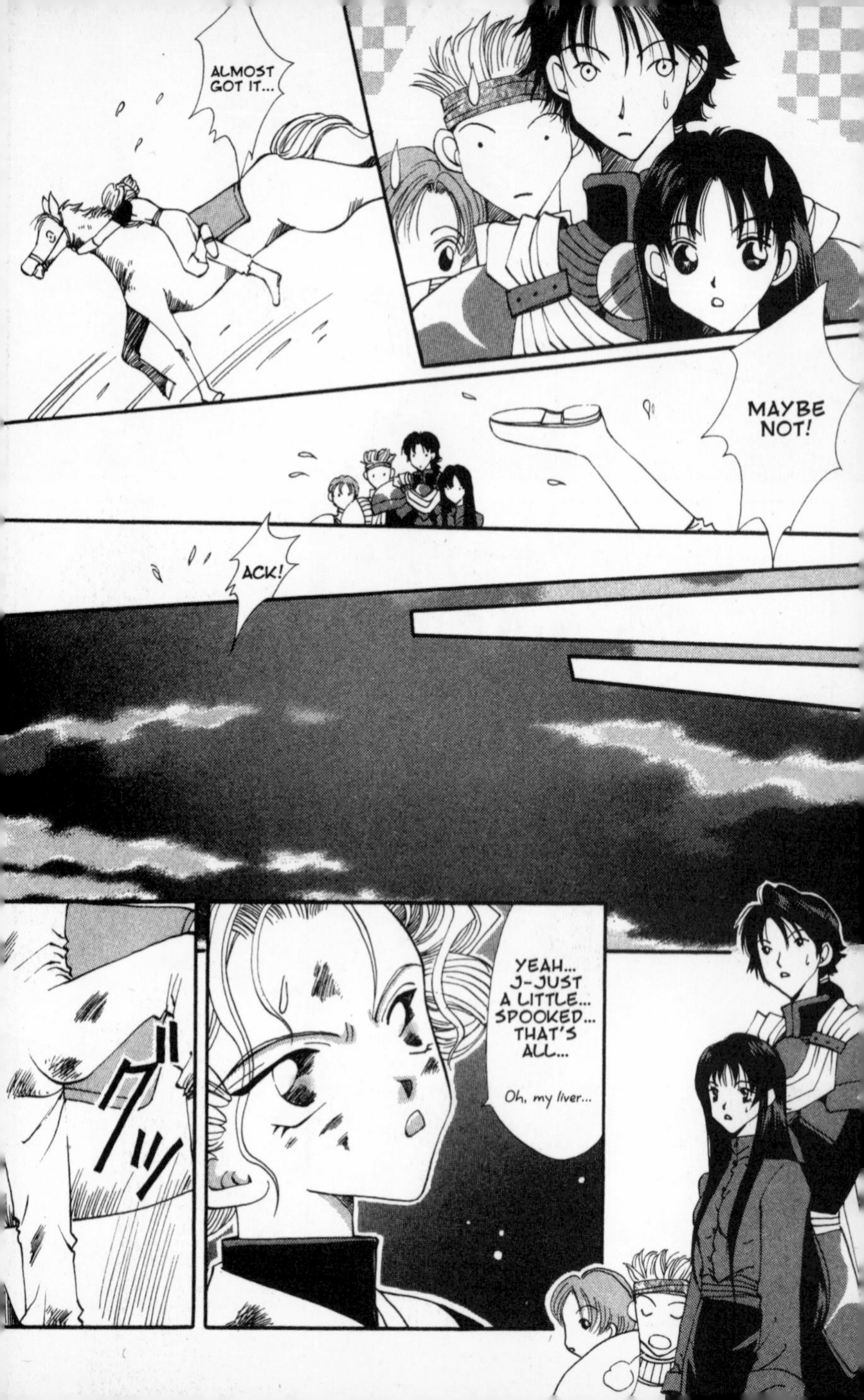
ALMOST GOT IT...
MAYBE NOT!
ACK!
YEAH... J-JUST A LITTLE... SPOOKED... THAT'S ALL...
Oh, my liver...
グッ

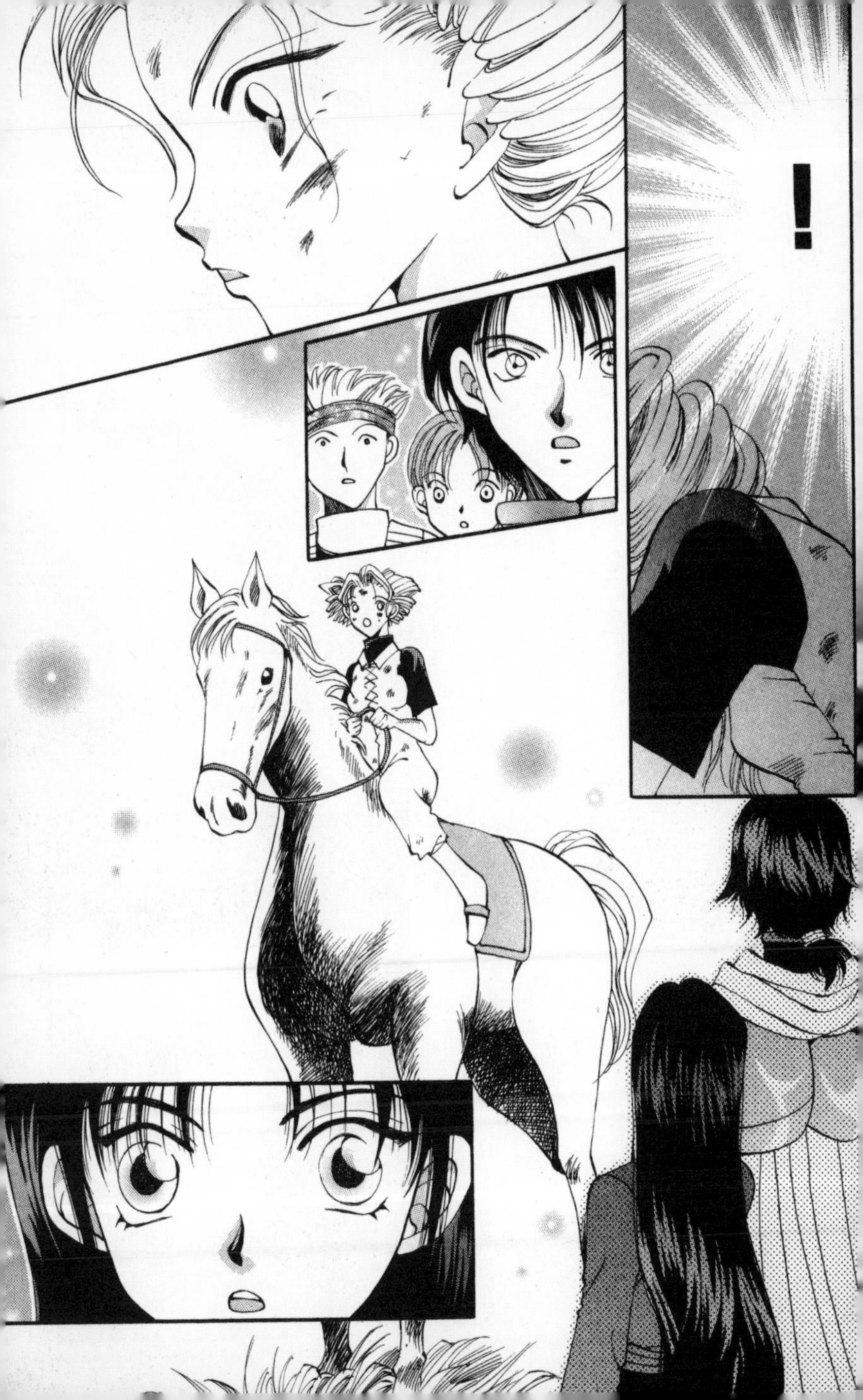
!

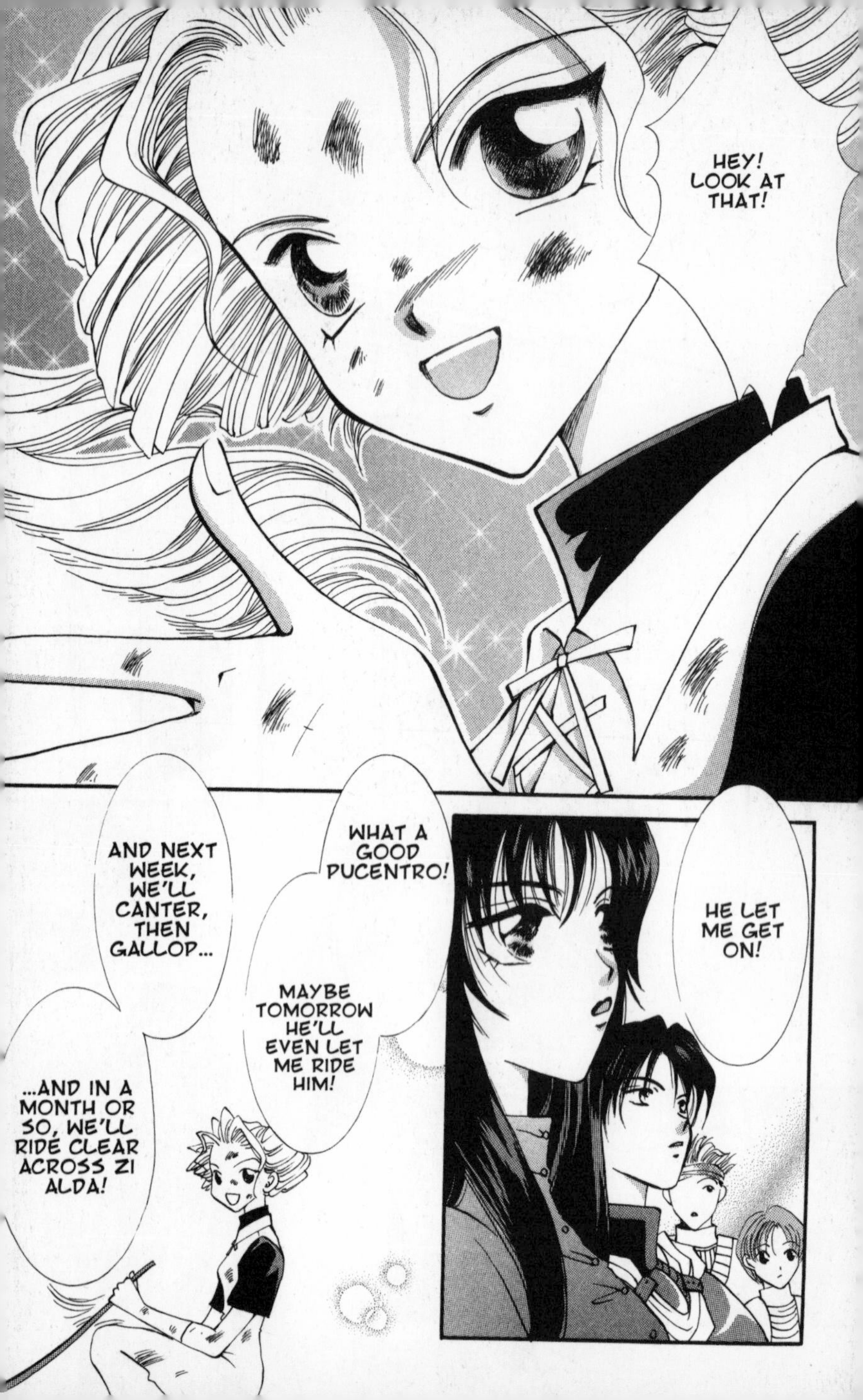
HEY! LOOK AT THAT!
HE LET ME GET ON!
WHAT A GOOD PUCENTRO!
MAYBE TOMORROW HE'LL EVEN LET ME RIDE HIM!
AND NEXT WEEK, WE'LL CANTER, THEN GALLOP...
...AND IN A MONTH OR SO, WE'LL RIDE CLEAR ACROSS ZI ALDA!

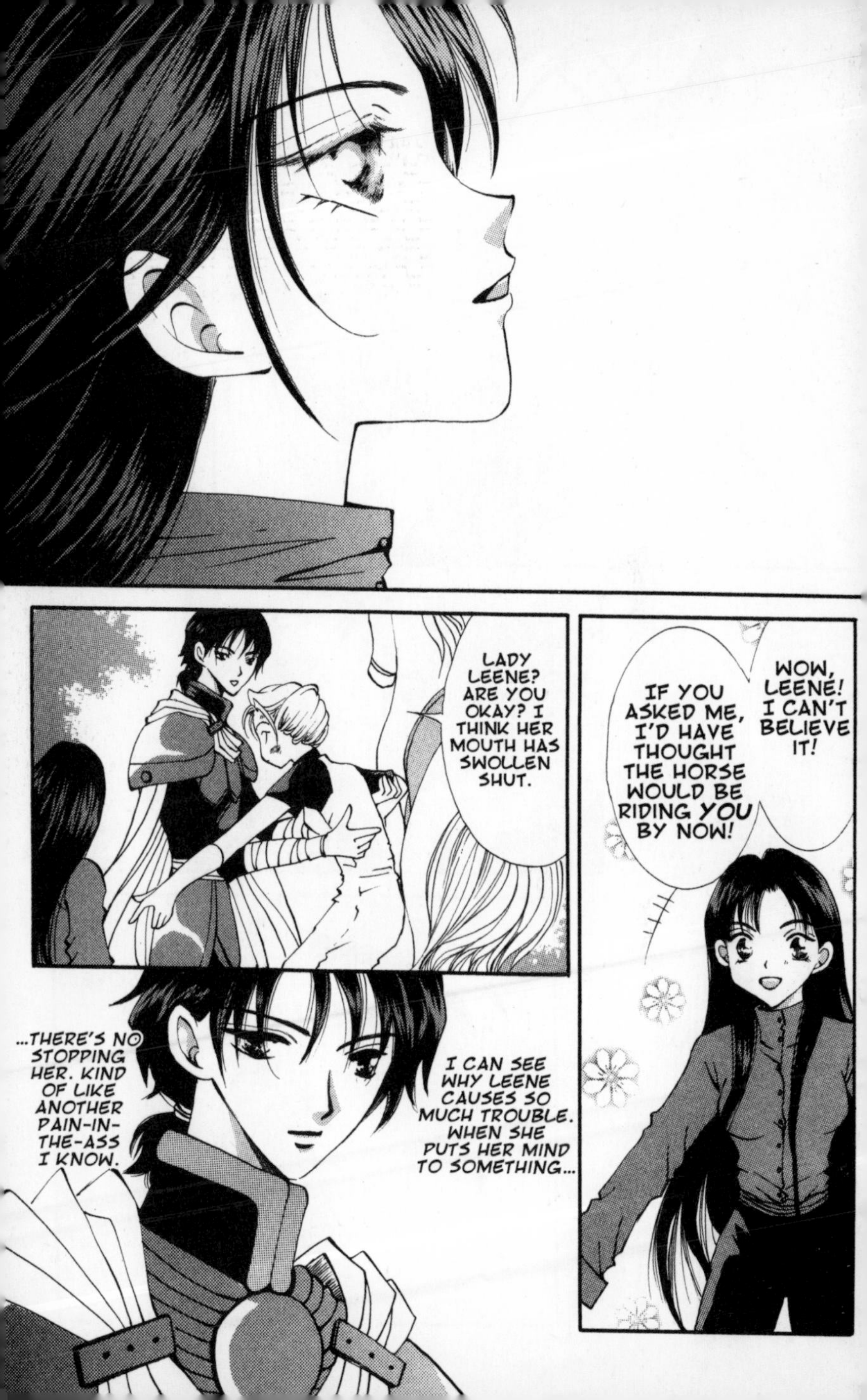
WOW, LEENE! I CAN'T BELIEVE IT!
IF YOU ASKED ME, I'D HAVE THOUGHT THE HORSE WOULD BE RIDING YOU BY NOW!
LADY LEENE? ARE YOU OKAY? I THINK HER MOUTH HAS SWOLLEN SHUT.
I CAN SEE WHY LEENE CAUSES SO MUCH TROUBLE. WHEN SHE PUTS HER MIND TO SOMETHING...
...THERE'S NO STOPPING HER. KIND OF LIKE ANOTHER PAIN-IN-THE-ASS I KNOW.

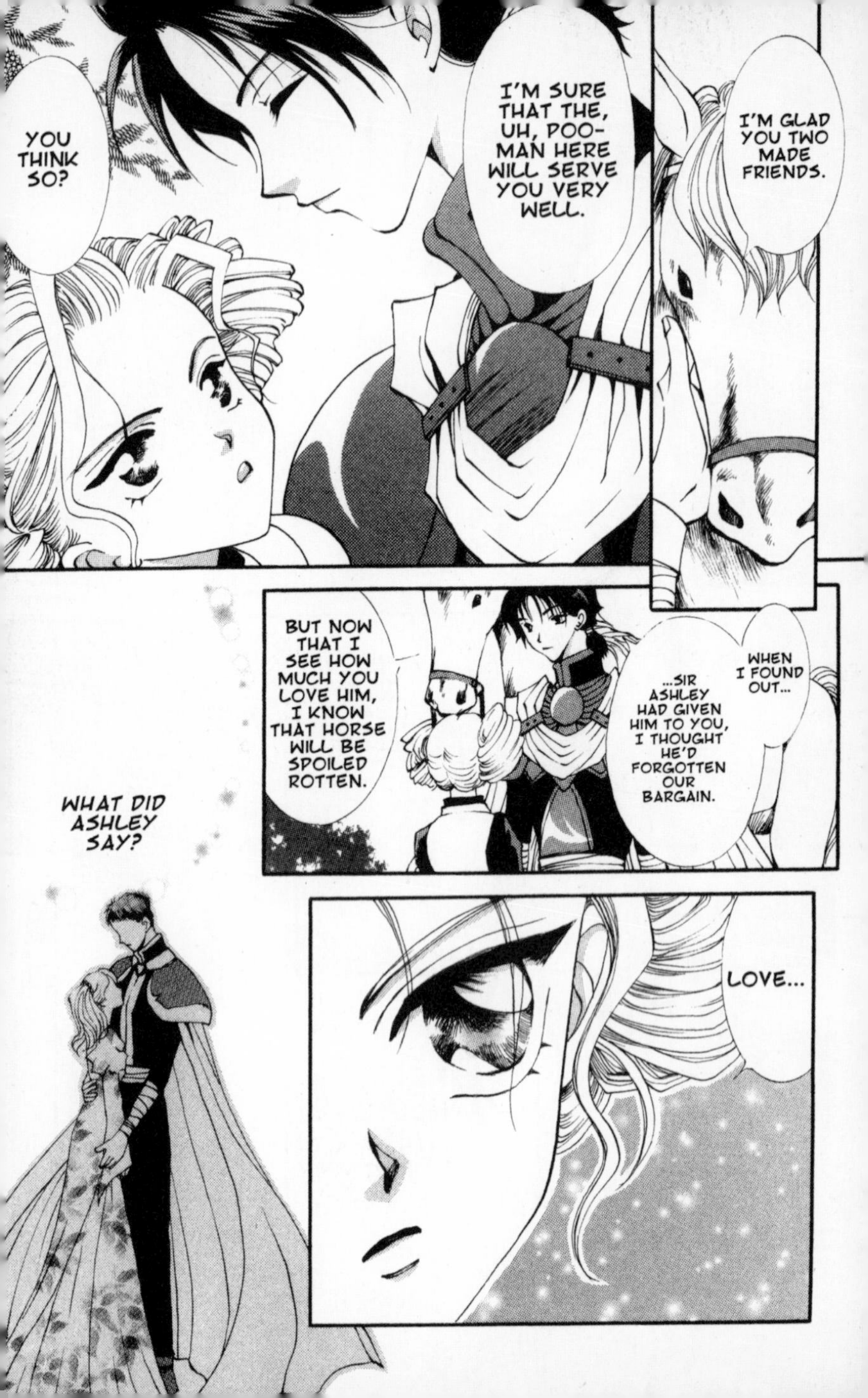
I'M GLAD YOU TWO MADE FRIENDS.
I'M SURE THAT THE, UH, POO-MAN HERE WILL SERVE YOU VERY WELL.
YOU THINK SO?
WHEN I FOUND OUT...
...SIR ASHLEY HAD GIVEN HIM TO YOU, I THOUGHT HE'D FORGOTTEN OUR BARGAIN.
BUT NOW THAT I SEE HOW MUCH YOU LOVE HIM, I KNOW THAT HORSE WILL BE SPOILED ROTTEN.
WHAT DID ASHLEY SAY?
LOVE...

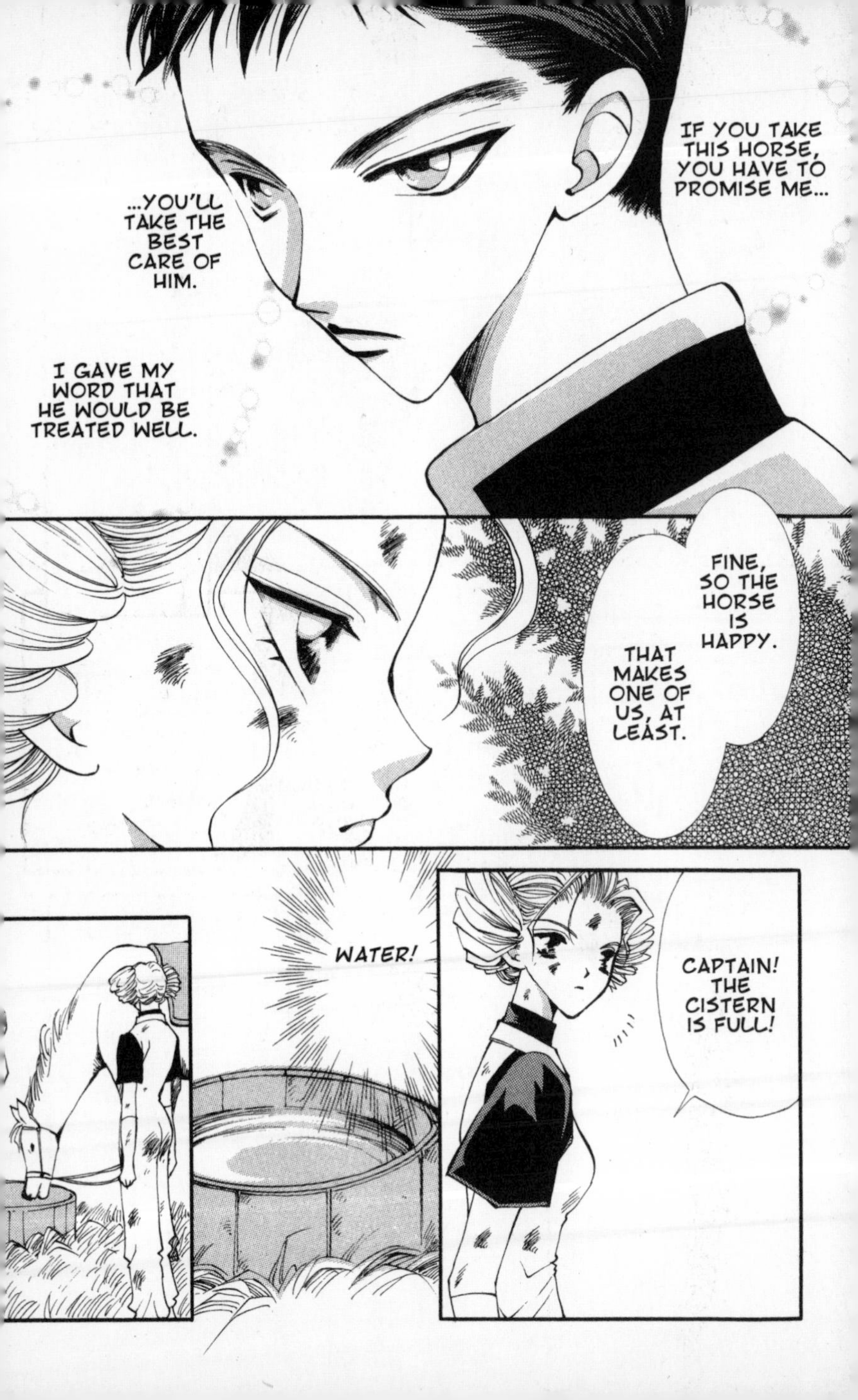
IF YOU TAKE THIS HORSE, YOU HAVE TO PROMISE ME...
...YOU'LL TAKE THE BEST CARE OF HIM.
I GAVE MY WORD THAT HE WOULD BE TREATED WELL.
FINE, SO THE HORSE IS HAPPY.
THAT MAKES ONE OF US, AT LEAST.
CAPTAIN! THE CISTERN IS FULL!
WATER!

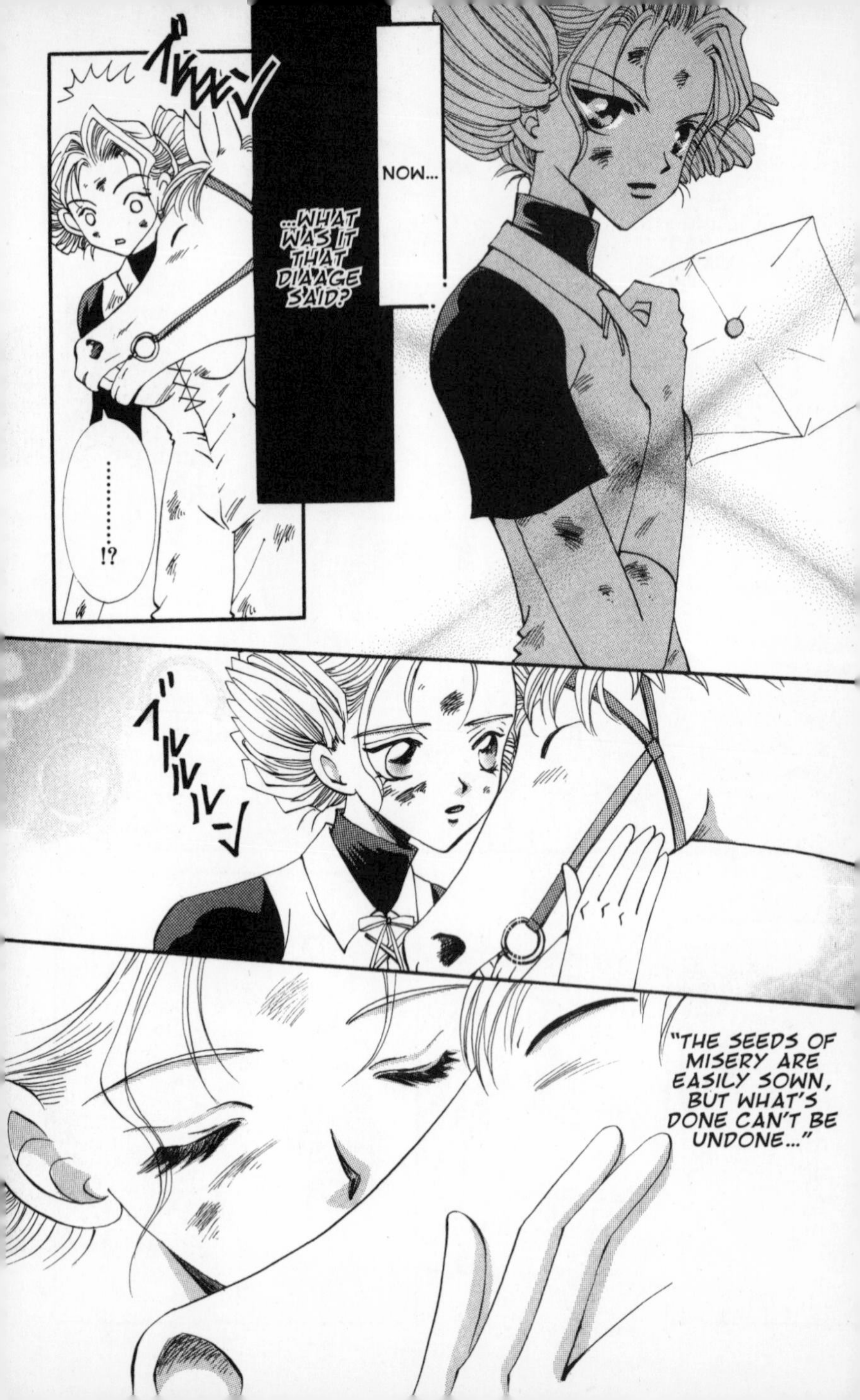
NOW...
...WHAT WAS IT THAT DIAAGE SAID?
......!?
"THE SEEDS OF MISERY ARE EASILY SOWN, BUT WHAT'S DONE CAN'T BE UNDONE..."

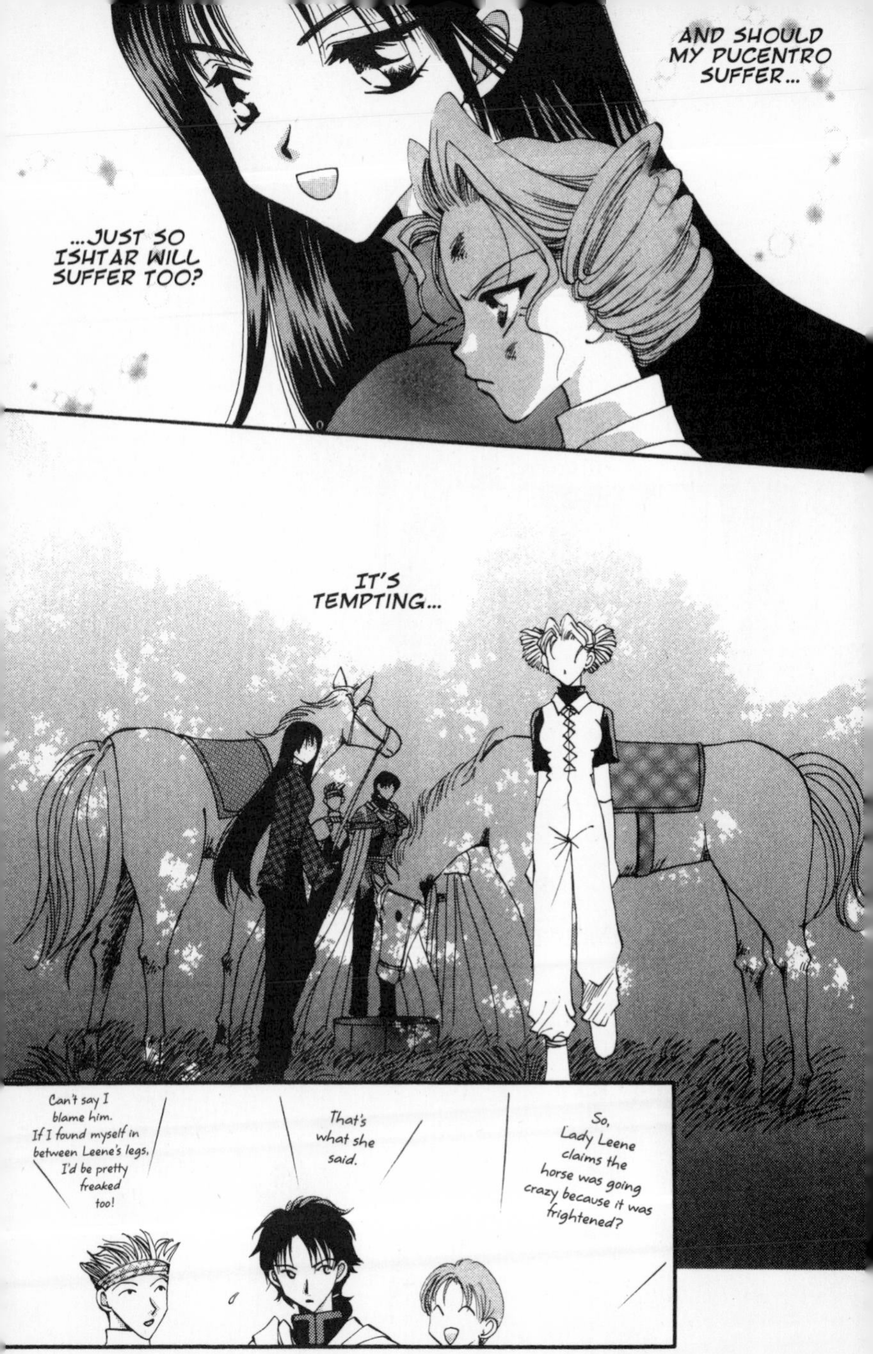
AND SHOULD MY PUCENTRO SUFFER...
...JUST SO ISHTAR WILL SUFFER TOO?
IT'S TEMPTING...
So, Lady Leene claims the horse was going crazy because it was frightened?
That's what she said.
Can't say I blame him. If I found myself in between Leene's legs, I'd be pretty freaked too!

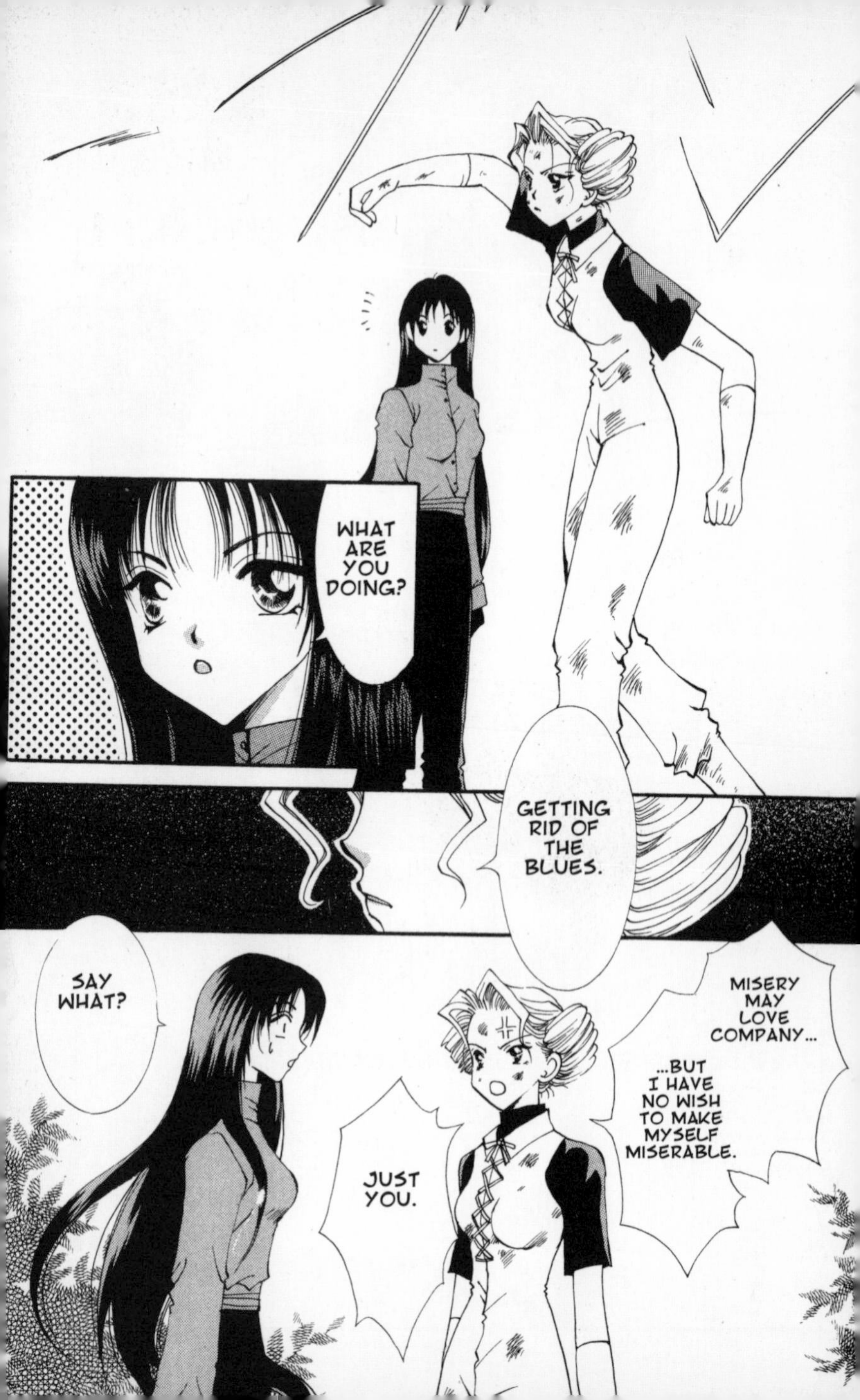
WHAT ARE YOU DOING?
GETTING RID OF THE BLUES.
MISERY MAY LOVE COMPANY...
...BUT I HAVE NO WISH TO MAKE MYSELF MISERABLE.
SAY WHAT?
JUST YOU.

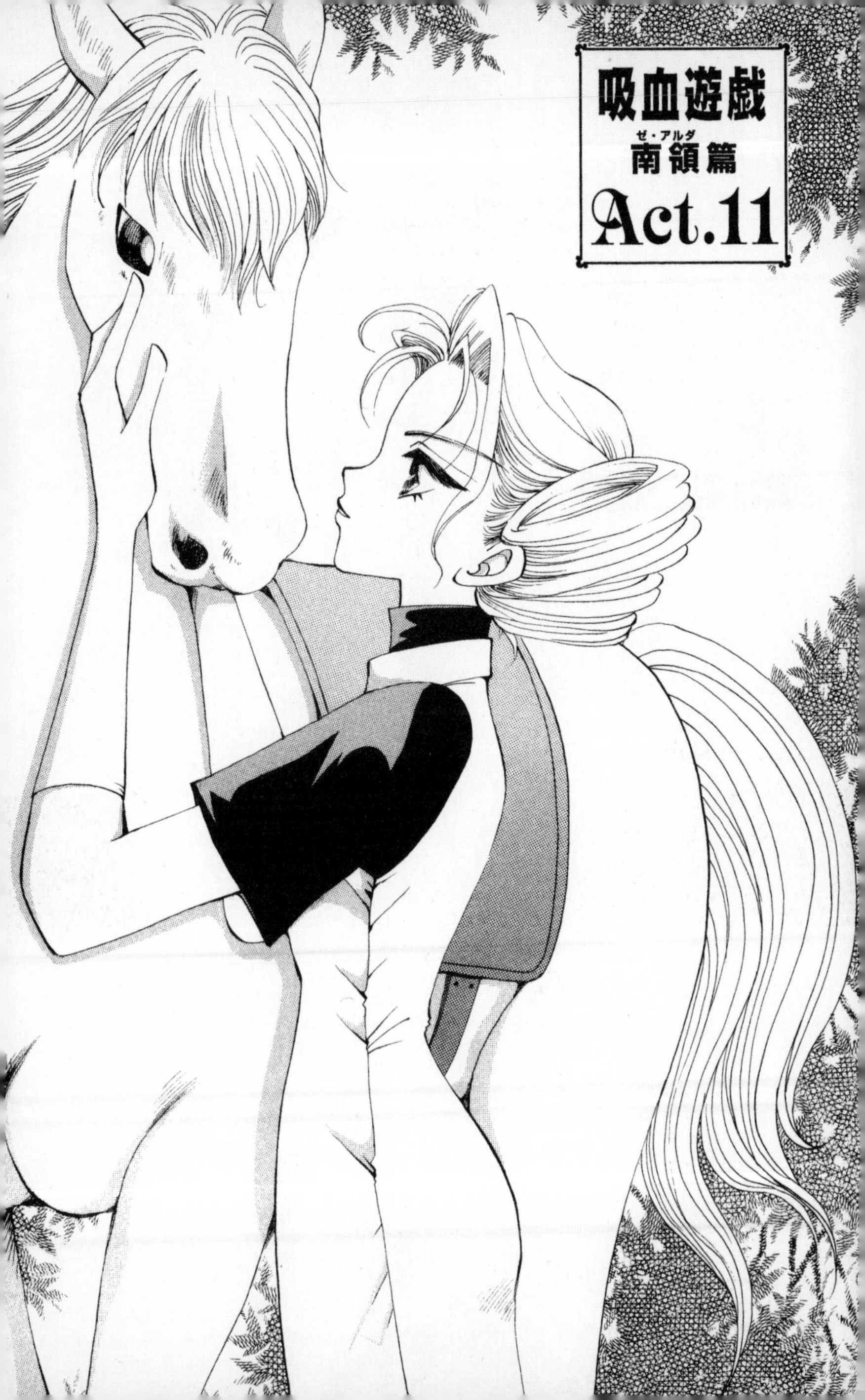
吸血遊戯
ゼ・アルダ
南領篇
Act.11

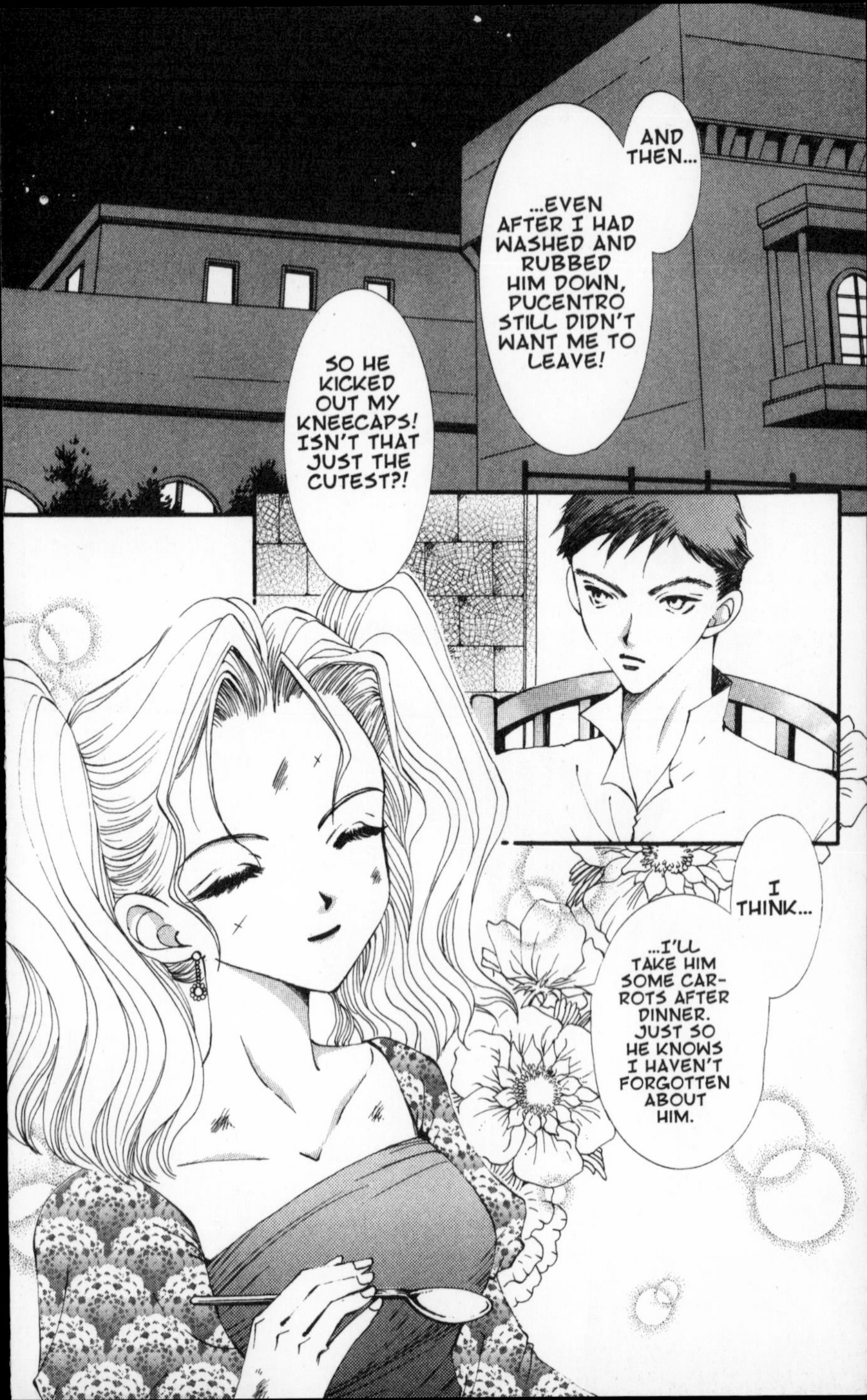
AND THEN...
...EVEN AFTER I HAD WASHED AND RUBBED HIM DOWN, PUCENTRO STILL DIDN'T WANT ME TO LEAVE!
SO HE KICKED OUT MY KNEECAPS! ISN'T THAT JUST THE CUTEST?!
I THINK...
...I'LL TAKE HIM SOME CAR-ROTS AFTER DINNER. JUST SO HE KNOWS I HAVEN'T FORGOTTEN ABOUT HIM.

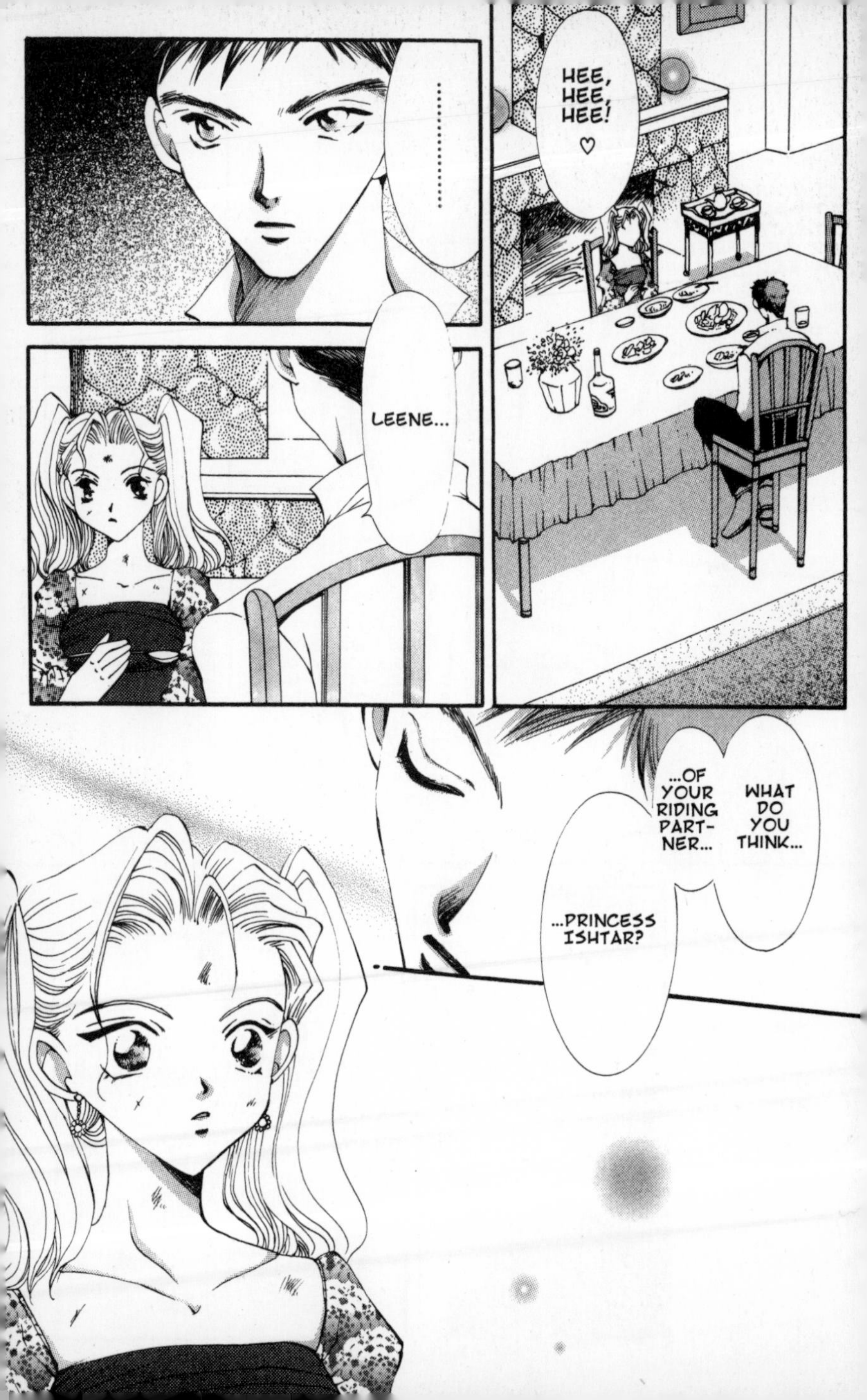
HEE, HEE, HEE! ♡
....
LEENE...
WHAT DO YOU THINK...
...OF YOUR RIDING PARTNER...
...PRINCESS ISHTAR?

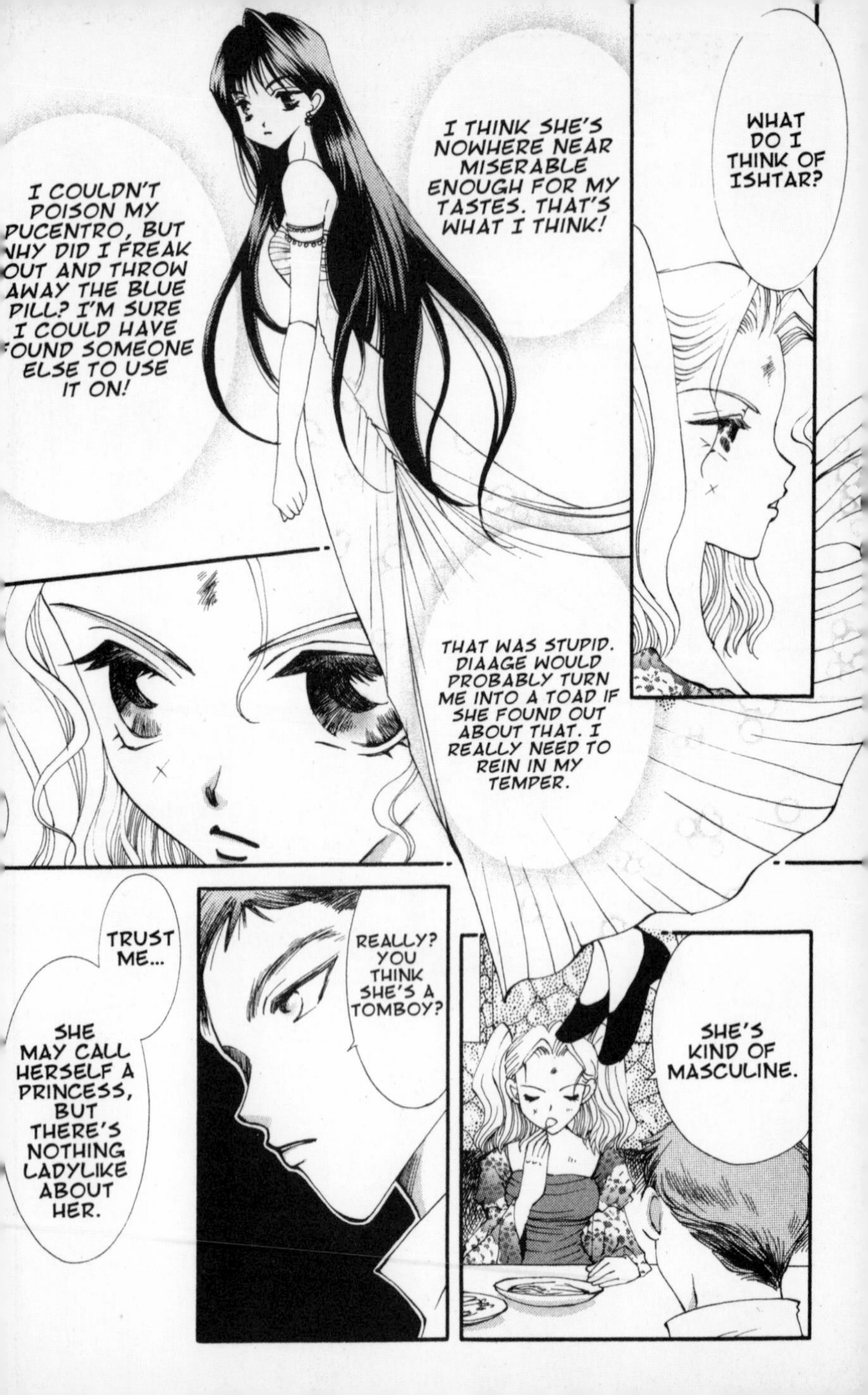
WHAT DO I THINK OF ISHTAR?
I THINK SHE'S NOWHERE NEAR MISERABLE ENOUGH FOR MY TASTES. THAT'S WHAT I THINK!
I COULDN'T POISON MY PUCENTRO, BUT WHY DID I FREAK OUT AND THROW AWAY THE BLUE PILL? I'M SURE I COULD HAVE FOUND SOMEONE ELSE TO USE IT ON!
THAT WAS STUPID. DIAAGE WOULD PROBABLY TURN ME INTO A TOAD IF SHE FOUND OUT ABOUT THAT. I REALLY NEED TO REIN IN MY TEMPER.
SHE'S KIND OF MASCULINE.
REALLY? YOU THINK SHE'S A TOMBOY?
TRUST ME...
SHE MAY CALL HERSELF A PRINCESS, BUT THERE'S NOTHING LADYLIKE ABOUT HER.

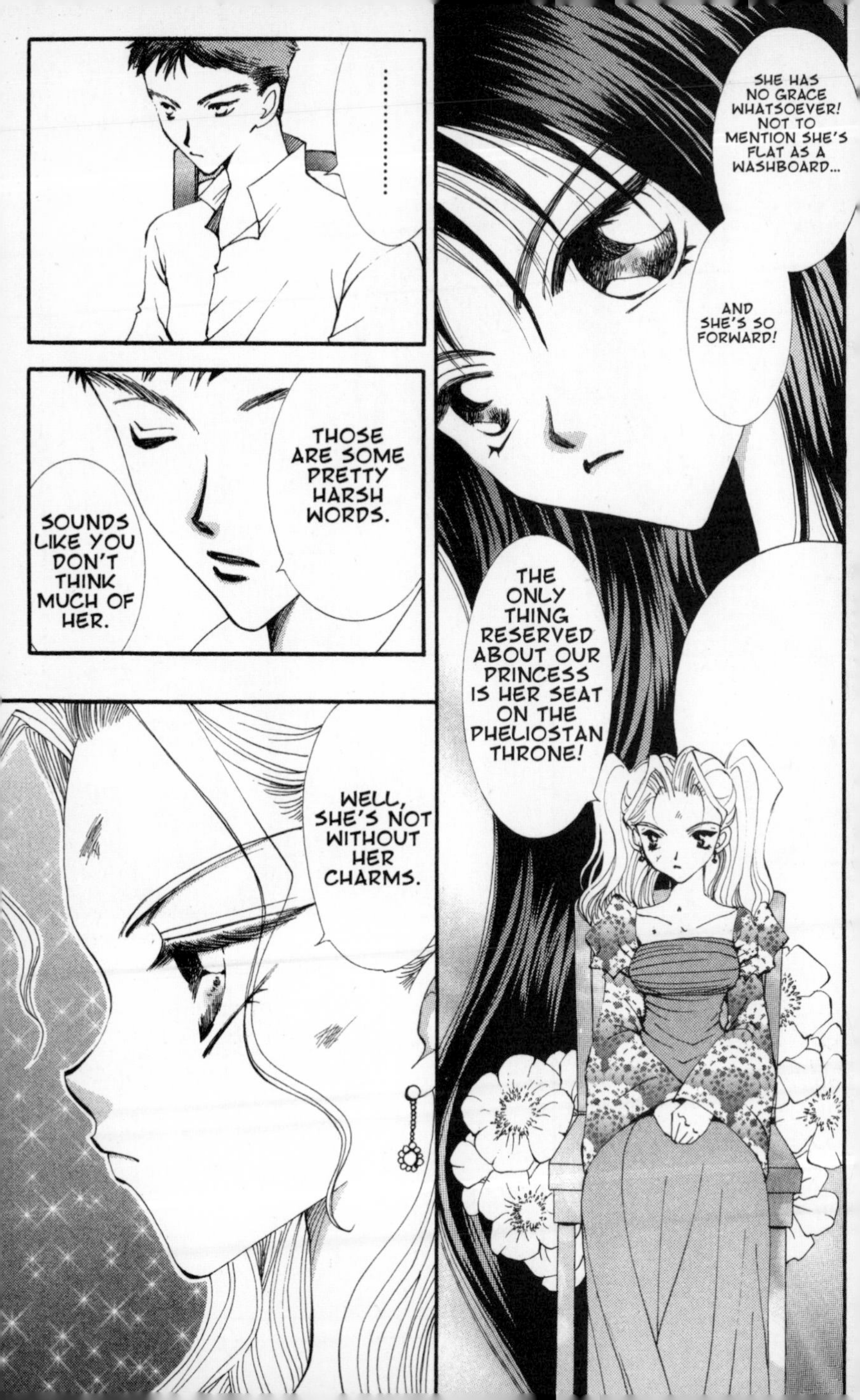
SHE HAS NO GRACE WHATSOEVER! NOT TO MENTION SHE'S FLAT AS A WASHBOARD...
AND SHE'S SO FORWARD!
THE ONLY THING RESERVED ABOUT OUR PRINCESS IS HER SEAT ON THE PHELIOSTAN THRONE!
......
THOSE ARE SOME PRETTY HARSH WORDS.
SOUNDS LIKE YOU DON'T THINK MUCH OF HER.
WELL, SHE'S NOT WITHOUT HER CHARMS.

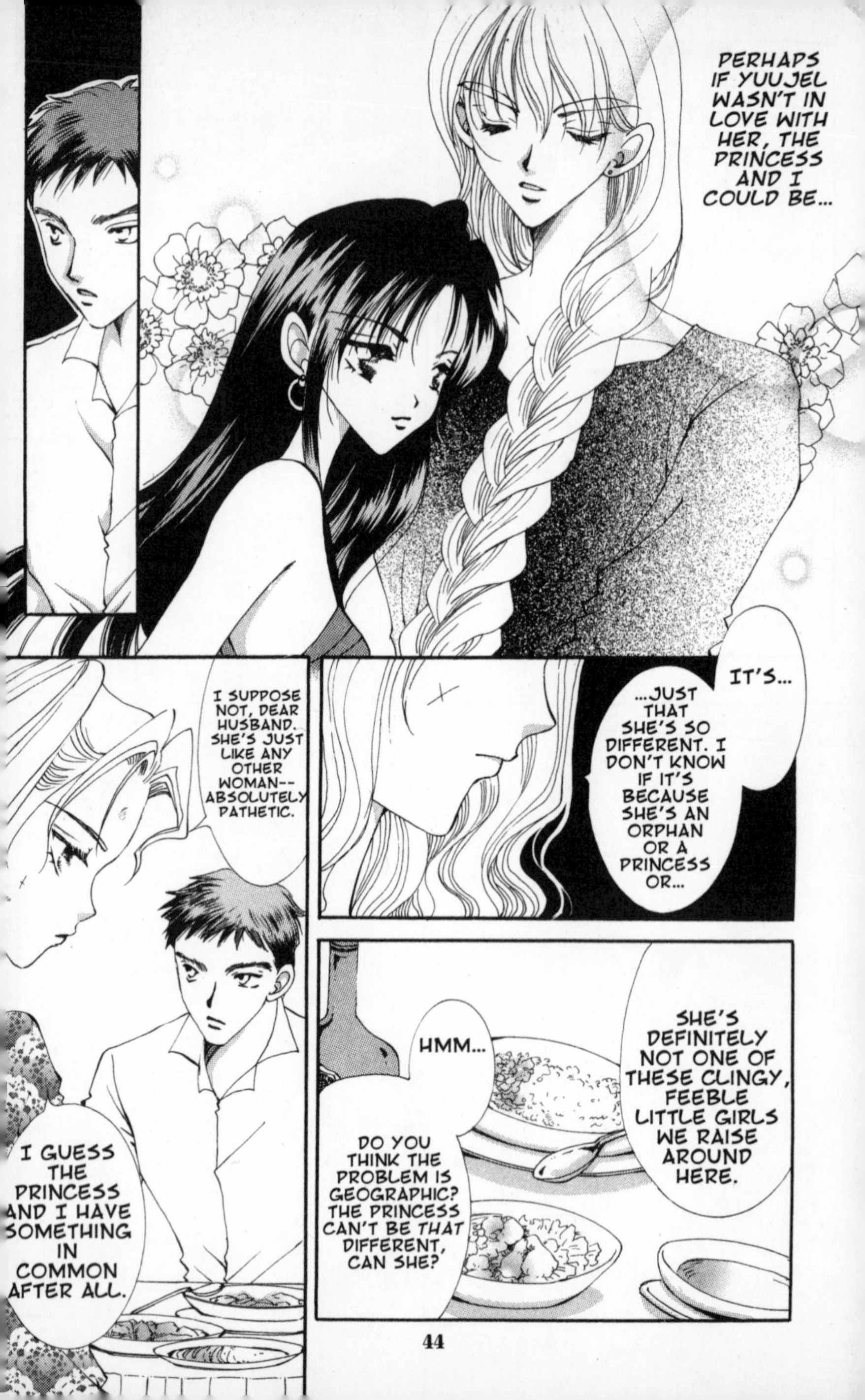
PERHAPS IF YUUJEL WASN'T IN LOVE WITH HER, THE PRINCESS AND I COULD BE...
IT'S...
...JUST THAT SHE'S SO DIFFERENT. I DON'T KNOW IF IT'S BECAUSE SHE'S AN ORPHAN OR A PRINCESS OR...
SHE'S DEFINITELY NOT ONE OF THESE CLINGY, FEEBLE LITTLE GIRLS WE RAISE AROUND HERE.
HMM...
DO YOU THINK THE PROBLEM IS GEOGRAPHIC? THE PRINCESS CAN'T BE *THAT* DIFFERENT, CAN SHE?
I SUPPOSE NOT, DEAR HUSBAND. SHE'S JUST LIKE ANY OTHER WOMAN--ABSOLUTELY PATHETIC.
I GUESS THE PRINCESS AND I HAVE SOMETHING IN COMMON AFTER ALL.

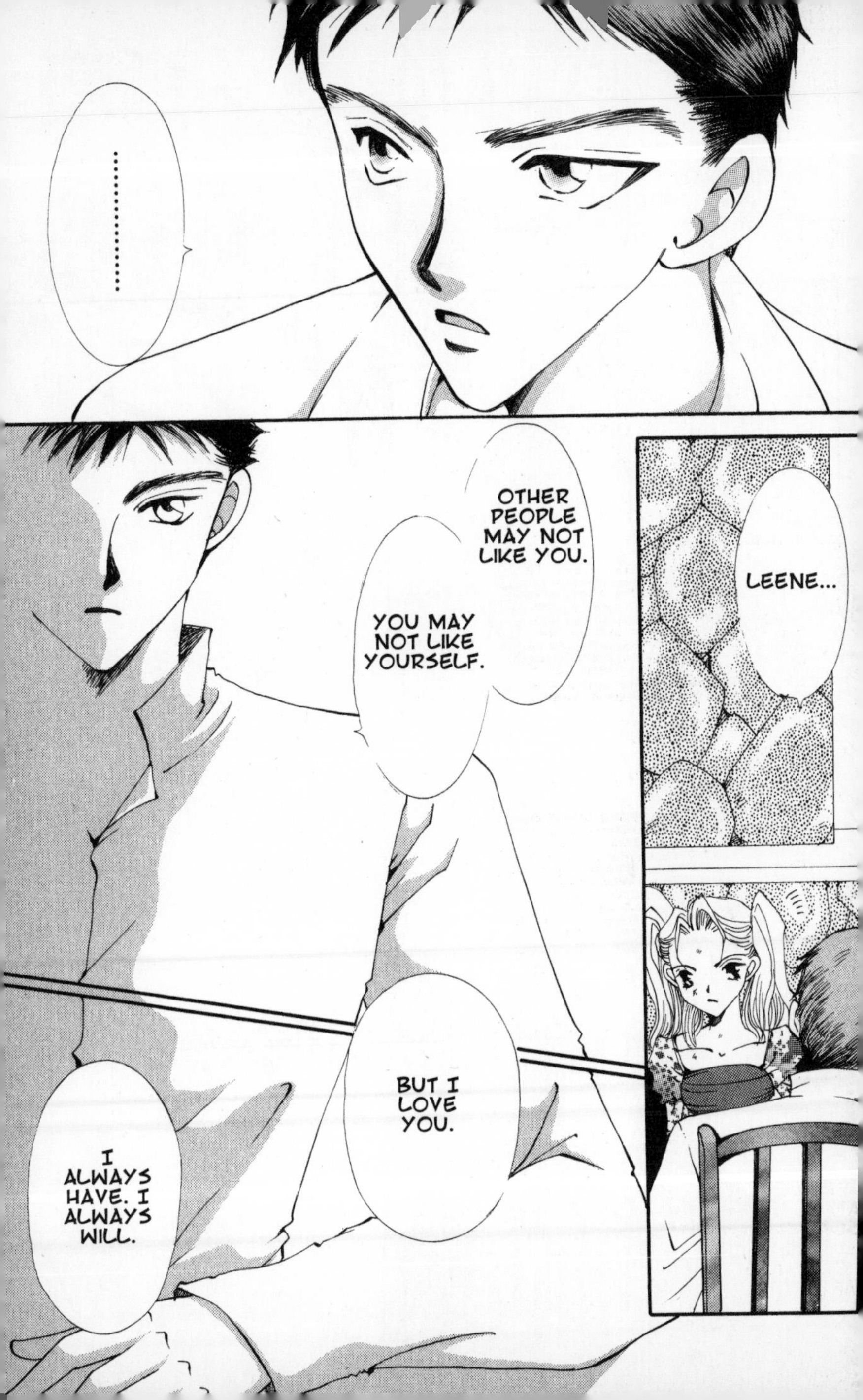
......
LEENE...
OTHER PEOPLE MAY NOT LIKE YOU.
YOU MAY NOT LIKE YOURSELF.
BUT I LOVE YOU.
I ALWAYS HAVE. I ALWAYS WILL.

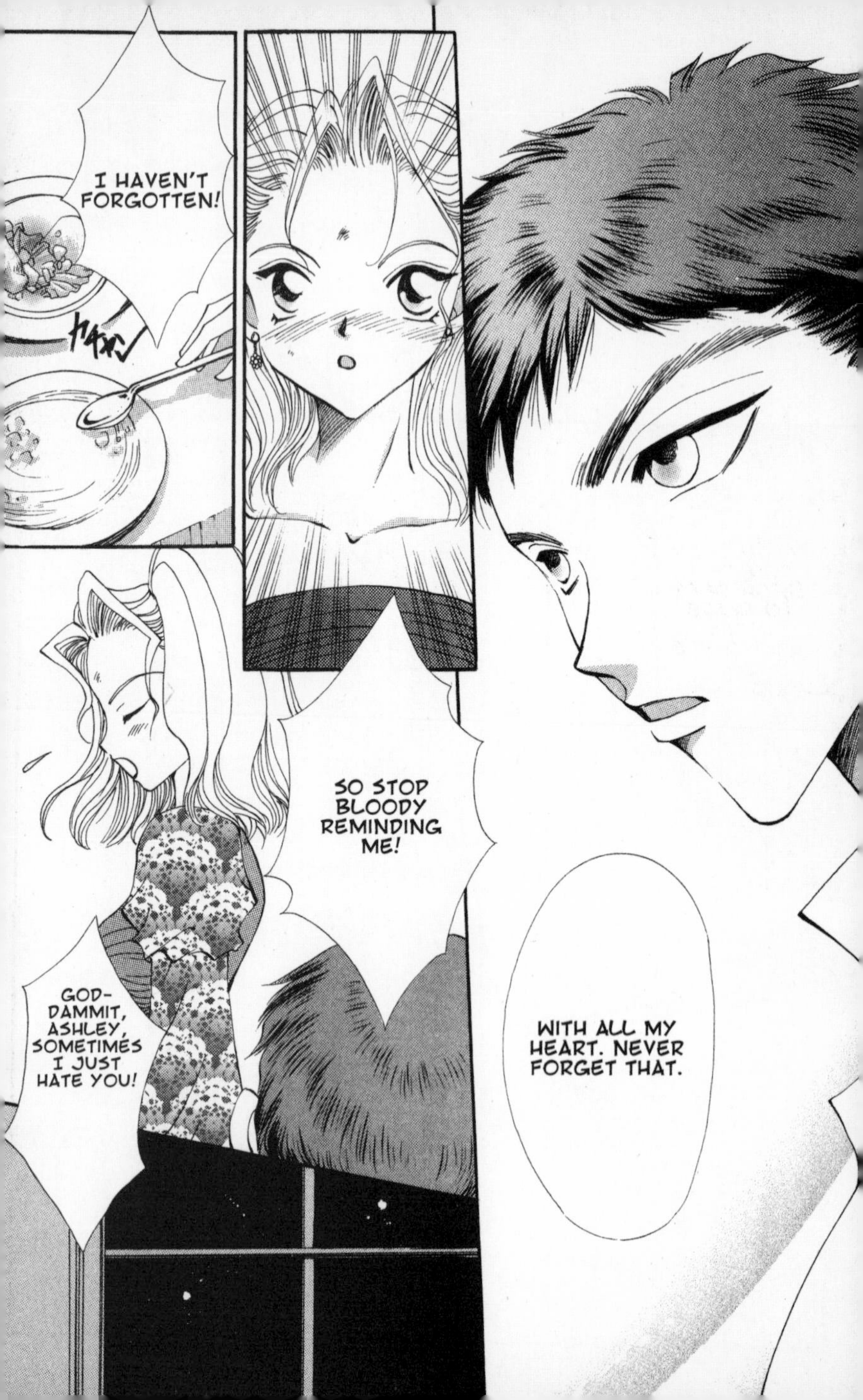
WITH ALL MY HEART. NEVER FORGET THAT.
I HAVEN'T FORGOTTEN!
SO STOP BLOODY REMINDING ME!
GOD-DAMMIT, ASHLEY, SOMETIMES I JUST HATE YOU!

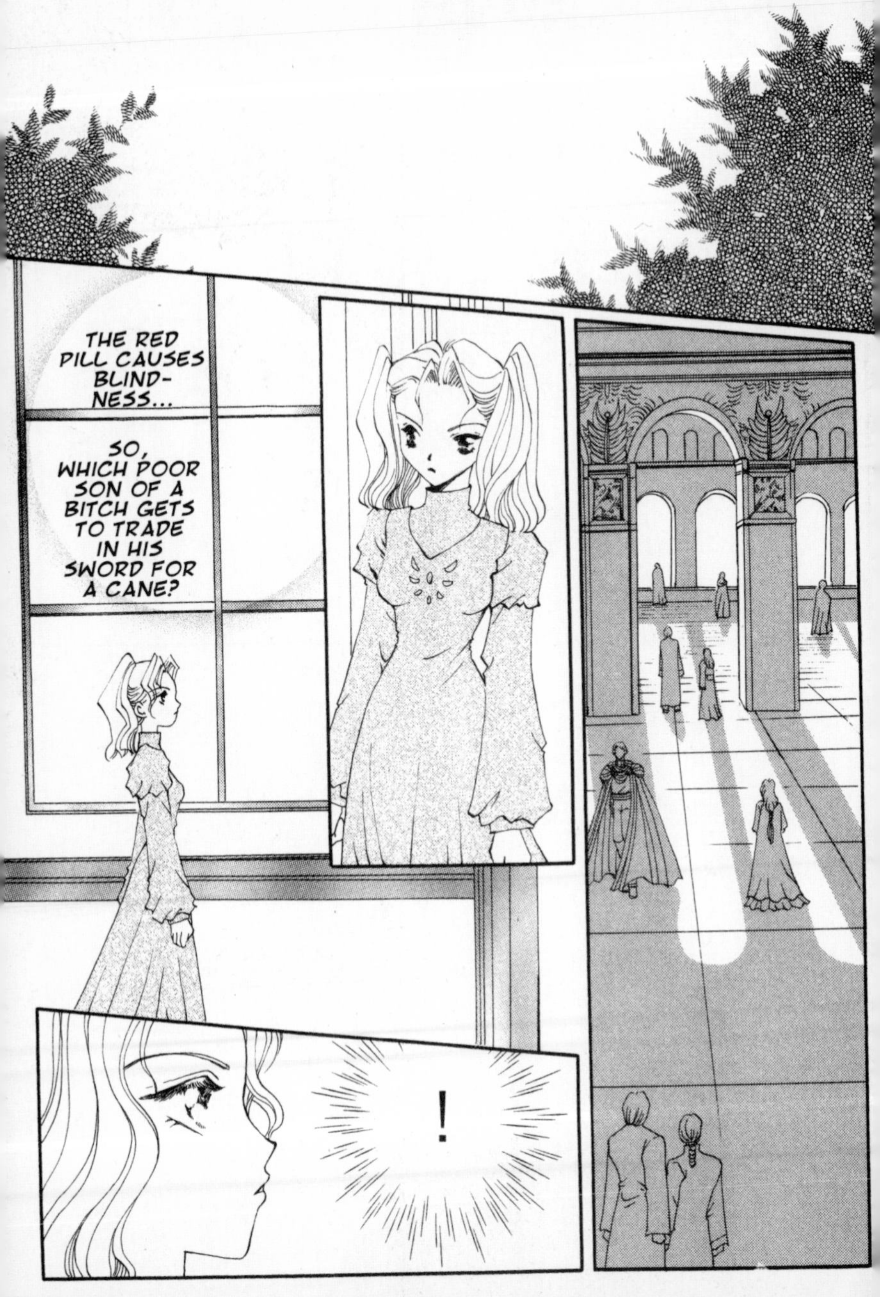
THE RED PILL CAUSES BLINDNESS...
SO, WHICH POOR SON OF A BITCH GETS TO TRADE IN HIS SWORD FOR A CANE?
!

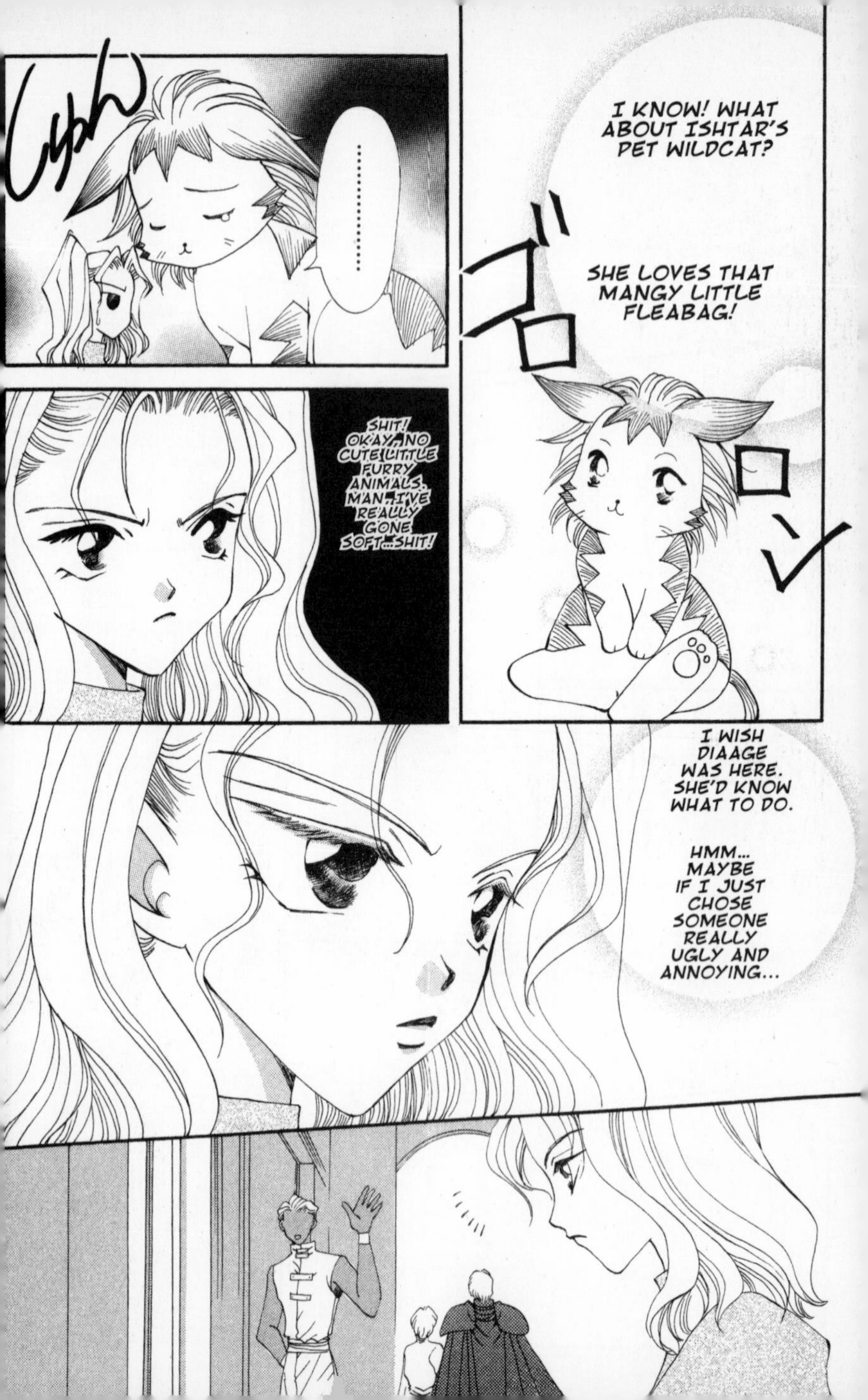
I KNOW! WHAT ABOUT ISHTAR'S PET WILDCAT?
SHE LOVES THAT MANGY LITTLE FLEABAG!
ゴロン
......
SHIT! OKAY, NO CUTE LITTLE FURRY ANIMALS. MAN, I'VE REALLY GONE SOFT...SHIT!
I WISH DIAAGE WAS HERE. SHE'D KNOW WHAT TO DO.
HMM... MAYBE IF I JUST CHOSE SOMEONE REALLY UGLY AND ANNOYING...

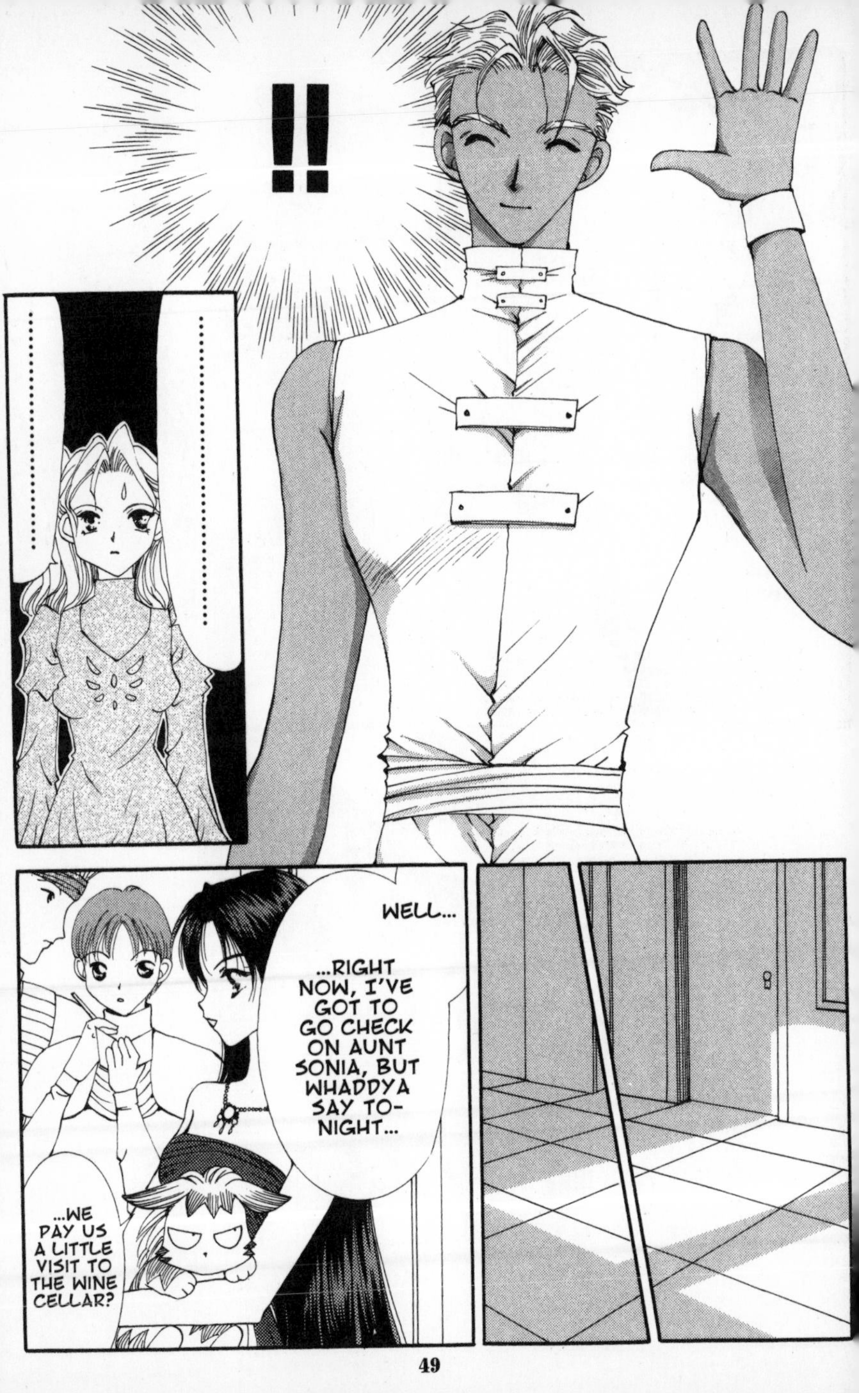
!!
......
......
WELL...
...RIGHT NOW, I'VE GOT TO GO CHECK ON AUNT SONIA, BUT WHADDYA SAY TO-NIGHT...
...WE PAY US A LITTLE VISIT TO THE WINE CELLAR?

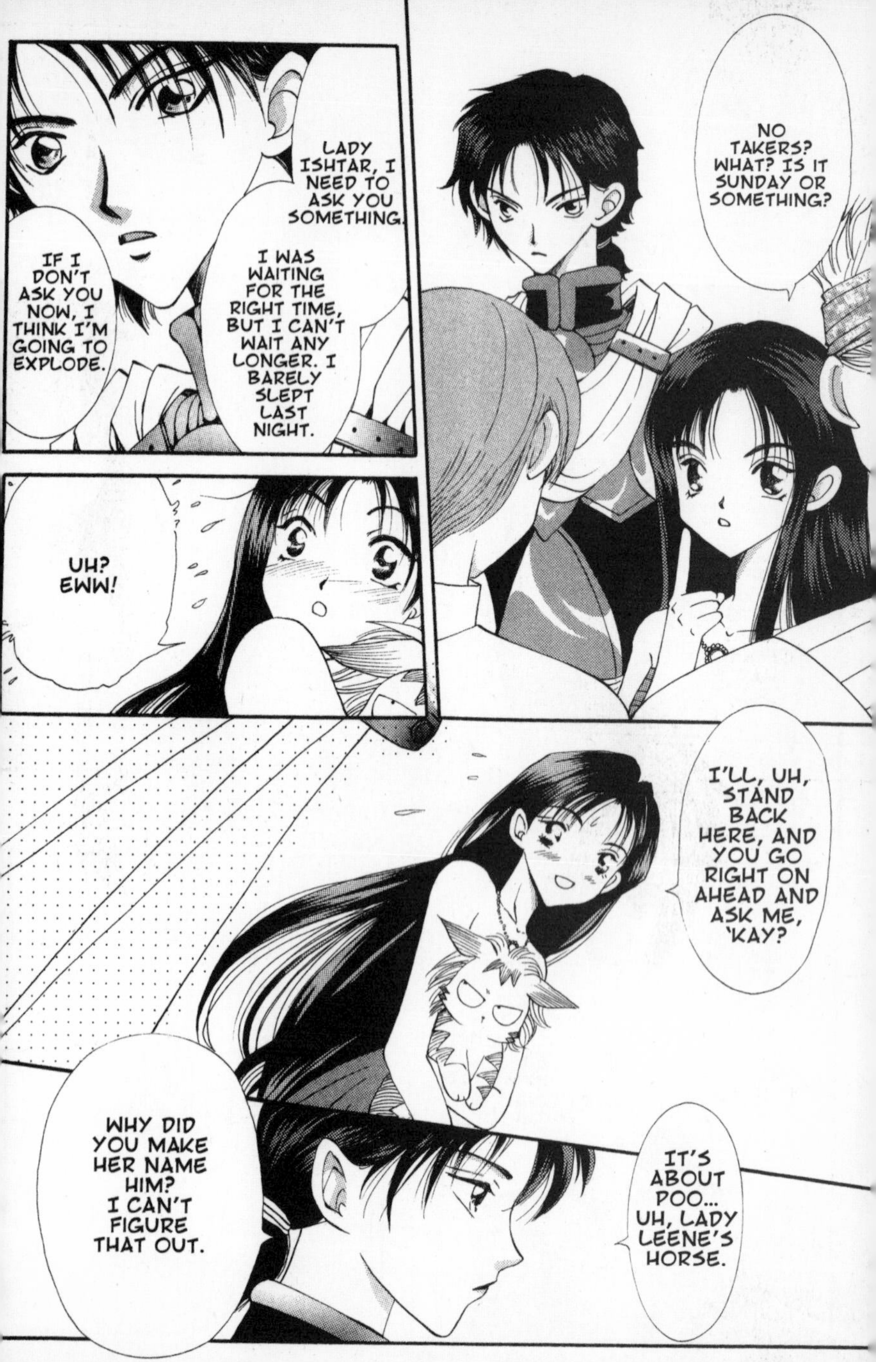
NO TAKERS? WHAT? IS IT SUNDAY OR SOMETHING?
LADY ISHTAR, I NEED TO ASK YOU SOMETHING.
I WAS WAITING FOR THE RIGHT TIME, BUT I CAN'T WAIT ANY LONGER. I BARELY SLEPT LAST NIGHT.
IF I DON'T ASK YOU NOW, I THINK I'M GOING TO EXPLODE.
UH? EWW!
I'LL, UH, STAND BACK HERE, AND YOU GO RIGHT ON AHEAD AND ASK ME, 'KAY?
IT'S ABOUT POO... UH, LADY LEENE'S HORSE.
WHY DID YOU MAKE HER NAME HIM? I CAN'T FIGURE THAT OUT.

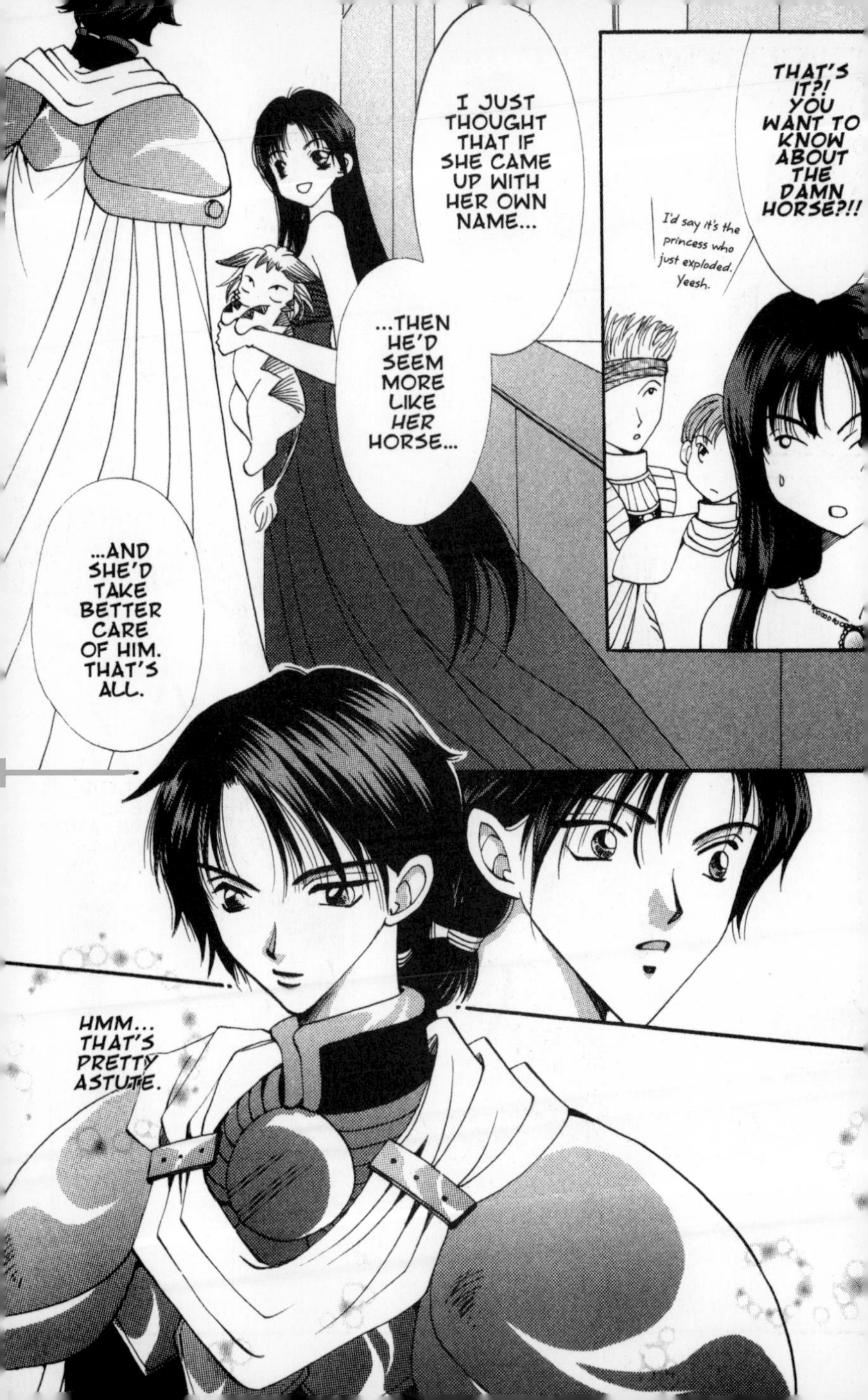
THAT'S IT?! YOU WANT TO KNOW ABOUT THE DAMN HORSE?!!
I'd say it's the princess who just exploded. Yeesh.
I JUST THOUGHT THAT IF SHE CAME UP WITH HER OWN NAME...
...THEN HE'D SEEM MORE LIKE HER HORSE...
...AND SHE'D TAKE BETTER CARE OF HIM. THAT'S ALL.
HMM... THAT'S PRETTY ASTUTE.

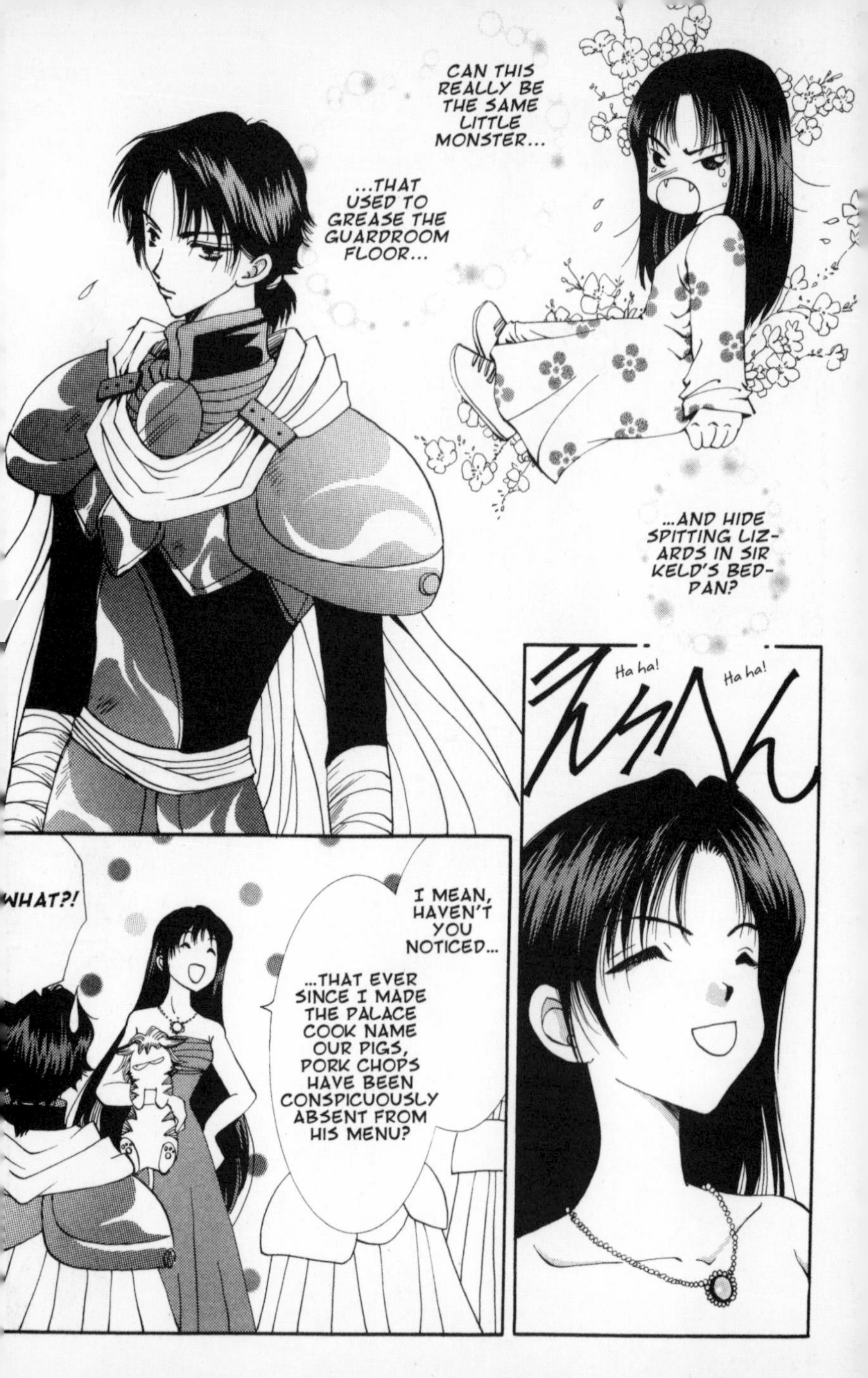
CAN THIS REALLY BE THE SAME LITTLE MONSTER...
...THAT USED TO GREASE THE GUARDROOM FLOOR...
...AND HIDE SPITTING LIZ-ARDS IN SIR KELD'S BED-PAN?
Ha ha!
Ha ha!
WHAT?!
I MEAN, HAVEN'T YOU NOTICED...
...THAT EVER SINCE I MADE THE PALACE COOK NAME OUR PIGS, PORK CHOPS HAVE BEEN CONSPICUOUSLY ABSENT FROM HIS MENU?

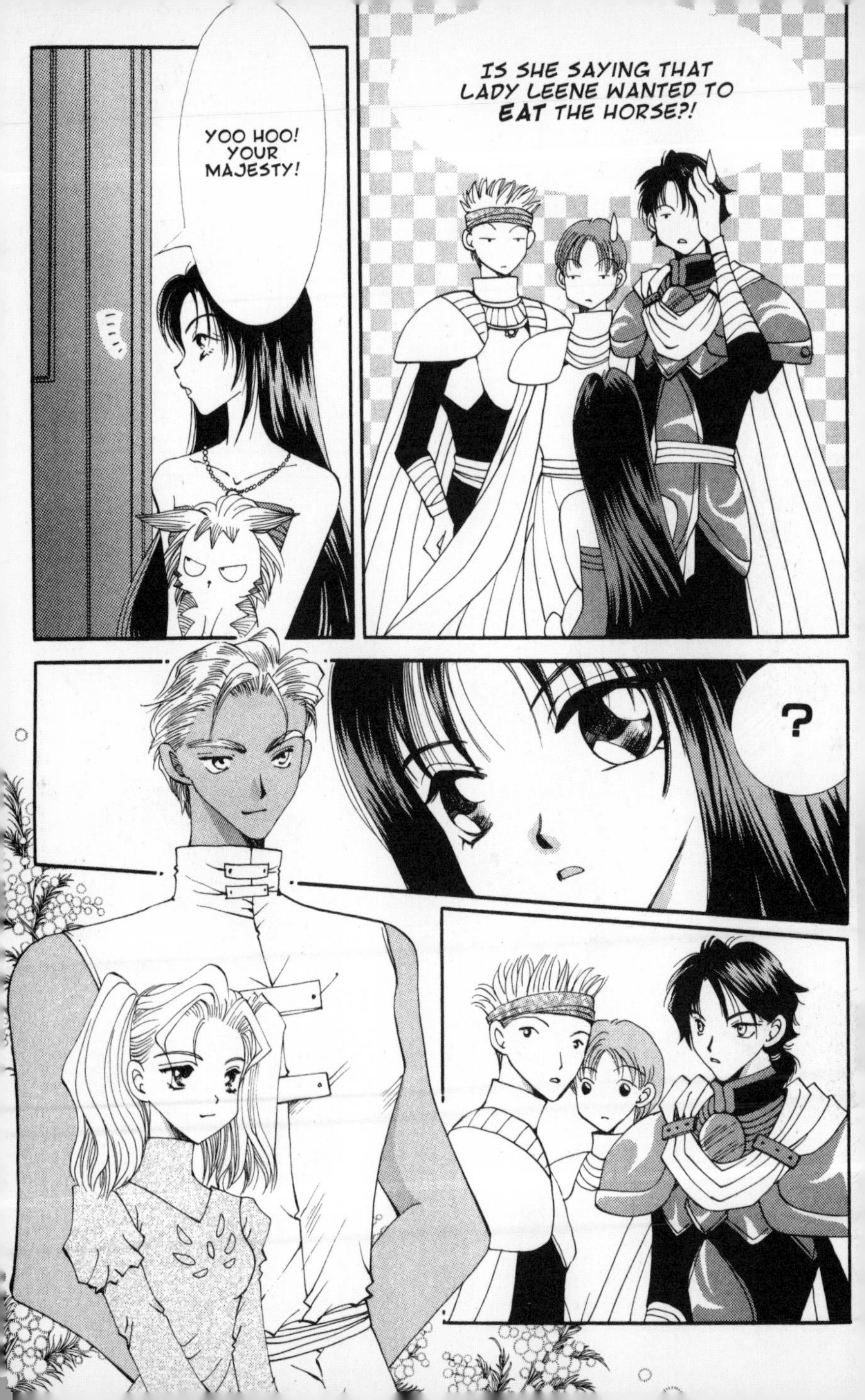
IS SHE SAYING THAT LADY LEENE WANTED TO **EAT** THE HORSE?!
YOO HOO! YOUR MAJESTY!
?

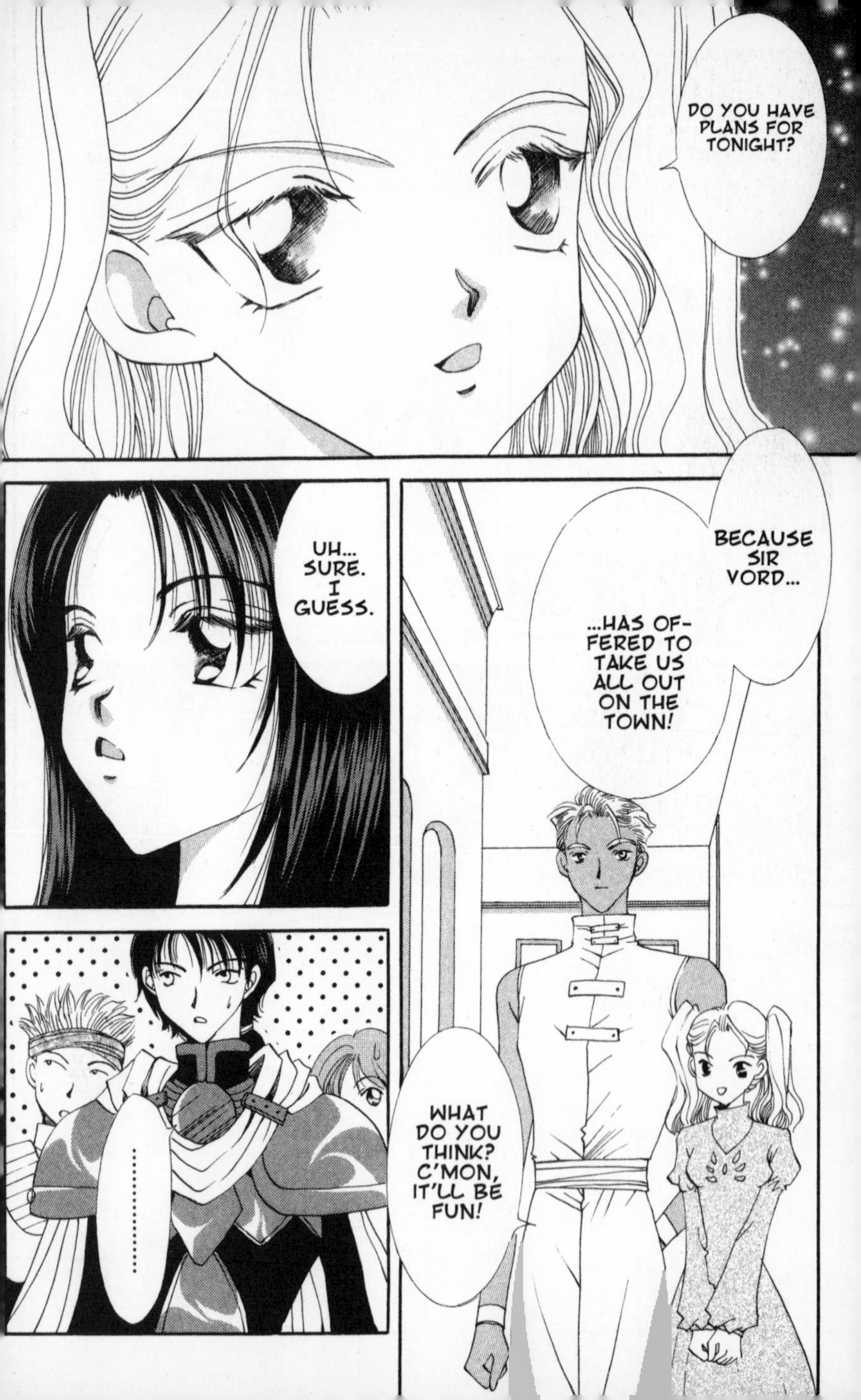
DO YOU HAVE PLANS FOR TONIGHT?
BECAUSE SIR VORD...
...HAS OF-FERED TO TAKE US ALL OUT ON THE TOWN!
WHAT DO YOU THINK? C'MON, IT'LL BE FUN!
UH... SURE. I GUESS.
....

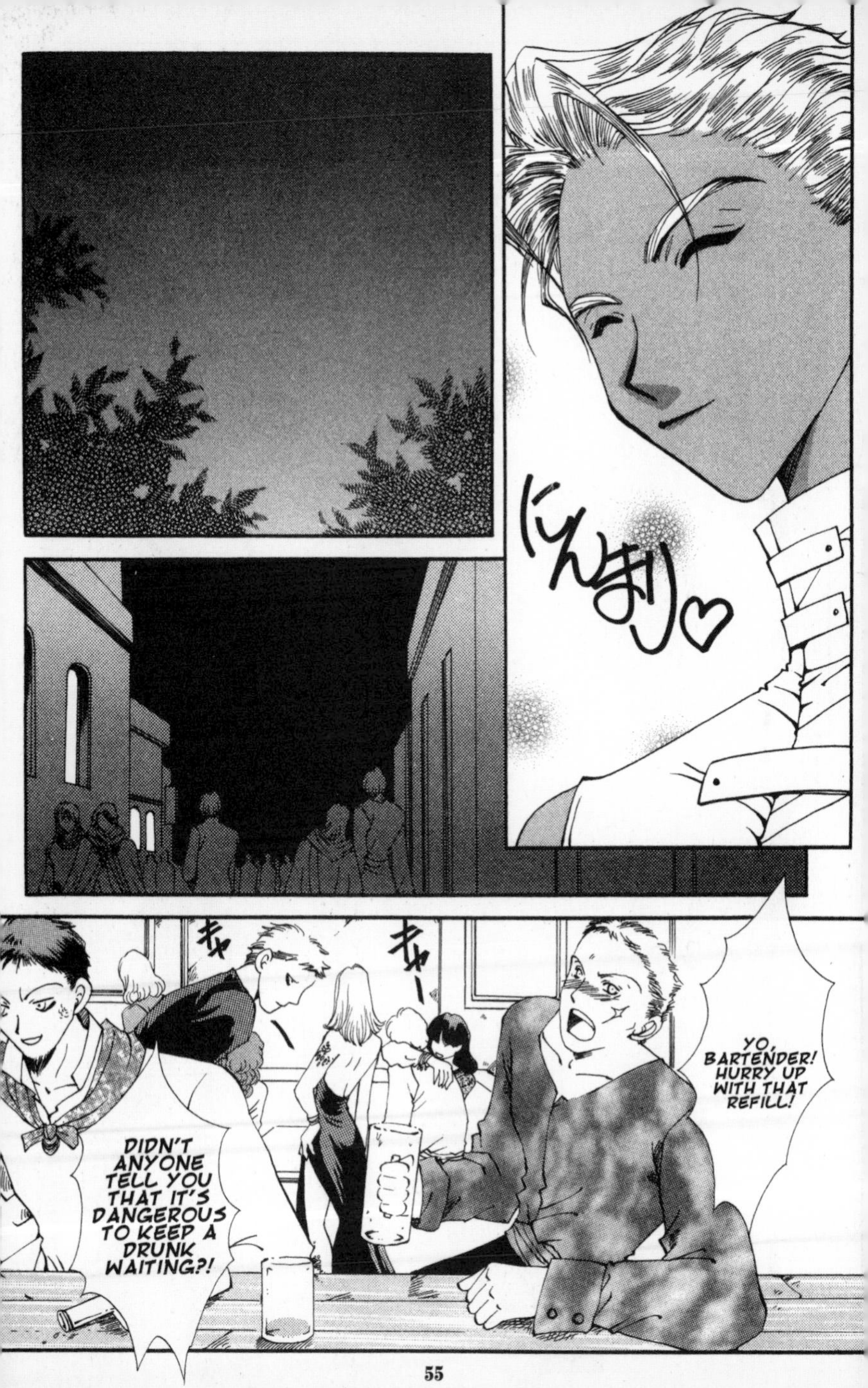
にんまり♡
キャー
キャ
YO, BARTENDER! HURRY UP WITH THAT REFILL!
DIDN'T ANYONE TELL YOU THAT IT'S DANGEROUS TO KEEP A DRUNK WAITING?!

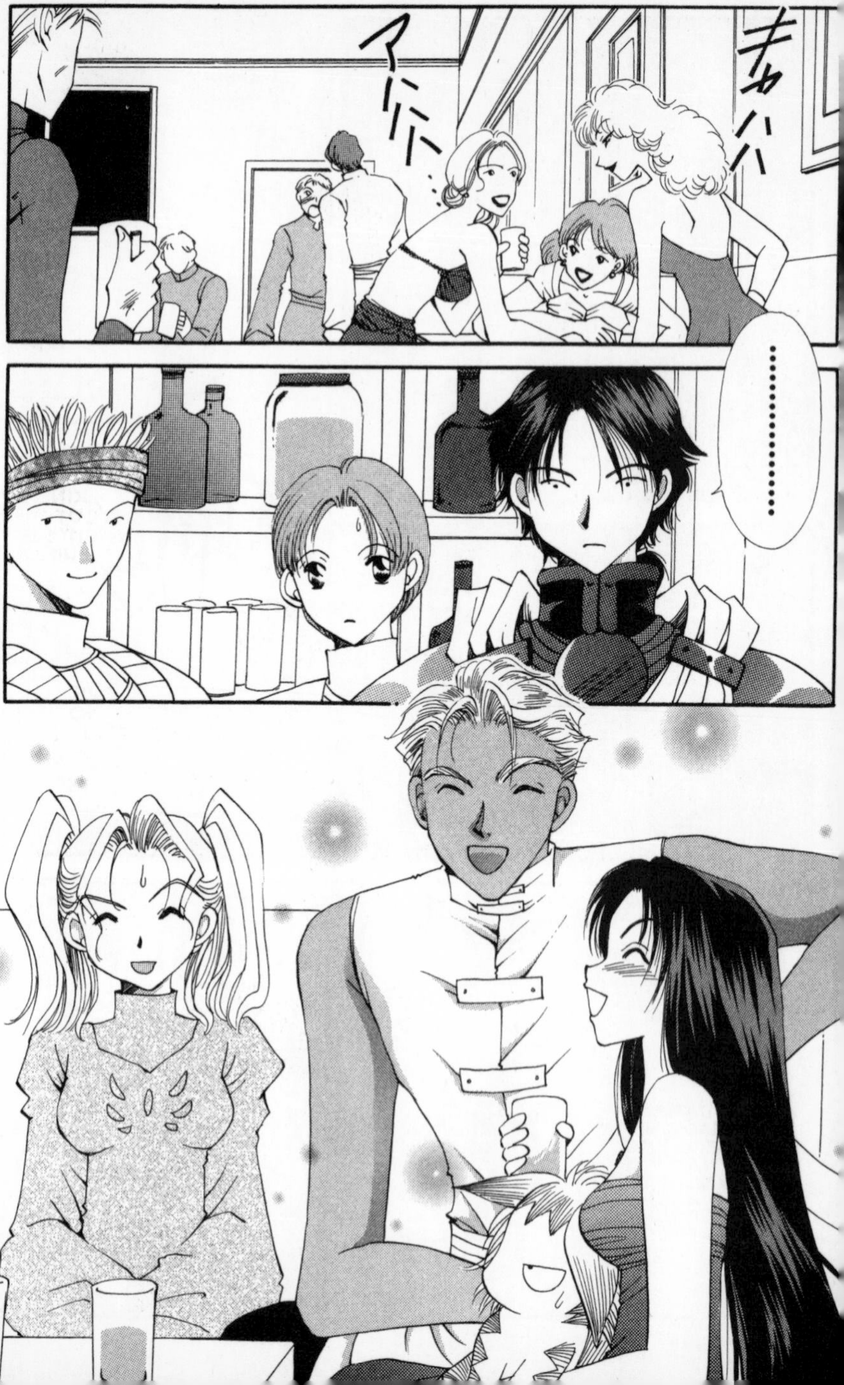
キャハハ
アハハー
………

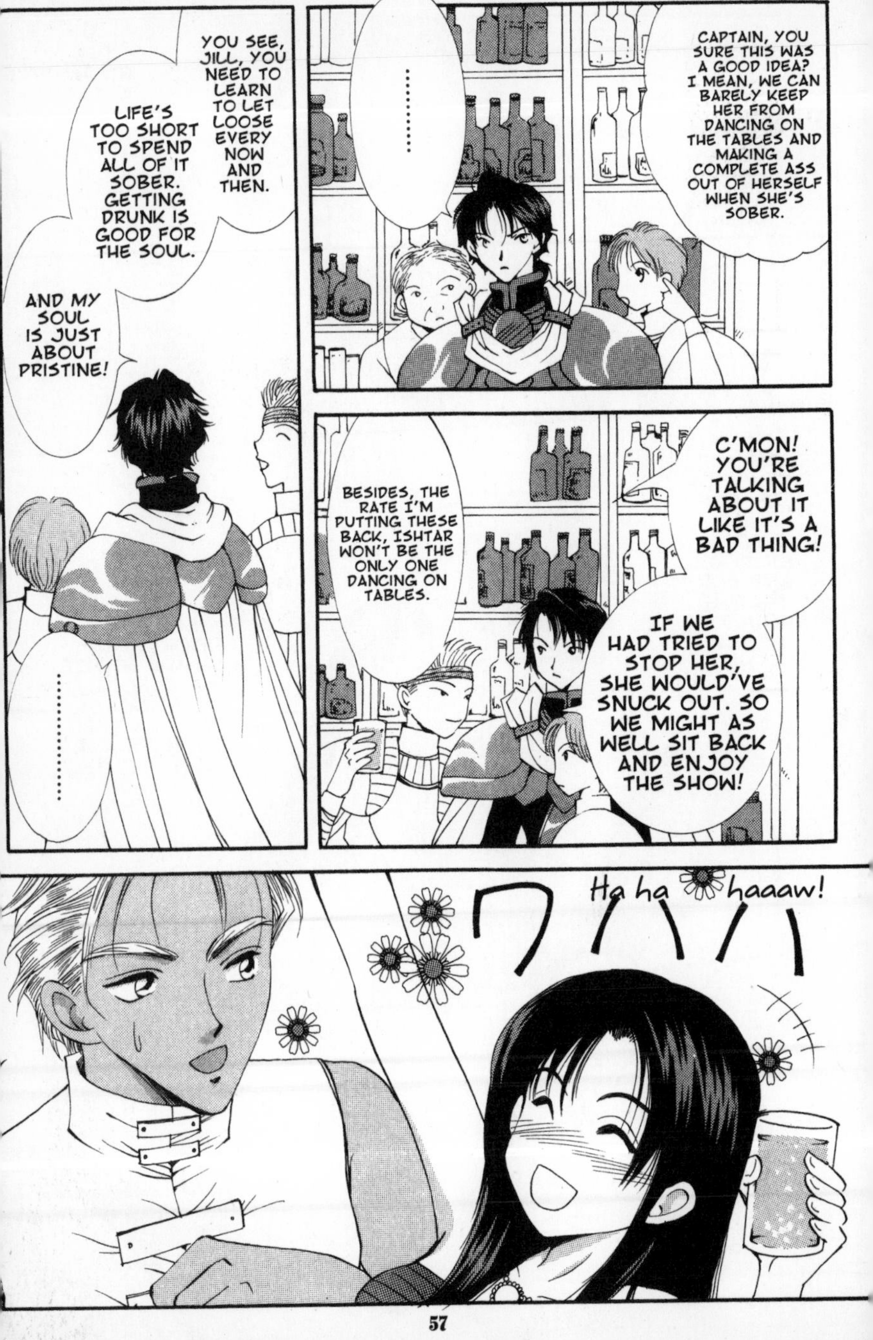
CAPTAIN, YOU SURE THIS WAS A GOOD IDEA? I MEAN, WE CAN BARELY KEEP HER FROM DANCING ON THE TABLES AND MAKING A COMPLETE ASS OUT OF HERSELF WHEN SHE'S SOBER.
......
C'MON! YOU'RE TALKING ABOUT IT LIKE IT'S A BAD THING!
IF WE HAD TRIED TO STOP HER, SHE WOULD'VE SNUCK OUT. SO WE MIGHT AS WELL SIT BACK AND ENJOY THE SHOW!
BESIDES, THE RATE I'M PUTTING THESE BACK, ISHTAR WON'T BE THE ONLY ONE DANCING ON TABLES.
YOU SEE, JILL, YOU NEED TO LEARN TO LET LOOSE EVERY NOW AND THEN.
LIFE'S TOO SHORT TO SPEND ALL OF IT SOBER. GETTING DRUNK IS GOOD FOR THE SOUL.
AND MY SOUL IS JUST ABOUT PRISTINE!
......
Ha ha haaaw!

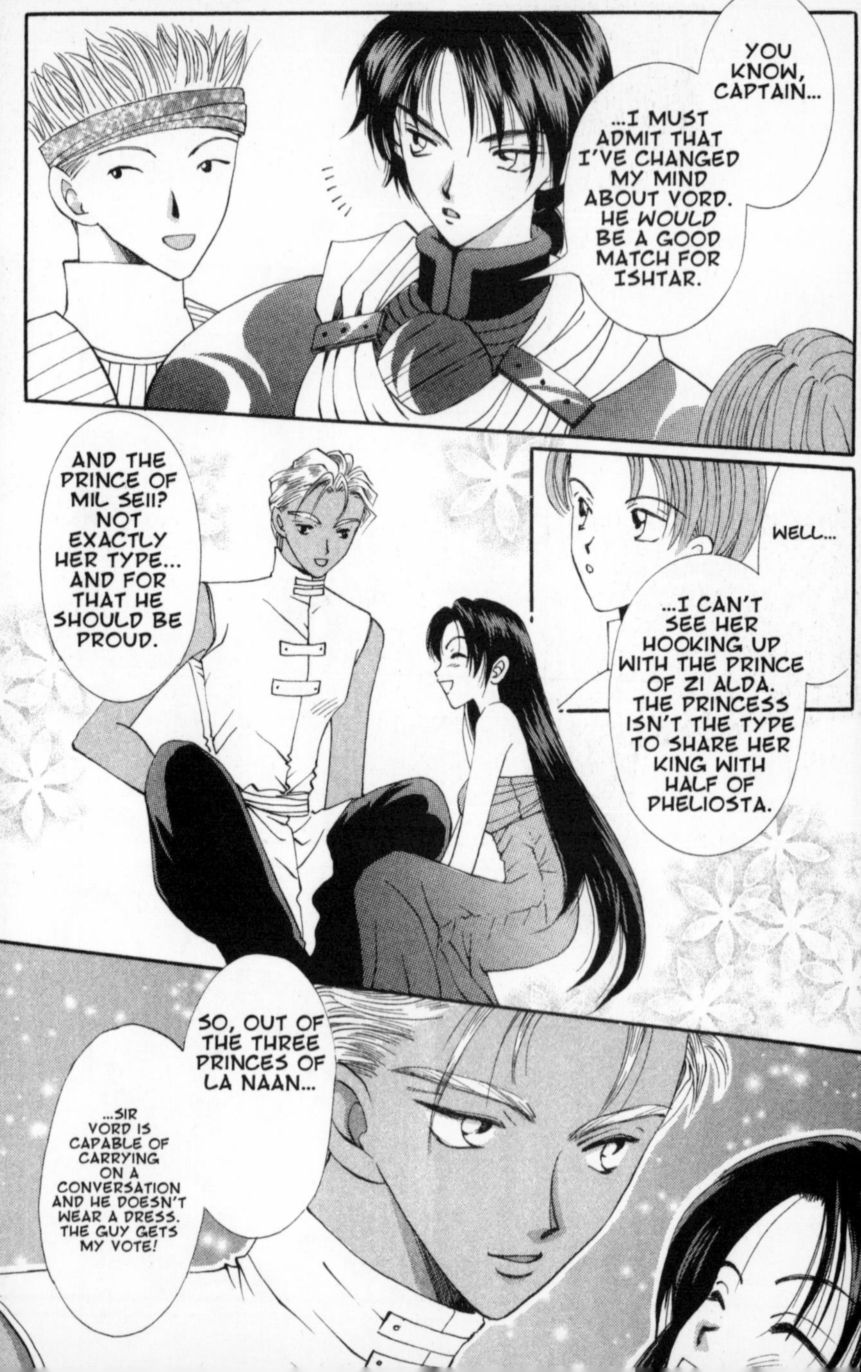
YOU KNOW, CAPTAIN...
...I MUST ADMIT THAT I'VE CHANGED MY MIND ABOUT VORD. HE *WOULD* BE A GOOD MATCH FOR ISHTAR.
WELL...
...I CAN'T SEE HER HOOKING UP WITH THE PRINCE OF ZI ALDA. THE PRINCESS ISN'T THE TYPE TO SHARE HER KING WITH HALF OF PHELIOSTA.
AND THE PRINCE OF MIL SEII? NOT EXACTLY HER TYPE... AND FOR THAT HE SHOULD BE PROUD.
SO, OUT OF THE THREE PRINCES OF LA NAAN...
...SIR VORD IS CAPABLE OF CARRYING ON A CONVERSATION AND HE DOESN'T WEAR A DRESS. THE GUY GETS MY VOTE!

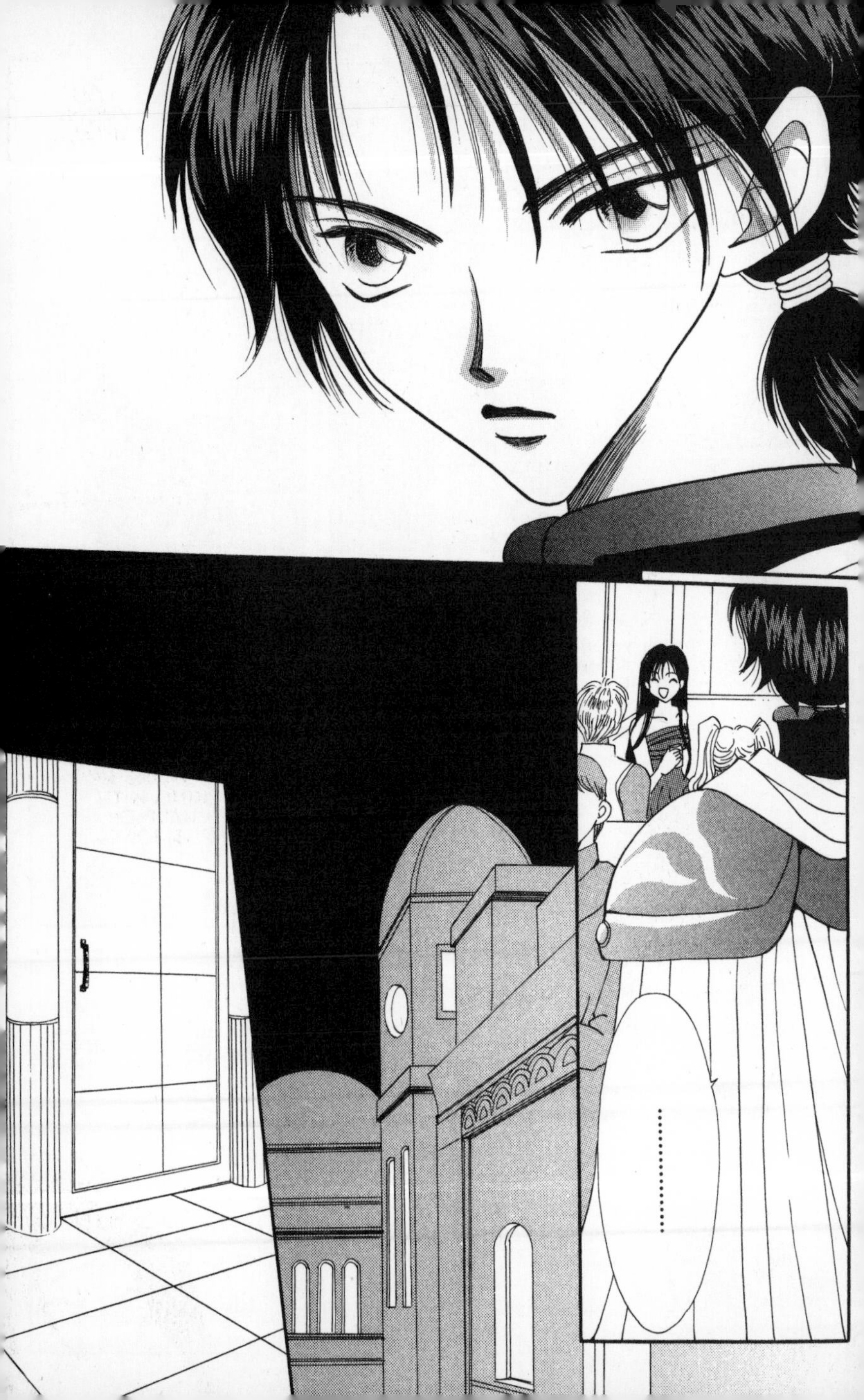
……

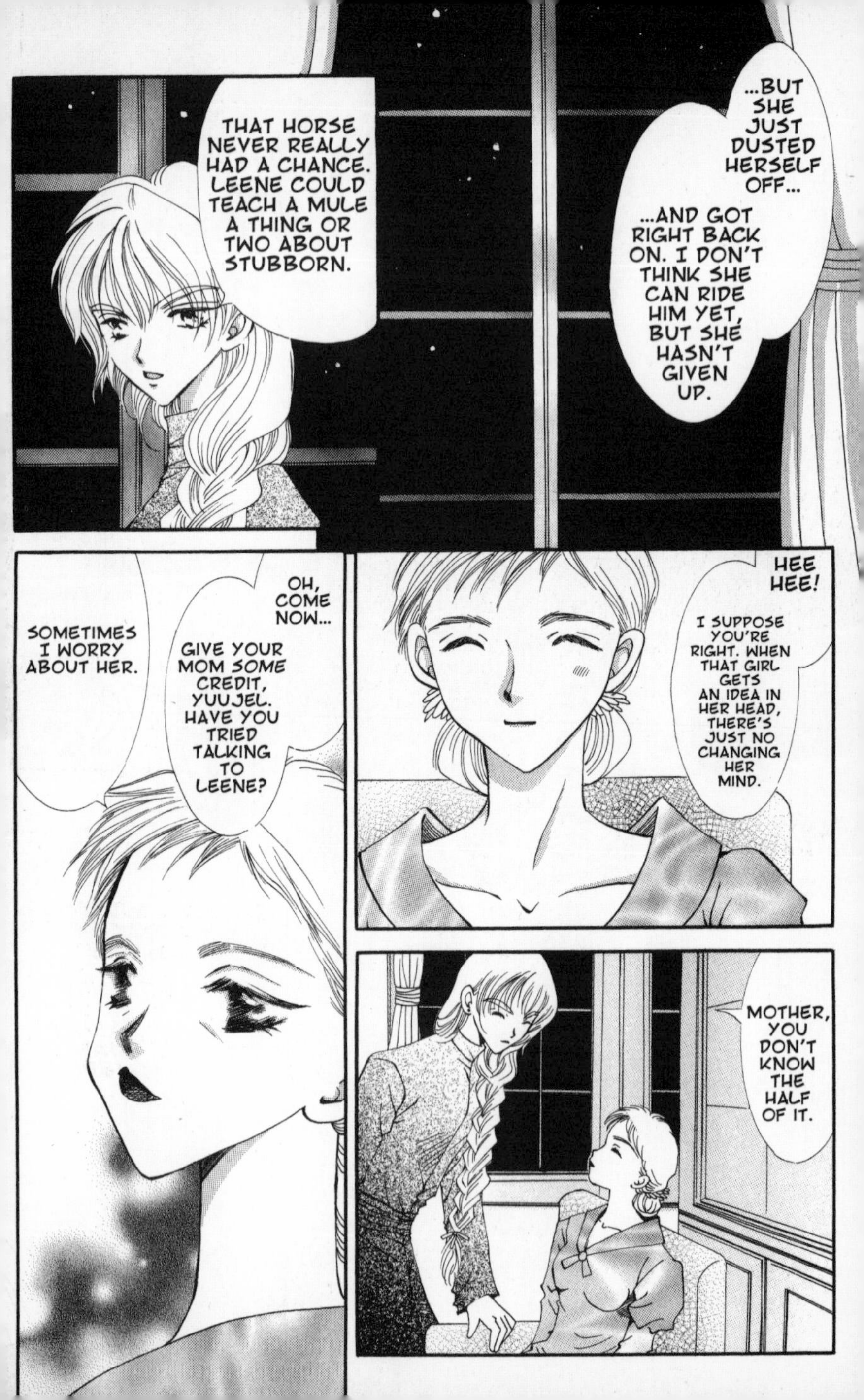
...BUT SHE JUST DUSTED HERSELF OFF...
...AND GOT RIGHT BACK ON. I DON'T THINK SHE CAN RIDE HIM YET, BUT SHE HASN'T GIVEN UP.
THAT HORSE NEVER REALLY HAD A CHANCE. LEENE COULD TEACH A MULE A THING OR TWO ABOUT STUBBORN.
HEE HEE!
I SUPPOSE YOU'RE RIGHT. WHEN THAT GIRL GETS AN IDEA IN HER HEAD, THERE'S JUST NO CHANGING HER MIND.
MOTHER, YOU DON'T KNOW THE HALF OF IT.
OH, COME NOW...
GIVE YOUR MOM SOME CREDIT, YUUJEL. HAVE YOU TRIED TALKING TO LEENE?
SOMETIMES I WORRY ABOUT HER.

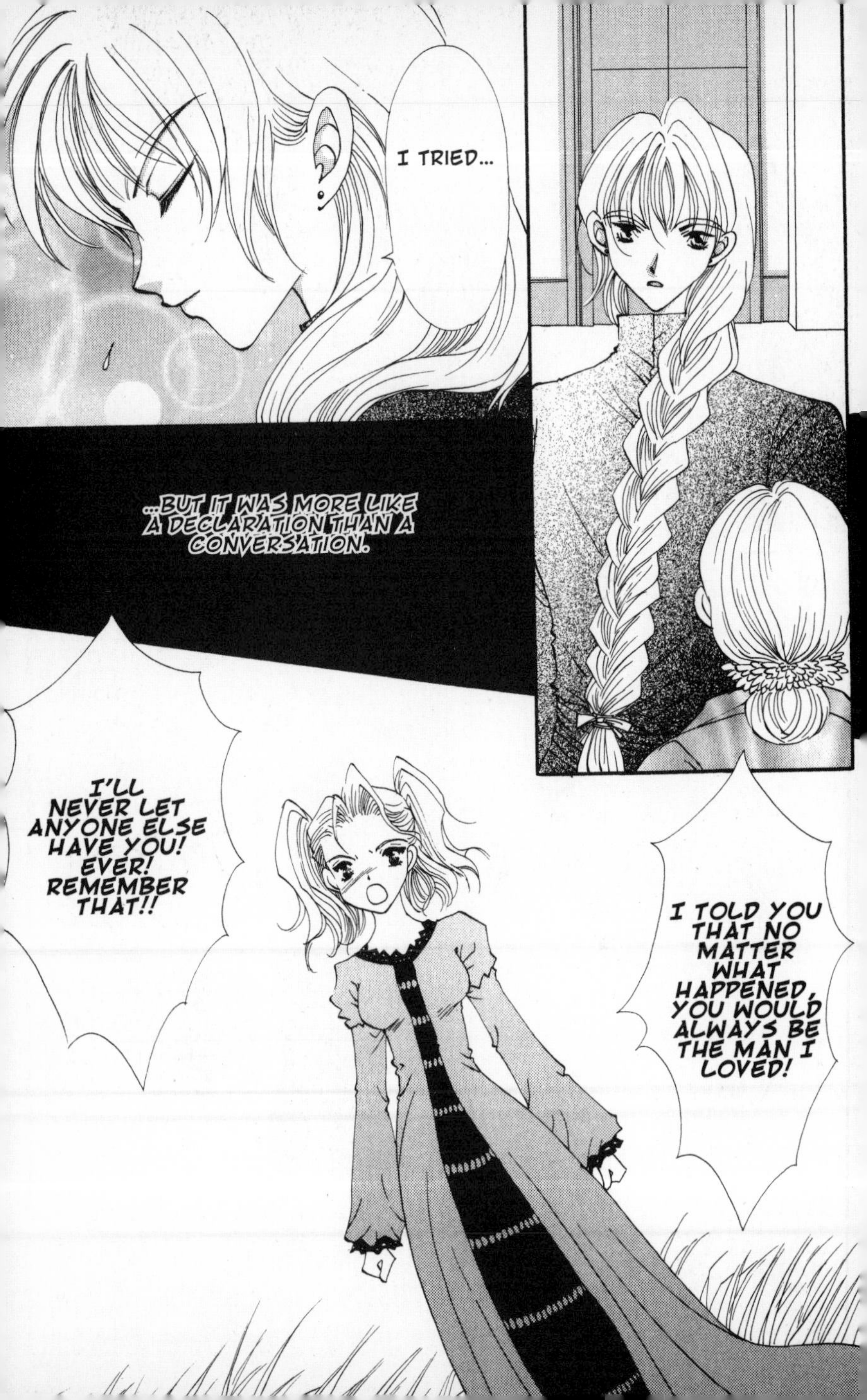
I TRIED...
...BUT IT WAS MORE LIKE A DECLARATION THAN A CONVERSATION.
I TOLD YOU THAT NO MATTER WHAT HAPPENED, YOU WOULD ALWAYS BE THE MAN I LOVED!
I'LL NEVER LET ANYONE ELSE HAVE YOU! EVER! REMEMBER THAT!!

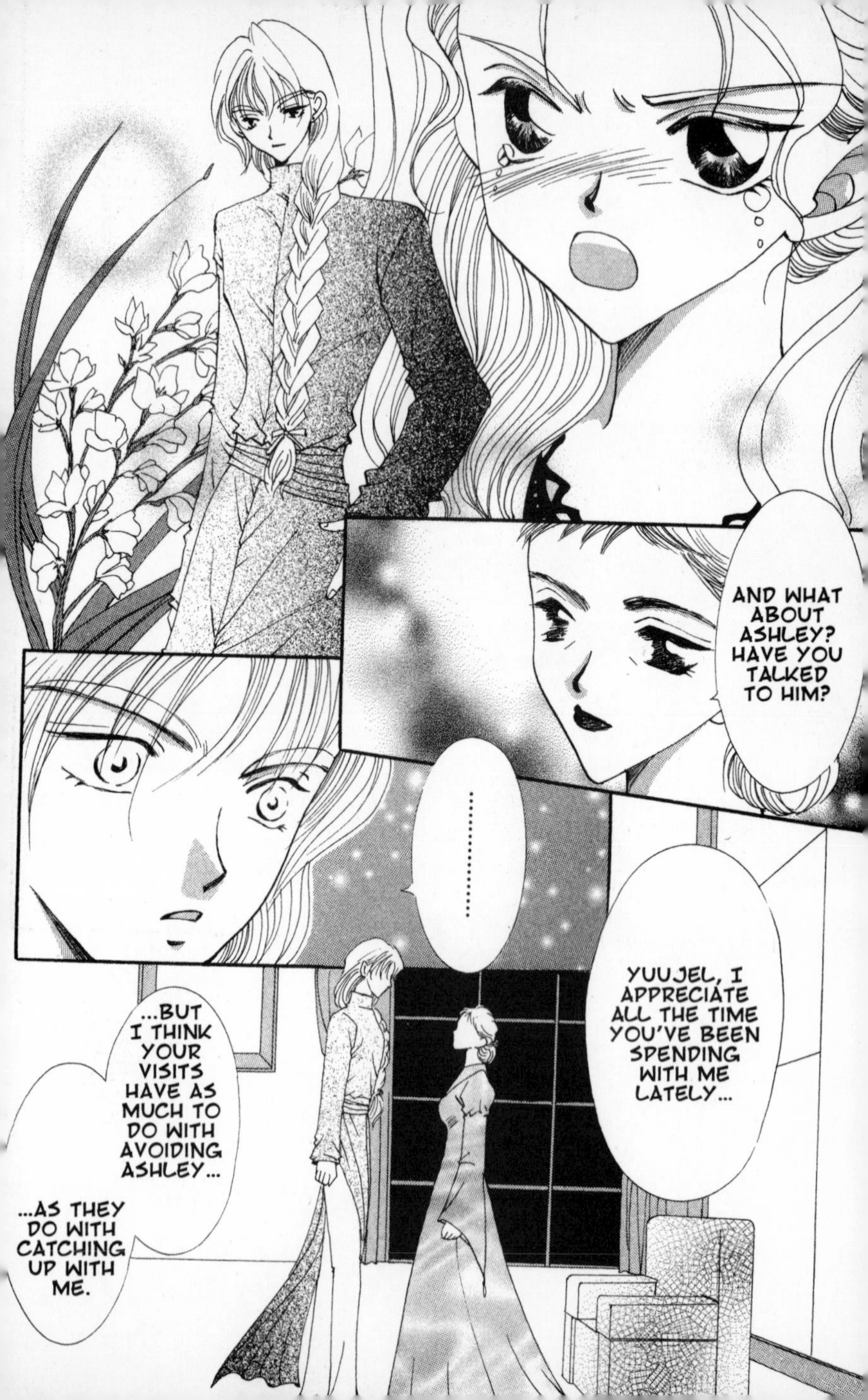
AND WHAT ABOUT ASHLEY? HAVE YOU TALKED TO HIM?
....
YUUJEL, I APPRECIATE ALL THE TIME YOU'VE BEEN SPENDING WITH ME LATELY...
...BUT I THINK YOUR VISITS HAVE AS MUCH TO DO WITH AVOIDING ASHLEY...
...AS THEY DO WITH CATCHING UP WITH ME.

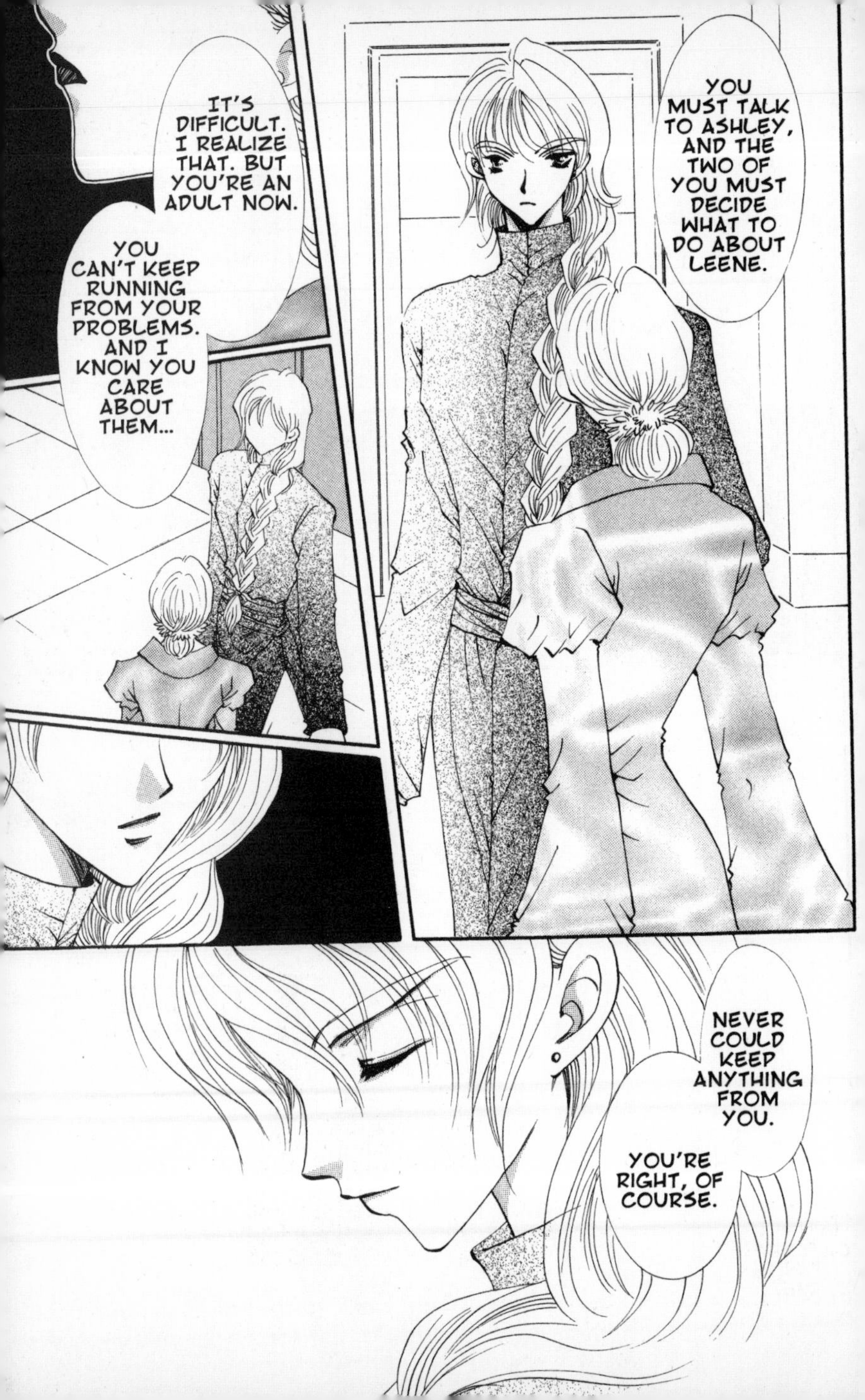
YOU MUST TALK TO ASHLEY, AND THE TWO OF YOU MUST DECIDE WHAT TO DO ABOUT LEENE.
IT'S DIFFICULT. I REALIZE THAT. BUT YOU'RE AN ADULT NOW.
YOU CAN'T KEEP RUNNING FROM YOUR PROBLEMS. AND I KNOW YOU CARE ABOUT THEM...
NEVER COULD KEEP ANYTHING FROM YOU.
YOU'RE RIGHT, OF COURSE.

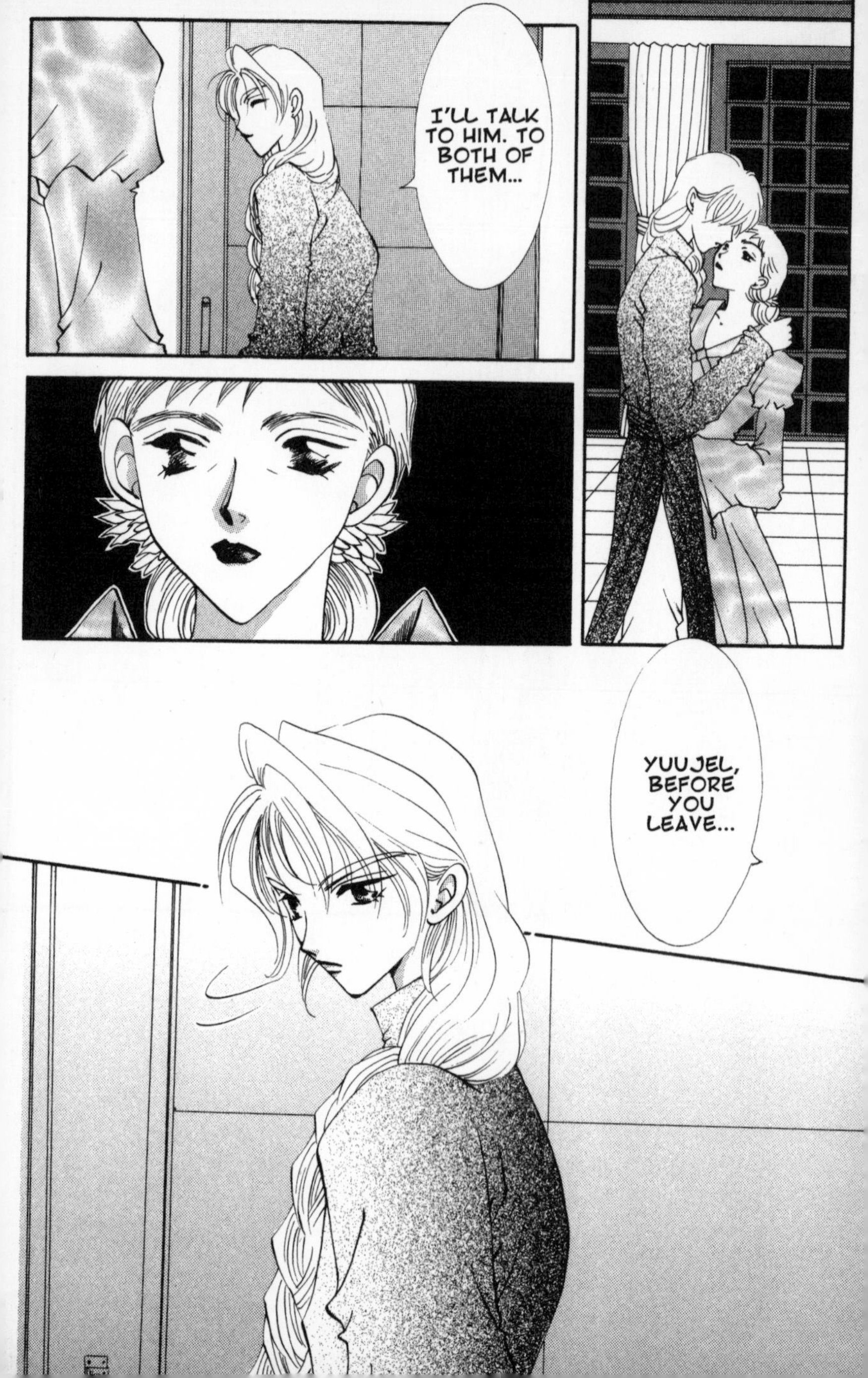
I'LL TALK TO HIM. TO BOTH OF THEM...
YUUJEL, BEFORE YOU LEAVE...

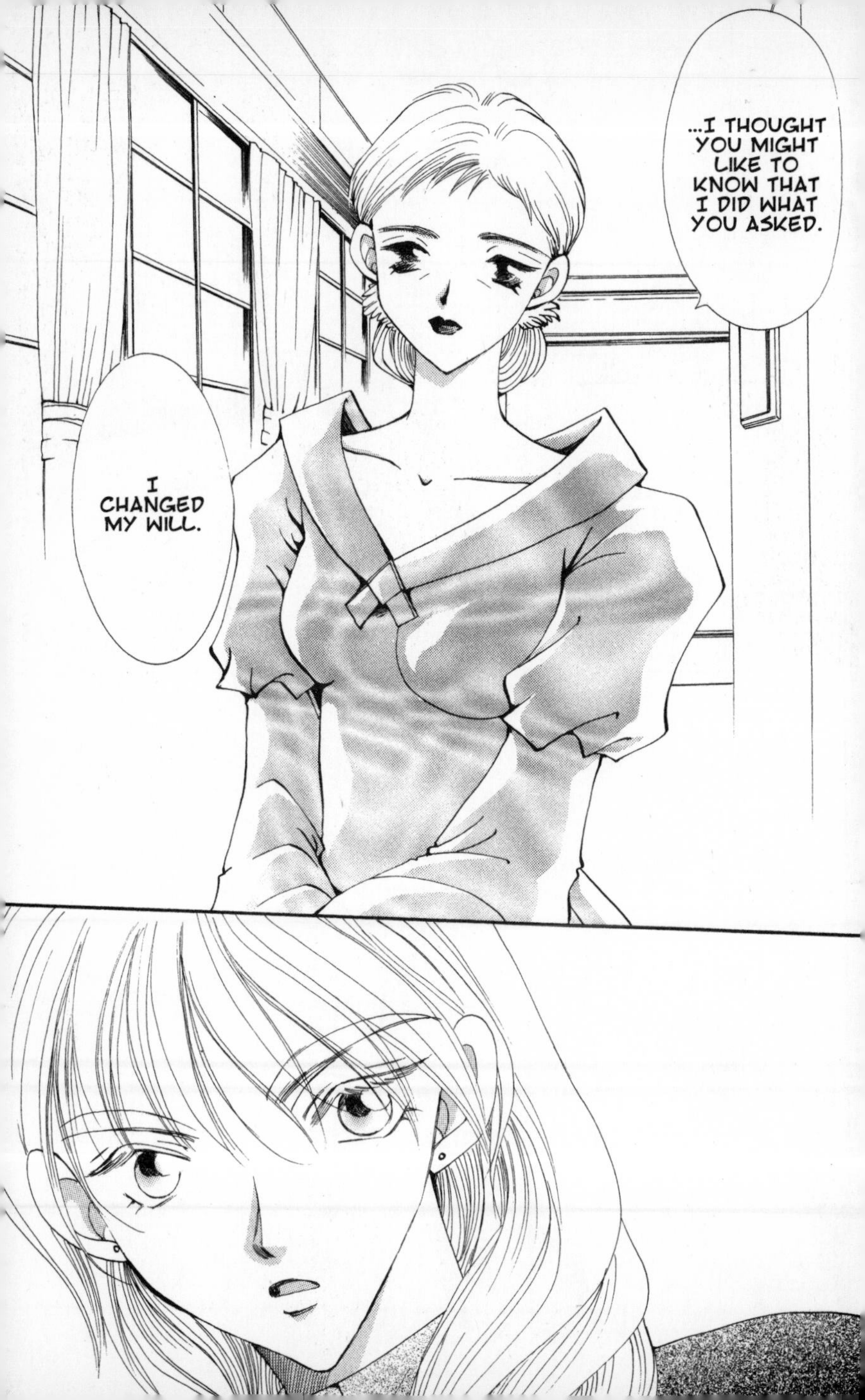
...I THOUGHT YOU MIGHT LIKE TO KNOW THAT I DID WHAT YOU ASKED.
I CHANGED MY WILL.

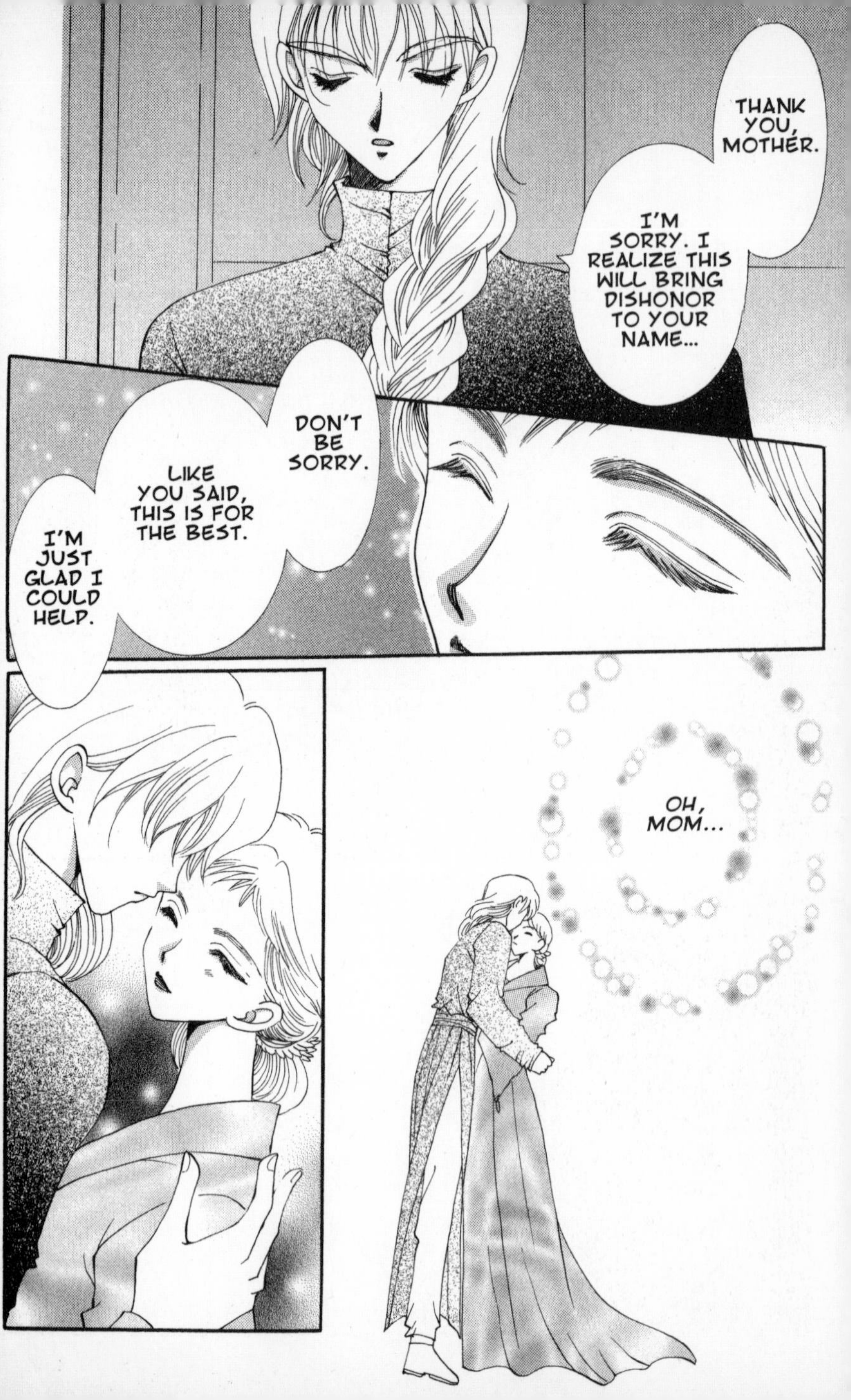
THANK YOU, MOTHER.
I'M SORRY. I REALIZE THIS WILL BRING DISHONOR TO YOUR NAME...
DON'T BE SORRY.
LIKE YOU SAID, THIS IS FOR THE BEST.
I'M JUST GLAD I COULD HELP.
OH, MOM...

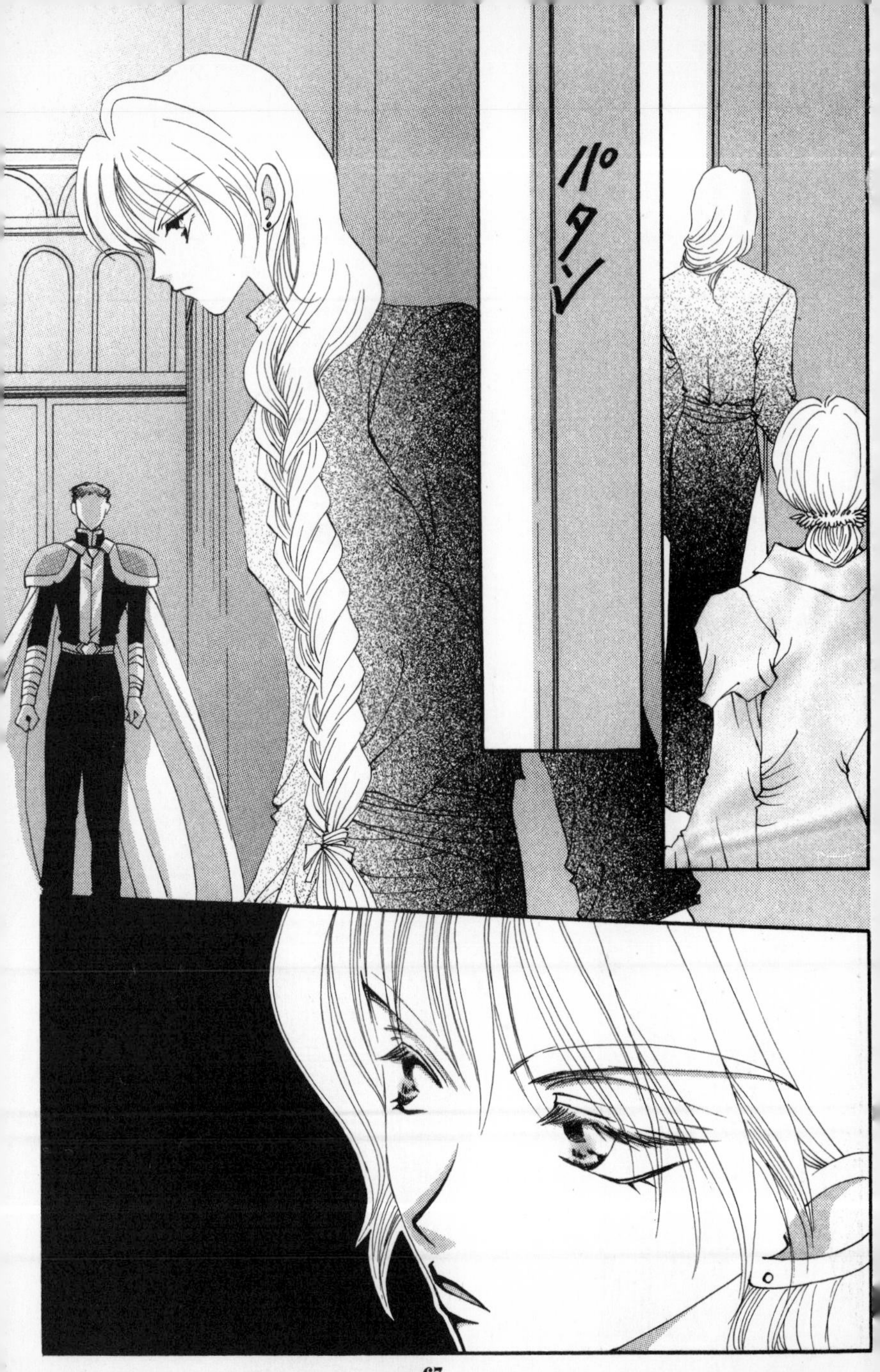
パタン

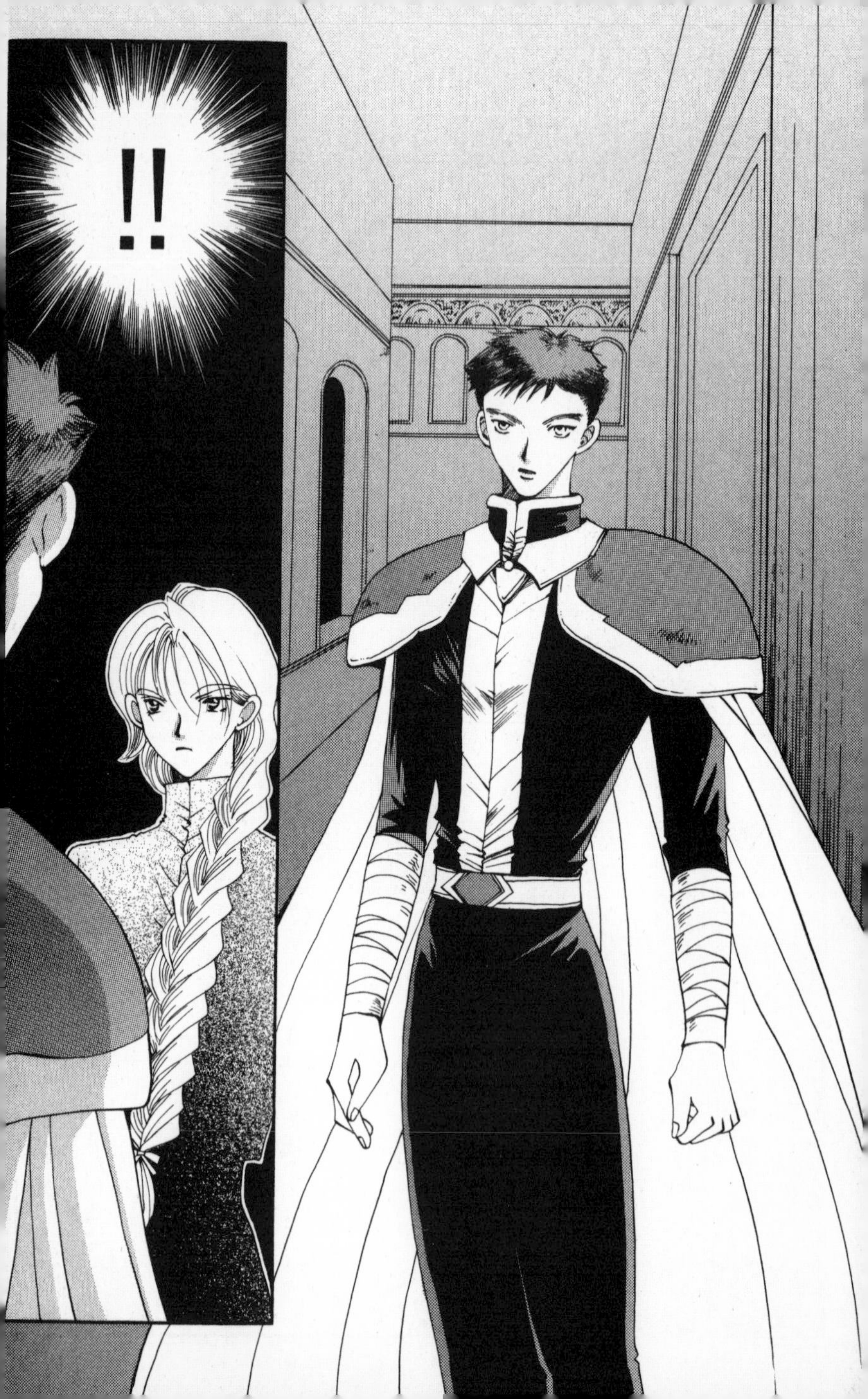
!!

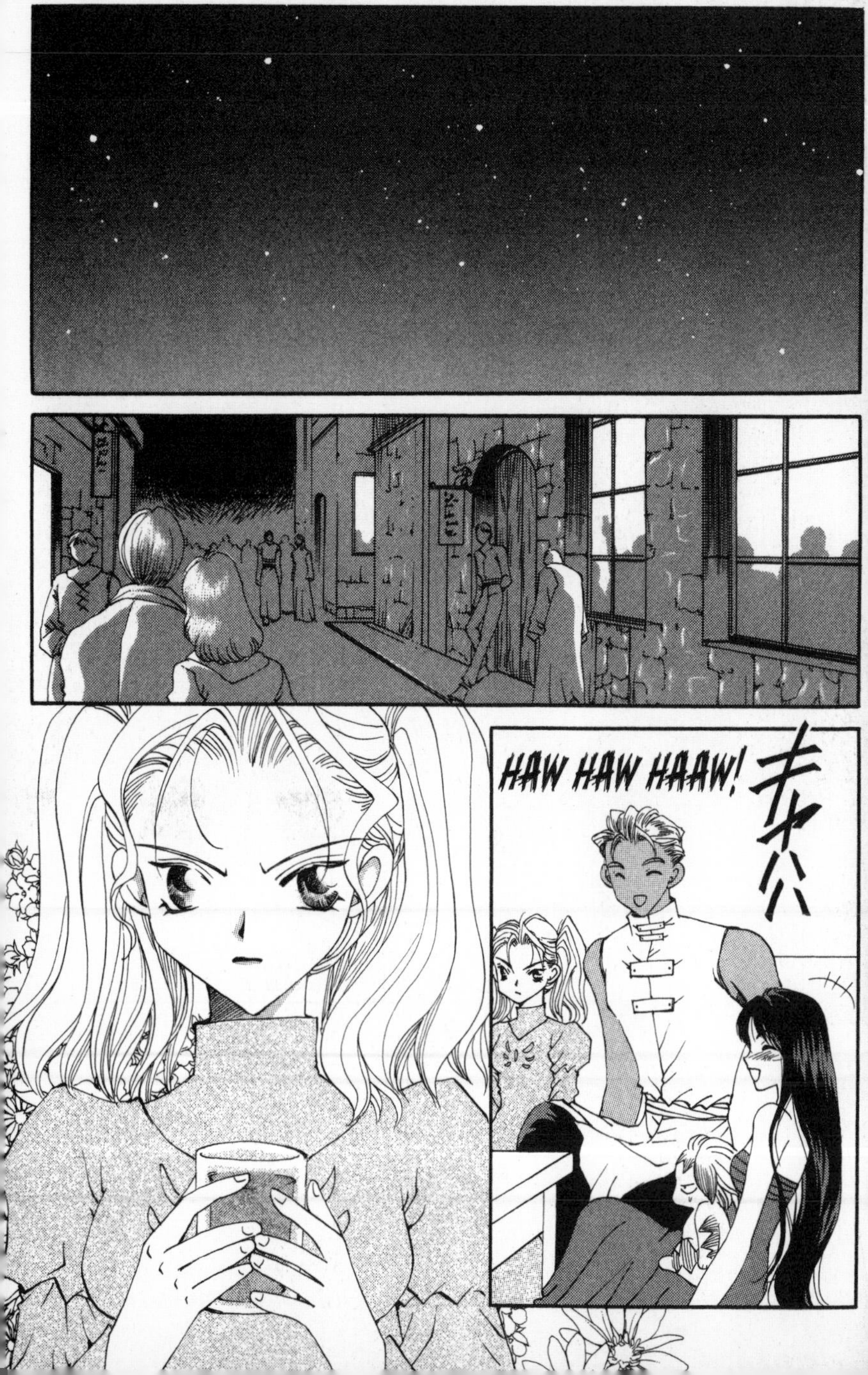
HAW HAW HAAW!
キャハハ

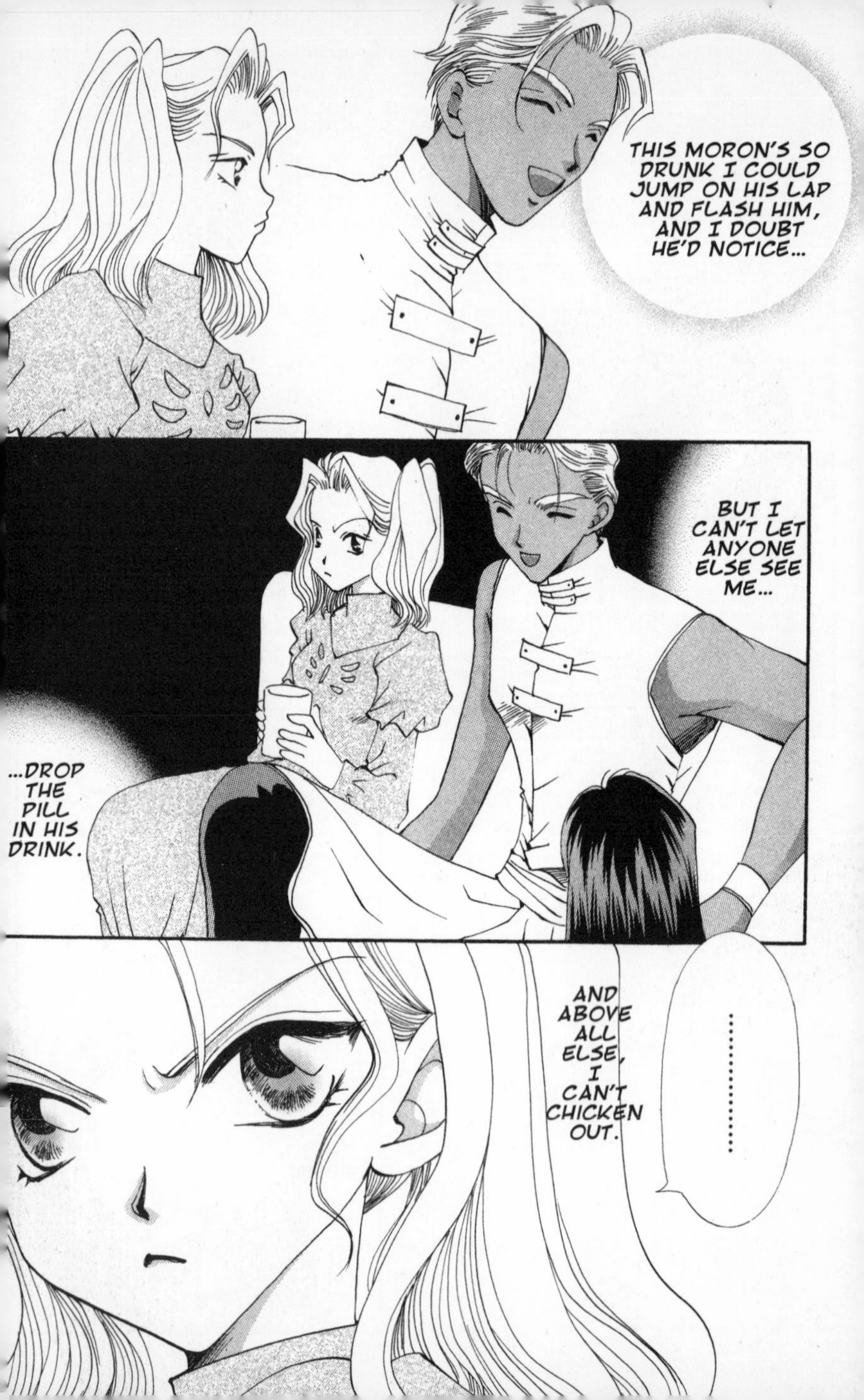
THIS MORON'S SO DRUNK I COULD JUMP ON HIS LAP AND FLASH HIM, AND I DOUBT HE'D NOTICE...
BUT I CAN'T LET ANYONE ELSE SEE ME...
...DROP THE PILL IN HIS DRINK.
....
AND ABOVE ALL ELSE, I CAN'T CHICKEN OUT.

吸血遊戯
南領篇(ゼ・アルダ)
Act.12

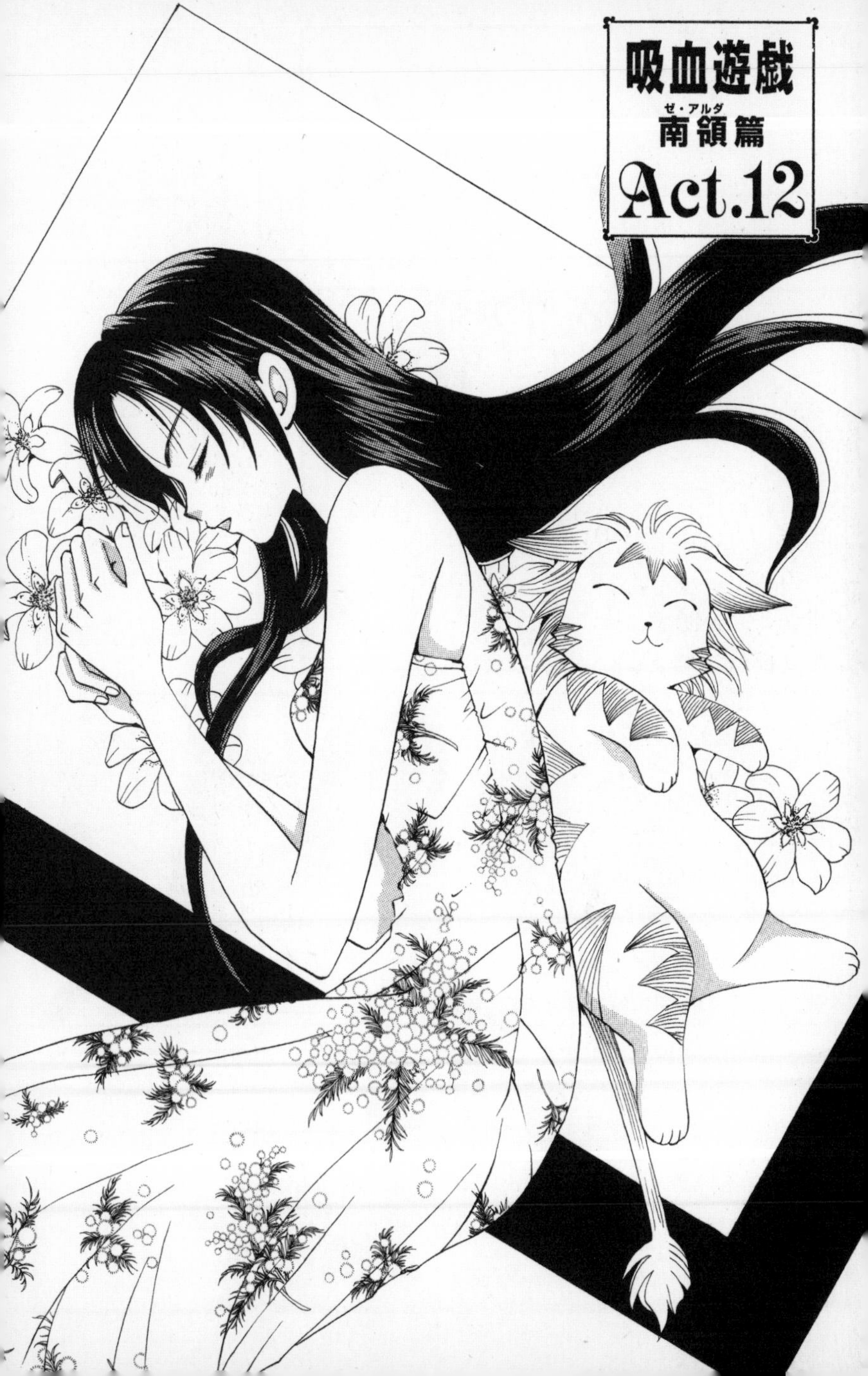

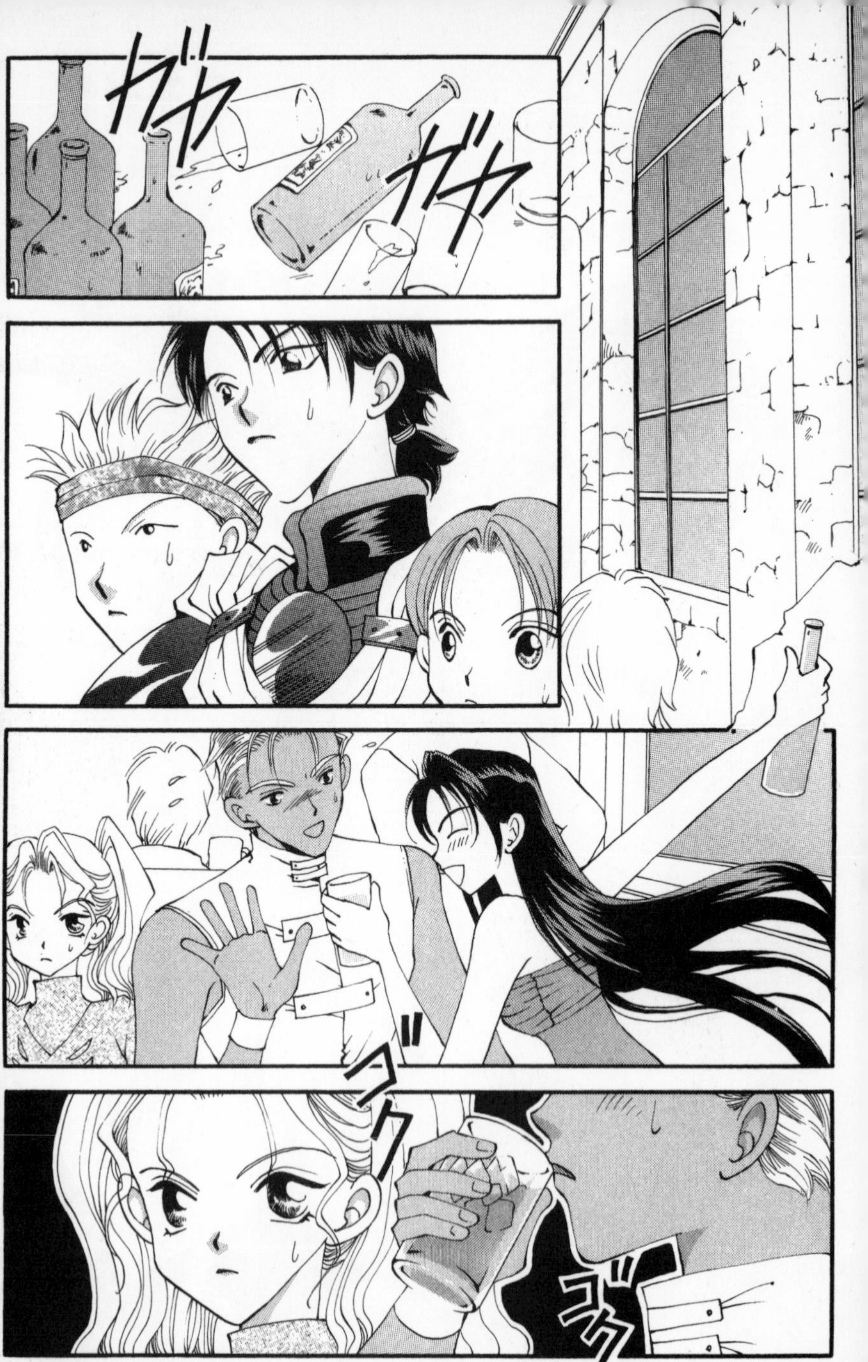
ガガ
ガガ
ゴク
ゴク

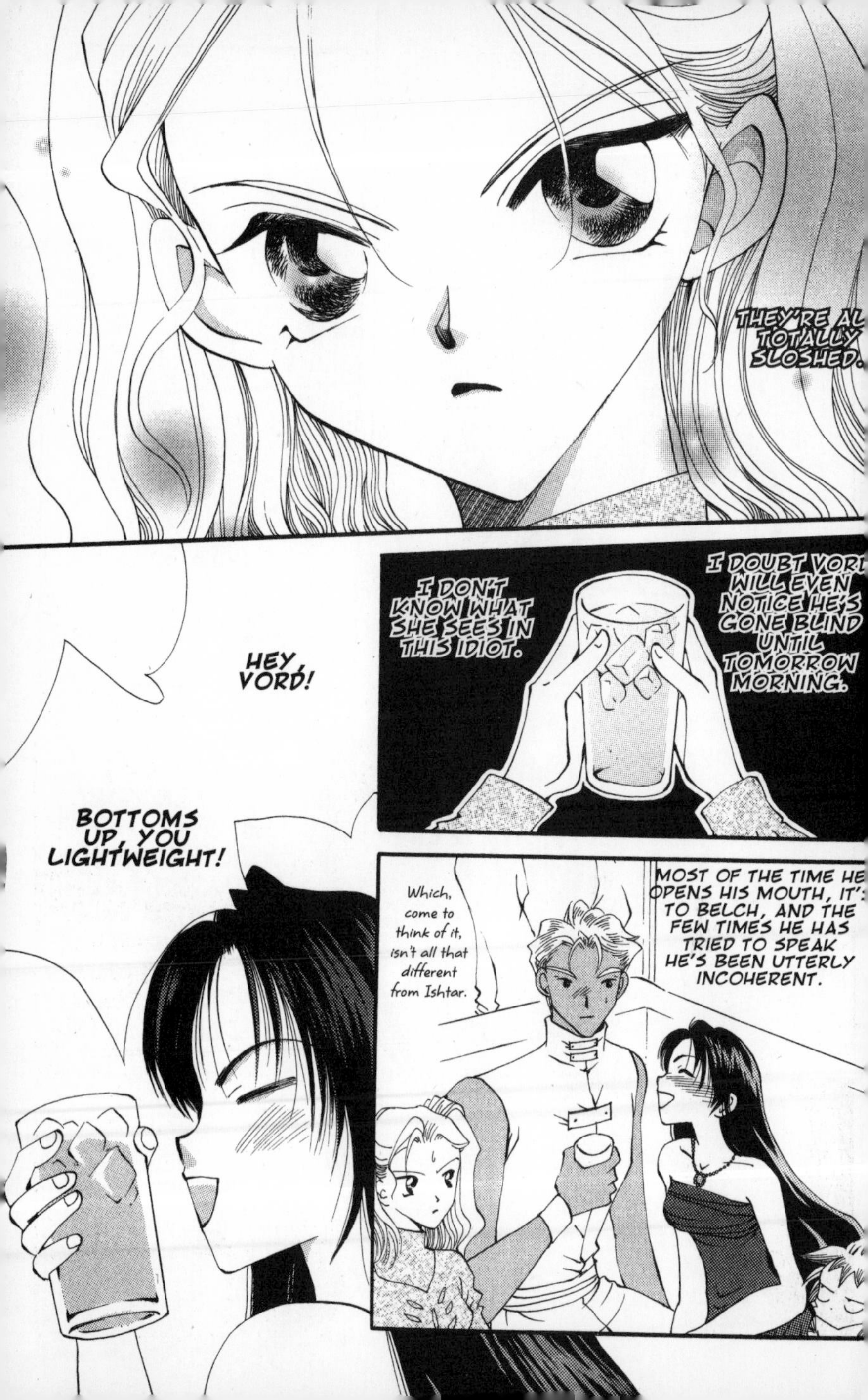
THEY'RE AL
TOTALLY SLOSHED.
I DOUBT VORD WILL EVEN NOTICE HE'S GONE BLIND UNTIL TOMORROW MORNING.
I DON'T KNOW WHAT SHE SEES IN THIS IDIOT.
MOST OF THE TIME HE OPENS HIS MOUTH, IT'S TO BELCH, AND THE FEW TIMES HE HAS TRIED TO SPEAK HE'S BEEN UTTERLY INCOHERENT.
Which, come to think of it, isn't all that different from Ishtar.
HEY, VORD!
BOTTOMS UP, YOU LIGHTWEIGHT!

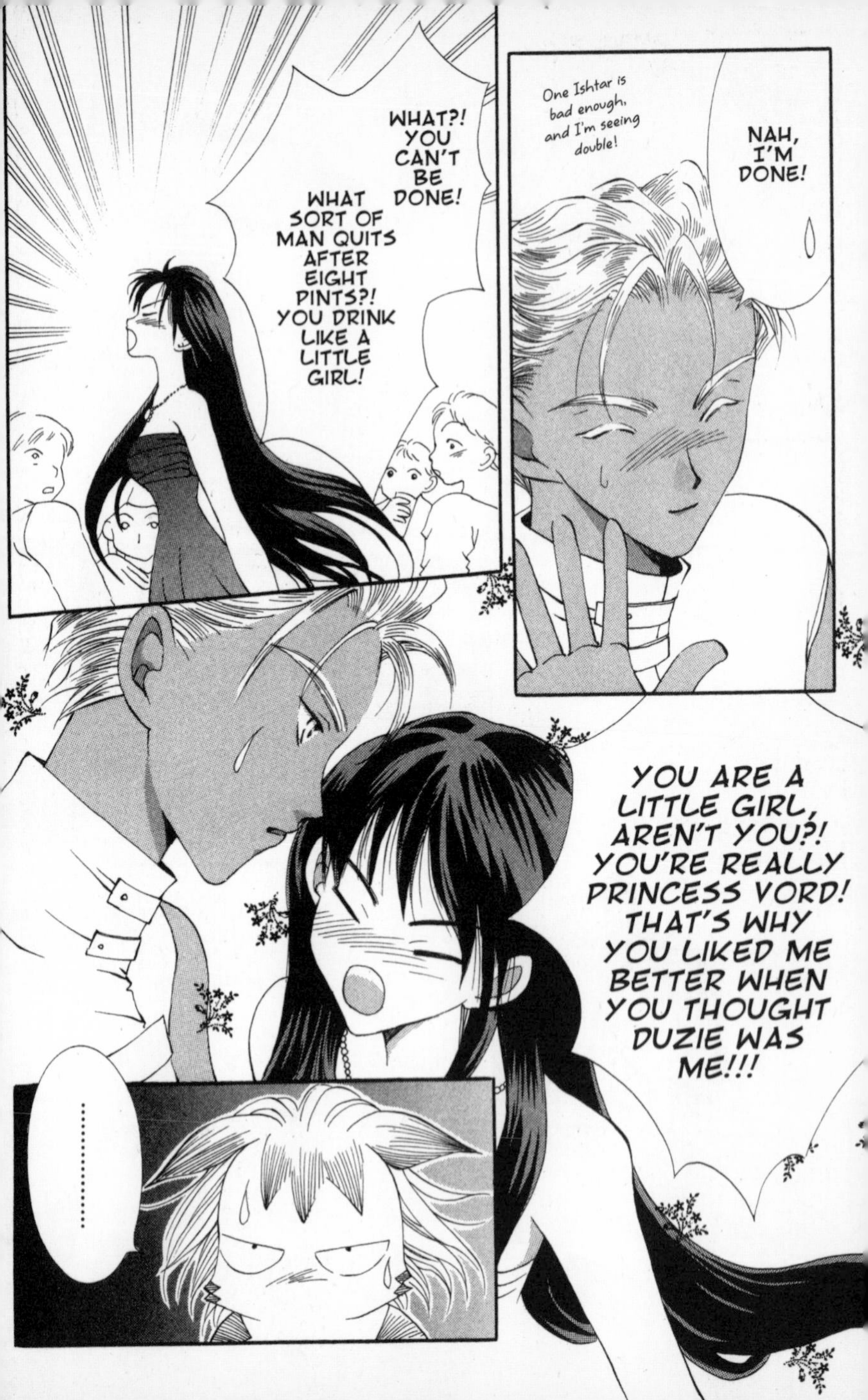
NAH, I'M DONE!
One Ishtar is bad enough, and I'm seeing double!
WHAT?! YOU CAN'T BE DONE!
WHAT SORT OF MAN QUITS AFTER EIGHT PINTS?! YOU DRINK LIKE A LITTLE GIRL!
YOU ARE A LITTLE GIRL, AREN'T YOU?! YOU'RE REALLY PRINCESS VORD! THAT'S WHY YOU LIKED ME BETTER WHEN YOU THOUGHT DUZIE WAS ME!!!
......

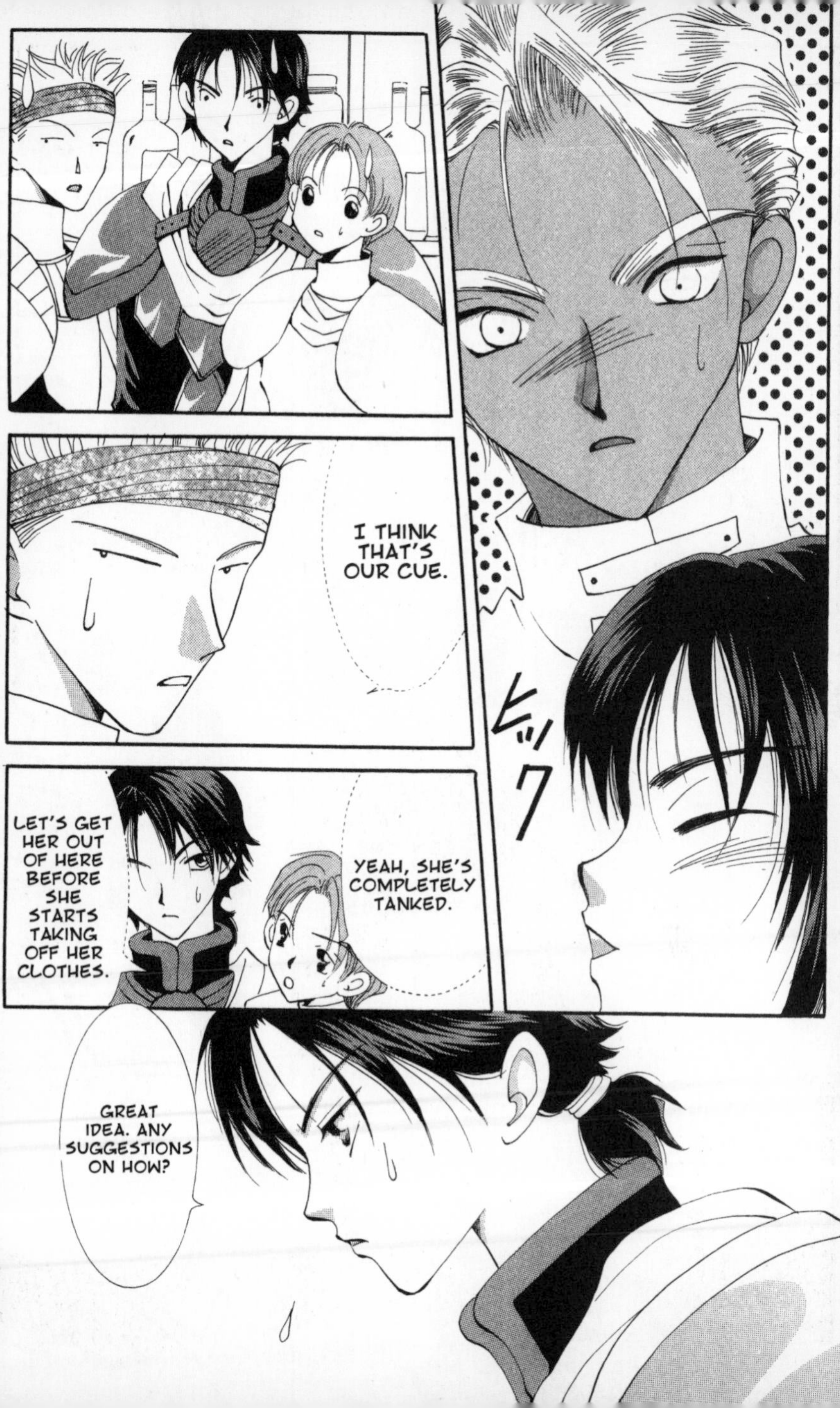
I THINK THAT'S OUR CUE.
YEAH, SHE'S COMPLETELY TANKED.
LET'S GET HER OUT OF HERE BEFORE SHE STARTS TAKING OFF HER CLOTHES.
GREAT IDEA. ANY SUGGESTIONS ON HOW?

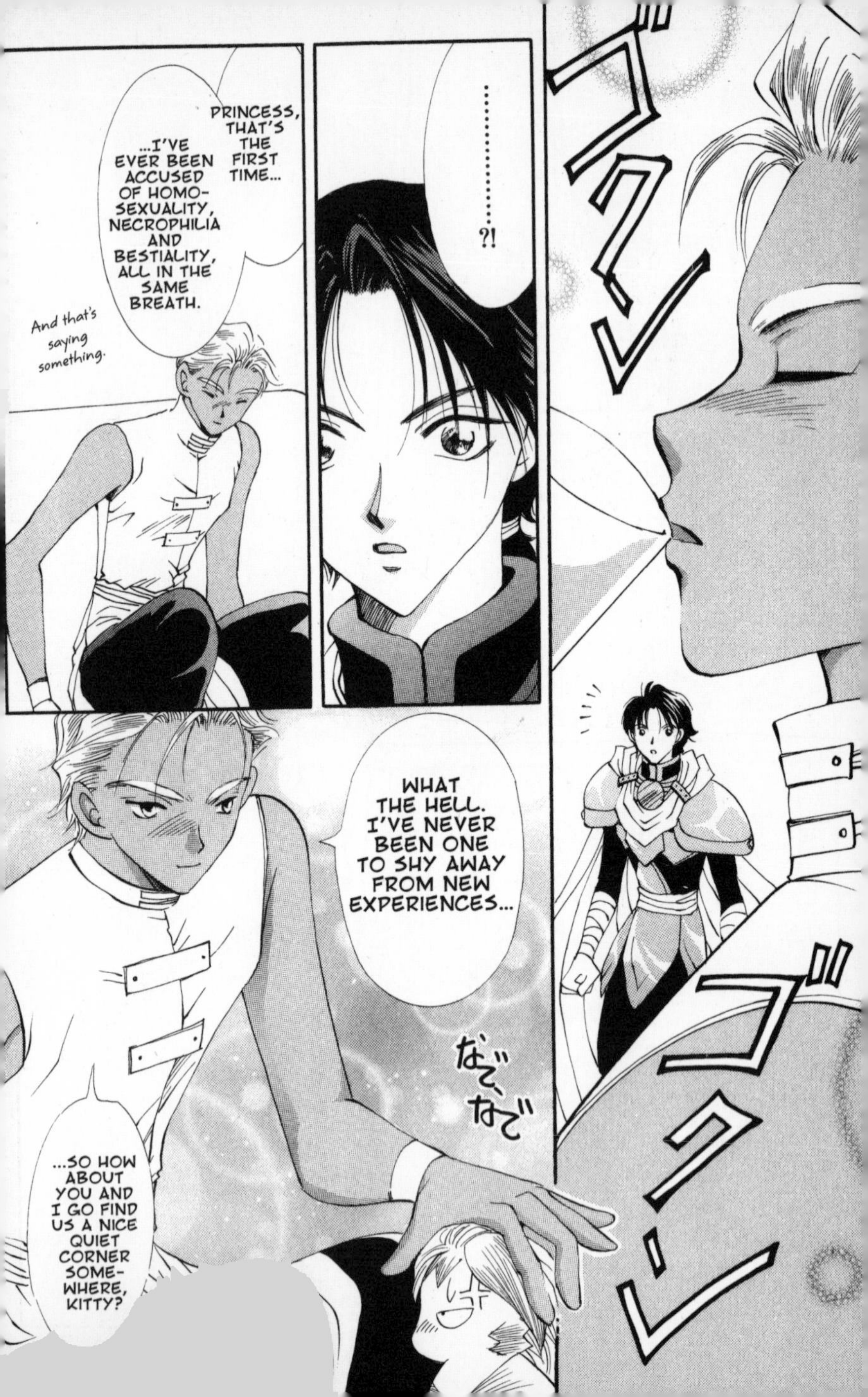

ズクン
ゴクン
........?!
PRINCESS, THAT'S THE FIRST TIME...
...I'VE EVER BEEN ACCUSED OF HOMOSEXUALITY, NECROPHILIA AND BESTIALITY, ALL IN THE SAME BREATH.
And that's saying something.
WHAT THE HELL. I'VE NEVER BEEN ONE TO SHY AWAY FROM NEW EXPERIENCES...
なで なで
...SO HOW ABOUT YOU AND I GO FIND US A NICE QUIET CORNER SOMEWHERE, KITTY?

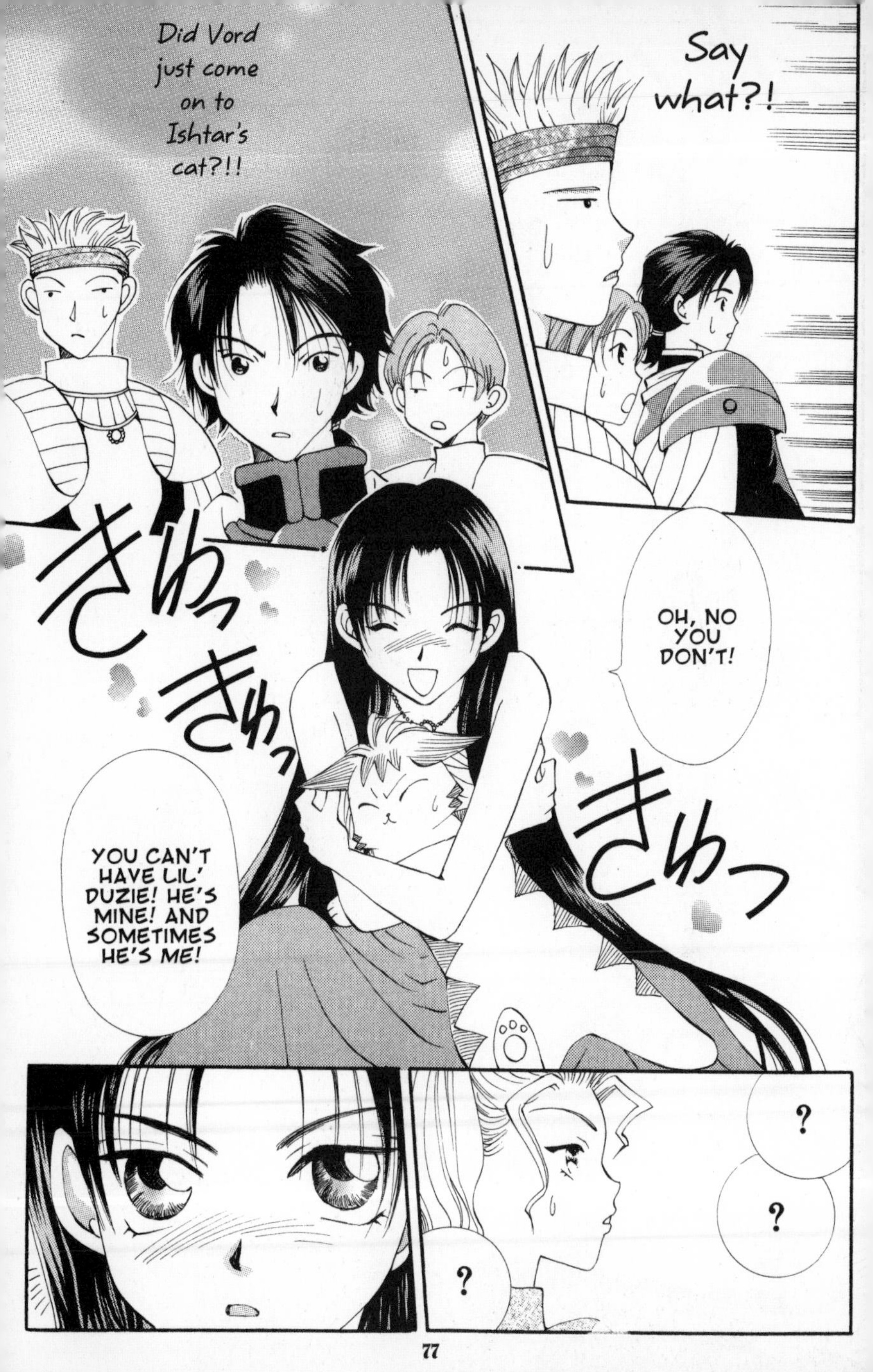

Say what?!
Did Vord just come on to Ishtar's cat?!!
きゅっ
OH, NO YOU DON'T!
きゅっ きゅっ
YOU CAN'T HAVE LIL' DUZIE! HE'S MINE! AND SOMETIMES HE'S ME!
?
?
?

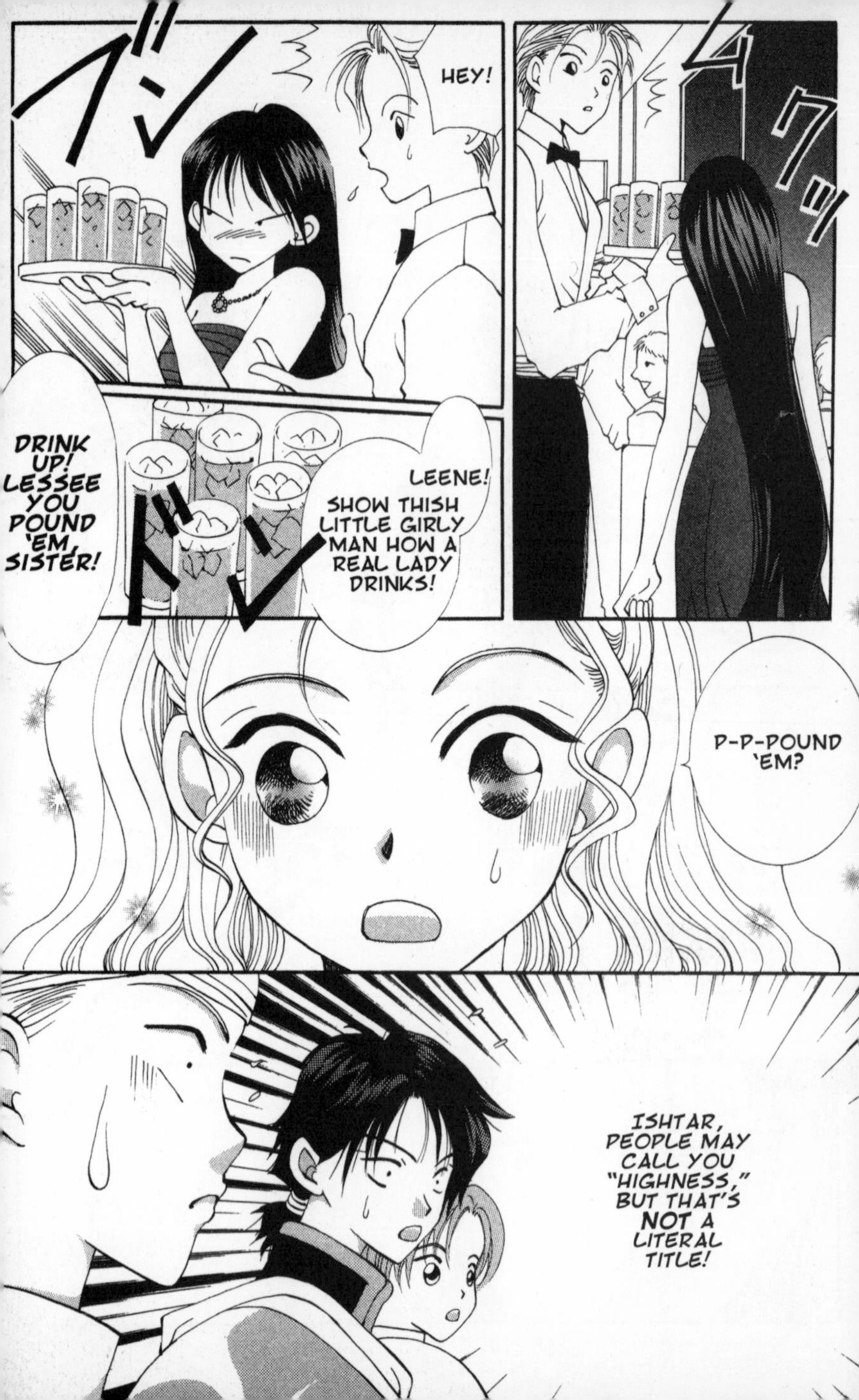
ムクッ
ブン
HEY!
LEENE! SHOW THISH LITTLE GIRLY MAN HOW A REAL LADY DRINKS!
DRINK UP! LESSEE YOU POUND 'EM, SISTER!
ドン
P-P-POUND 'EM?
ISHTAR, PEOPLE MAY CALL YOU "HIGHNESS," BUT THAT'S NOT A LITERAL TITLE!

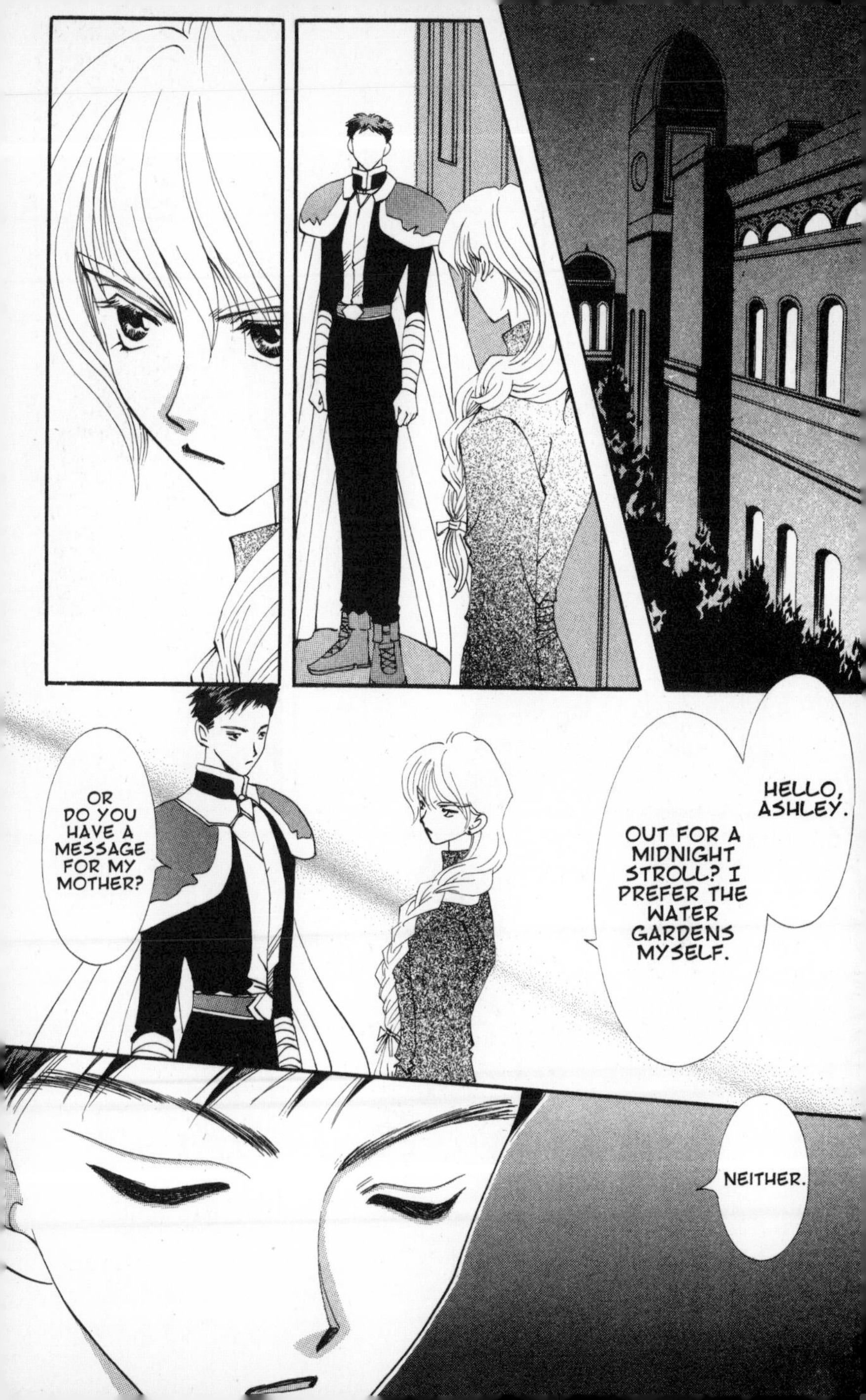
HELLO, ASHLEY.
OUT FOR A MIDNIGHT STROLL? I PREFER THE WATER GARDENS MYSELF.
OR DO YOU HAVE A MESSAGE FOR MY MOTHER?
NEITHER.

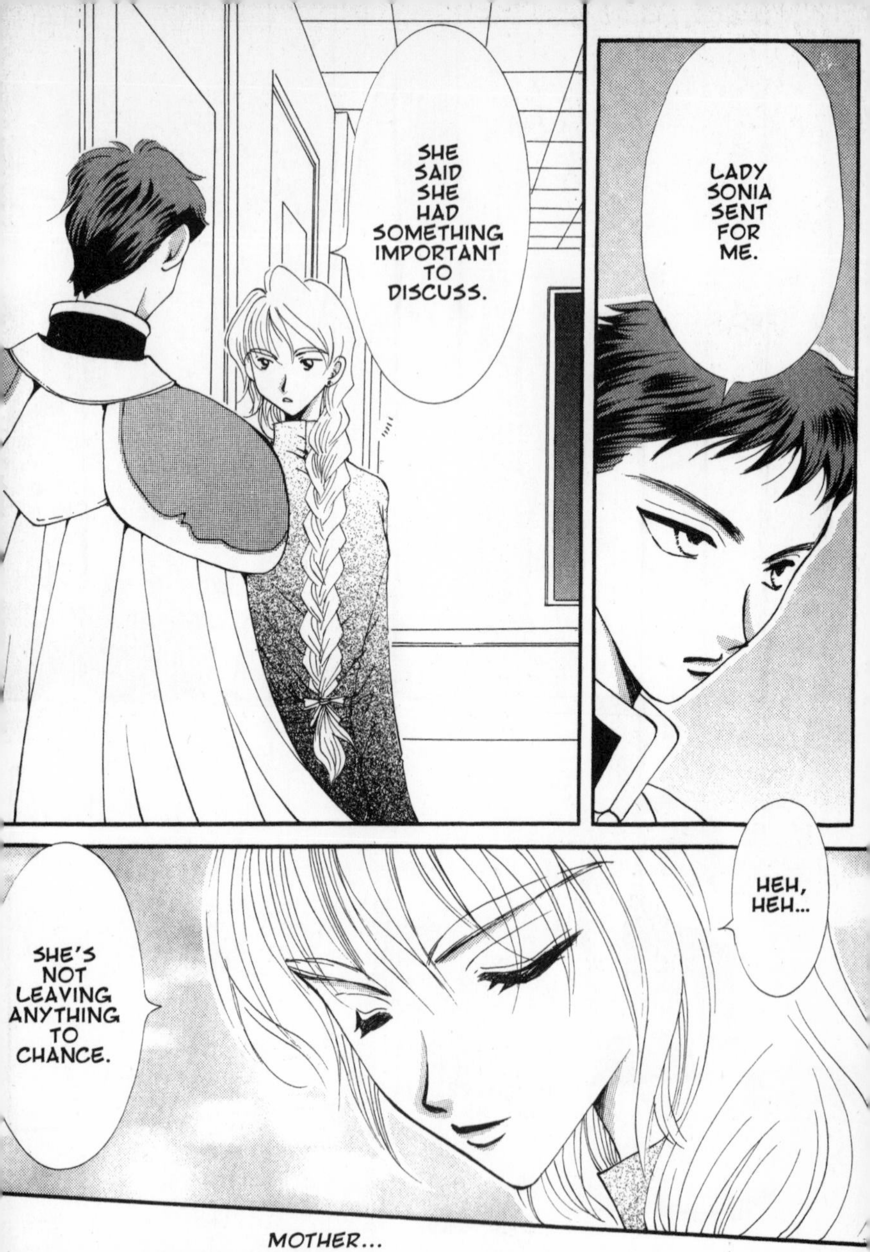
LADY SONIA SENT FOR ME.
SHE SAID SHE HAD SOMETHING IMPORTANT TO DISCUSS.
HEH, HEH...
SHE'S NOT LEAVING ANYTHING TO CHANCE.

MOTHER...

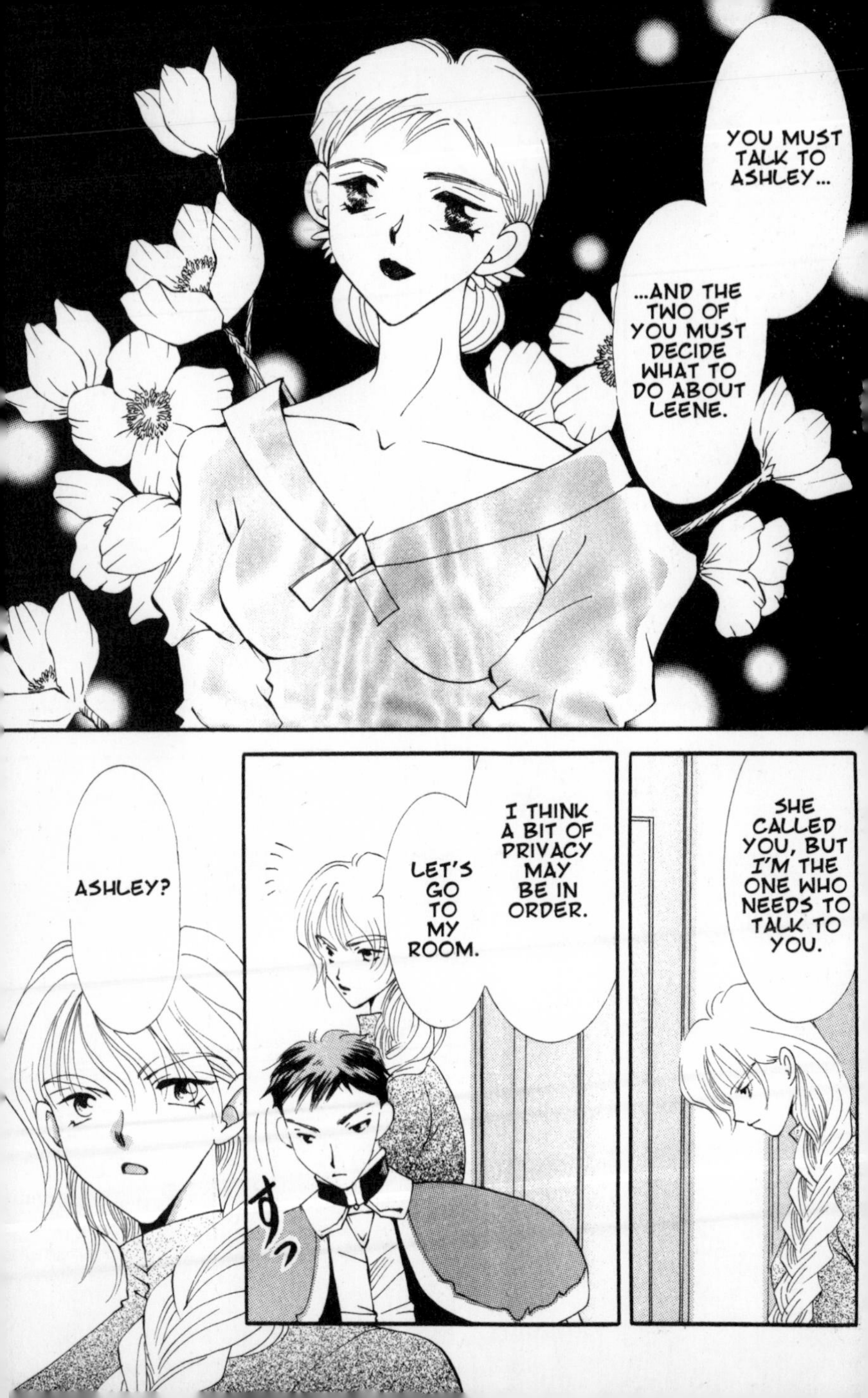
YOU MUST TALK TO ASHLEY...
...AND THE TWO OF YOU MUST DECIDE WHAT TO DO ABOUT LEENE.
SHE CALLED YOU, BUT I'M THE ONE WHO NEEDS TO TALK TO YOU.
I THINK A BIT OF PRIVACY MAY BE IN ORDER.
LET'S GO TO MY ROOM.
すっ
ASHLEY?

LET ME JUST MAKE SURE LEENE DOESN'T NEED ANYTHING ELSE.

HE DOESN'T TRUST ME ANYMORE. NOT THAT I BLAME HIM.

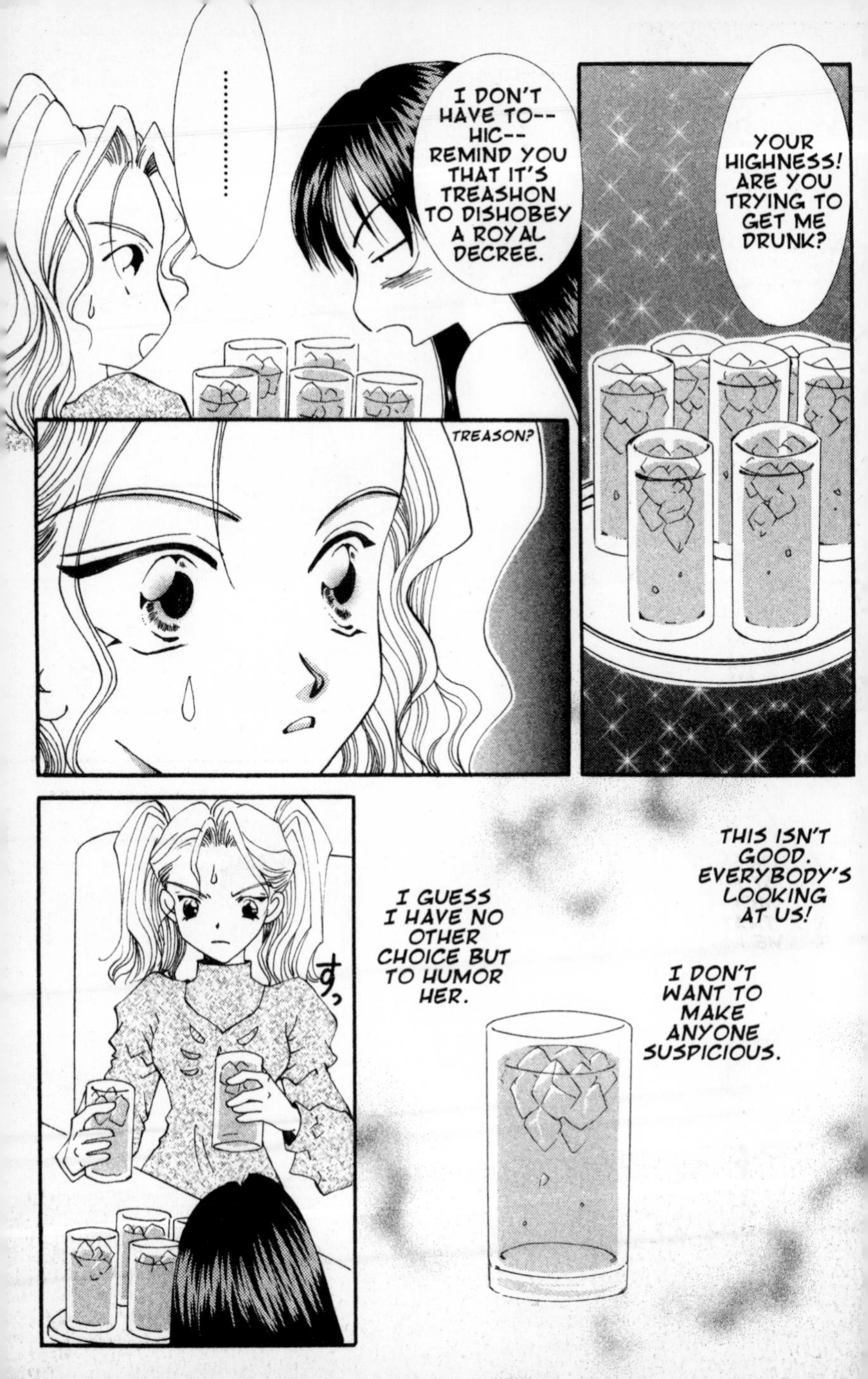
YOUR HIGHNESS! ARE YOU TRYING TO GET ME DRUNK?
I DON'T HAVE TO-- HIC-- REMIND YOU THAT IT'S TREASHON TO DISHOBEY A ROYAL DECREE.
......
TREASON?
THIS ISN'T GOOD. EVERYBODY'S LOOKING AT US!
I DON'T WANT TO MAKE ANYONE SUSPICIOUS.
I GUESS I HAVE NO OTHER CHOICE BUT TO HUMOR HER.
すっ

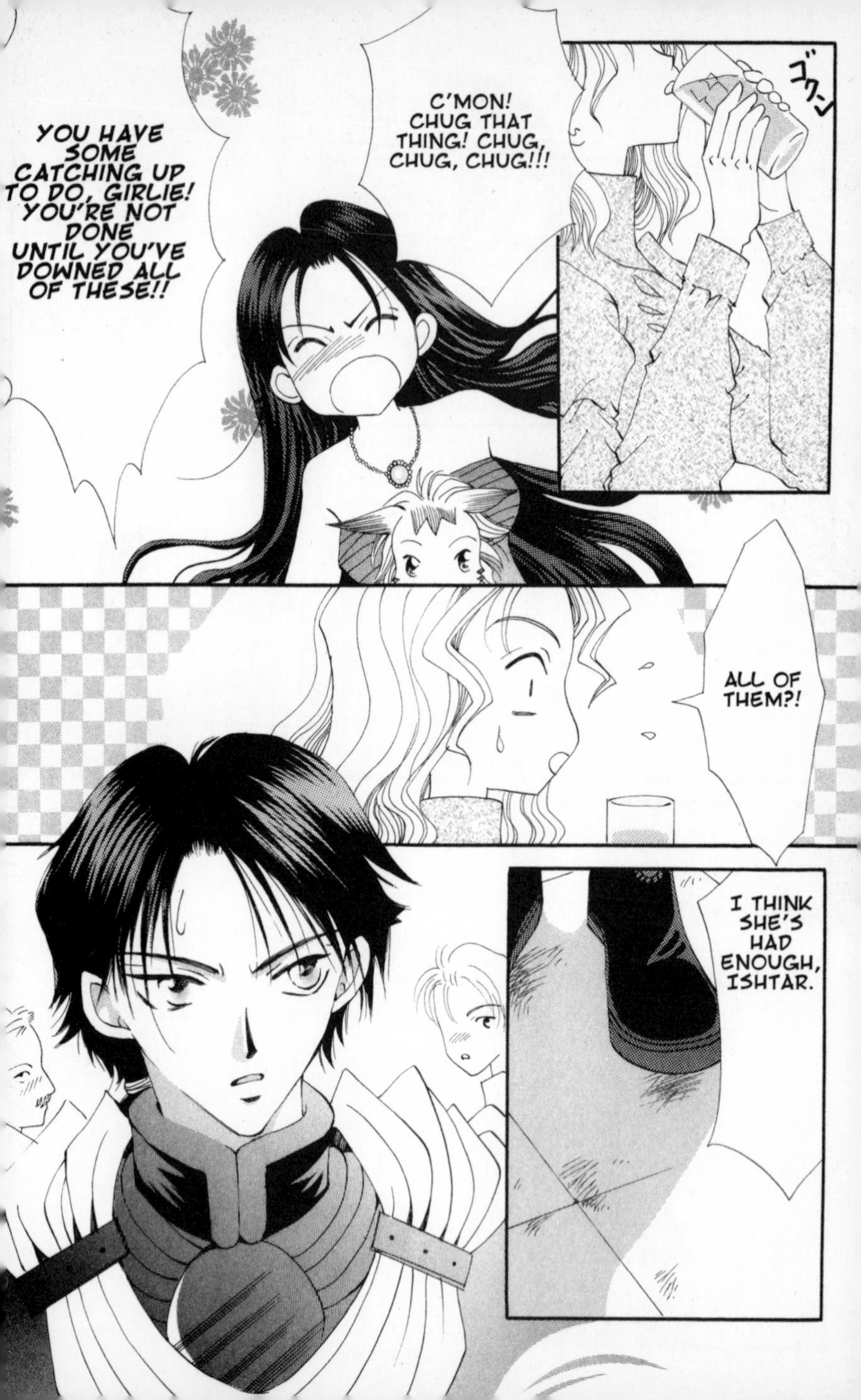
ゴクン
C'MON! CHUG THAT THING! CHUG, CHUG, CHUG!!!
YOU HAVE SOME CATCHING UP TO DO, GIRLIE! YOU'RE NOT DONE UNTIL YOU'VE DOWNED ALL OF THESE!!
ALL OF THEM?!
I THINK SHE'S HAD ENOUGH, ISHTAR.

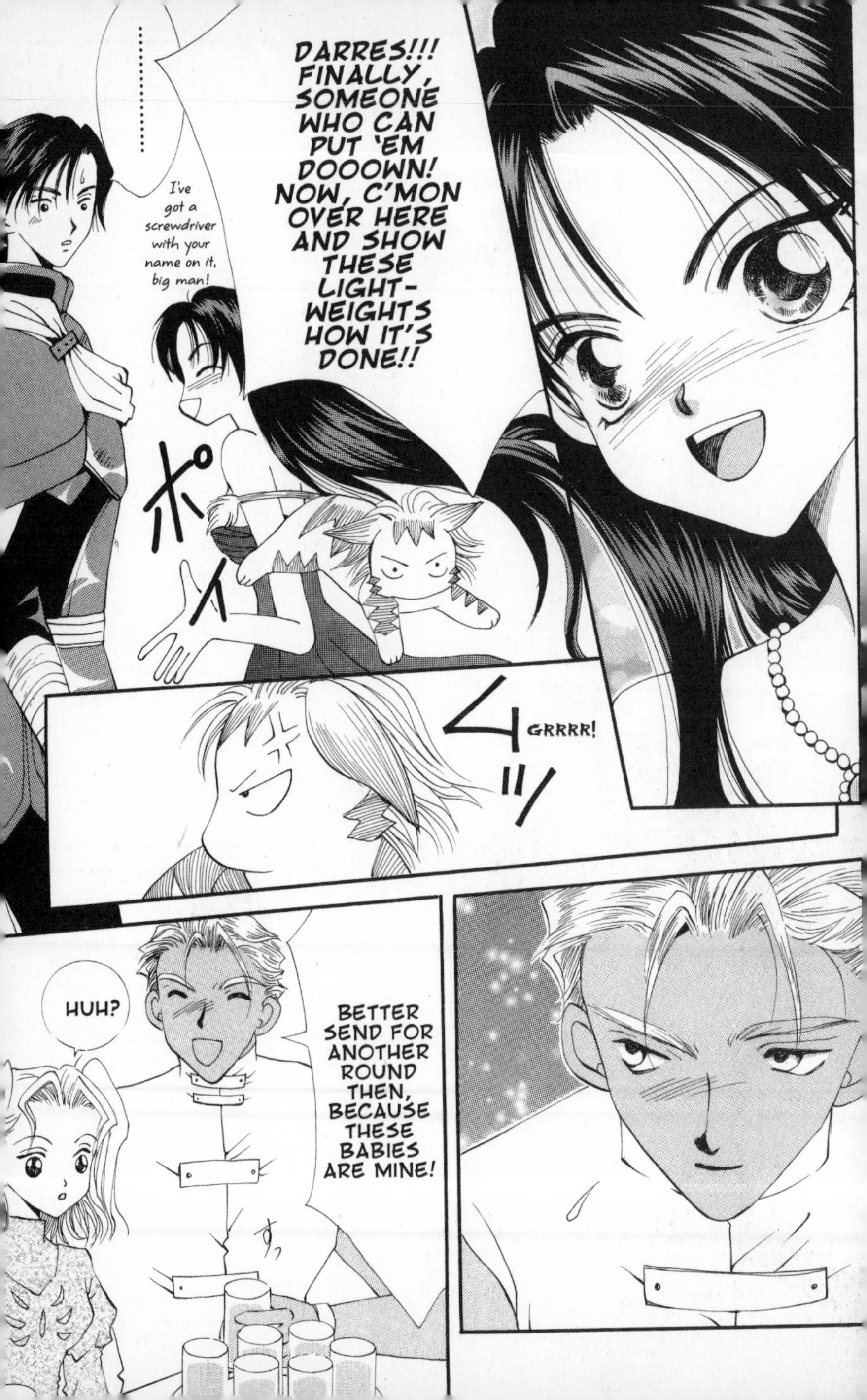
DARRES!!! FINALLY, SOMEONE WHO CAN PUT 'EM DOOOWN! NOW, C'MON OVER HERE AND SHOW THESE LIGHT-WEIGHTS HOW IT'S DONE!!
......
I've got a screwdriver with your name on it, big man!
ポイ
ムッ
GRRRR!
BETTER SEND FOR ANOTHER ROUND THEN, BECAUSE THESE BABIES ARE MINE!
HUH?

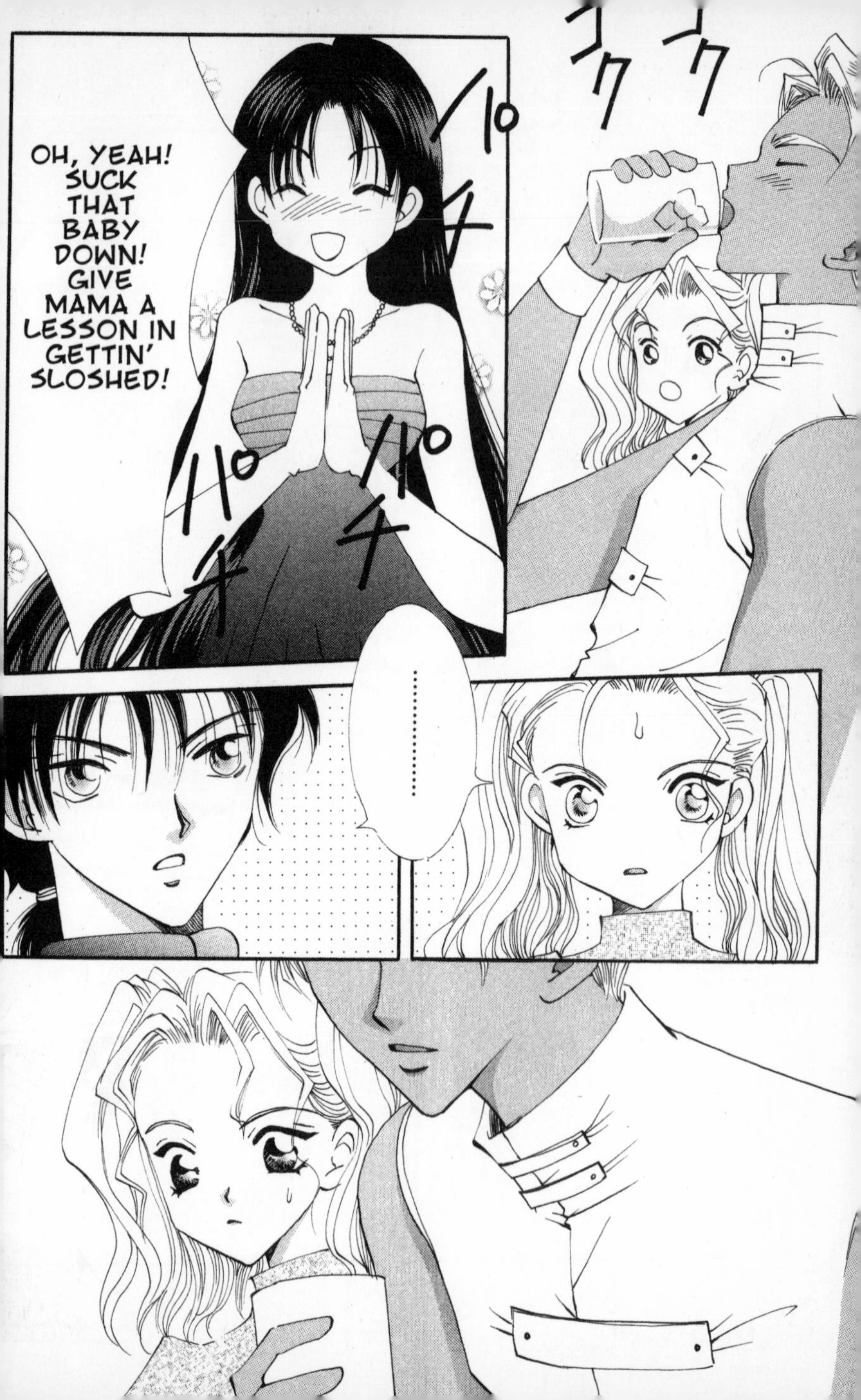

ゴク ゴク
パチ
パチ パチ
OH, YEAH! SUCK THAT BABY DOWN! GIVE MAMA A LESSON IN GETTIN' SLOSHED!
....

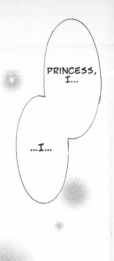

PRINCESS, I...

...I...

I'VE BEEN WANTING TO TELL YOU THAT FOR A LONG TIME.

I LOVE YOU.

I KNOW YOU DON'T LOVE ME, BUT I NEEDED TO GET IT OFF MY CHEST.

AND NOW, I THINK IT'S TIME THAT I LET GO, AND GET ON WITH MY LIFE.

⋮

!?

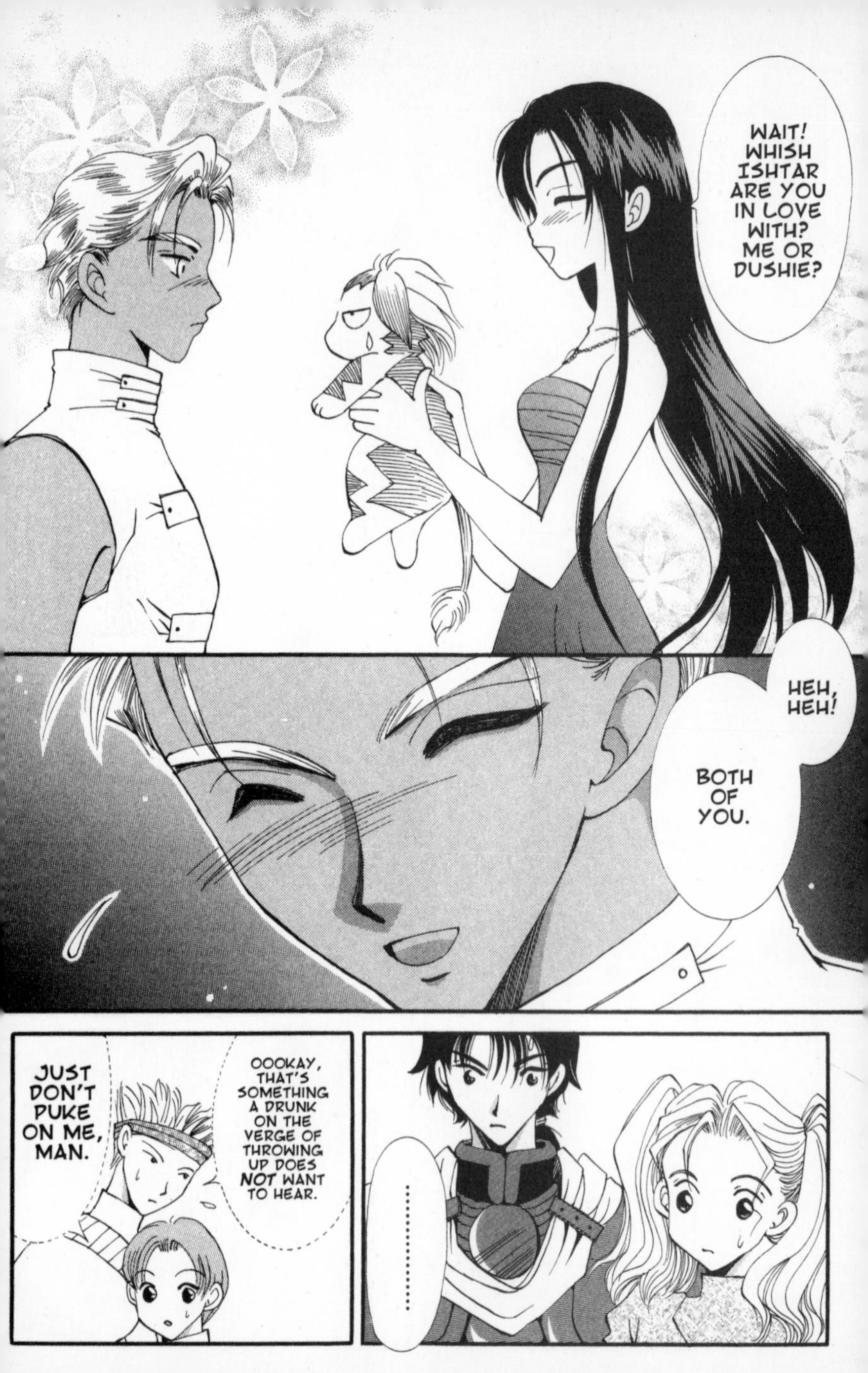
WAIT! WHISH ISHTAR ARE YOU IN LOVE WITH? ME OR DUSHIE?
HEH, HEH!
BOTH OF YOU.
....
OOOKAY, THAT'S SOMETHING A DRUNK ON THE VERGE OF THROWING UP DOES *NOT* WANT TO HEAR.
JUST DON'T PUKE ON ME, MAN.

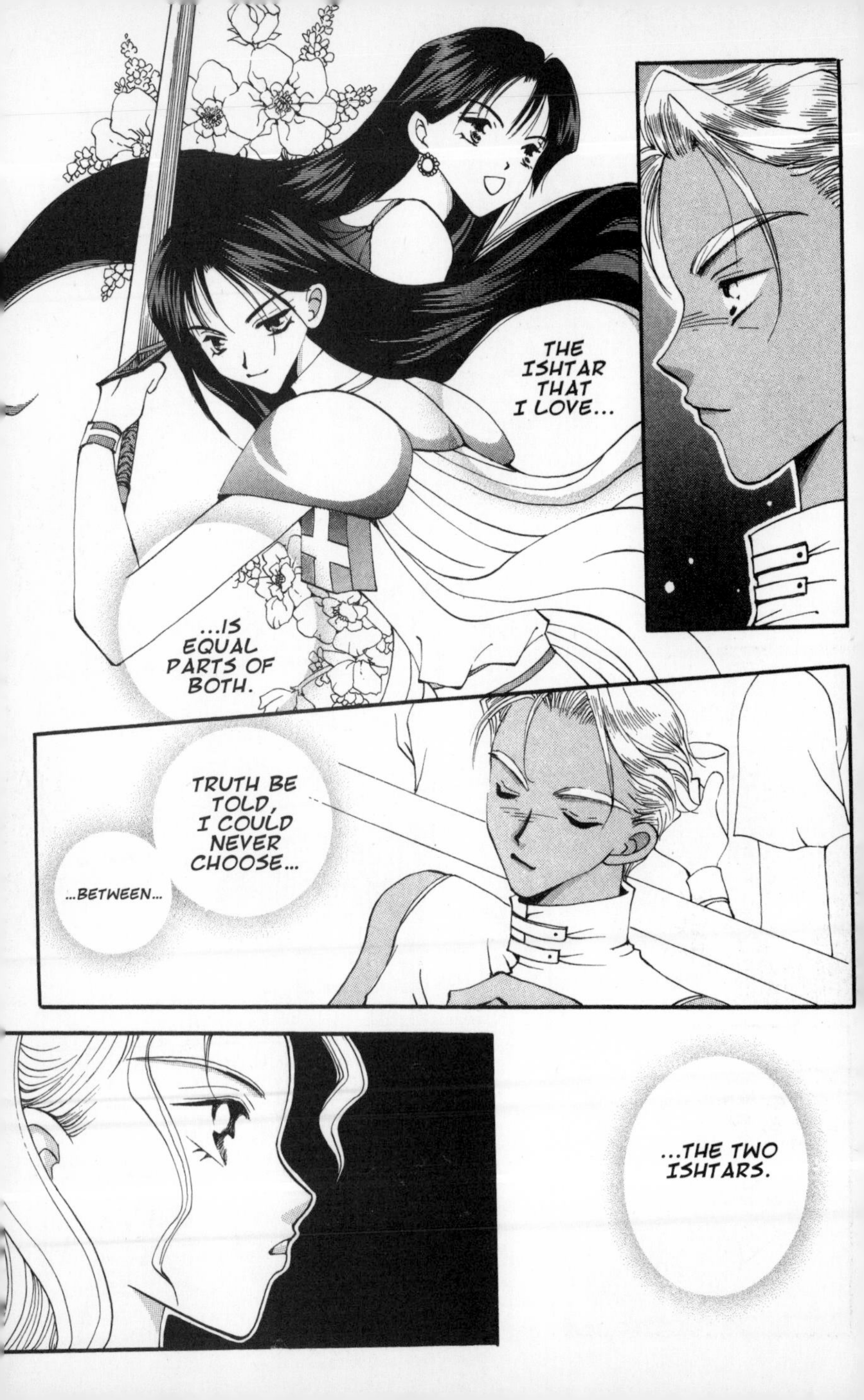
THE ISHTAR THAT I LOVE...
...IS EQUAL PARTS OF BOTH.
TRUTH BE TOLD, I COULD NEVER CHOOSE...
...BETWEEN...
...THE TWO ISHTARS.

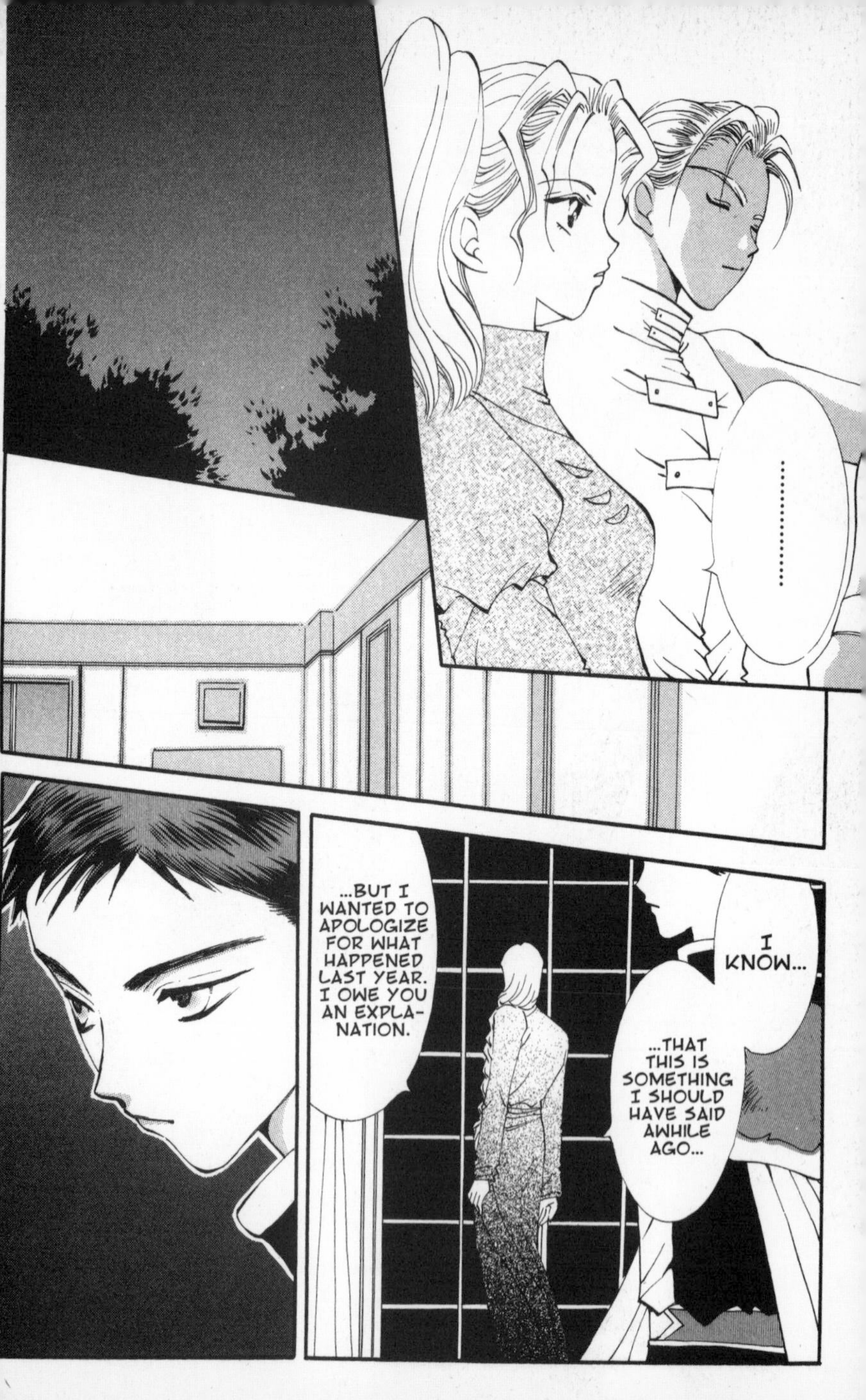
......
I KNOW...
...THAT THIS IS SOMETHING I SHOULD HAVE SAID AWHILE AGO...
...BUT I WANTED TO APOLOGIZE FOR WHAT HAPPENED LAST YEAR. I OWE YOU AN EXPLA-NATION.

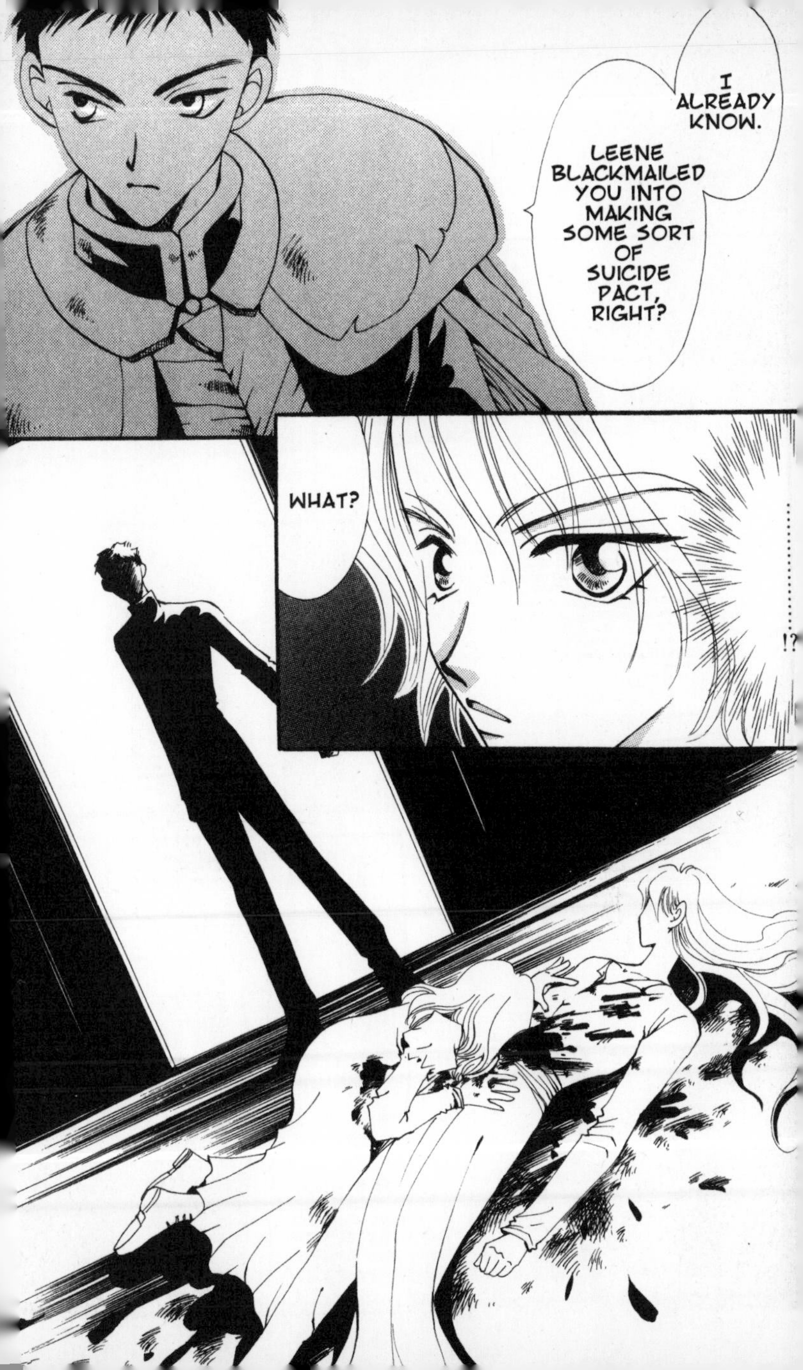
I ALREADY KNOW.
LEENE BLACKMAILED YOU INTO MAKING SOME SORT OF SUICIDE PACT, RIGHT?
......!?
WHAT?

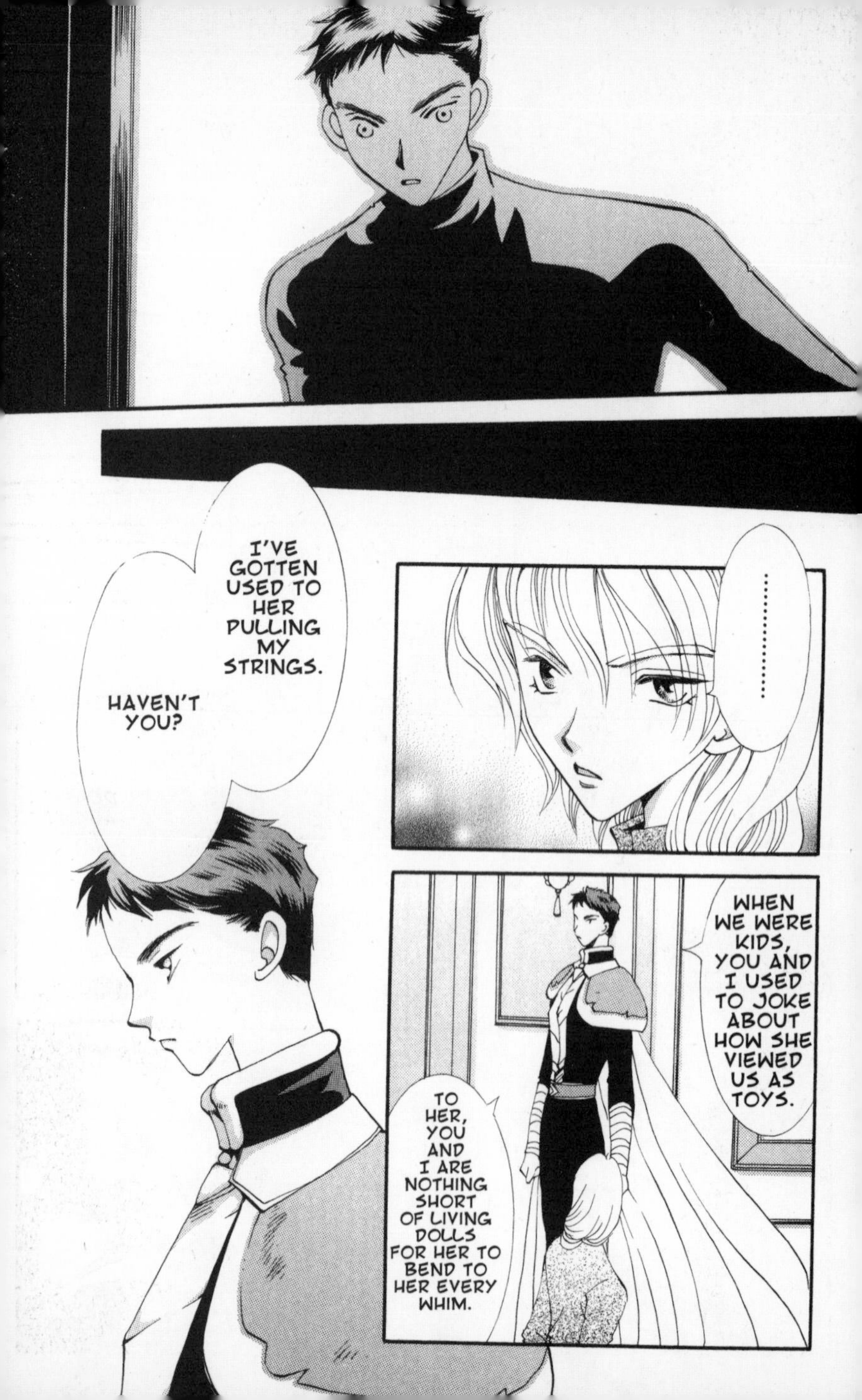
......
WHEN WE WERE KIDS, YOU AND I USED TO JOKE ABOUT HOW SHE VIEWED US AS TOYS.
TO HER, YOU AND I ARE NOTHING SHORT OF LIVING DOLLS FOR HER TO BEND TO HER EVERY WHIM.
I'VE GOTTEN USED TO HER PULLING MY STRINGS.
HAVEN'T YOU?

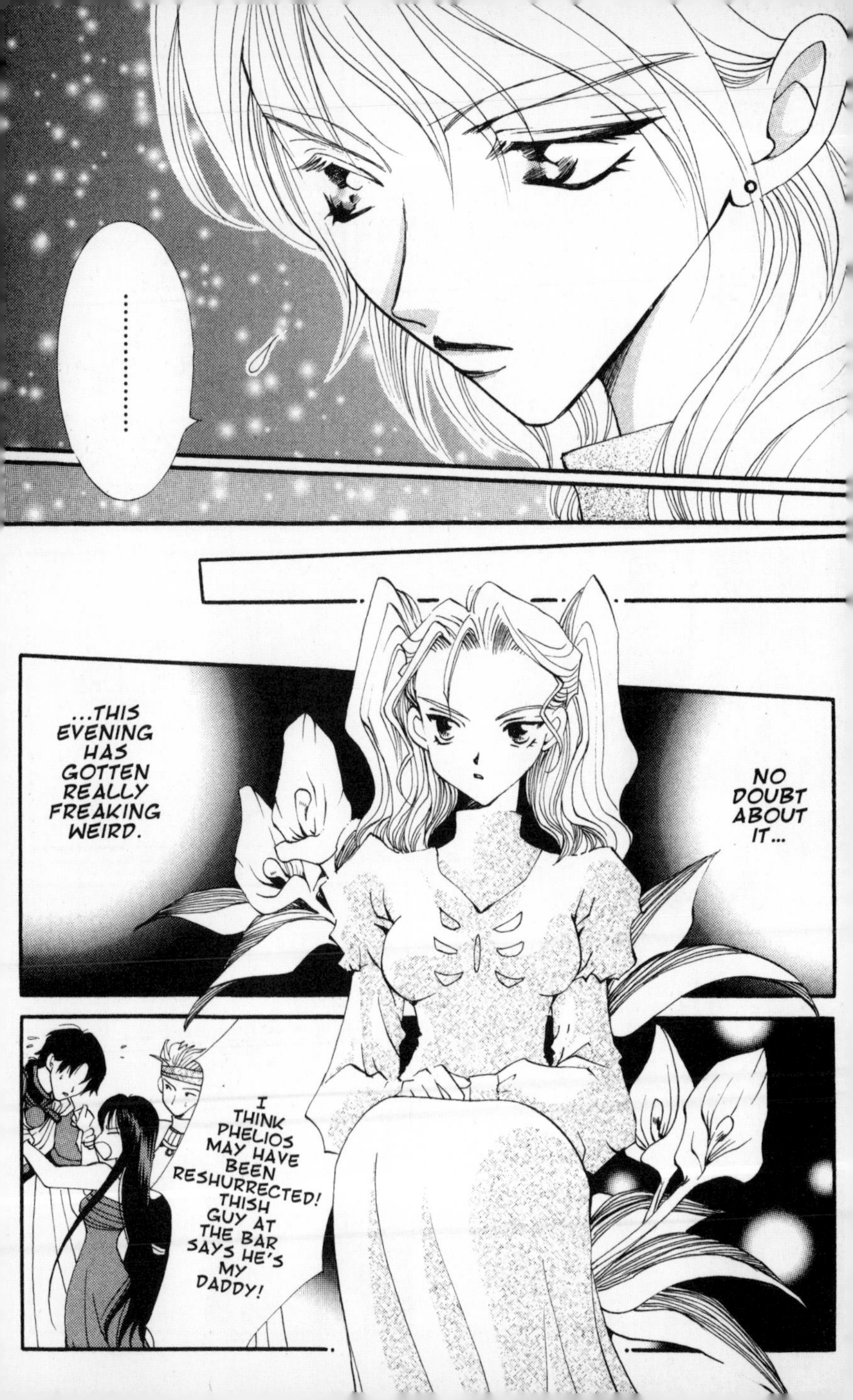
......
NO DOUBT ABOUT IT...
...THIS EVENING HAS GOTTEN REALLY FREAKING WEIRD.
I THINK PHELIOS MAY HAVE BEEN RESHURRECTED! THISH GUY AT THE BAR SAYS HE'S MY DADDY!

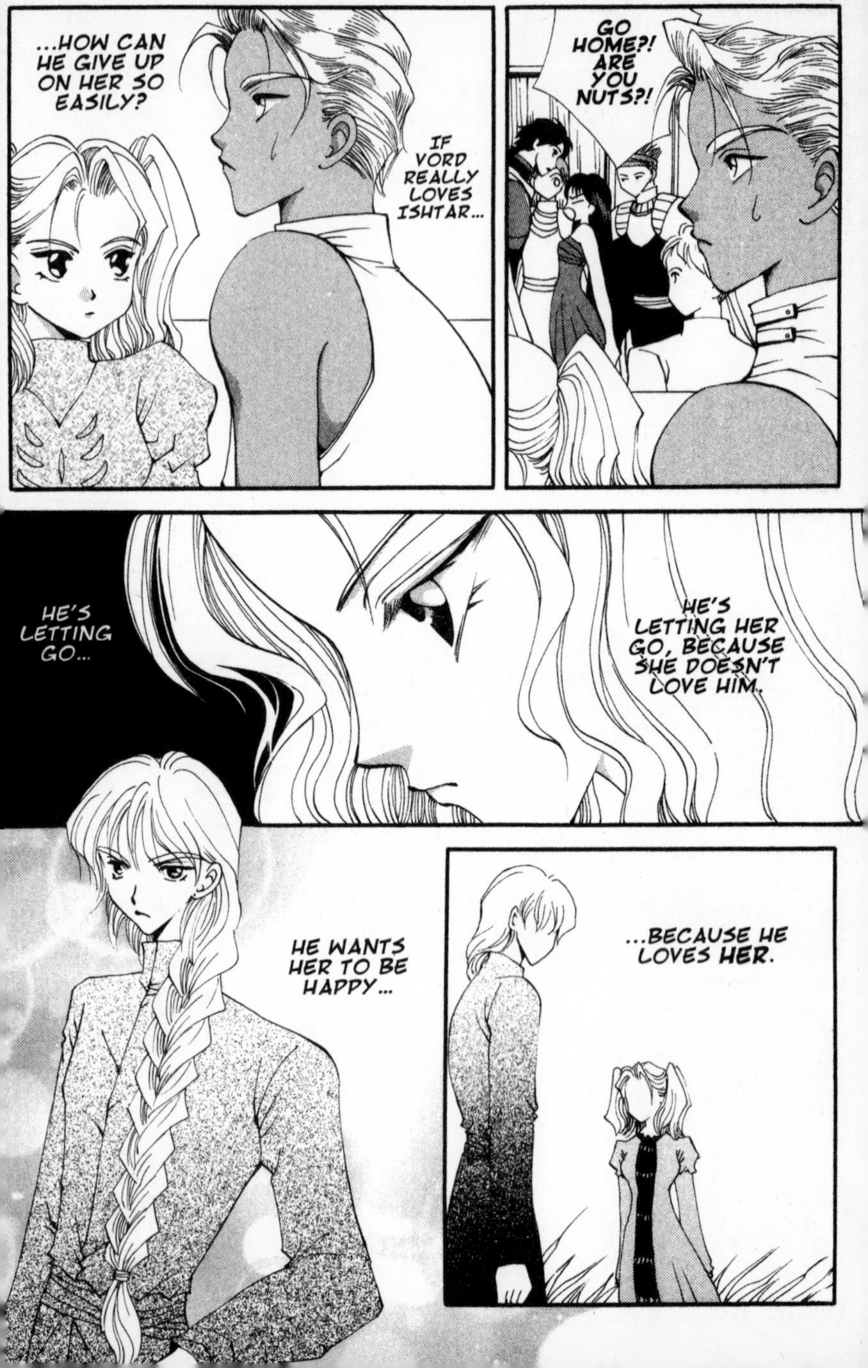
GO HOME?! ARE YOU NUTS?!
IF VORD REALLY LOVES ISHTAR...
...HOW CAN HE GIVE UP ON HER SO EASILY?
HE'S LETTING HER GO, BECAUSE SHE DOESN'T LOVE HIM.
HE'S LETTING GO...
...BECAUSE HE LOVES **HER**.
HE WANTS HER TO BE HAPPY...

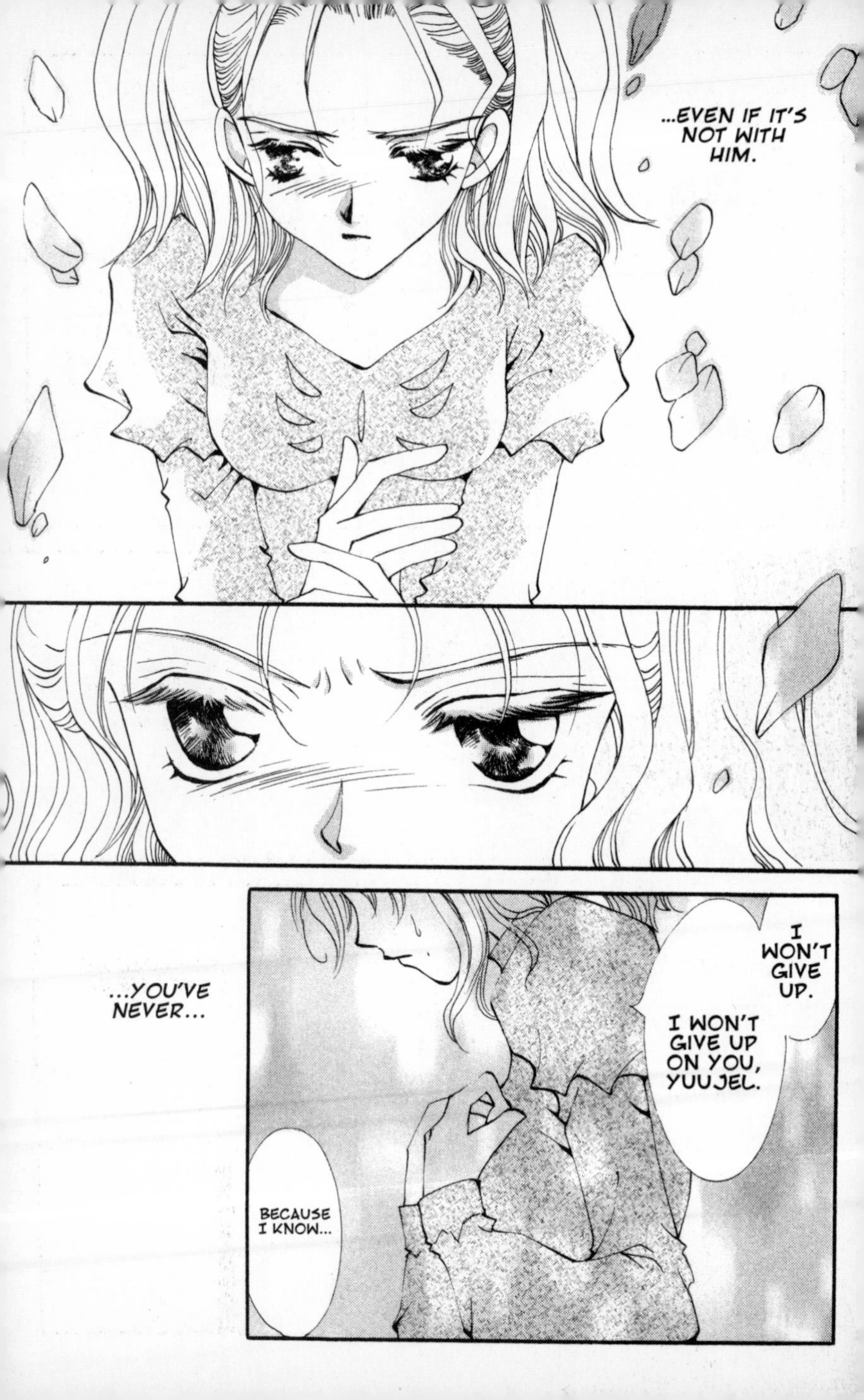
...EVEN IF IT'S NOT WITH HIM.
I WON'T GIVE UP.
I WON'T GIVE UP ON YOU, YUUJEL.
BECAUSE I KNOW...
...YOU'VE NEVER...

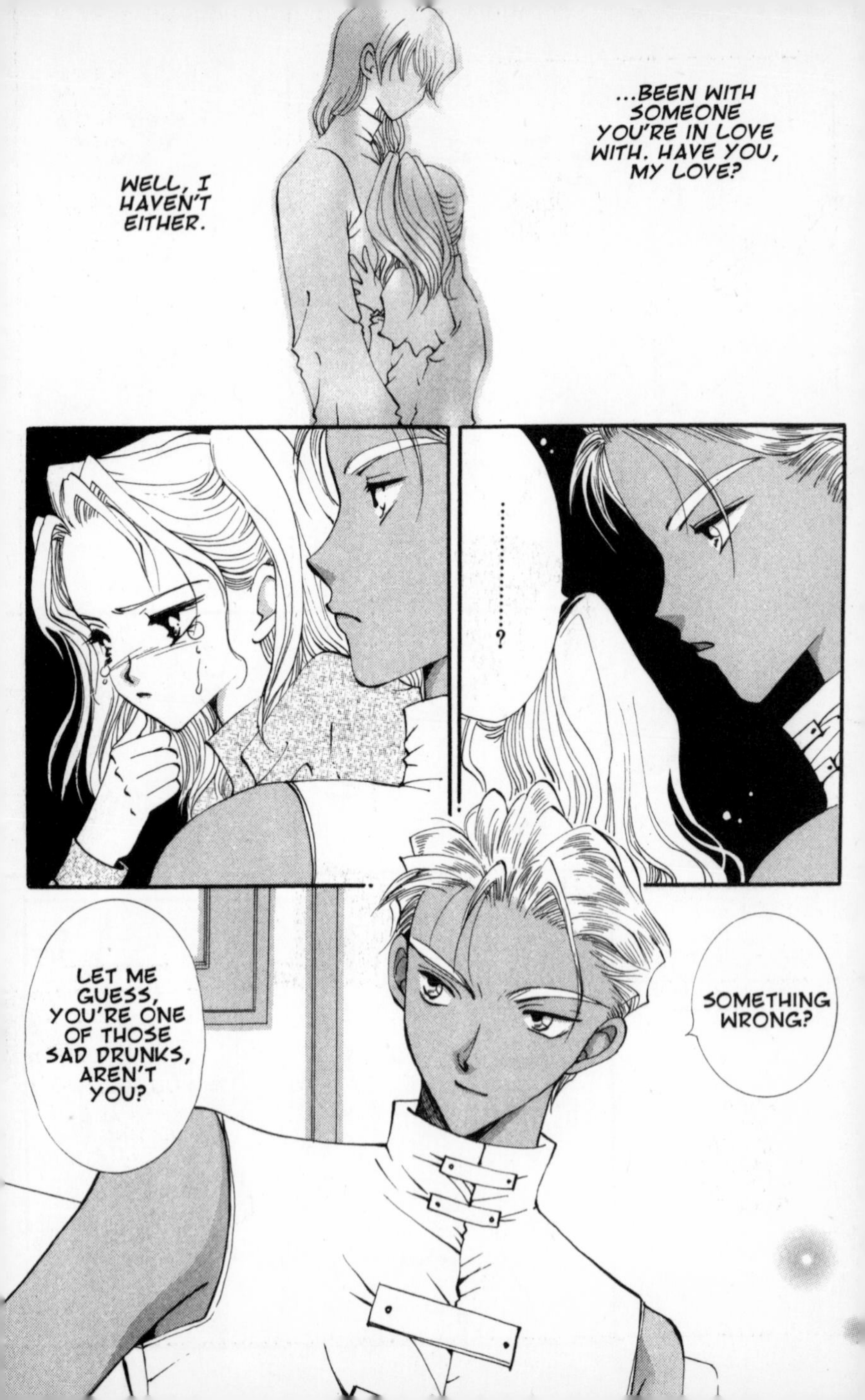
...BEEN WITH SOMEONE YOU'RE IN LOVE WITH. HAVE YOU, MY LOVE?
WELL, I HAVEN'T EITHER.
.........?
SOMETHING WRONG?
LET ME GUESS, YOU'RE ONE OF THOSE SAD DRUNKS, AREN'T YOU?

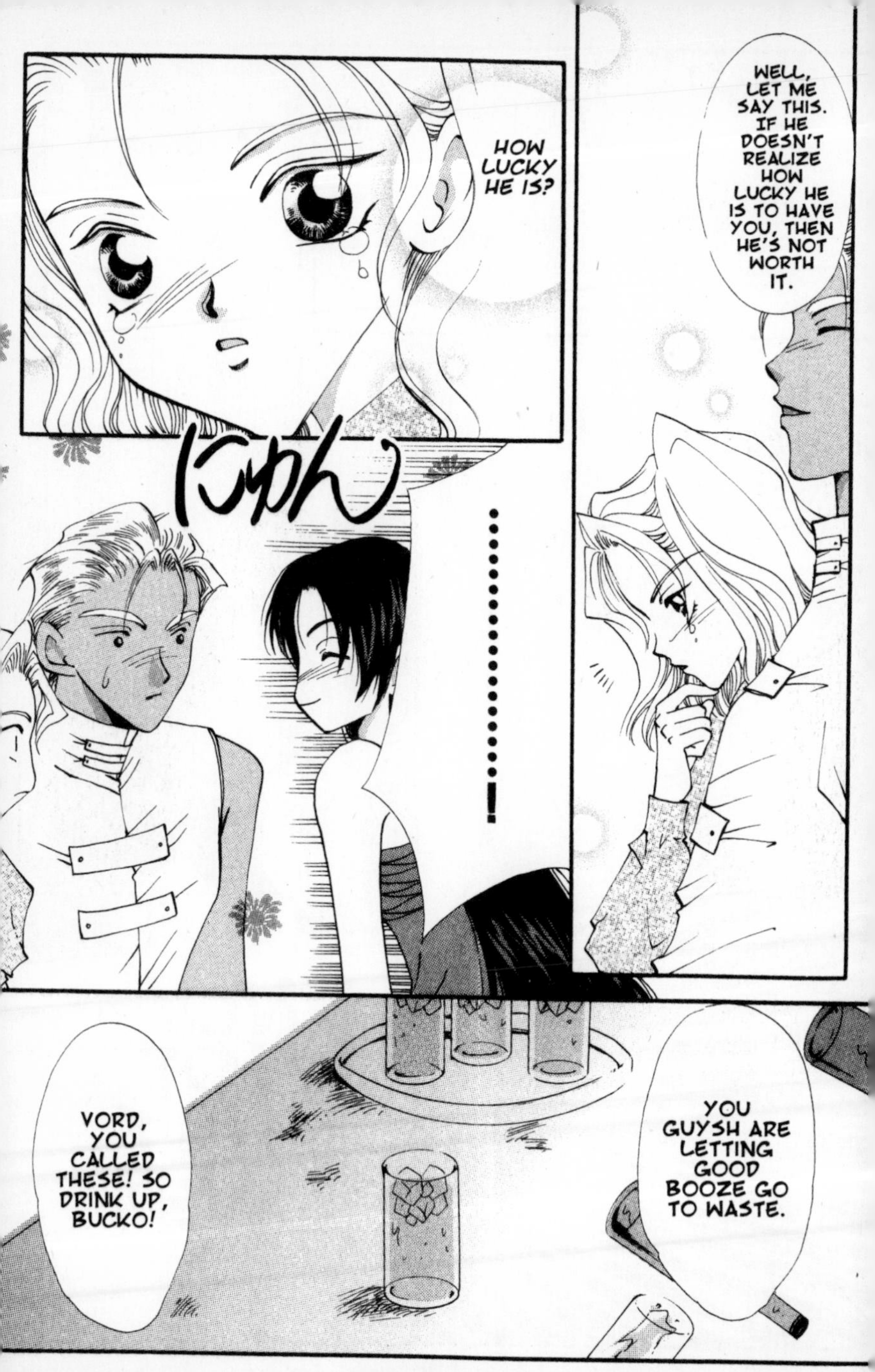
WELL, LET ME SAY THIS. IF HE DOESN'T REALIZE HOW LUCKY HE IS TO HAVE YOU, THEN HE'S NOT WORTH IT.
HOW LUCKY HE IS?
にゅん
……………!
YOU GUYSH ARE LETTING GOOD BOOZE GO TO WASTE.
VORD, YOU CALLED THESE! SO DRINK UP, BUCKO!

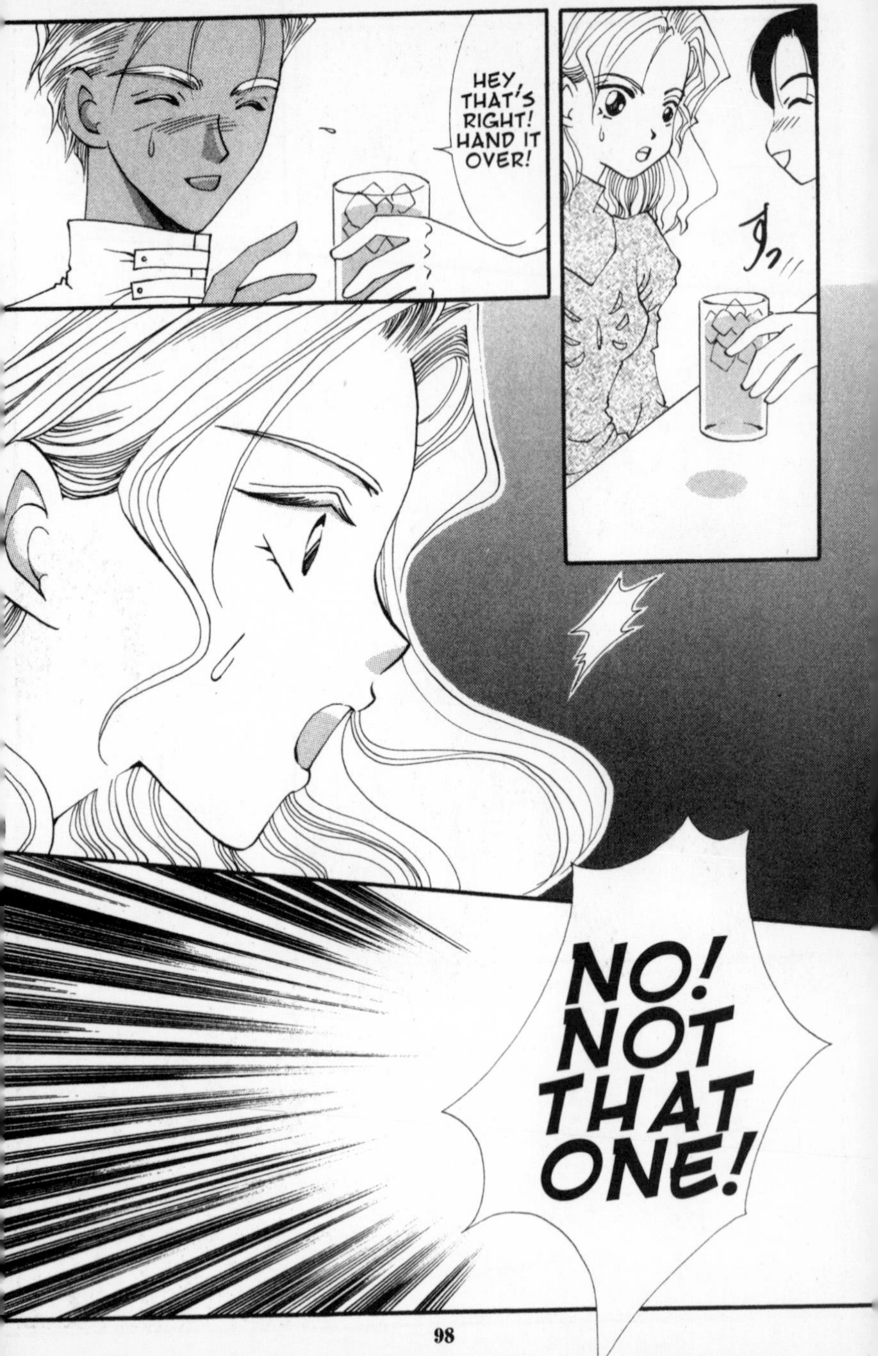
HEY, THAT'S RIGHT! HAND IT OVER!
NO! NOT THAT ONE!

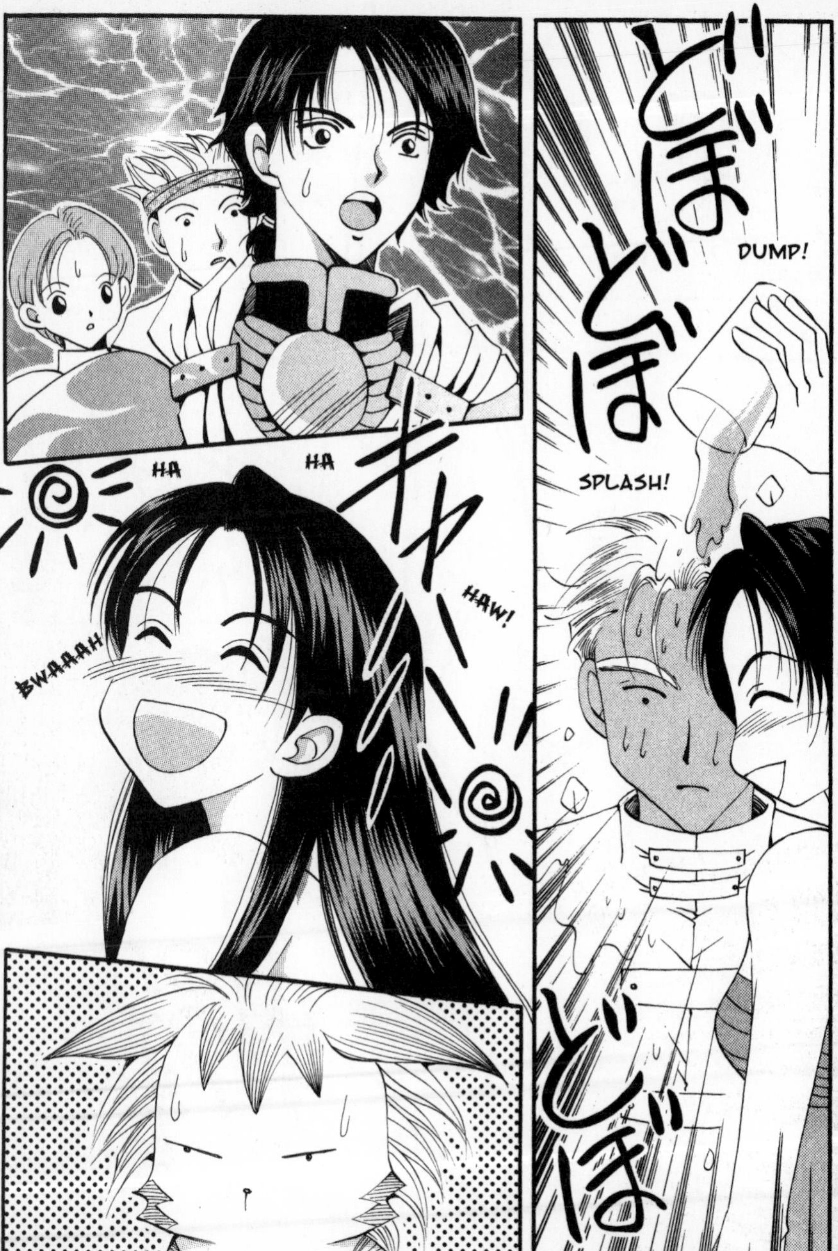
どぼどぼ
DUMP!
SPLASH!
どぼどぼ
HA
HA
キャハ
HAW!
BWAAAH

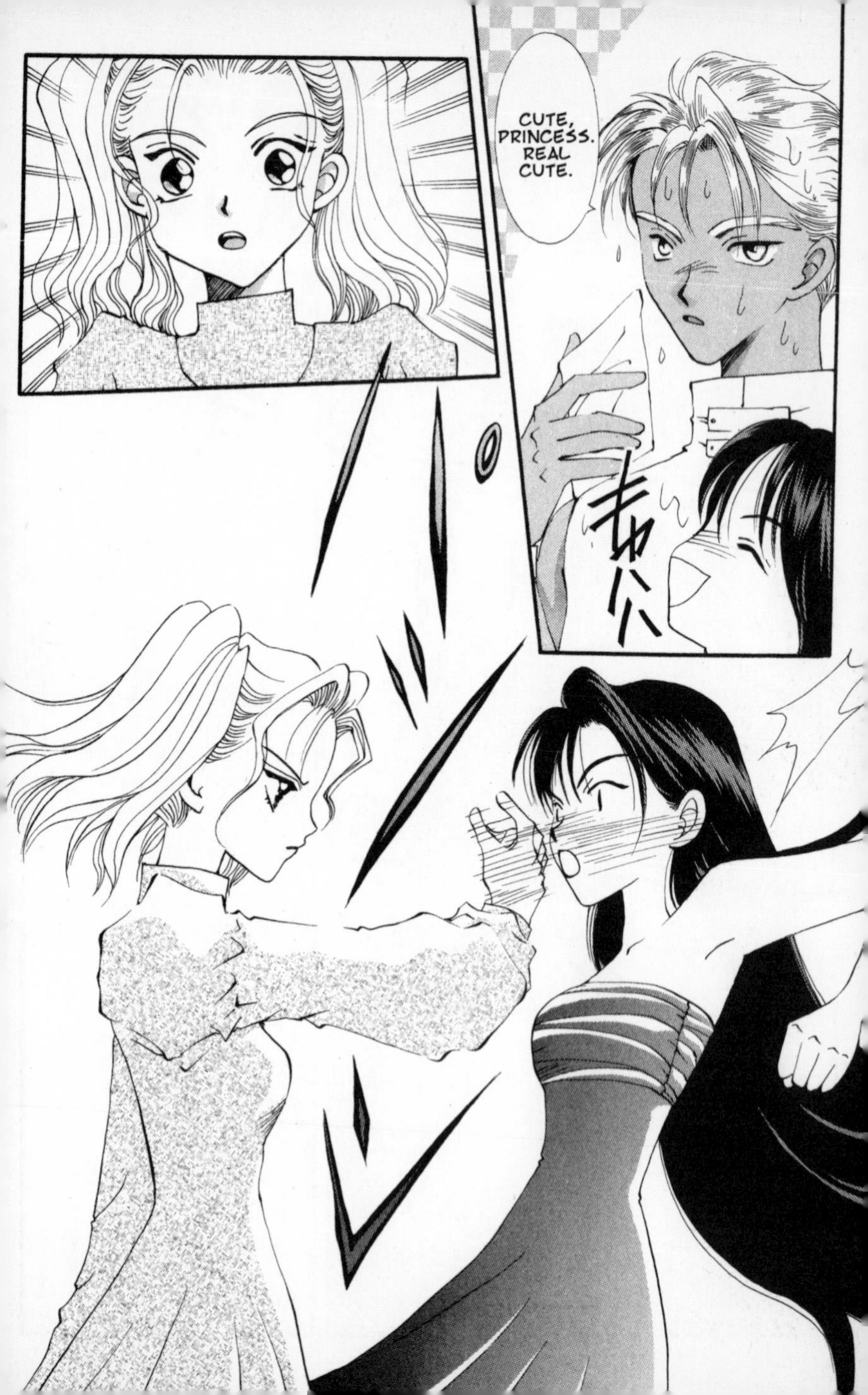
CUTE, PRINCESS. REAL CUTE.
キャハハ

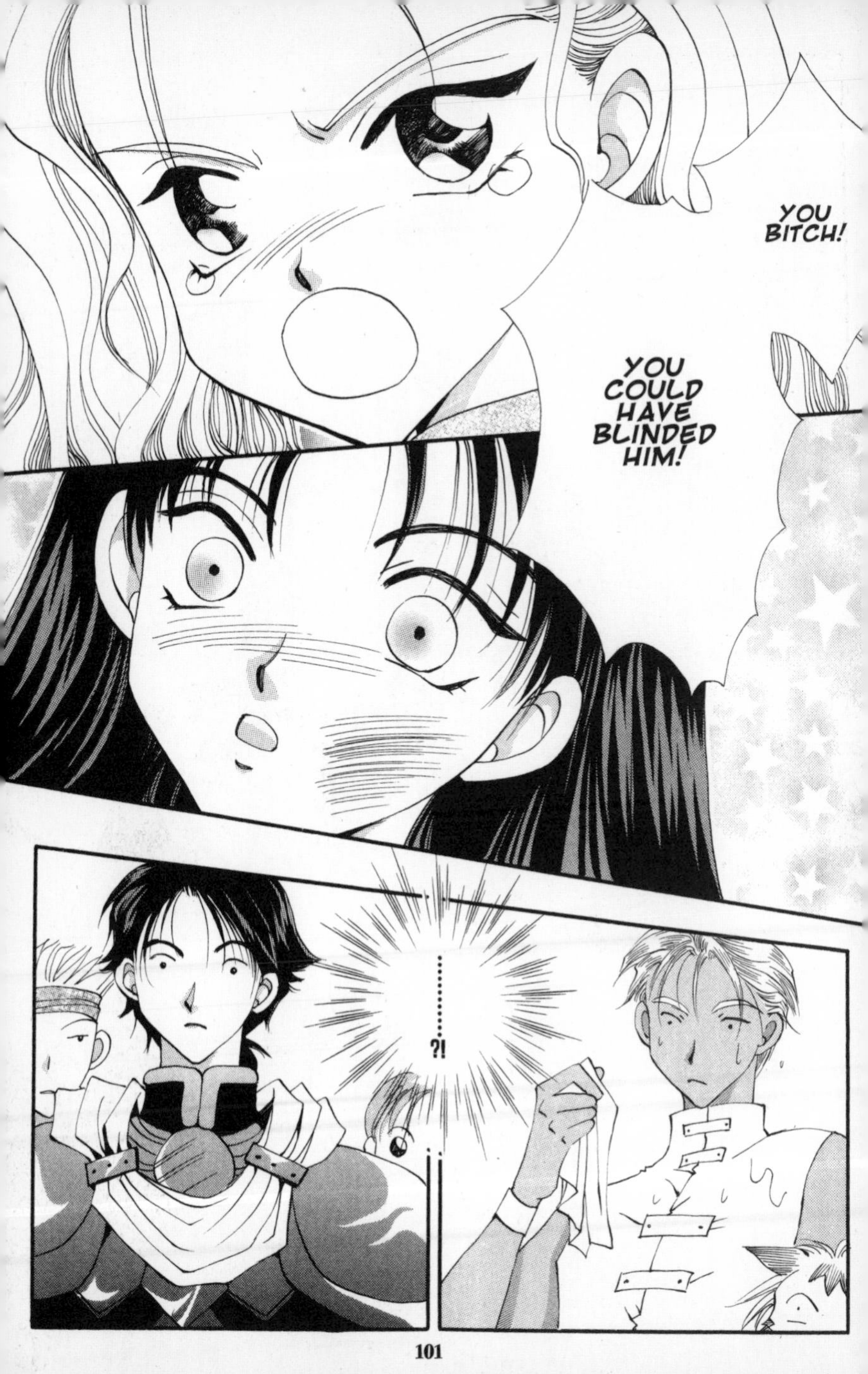
YOU BITCH!
YOU COULD HAVE BLINDED HIM!
......?!

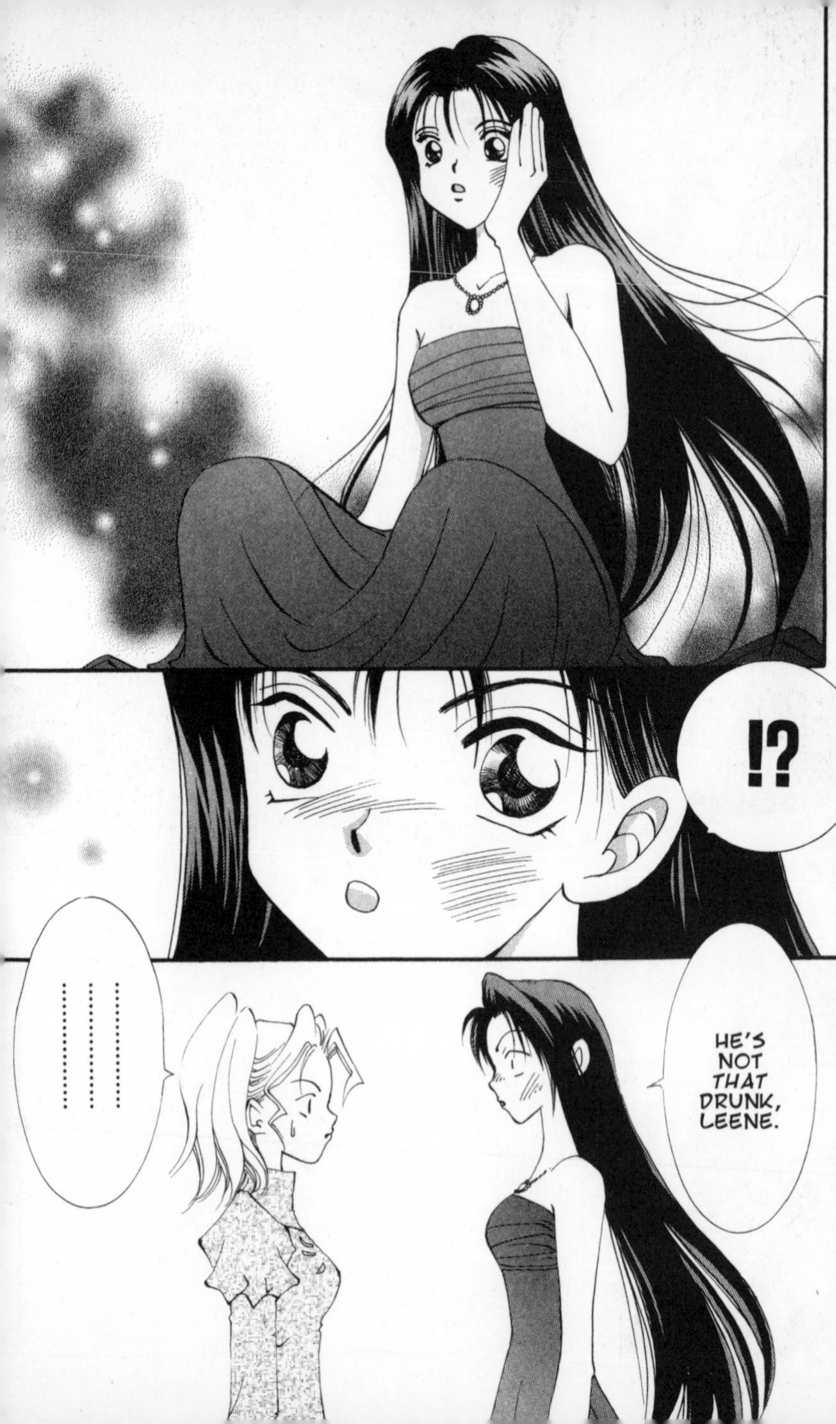
!?
HE'S NOT *THAT* DRUNK, LEENE.
......

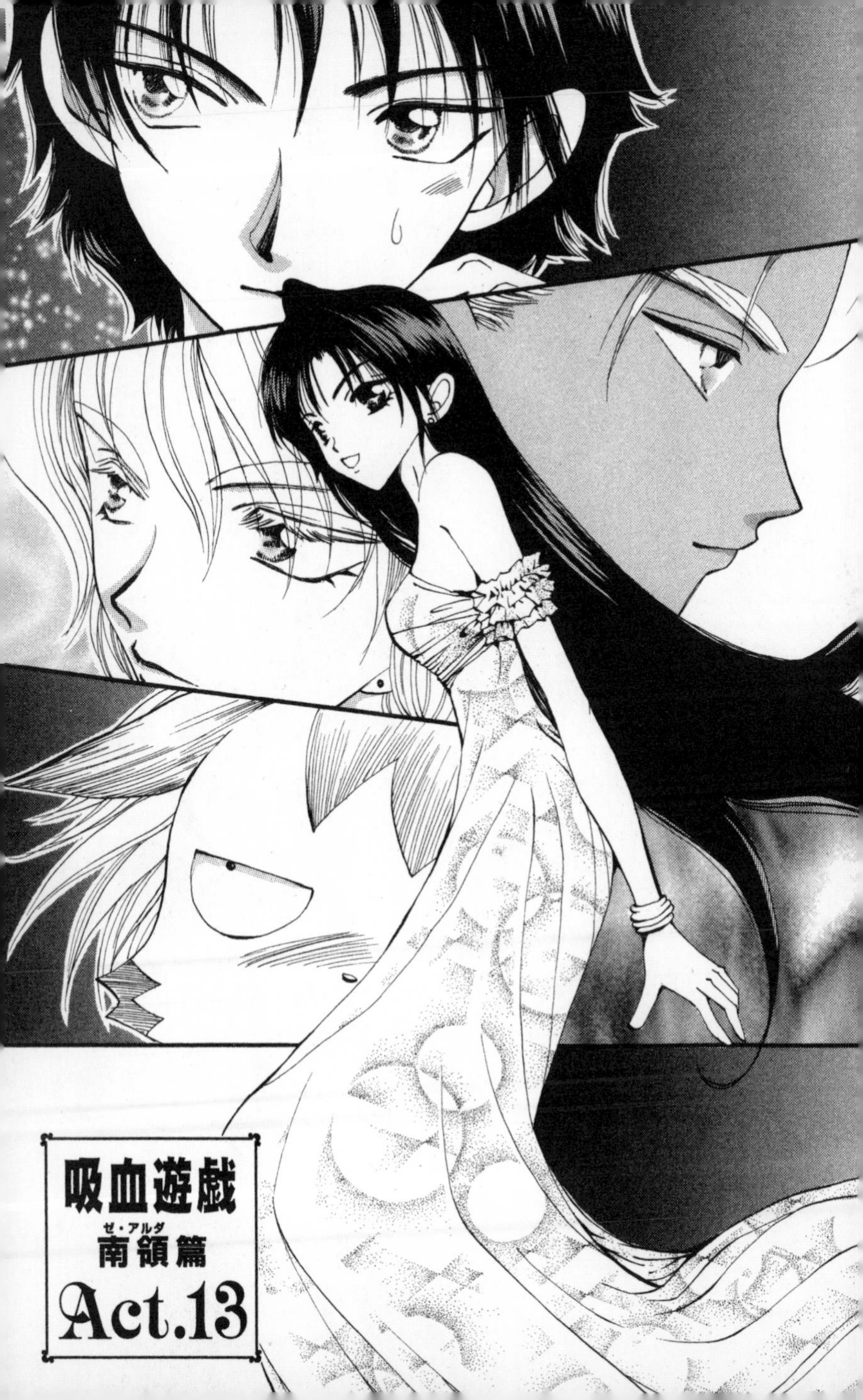
吸血遊戯
ゼ・アルダ
南領篇
Act.13

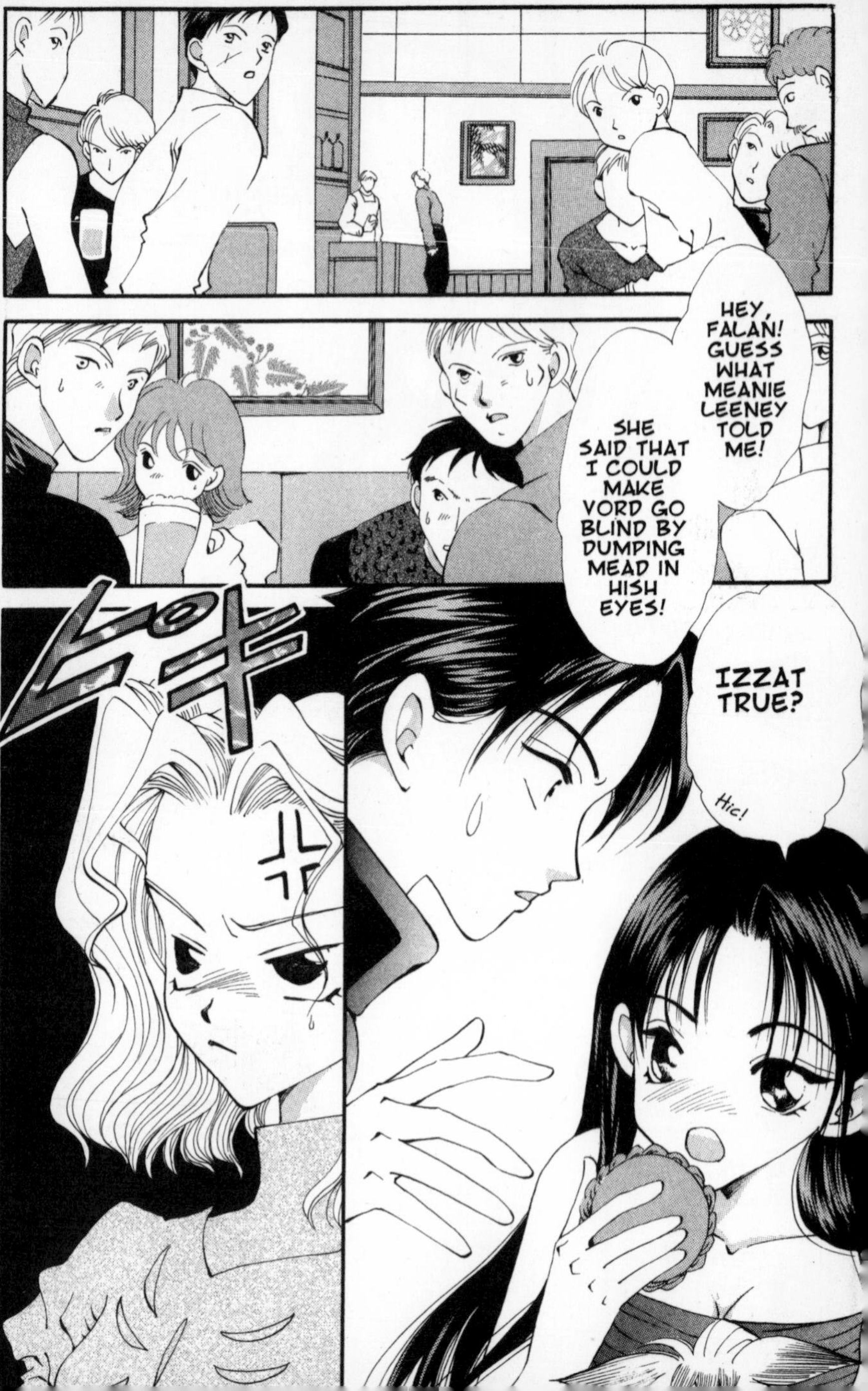
HEY, FALAN! GUESS WHAT MEANIE LEENEY TOLD ME!
SHE SAID THAT I COULD MAKE VORD GO BLIND BY DUMPING MEAD IN HISH EYES!
IZZAT TRUE?
Hic!

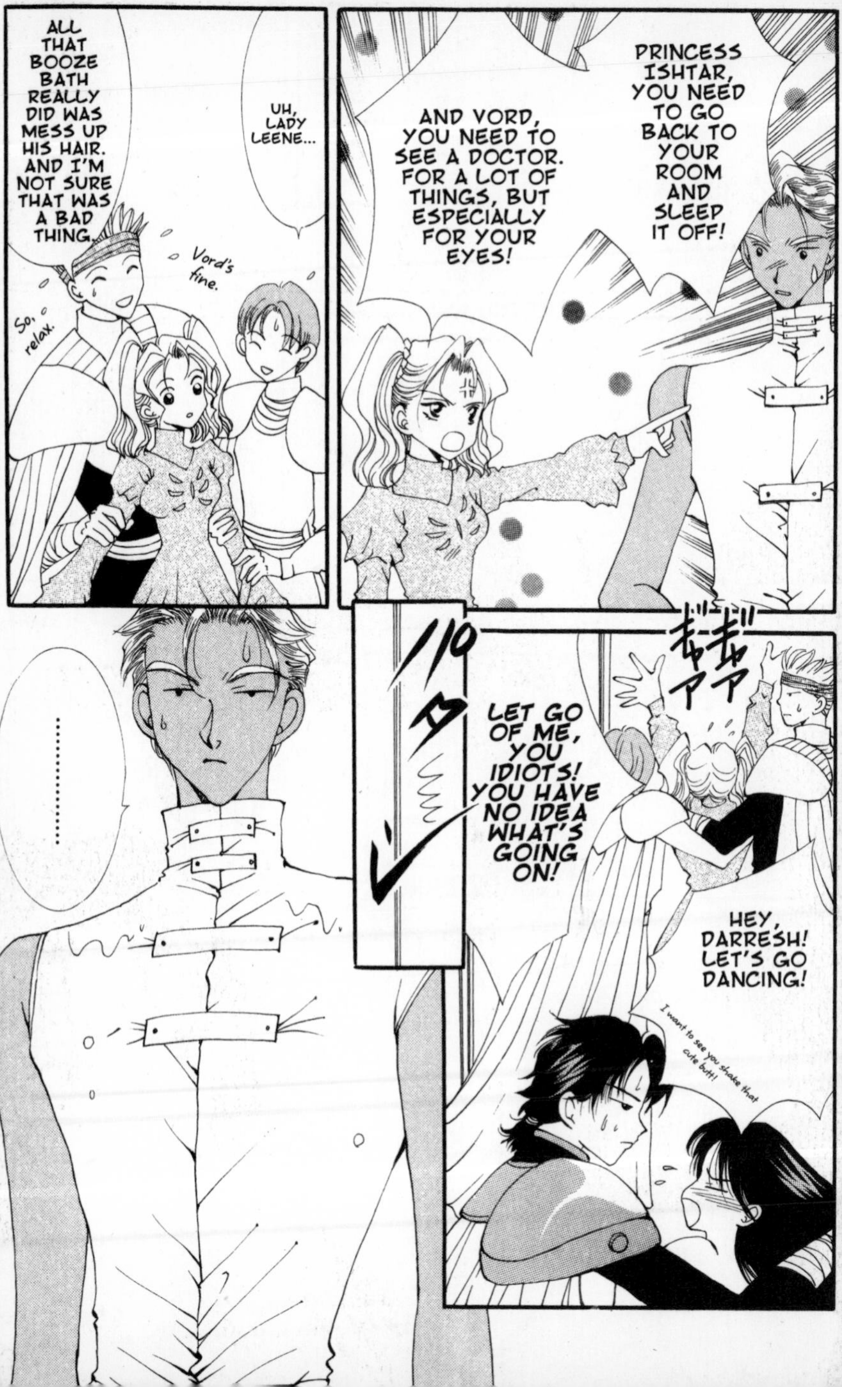
PRINCESS ISHTAR, YOU NEED TO GO BACK TO YOUR ROOM AND SLEEP IT OFF!
AND VORD, YOU NEED TO SEE A DOCTOR. FOR A LOT OF THINGS, BUT ESPECIALLY FOR YOUR EYES!
ALL THAT BOOZE BATH REALLY DID WAS MESS UP HIS HAIR. AND I'M NOT SURE THAT WAS A BAD THING.
UH, LADY LEENE...
Vord's fine.
So, relax.
ギャアギャア
LET GO OF ME, YOU IDIOTS! YOU HAVE NO IDEA WHAT'S GOING ON!
HEY, DARRESH! LET'S GO DANCING!
I want to see you shake that cute butt!
パタン
....

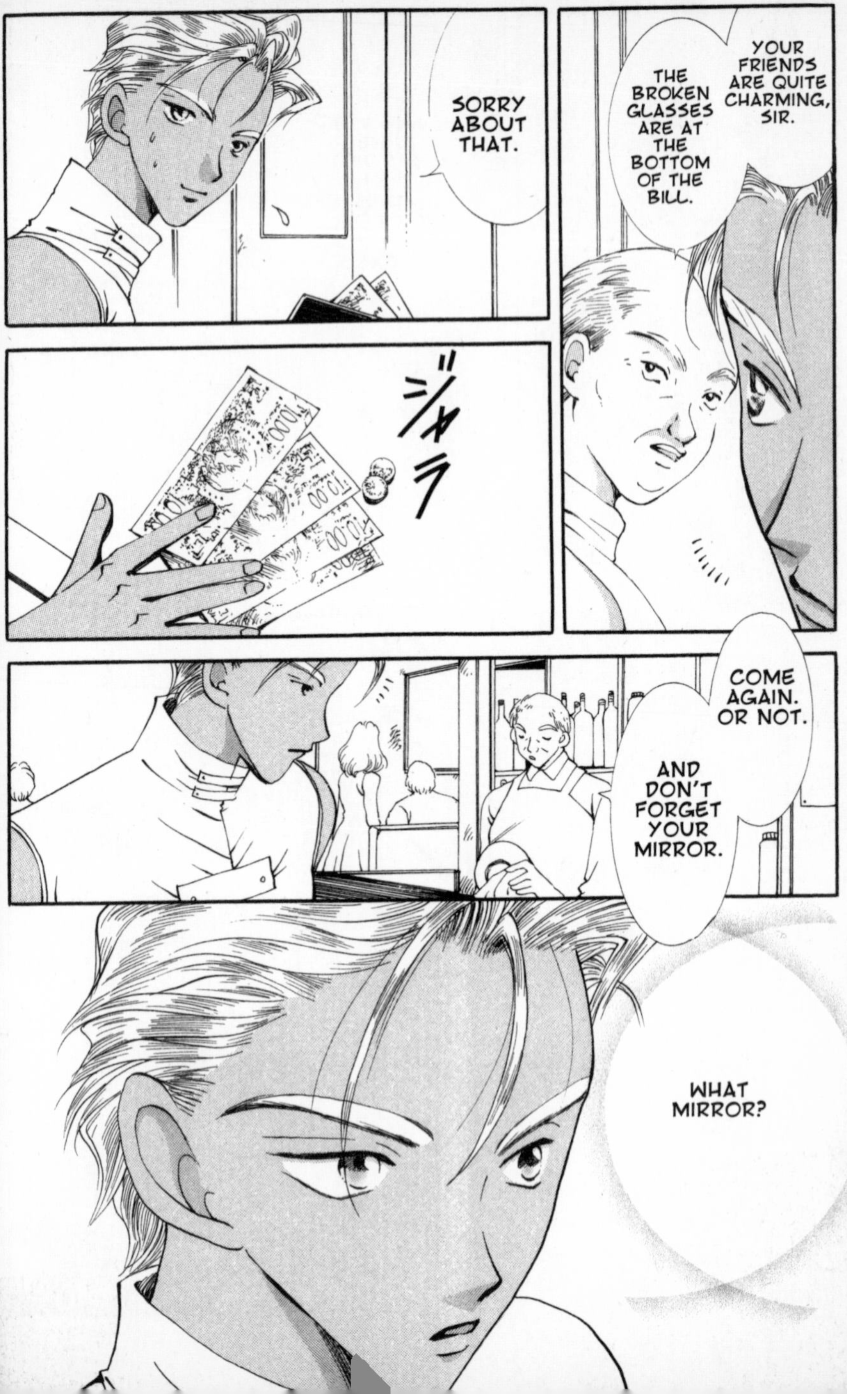
YOUR FRIENDS ARE QUITE CHARMING, SIR.
THE BROKEN GLASSES ARE AT THE BOTTOM OF THE BILL.
SORRY ABOUT THAT.
ジャラ
COME AGAIN. OR NOT.
AND DON'T FORGET YOUR MIRROR.
WHAT MIRROR?

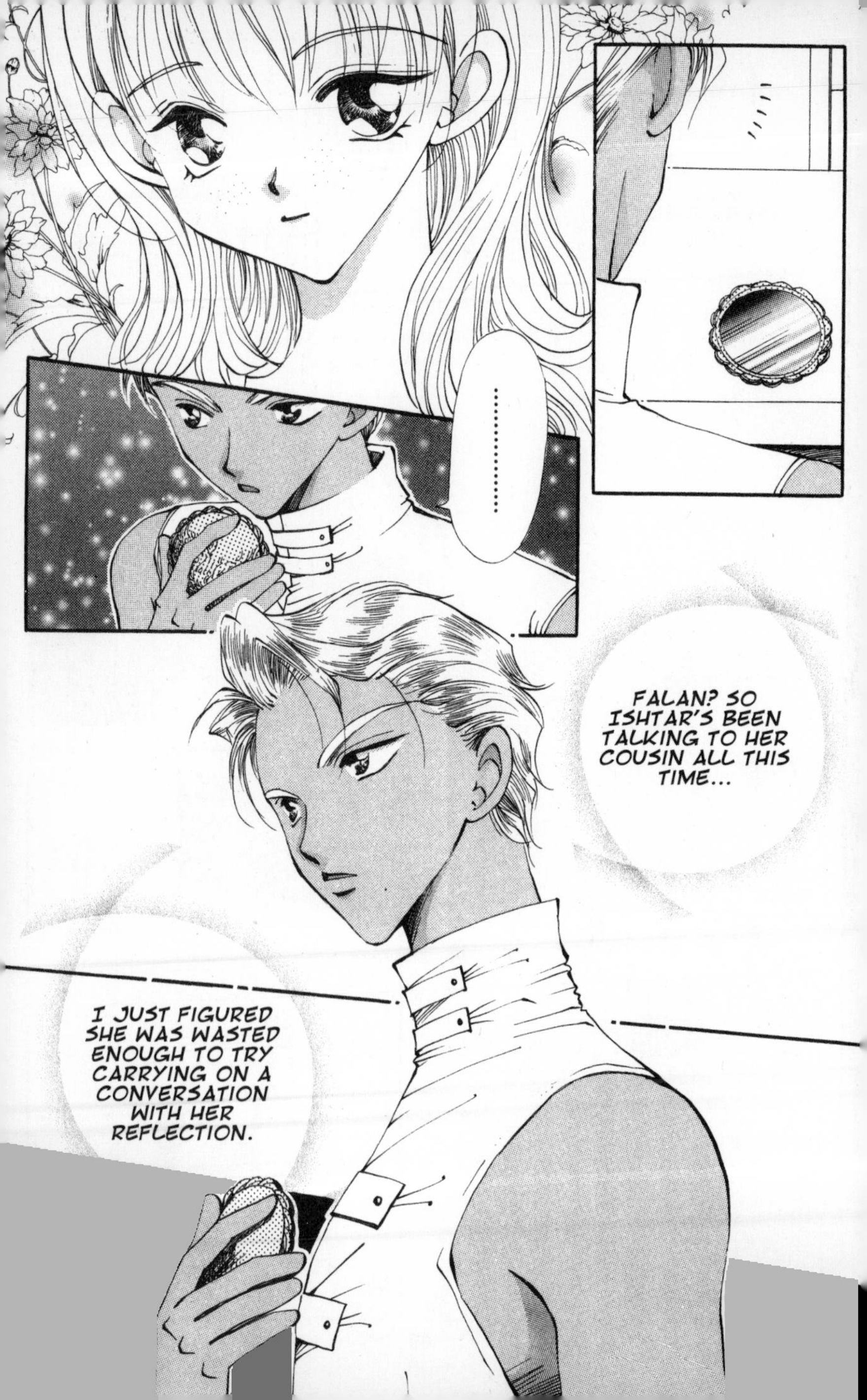
......
FALAN? SO ISHTAR'S BEEN TALKING TO HER COUSIN ALL THIS TIME...
I JUST FIGURED SHE WAS WASTED ENOUGH TO TRY CARRYING ON A CONVERSATION WITH HER REFLECTION.

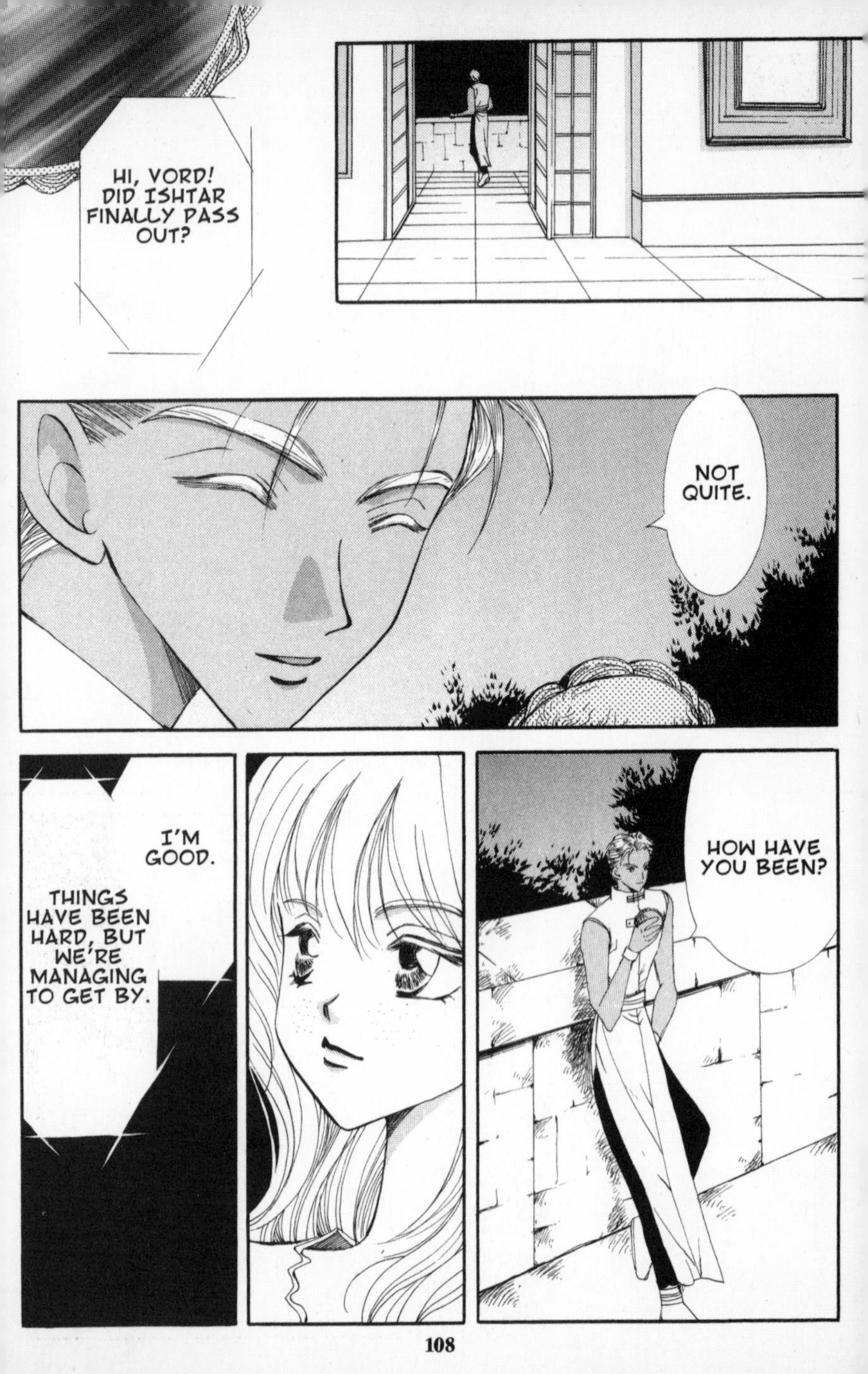
HI, VORD! DID ISHTAR FINALLY PASS OUT?
NOT QUITE.
HOW HAVE YOU BEEN?
I'M GOOD.
THINGS HAVE BEEN HARD, BUT WE'RE MANAGING TO GET BY.

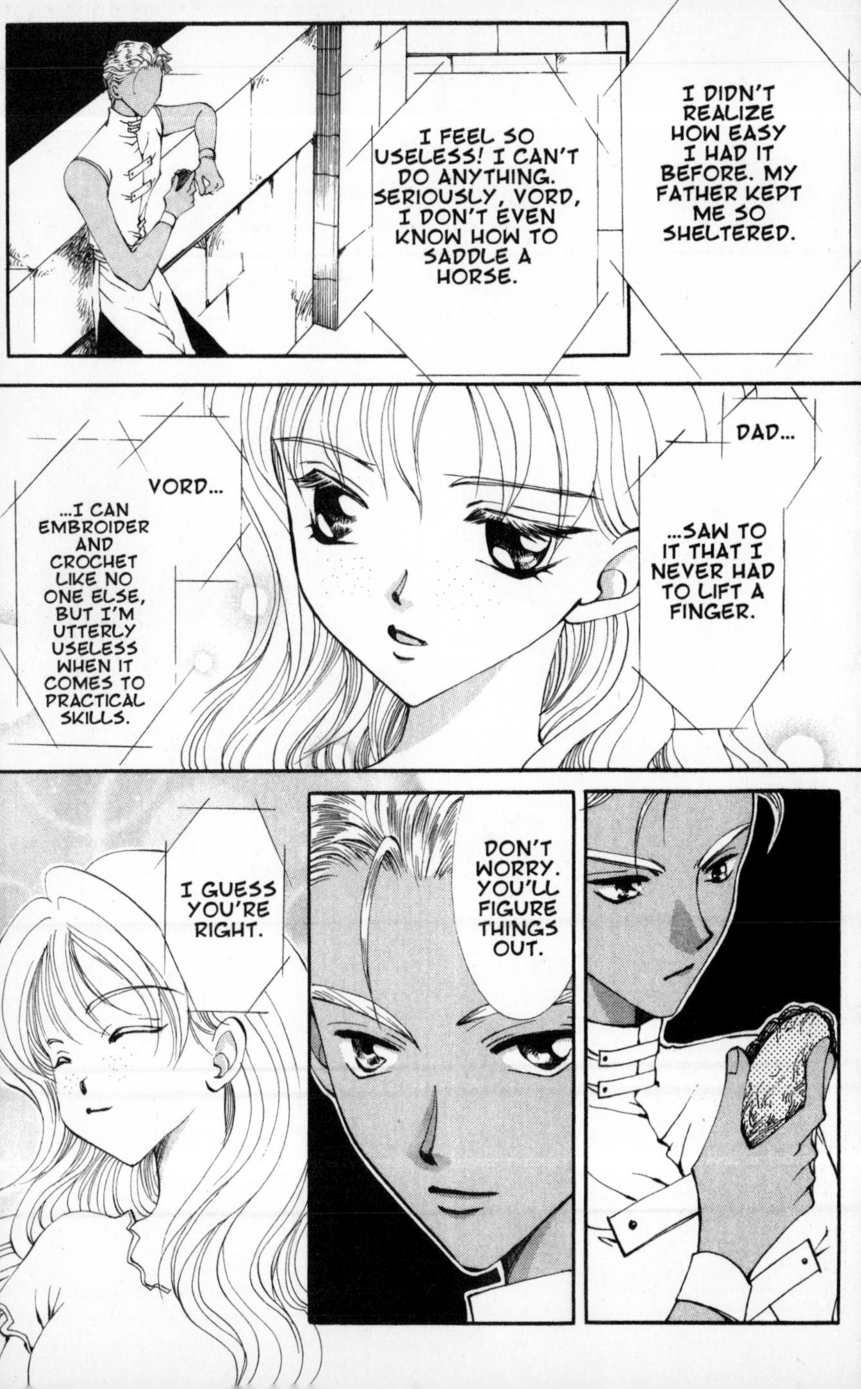
I DIDN'T REALIZE HOW EASY I HAD IT BEFORE. MY FATHER KEPT ME SO SHELTERED.
I FEEL SO USELESS! I CAN'T DO ANYTHING. SERIOUSLY, VORD, I DON'T EVEN KNOW HOW TO SADDLE A HORSE.
DAD...
...SAW TO IT THAT I NEVER HAD TO LIFT A FINGER.
VORD...
...I CAN EMBROIDER AND CROCHET LIKE NO ONE ELSE, BUT I'M UTTERLY USELESS WHEN IT COMES TO PRACTICAL SKILLS.
DON'T WORRY. YOU'LL FIGURE THINGS OUT.
I GUESS YOU'RE RIGHT.

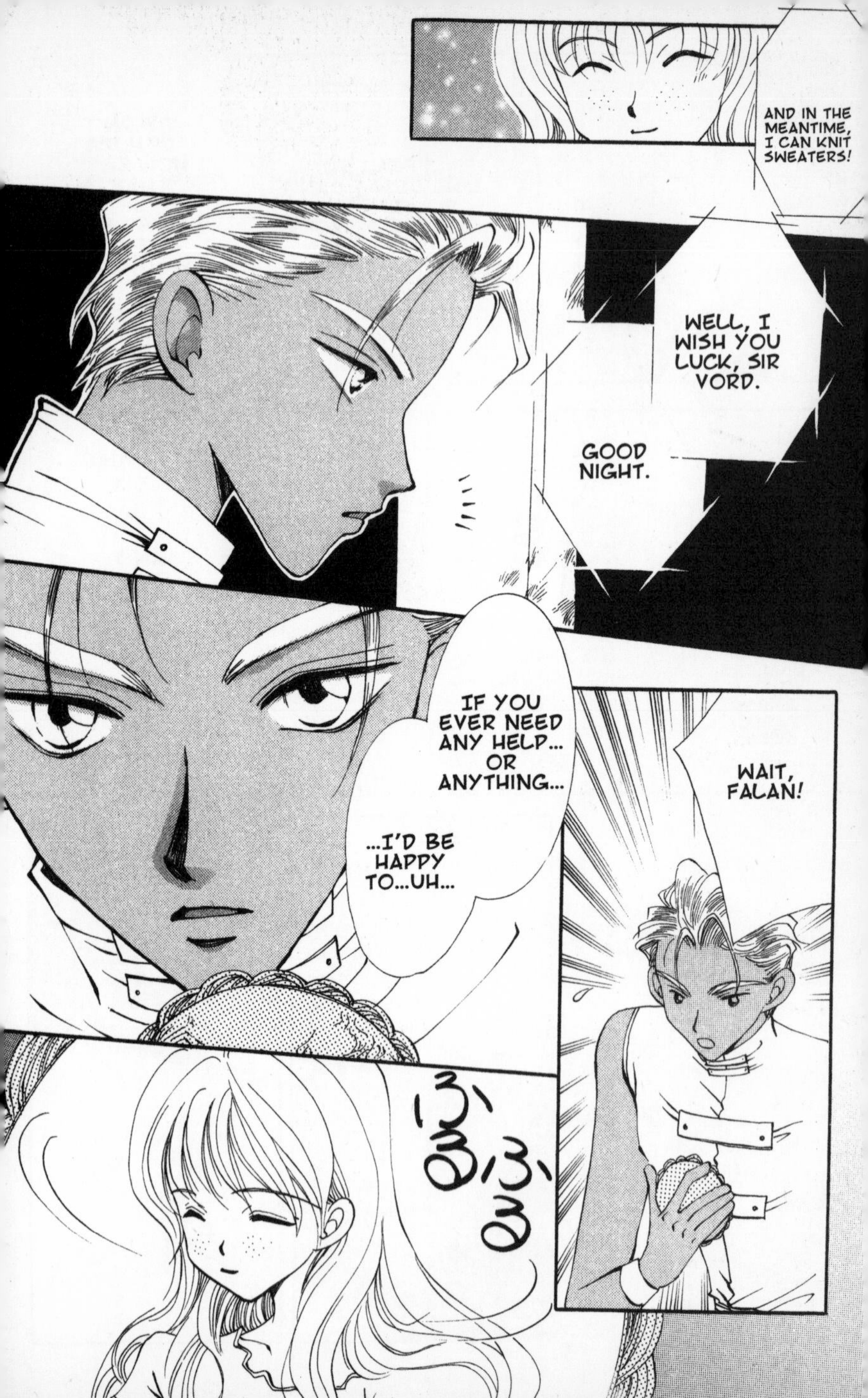
AND IN THE MEANTIME, I CAN KNIT SWEATERS!
WELL, I WISH YOU LUCK, SIR VORD.
GOOD NIGHT.
WAIT, FALAN!
IF YOU EVER NEED ANY HELP... OR ANYTHING...
...I'D BE HAPPY TO...UH...
ふ、ふふ、ふ

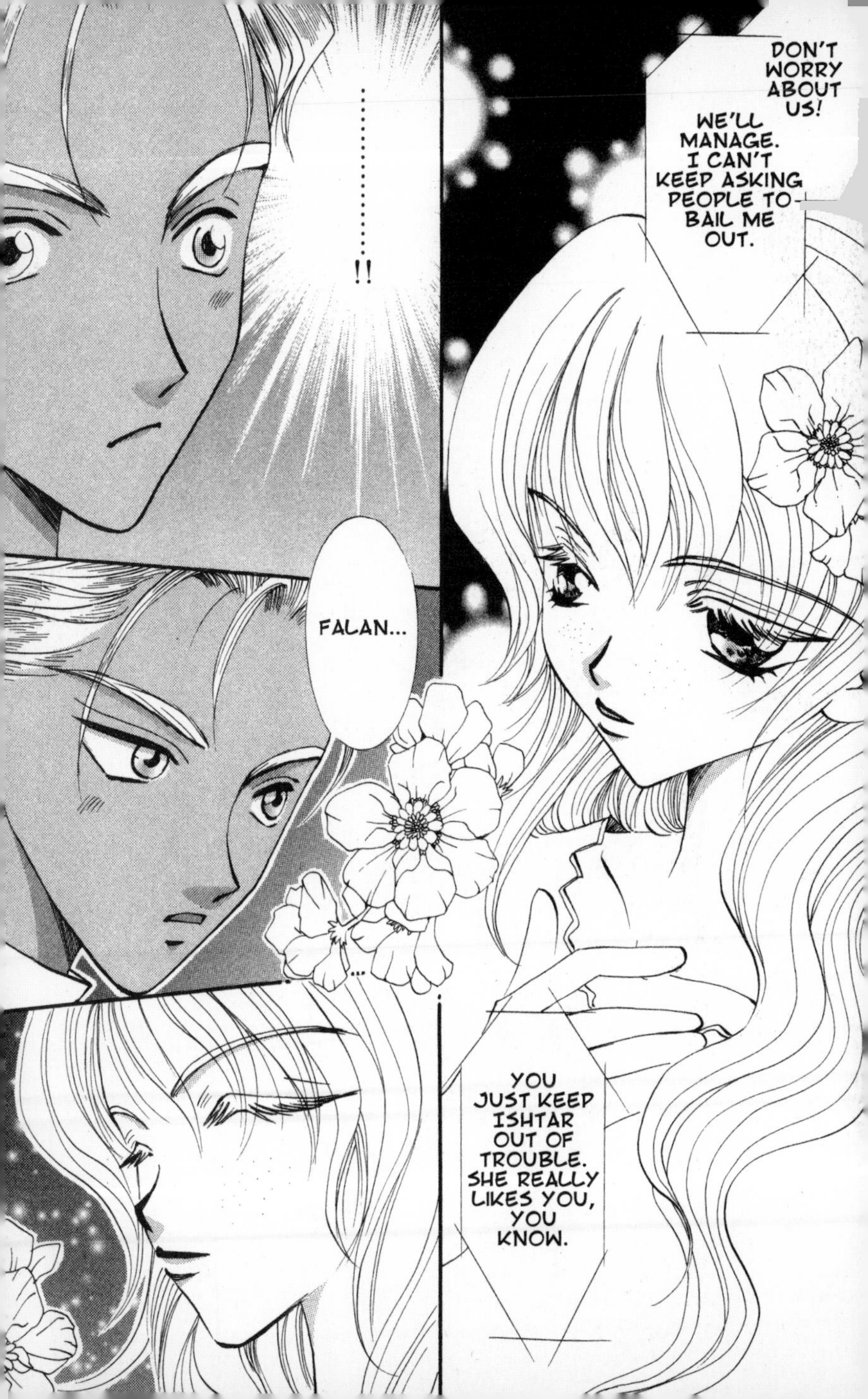
DON'T WORRY ABOUT US!
WE'LL MANAGE. I CAN'T KEEP ASKING PEOPLE TO-BAIL ME OUT.
YOU JUST KEEP ISHTAR OUT OF TROUBLE. SHE REALLY LIKES YOU, YOU KNOW.
.........!!
FALAN...
...

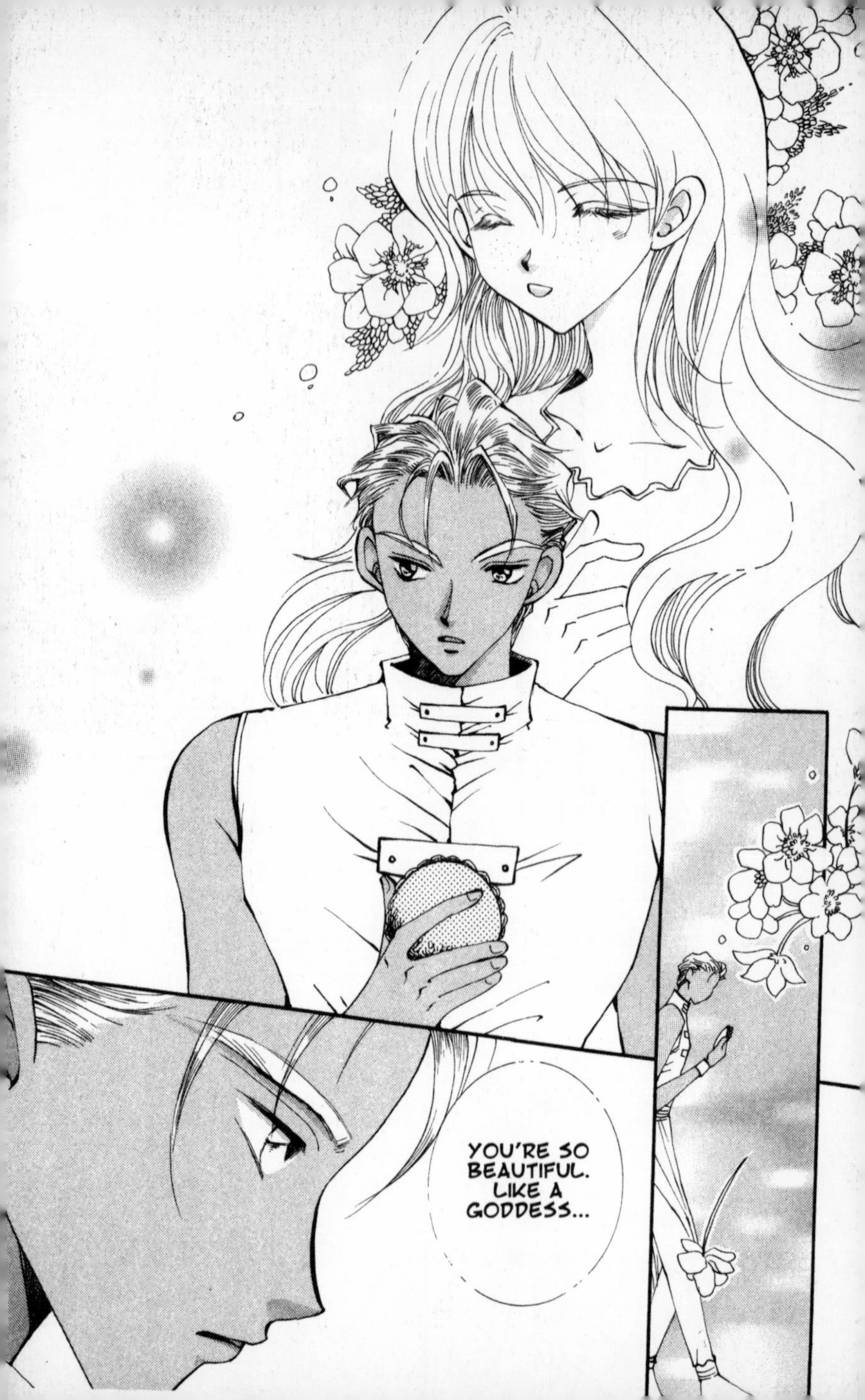
YOU'RE SO BEAUTIFUL. LIKE A GODDESS...

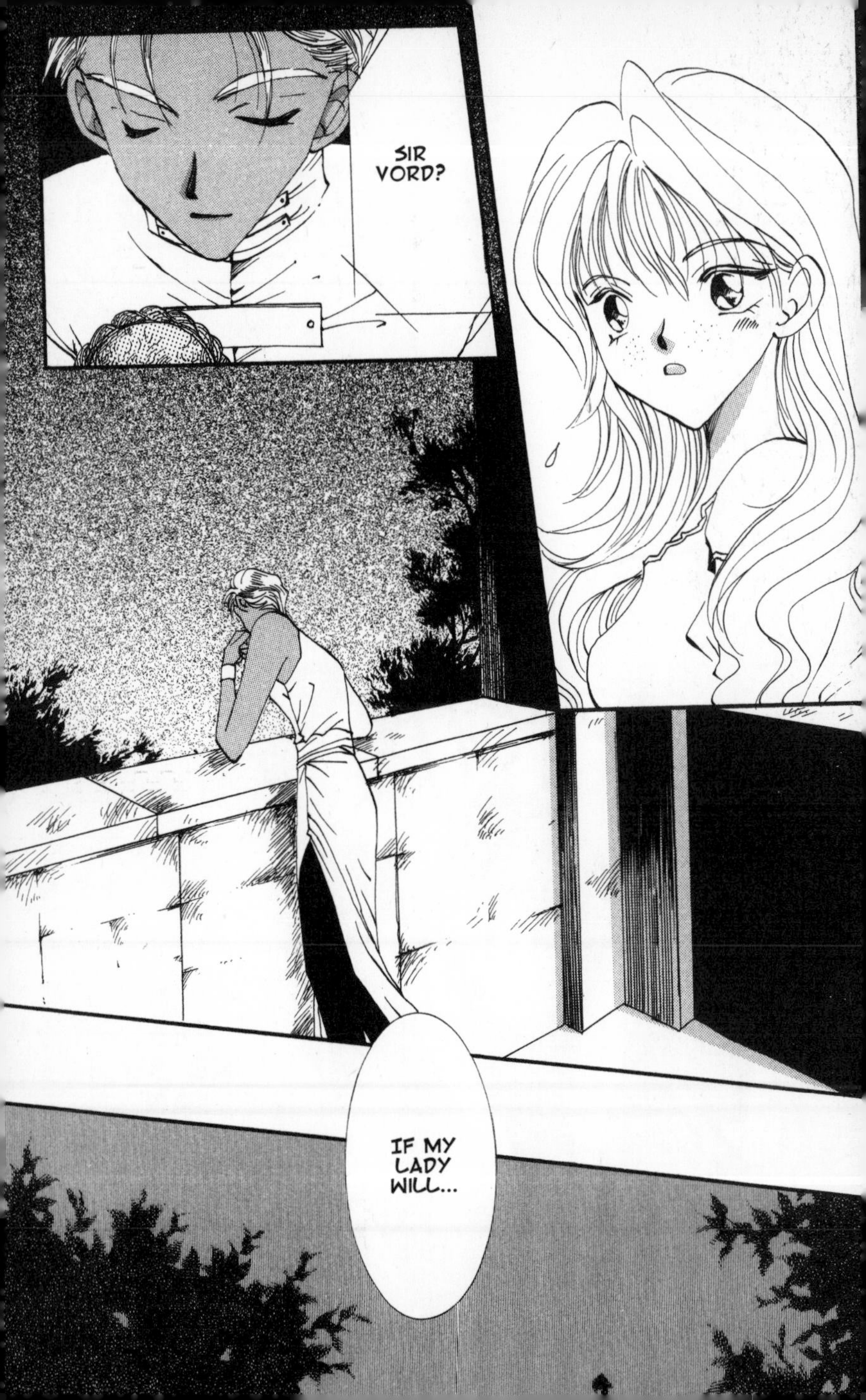

SIR VORD?
IF MY LADY WILL...

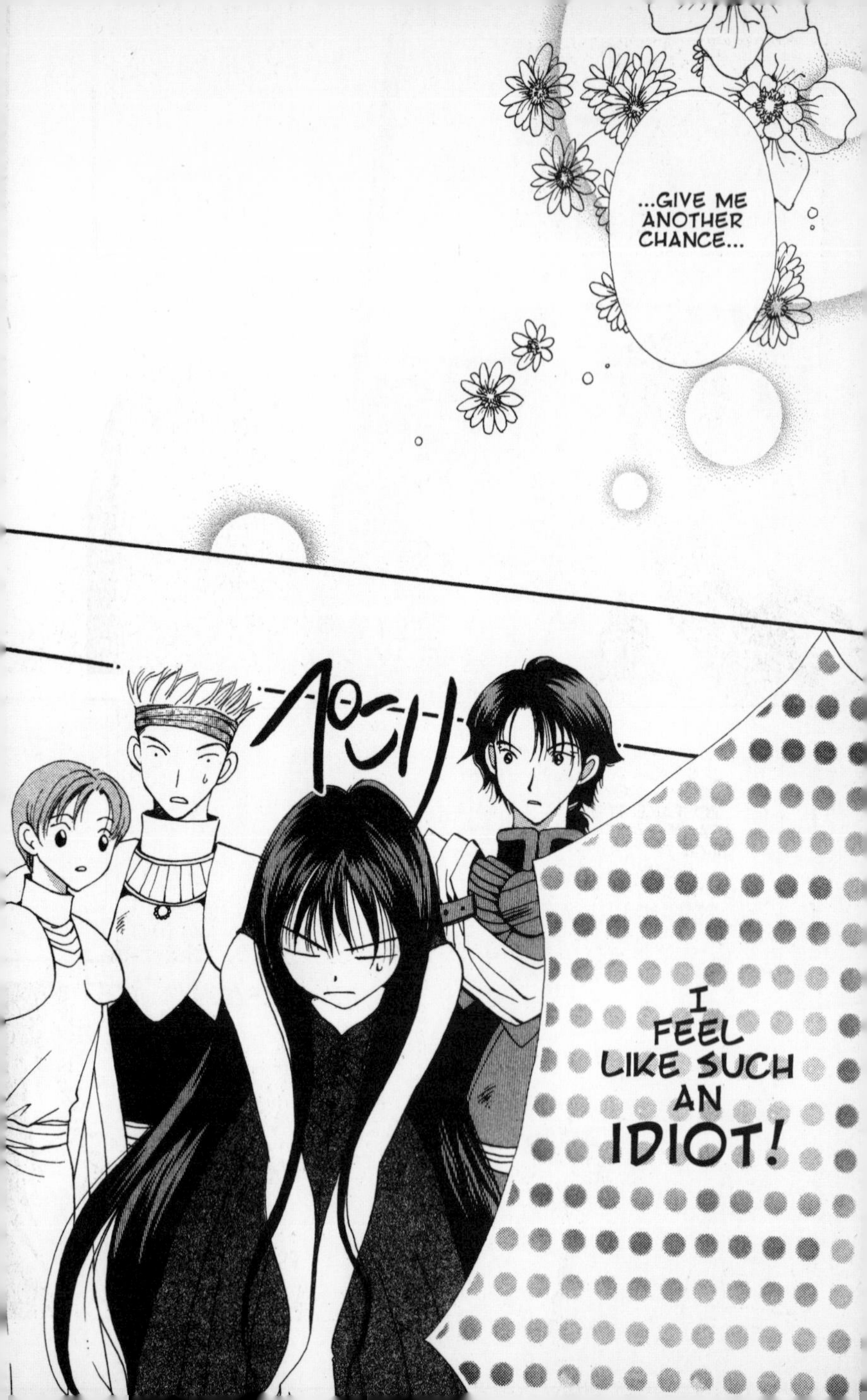
...GIVE ME ANOTHER CHANCE...
I FEEL LIKE SUCH AN IDIOT!

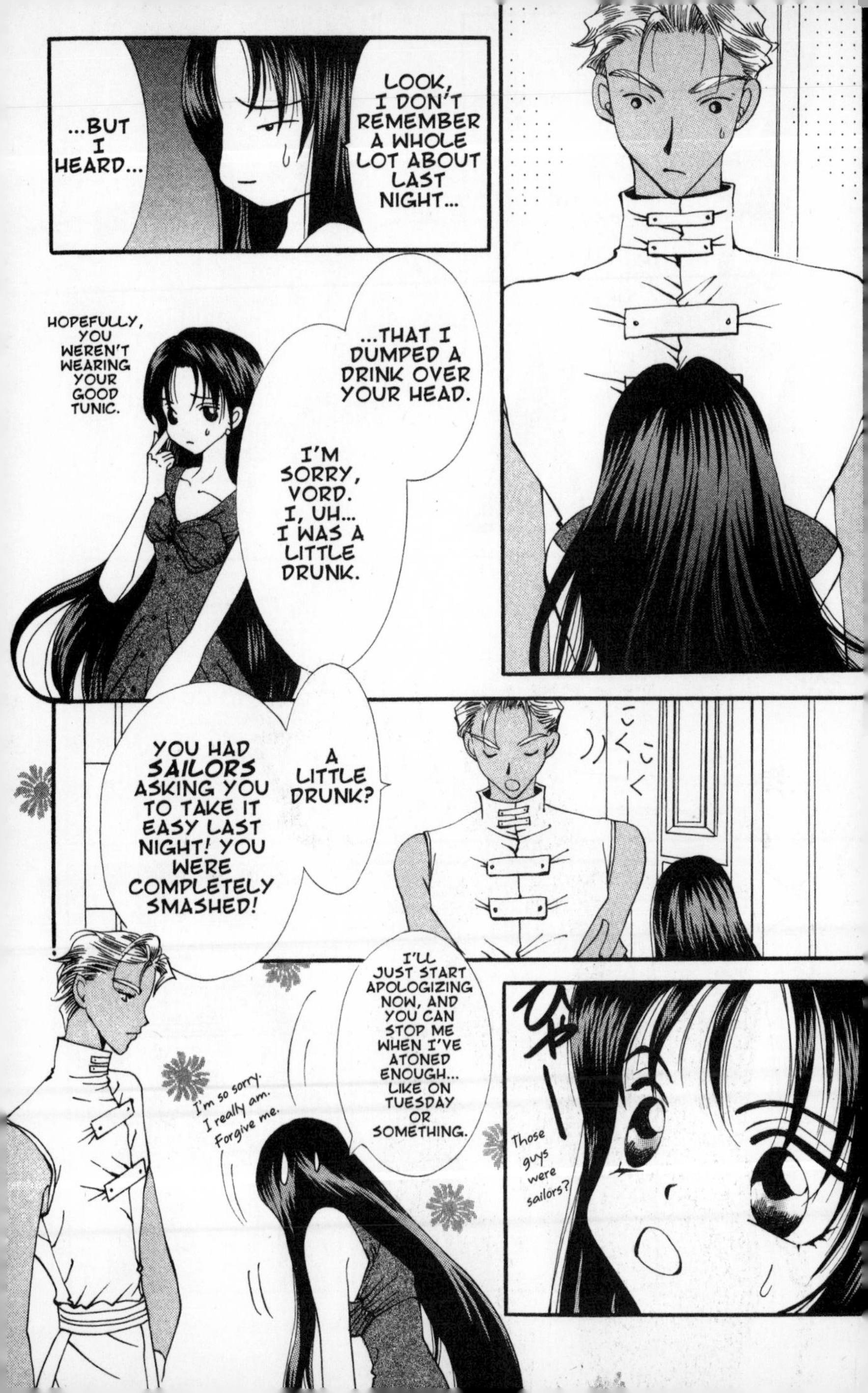

LOOK, I DON'T REMEMBER A WHOLE LOT ABOUT LAST NIGHT...
...BUT I HEARD...
...THAT I DUMPED A DRINK OVER YOUR HEAD.
HOPEFULLY, YOU WEREN'T WEARING YOUR GOOD TUNIC.
I'M SORRY, VORD. I, UH... I WAS A LITTLE DRUNK.
こくこく
A LITTLE DRUNK?
YOU HAD **SAILORS** ASKING YOU TO TAKE IT EASY LAST NIGHT! YOU WERE COMPLETELY SMASHED!
ひゃー
Those guys were sailors?
I'LL JUST START APOLOGIZING NOW, AND YOU CAN STOP ME WHEN I'VE ATONED ENOUGH... LIKE ON TUESDAY OR SOMETHING.
I'm so sorry. I really am. Forgive me.

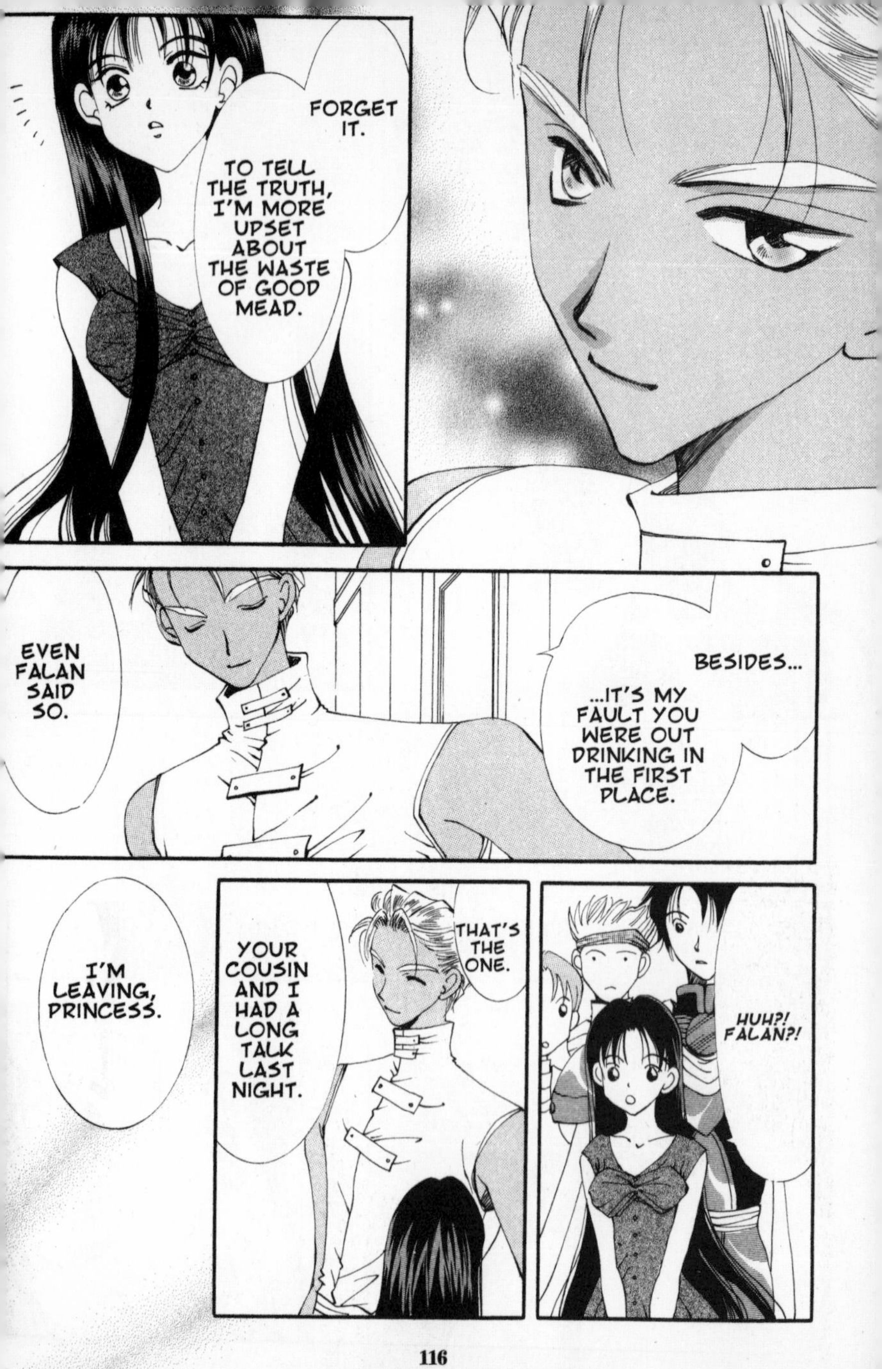
FORGET IT.
TO TELL THE TRUTH, I'M MORE UPSET ABOUT THE WASTE OF GOOD MEAD.
BESIDES...
...IT'S MY FAULT YOU WERE OUT DRINKING IN THE FIRST PLACE.
EVEN FALAN SAID SO.
HUH?! FALAN?!
THAT'S THE ONE.
YOUR COUSIN AND I HAD A LONG TALK LAST NIGHT.
I'M LEAVING, PRINCESS.

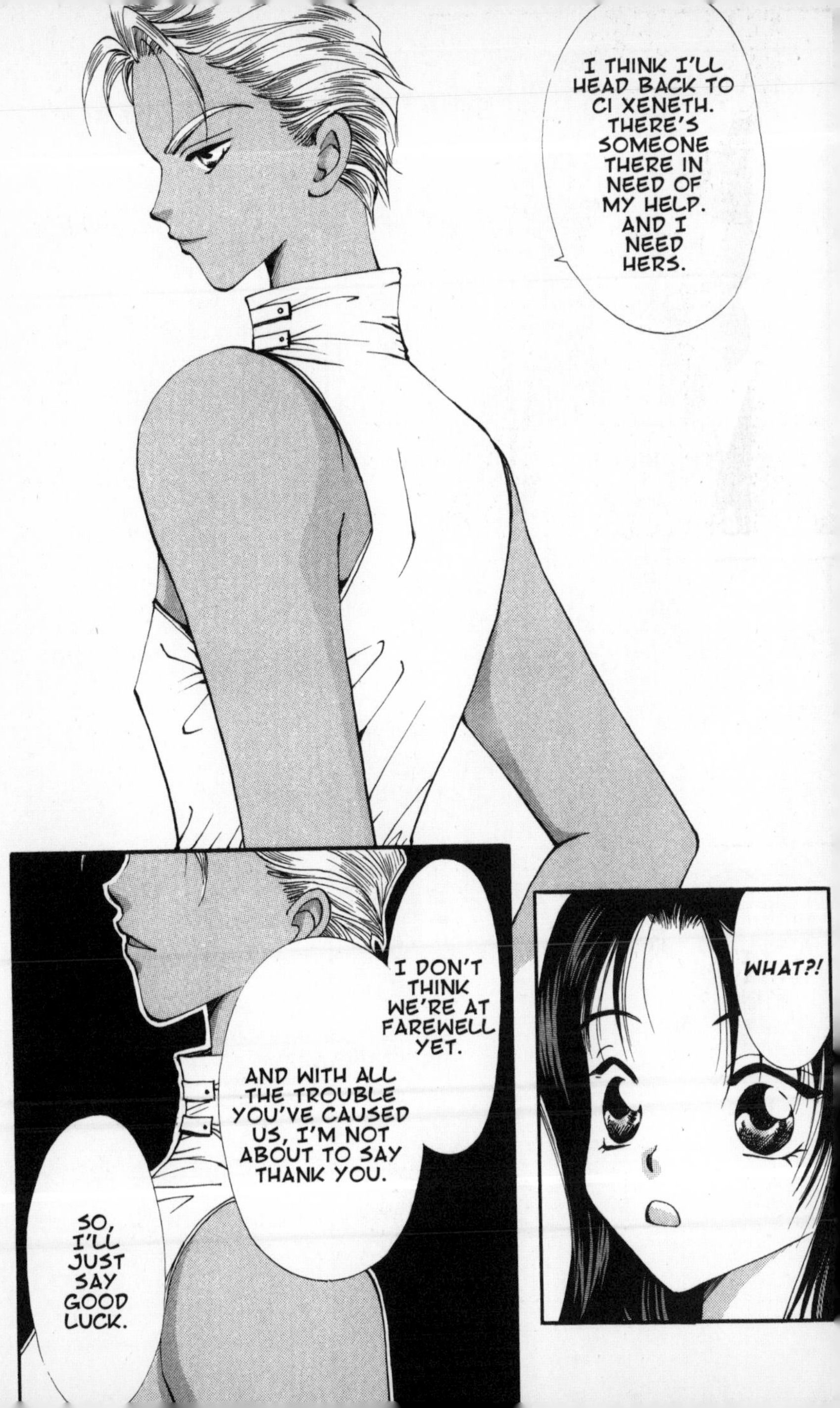

I THINK I'LL HEAD BACK TO CI XENETH. THERE'S SOMEONE THERE IN NEED OF MY HELP. AND I NEED HERS.
WHAT?!
I DON'T THINK WE'RE AT FAREWELL YET.
AND WITH ALL THE TROUBLE YOU'VE CAUSED US, I'M NOT ABOUT TO SAY THANK YOU.
SO, I'LL JUST SAY GOOD LUCK.

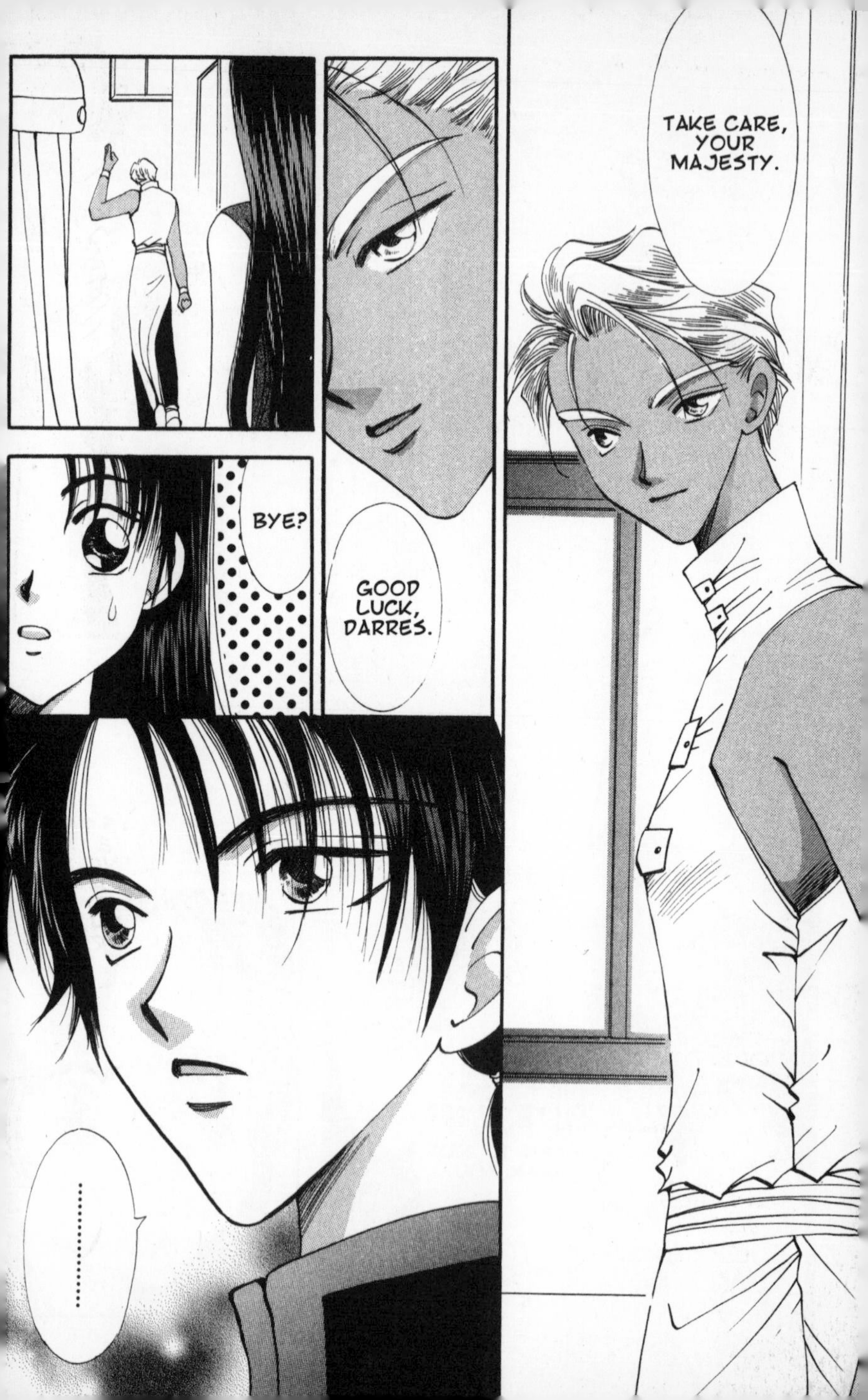
TAKE CARE, YOUR MAJESTY.
GOOD LUCK, DARRES.
BYE?
......

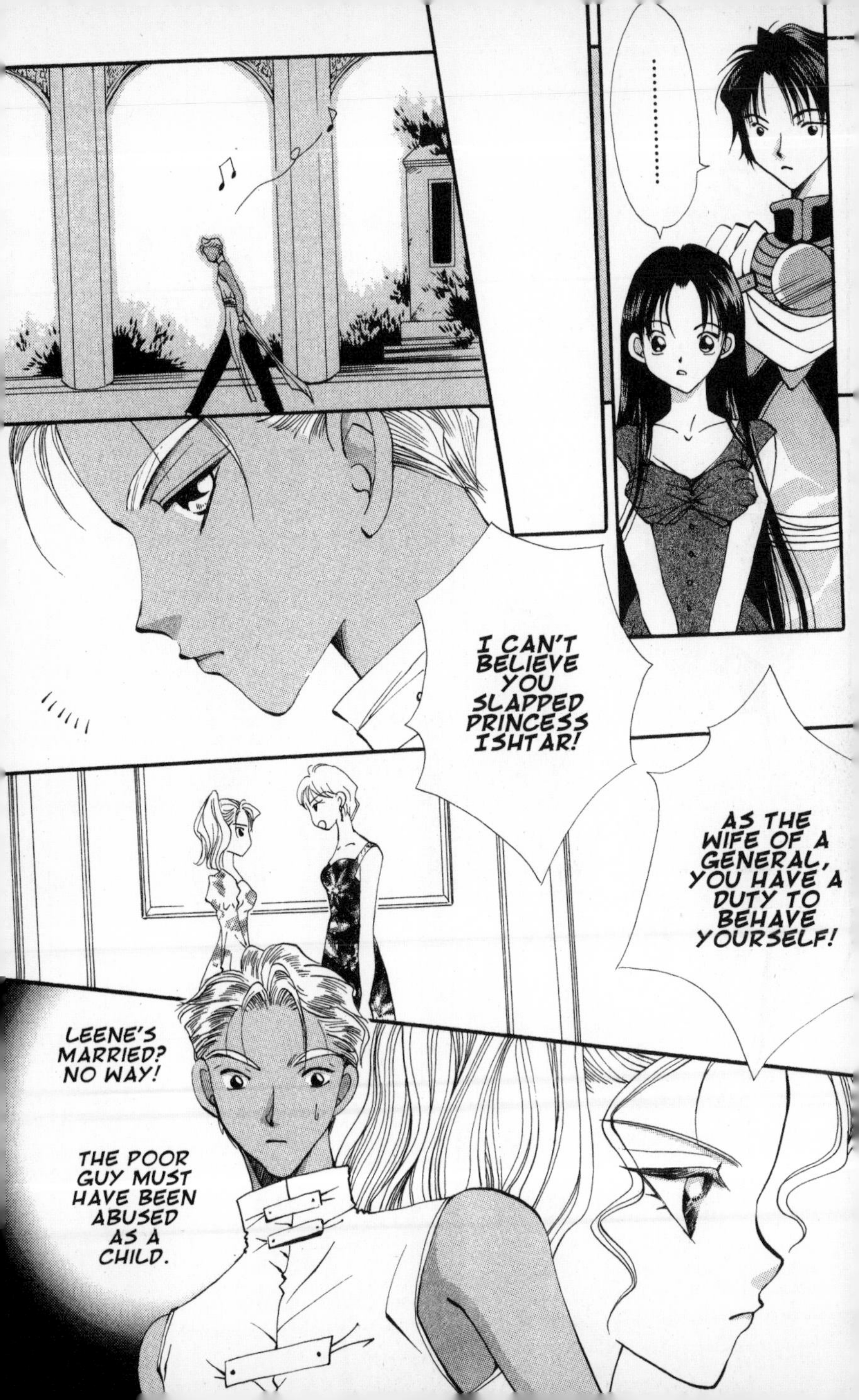
......
I CAN'T BELIEVE YOU SLAPPED PRINCESS ISHTAR!
AS THE WIFE OF A GENERAL, YOU HAVE A DUTY TO BEHAVE YOURSELF!
LEENE'S MARRIED? NO WAY!
THE POOR GUY MUST HAVE BEEN ABUSED AS A CHILD.

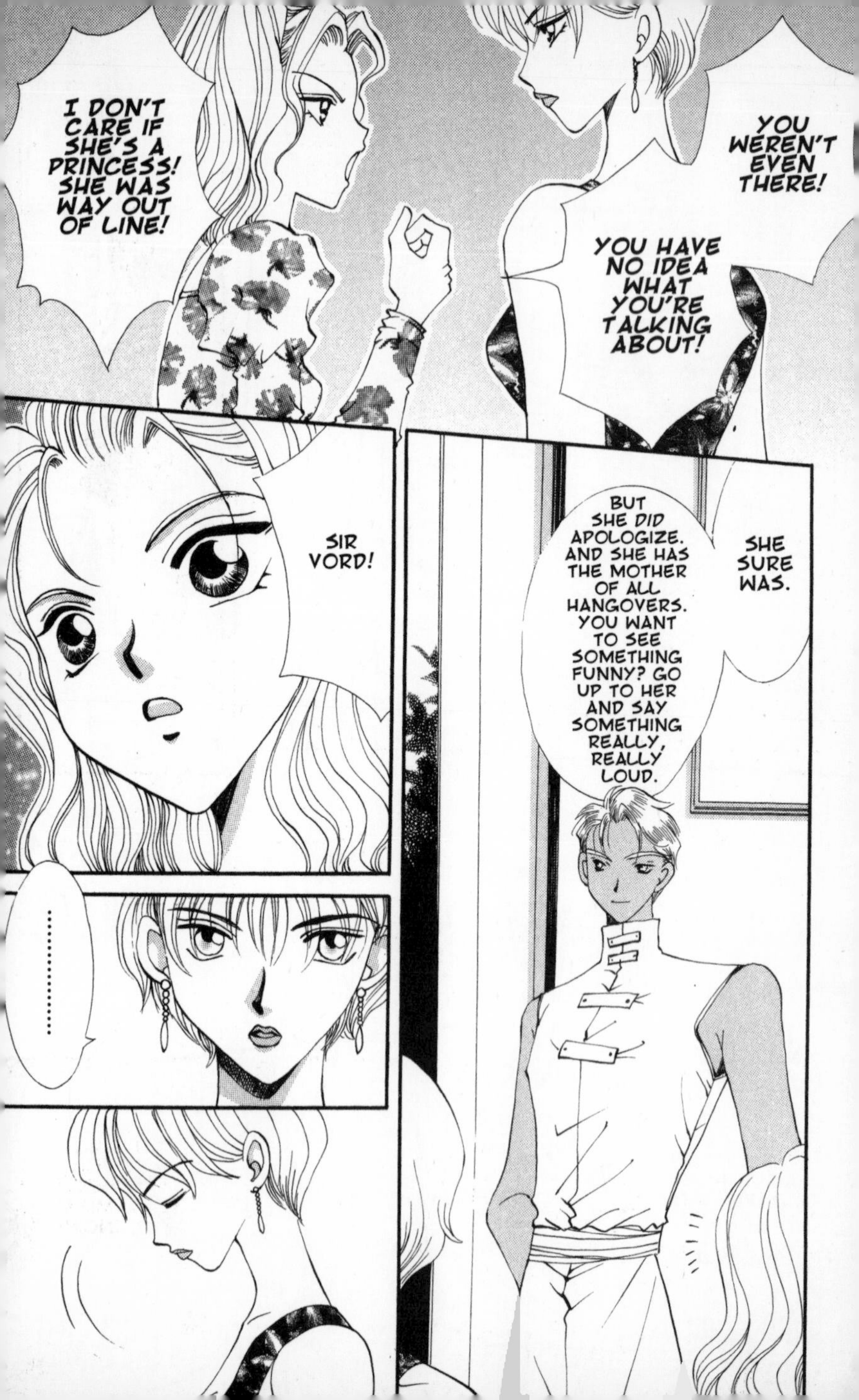

YOU WEREN'T EVEN THERE!
YOU HAVE NO IDEA WHAT YOU'RE TALKING ABOUT!
I DON'T CARE IF SHE'S A PRINCESS! SHE WAS WAY OUT OF LINE!
SHE SURE WAS.
BUT SHE *DID* APOLOGIZE. AND SHE HAS THE MOTHER OF ALL HANGOVERS. YOU WANT TO SEE SOMETHING FUNNY? GO UP TO HER AND SAY SOMETHING REALLY, REALLY LOUD.
SIR VORD!
......

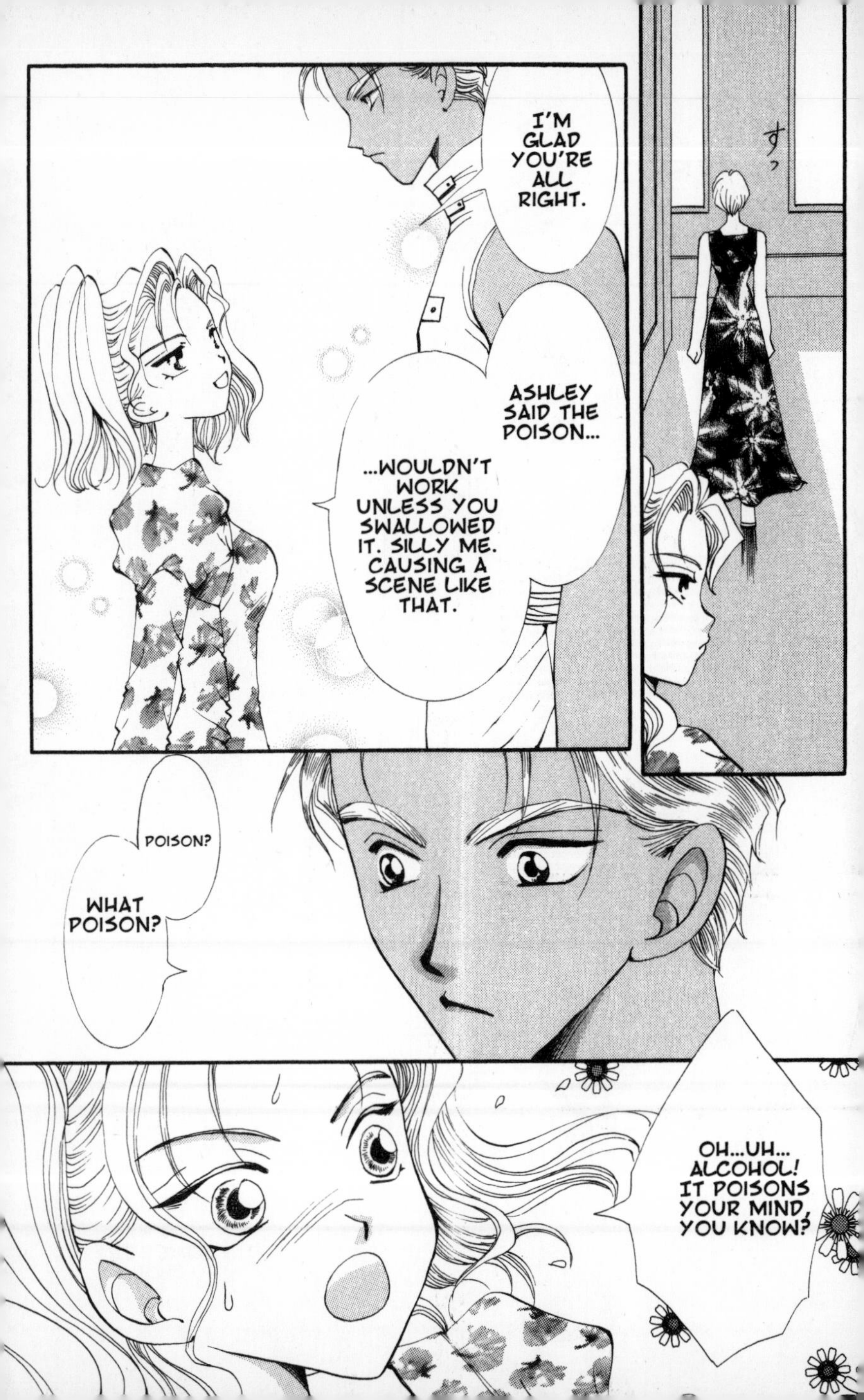

すっ
I'M GLAD YOU'RE ALL RIGHT.
ASHLEY SAID THE POISON...
...WOULDN'T WORK UNLESS YOU SWALLOWED IT. SILLY ME. CAUSING A SCENE LIKE THAT.
POISON?
WHAT POISON?
OH...UH... ALCOHOL! IT POISONS YOUR MIND, YOU KNOW?

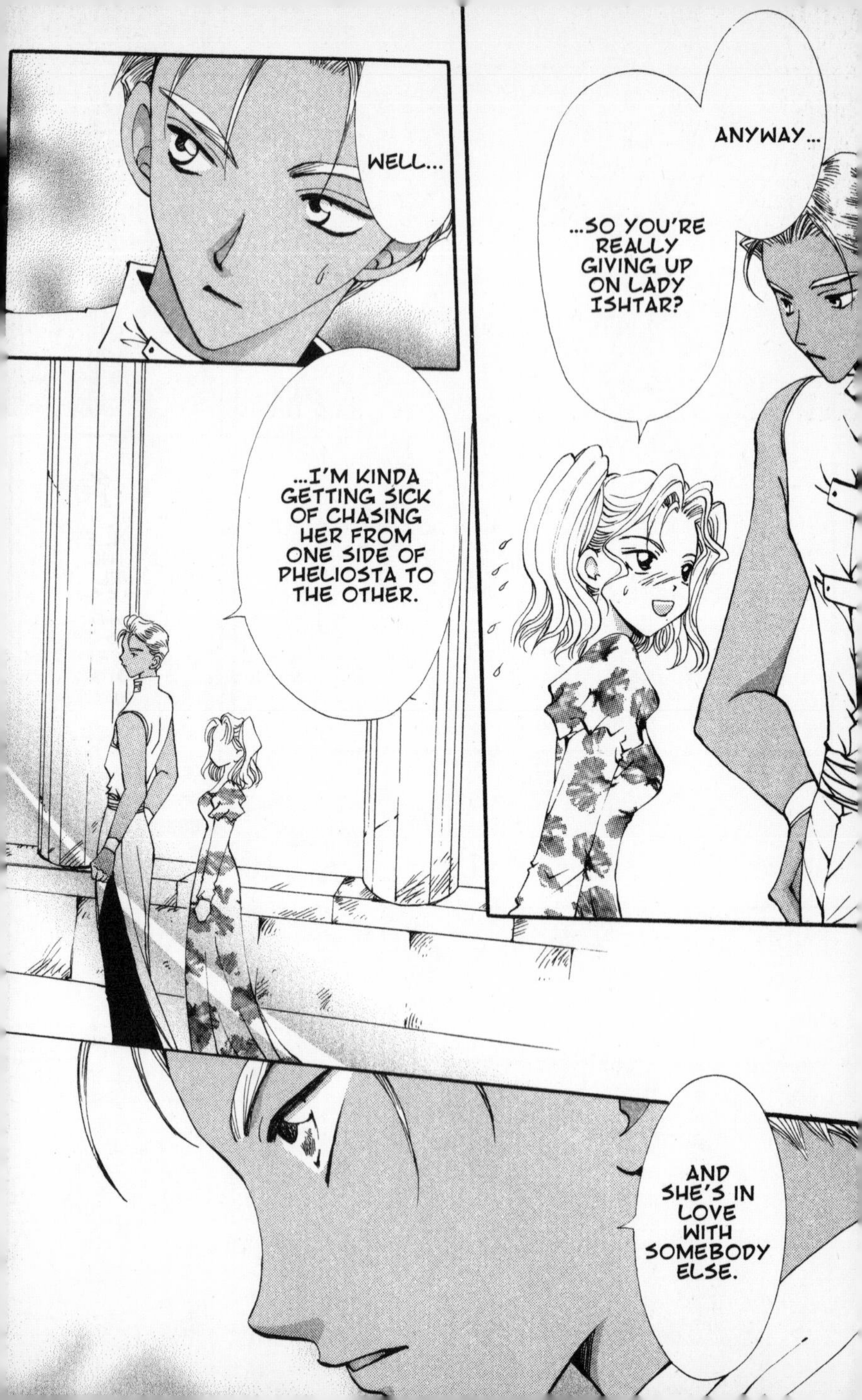
ANYWAY...
...SO YOU'RE REALLY GIVING UP ON LADY ISHTAR?
WELL...
...I'M KINDA GETTING SICK OF CHASING HER FROM ONE SIDE OF PHELIOSTA TO THE OTHER.
AND SHE'S IN LOVE WITH SOMEBODY ELSE.

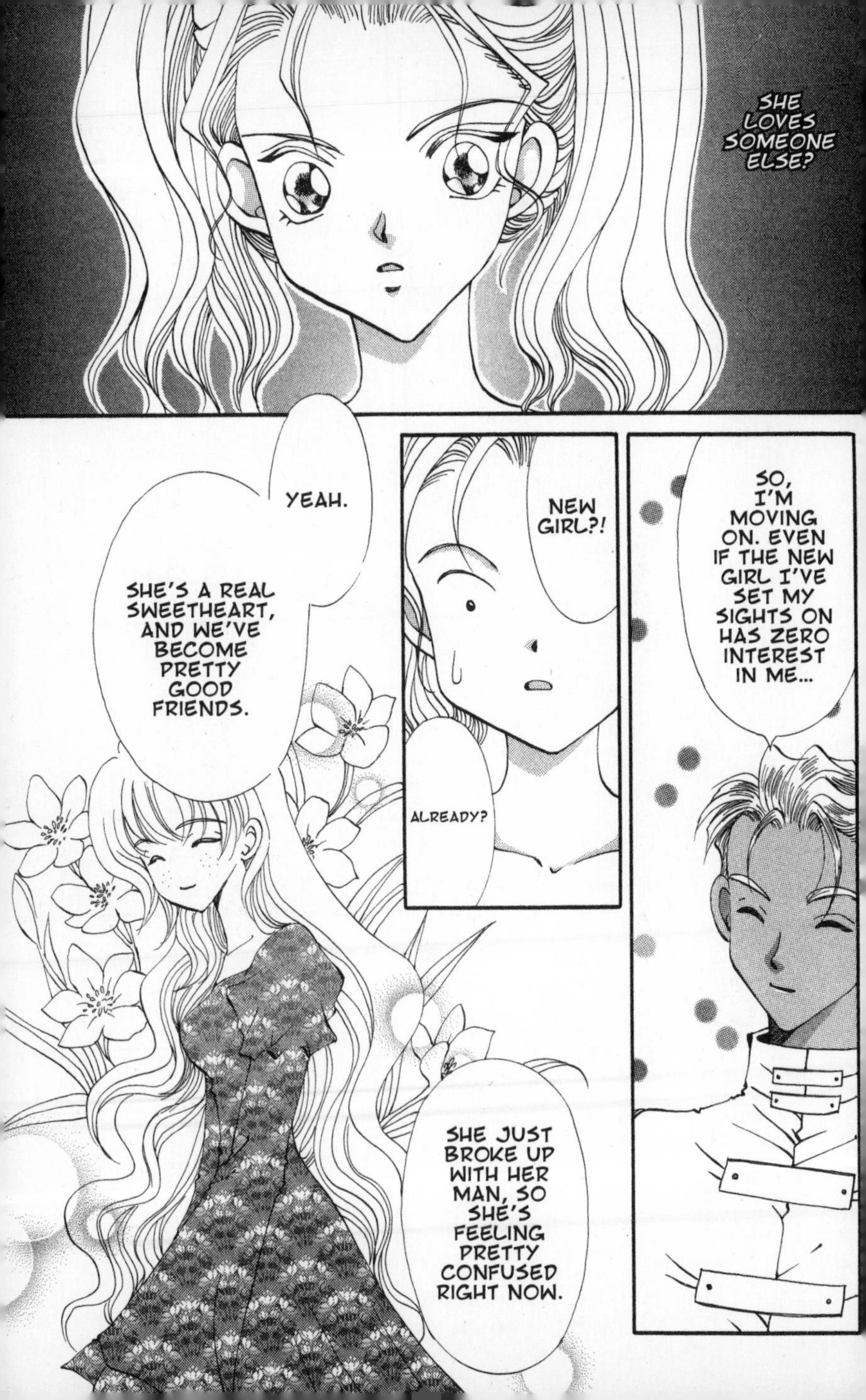
SHE LOVES SOMEONE ELSE?
SO, I'M MOVING ON. EVEN IF THE NEW GIRL I'VE SET MY SIGHTS ON HAS ZERO INTEREST IN ME...
NEW GIRL?!
ALREADY?
YEAH.
SHE'S A REAL SWEETHEART, AND WE'VE BECOME PRETTY GOOD FRIENDS.
SHE JUST BROKE UP WITH HER MAN, SO SHE'S FEELING PRETTY CONFUSED RIGHT NOW.

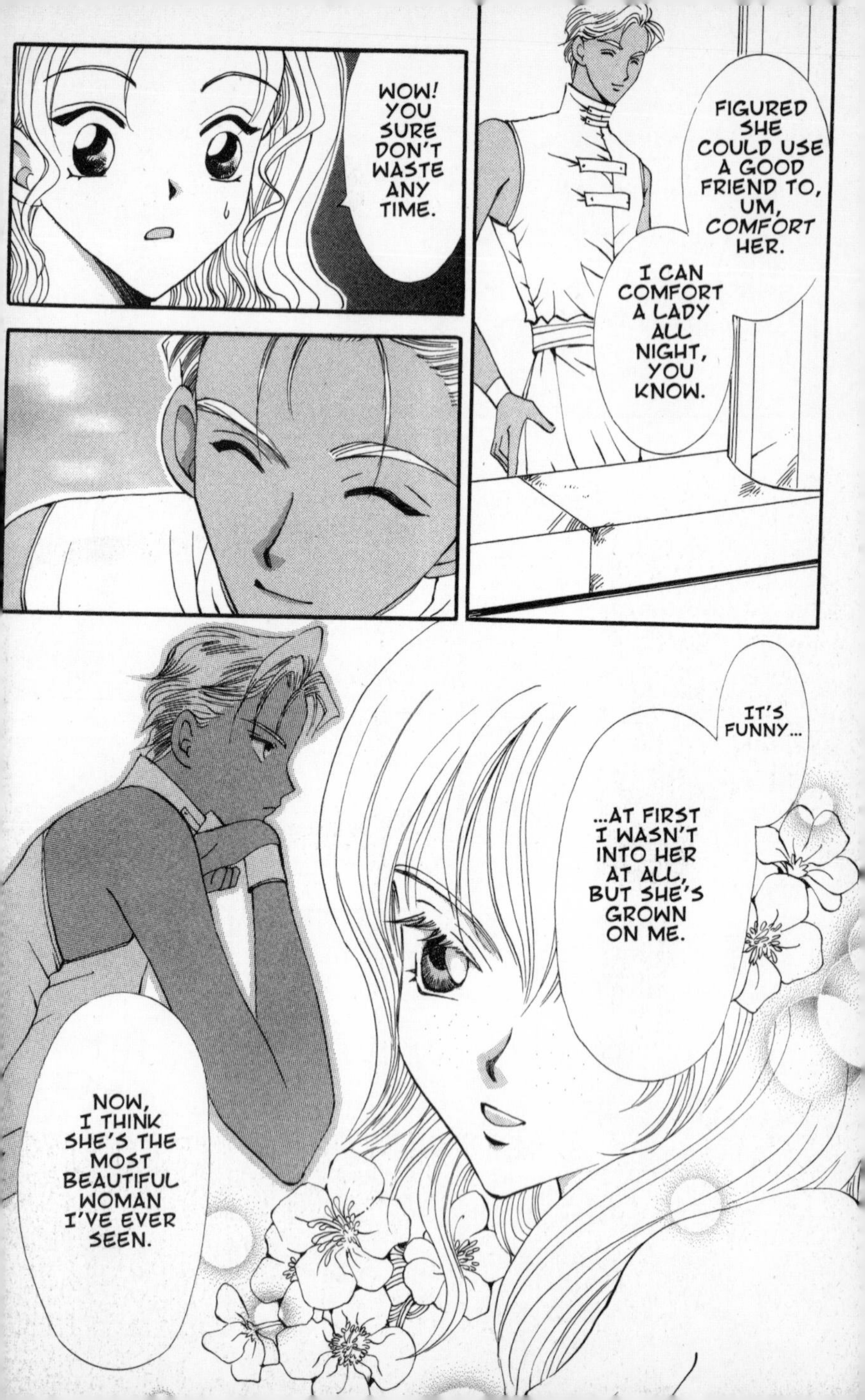
FIGURED SHE COULD USE A GOOD FRIEND TO, UM, COMFORT HER.
I CAN COMFORT A LADY ALL NIGHT, YOU KNOW.
WOW! YOU SURE DON'T WASTE ANY TIME.
IT'S FUNNY...
...AT FIRST I WASN'T INTO HER AT ALL, BUT SHE'S GROWN ON ME.
NOW, I THINK SHE'S THE MOST BEAUTIFUL WOMAN I'VE EVER SEEN.

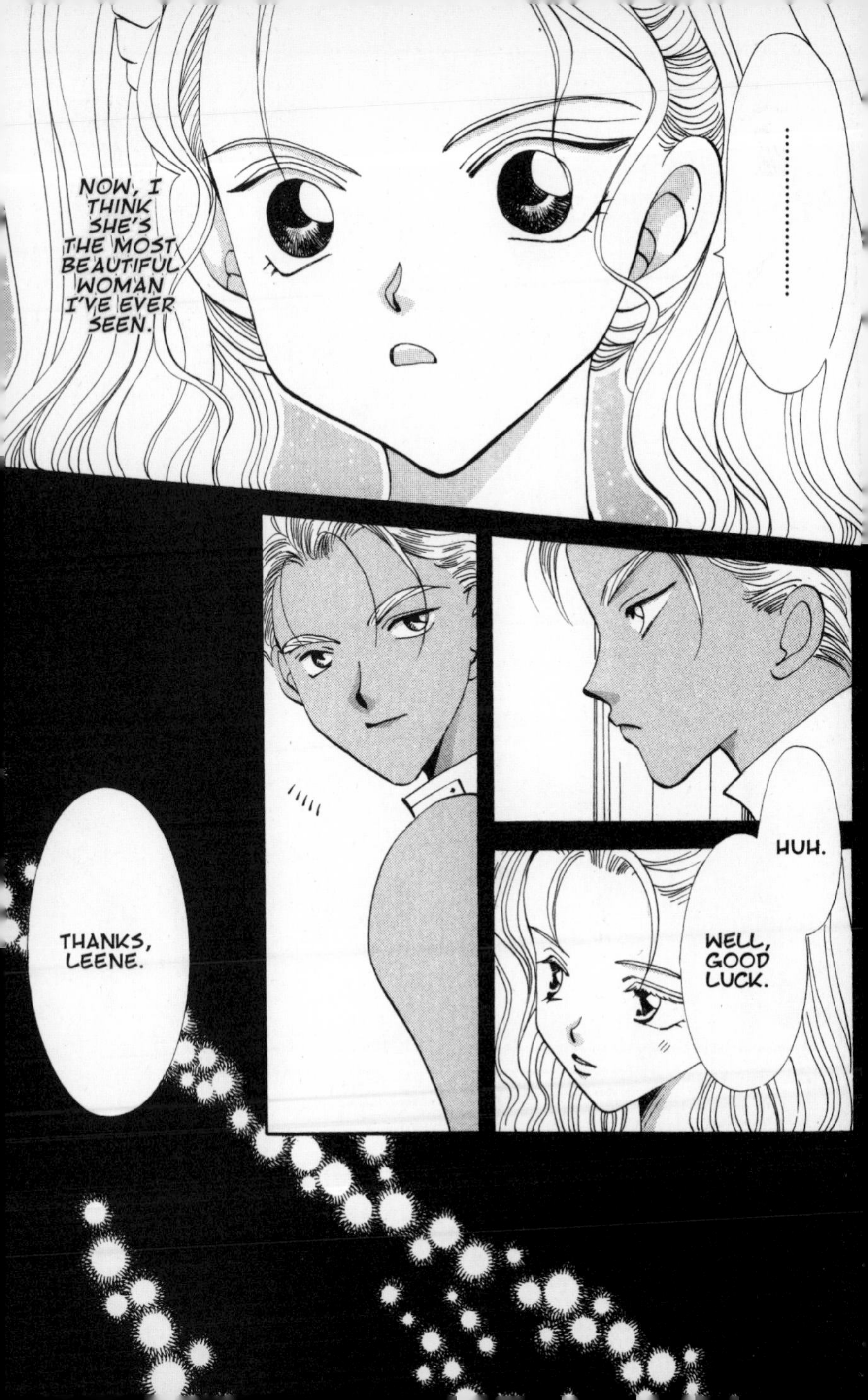
......
NOW, I THINK SHE'S THE MOST BEAUTIFUL WOMAN I'VE EVER SEEN.
HUH.
WELL, GOOD LUCK.
THANKS, LEENE.

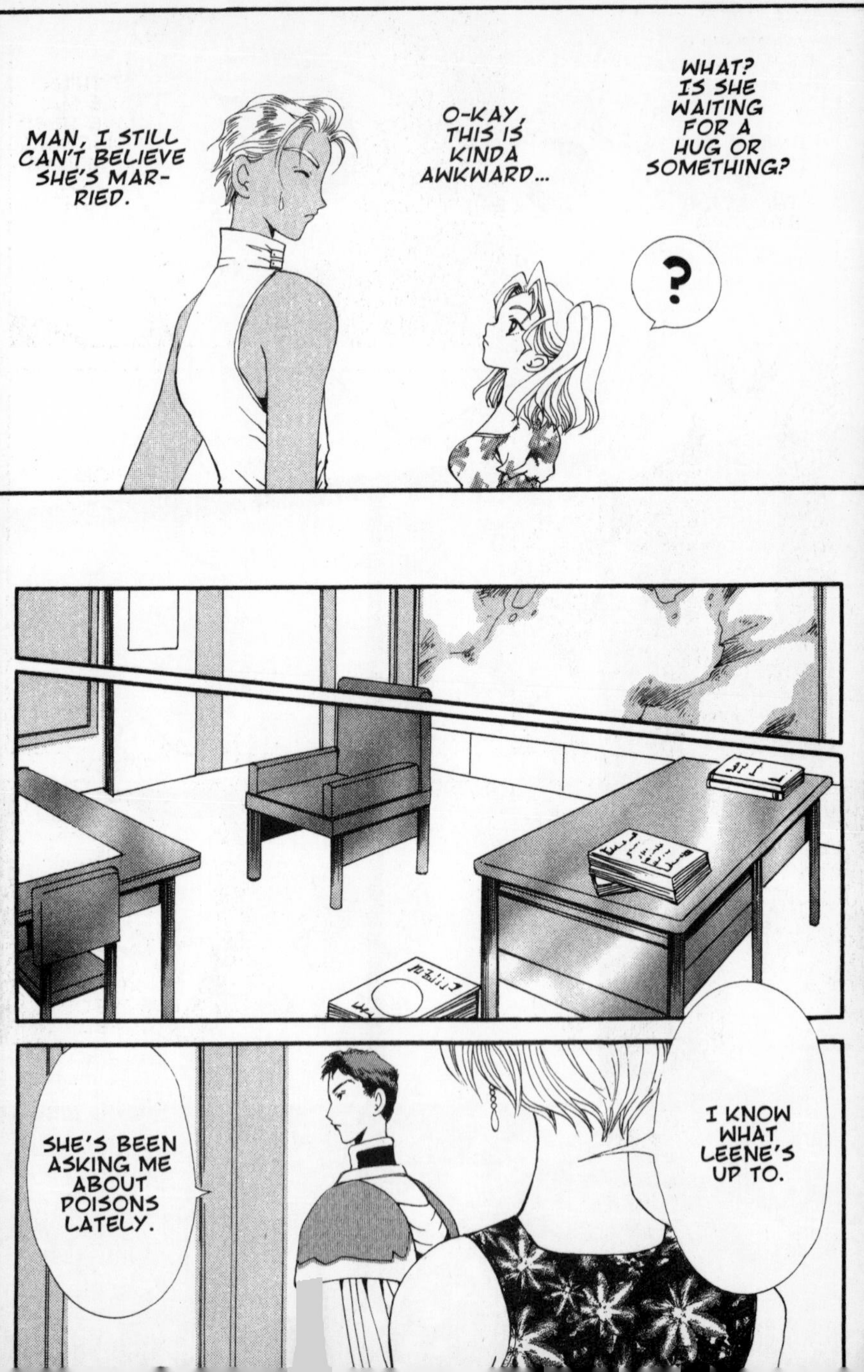
WHAT? IS SHE WAITING FOR A HUG OR SOMETHING?
O-KAY, THIS IS KINDA AWKWARD...
MAN, I STILL CAN'T BELIEVE SHE'S MAR-RIED.
?
I KNOW WHAT LEENE'S UP TO.
SHE'S BEEN ASKING ME ABOUT POISONS LATELY.

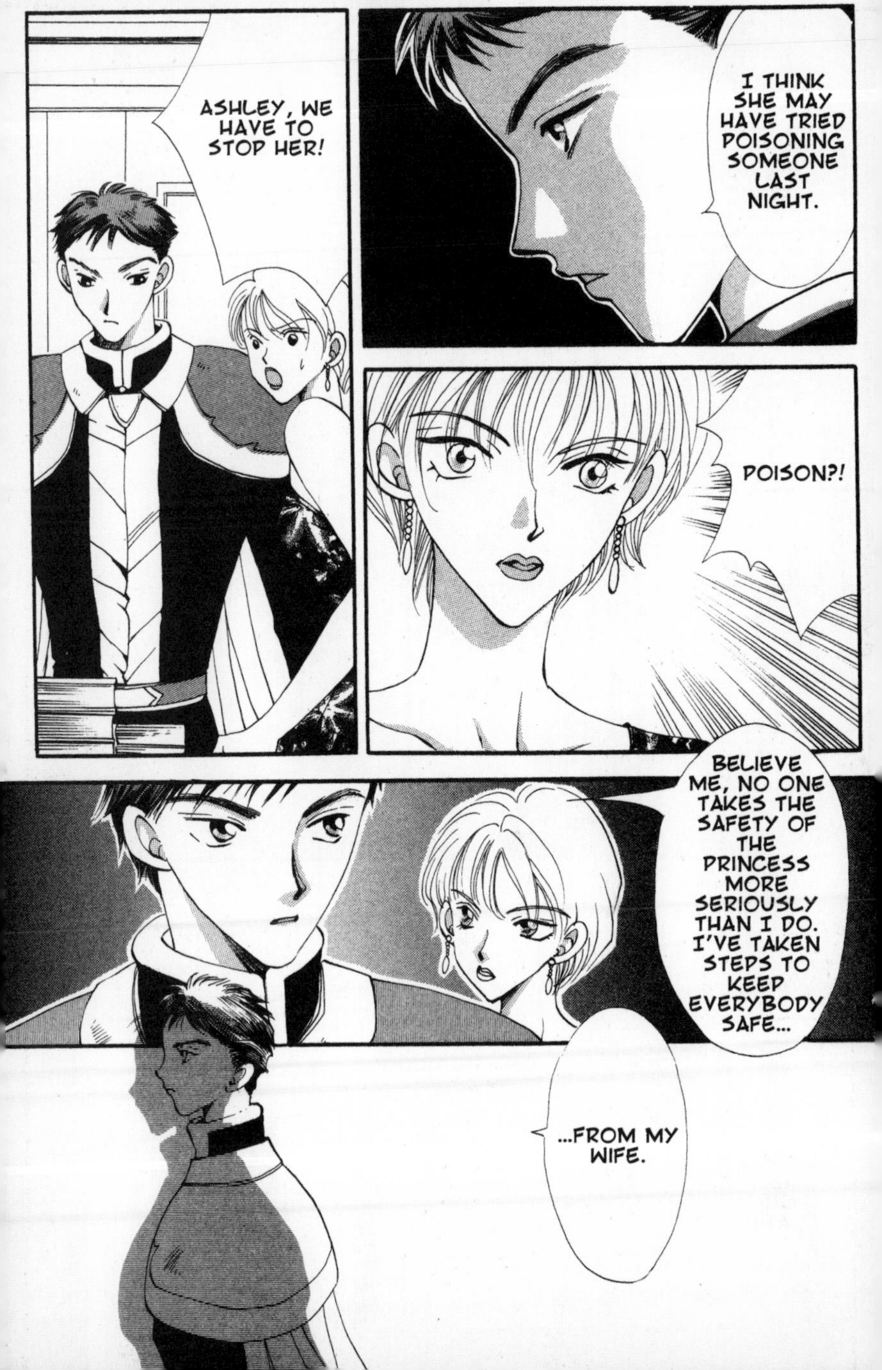
I THINK SHE MAY HAVE TRIED POISONING SOMEONE LAST NIGHT.
POISON?!
ASHLEY, WE HAVE TO STOP HER!
BELIEVE ME, NO ONE TAKES THE SAFETY OF THE PRINCESS MORE SERIOUSLY THAN I DO. I'VE TAKEN STEPS TO KEEP EVERYBODY SAFE...
...FROM MY WIFE.

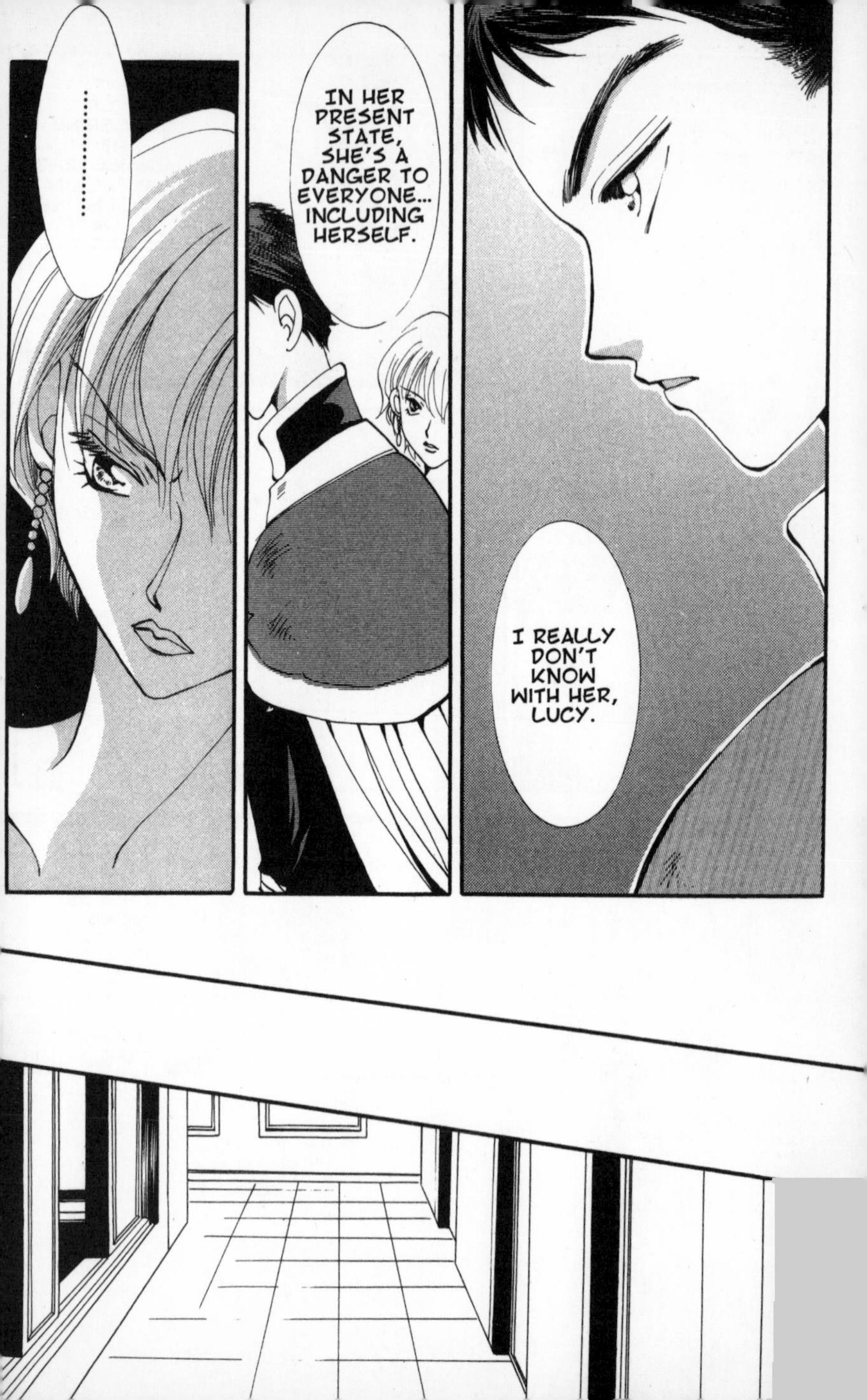
I REALLY DON'T KNOW WITH HER, LUCY.
IN HER PRESENT STATE, SHE'S A DANGER TO EVERYONE... INCLUDING HERSELF.
....

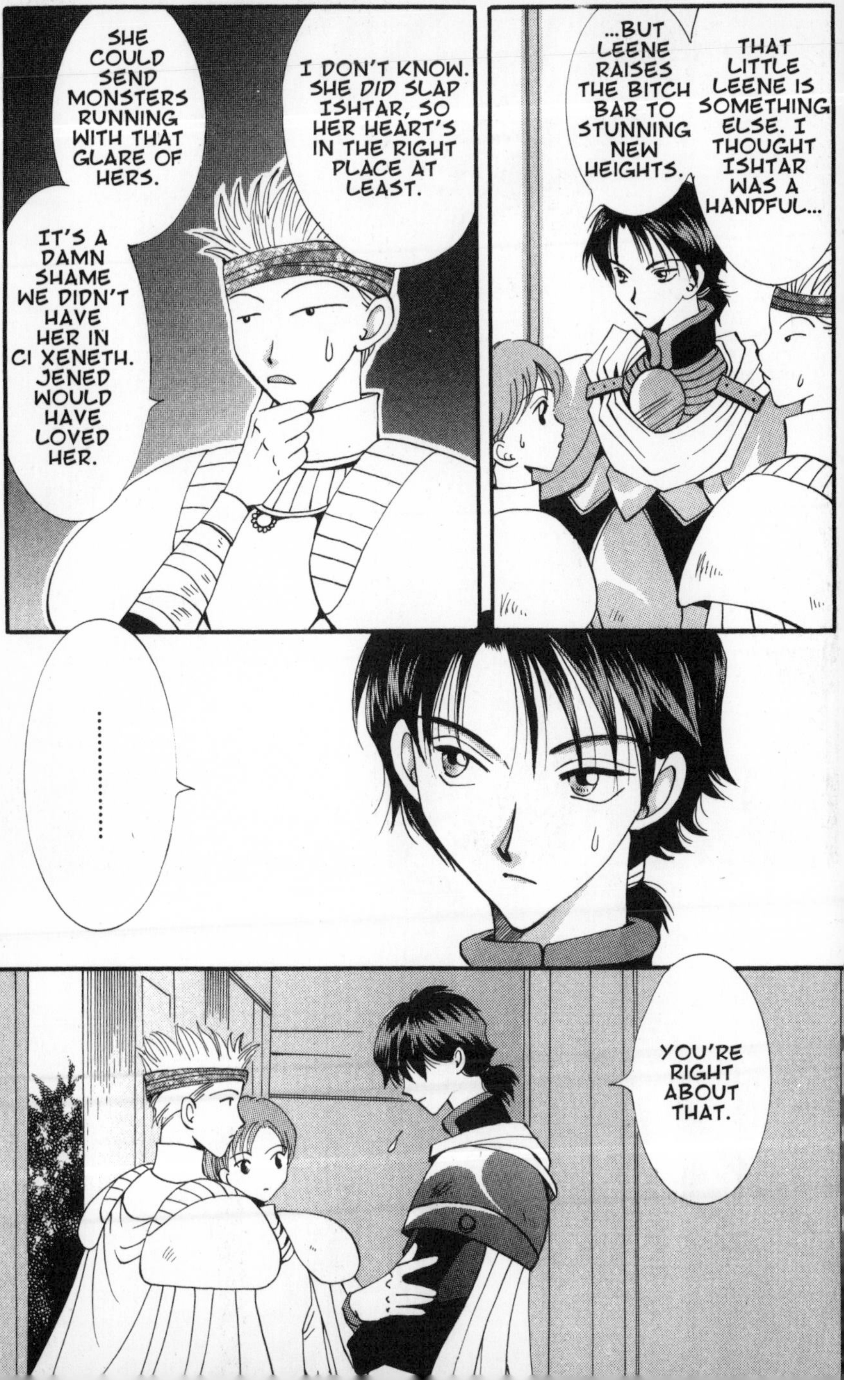
THAT LITTLE LEENE IS SOMETHING ELSE. I THOUGHT ISHTAR WAS A HANDFUL...
...BUT LEENE RAISES THE BITCH BAR TO STUNNING NEW HEIGHTS.
I DON'T KNOW. SHE *DID* SLAP ISHTAR, SO HER HEART'S IN THE RIGHT PLACE AT LEAST.
SHE COULD SEND MONSTERS RUNNING WITH THAT GLARE OF HERS.
IT'S A DAMN SHAME WE DIDN'T HAVE HER IN CI XENETH. JENED WOULD HAVE LOVED HER.
......
YOU'RE RIGHT ABOUT THAT.

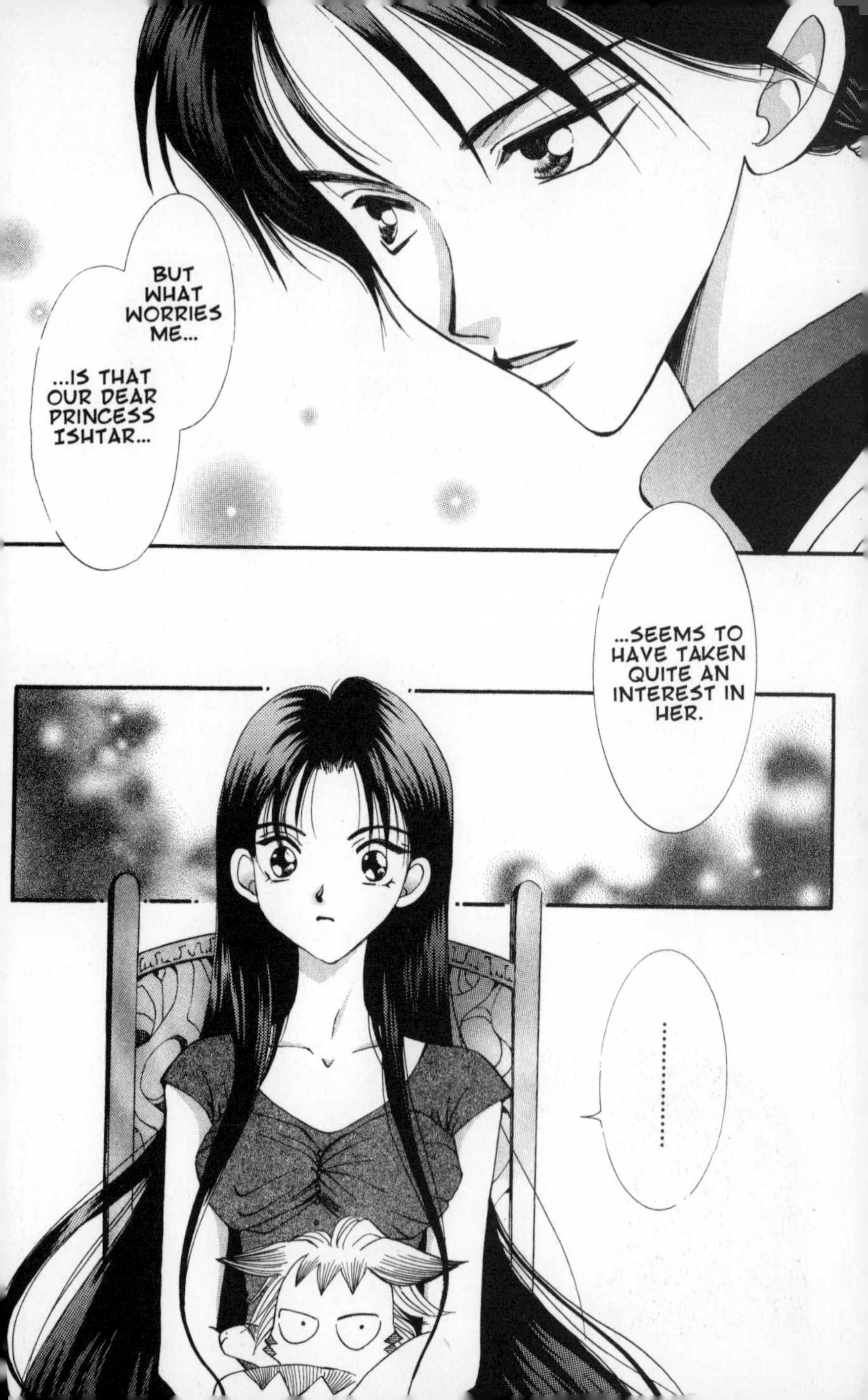
BUT WHAT WORRIES ME...
...IS THAT OUR DEAR PRINCESS ISHTAR...
...SEEMS TO HAVE TAKEN QUITE AN INTEREST IN HER.
......

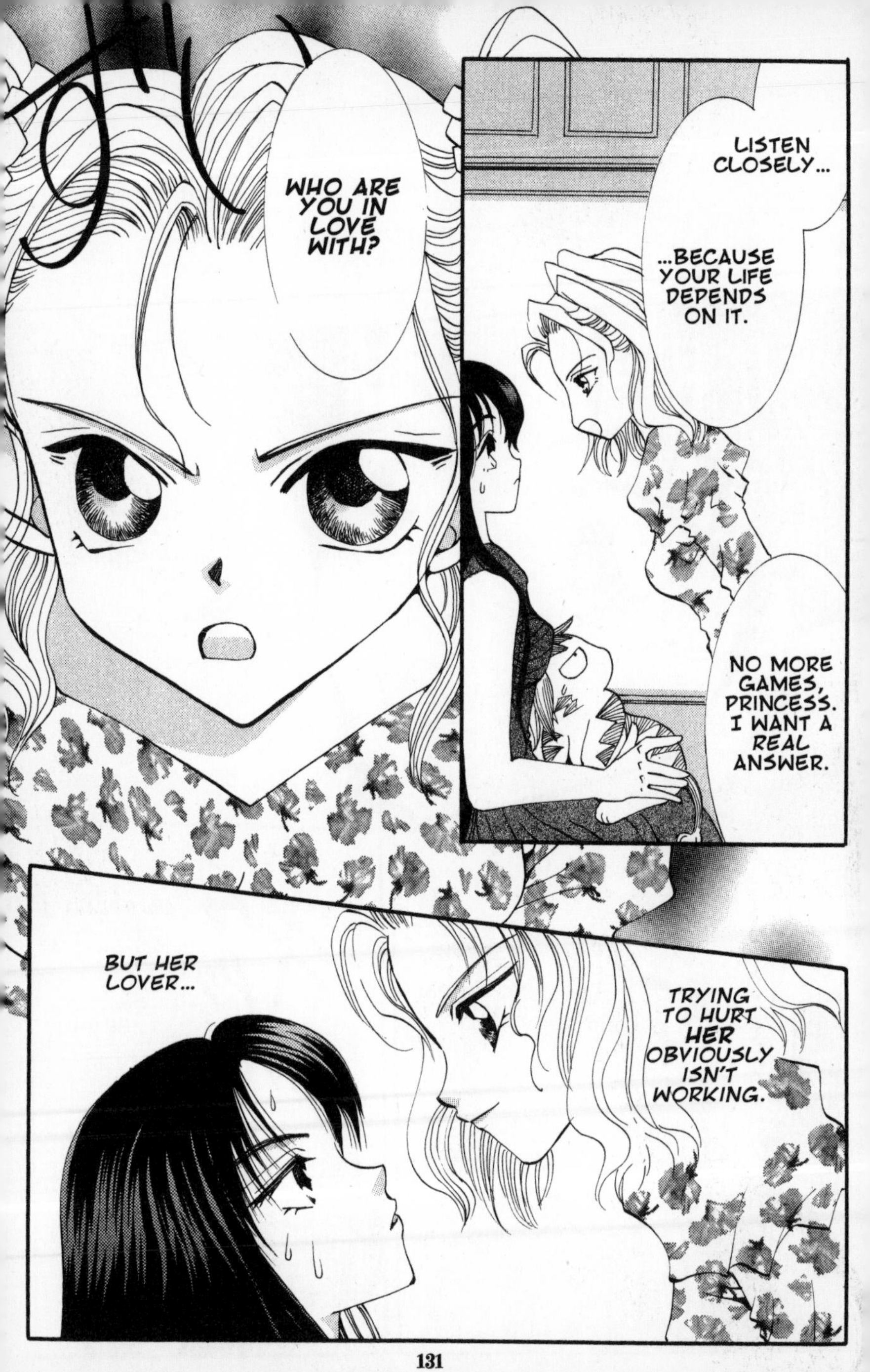
LISTEN CLOSELY...
...BECAUSE YOUR LIFE DEPENDS ON IT.
NO MORE GAMES, PRINCESS. I WANT A REAL ANSWER.
WHO ARE YOU IN LOVE WITH?
TRYING TO HURT HER OBVIOUSLY ISN'T WORKING.
BUT HER LOVER...

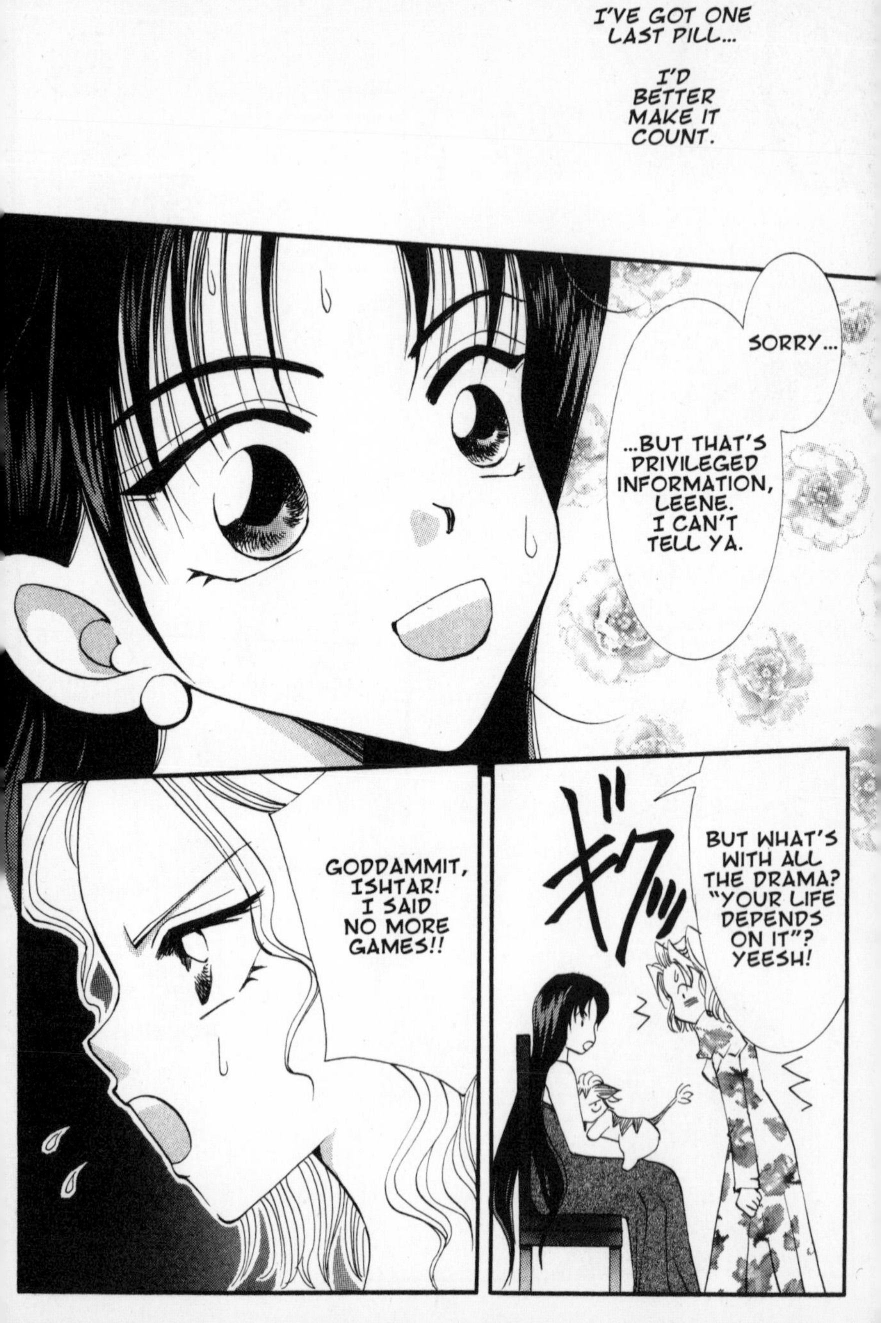
I'VE GOT ONE LAST PILL...
I'D BETTER MAKE IT COUNT.
SORRY...
...BUT THAT'S PRIVILEGED INFORMATION, LEENE. I CAN'T TELL YA.
ギクッ
BUT WHAT'S WITH ALL THE DRAMA? "YOUR LIFE DEPENDS ON IT"? YEESH!
GODDAMMIT, ISHTAR! I SAID NO MORE GAMES!!

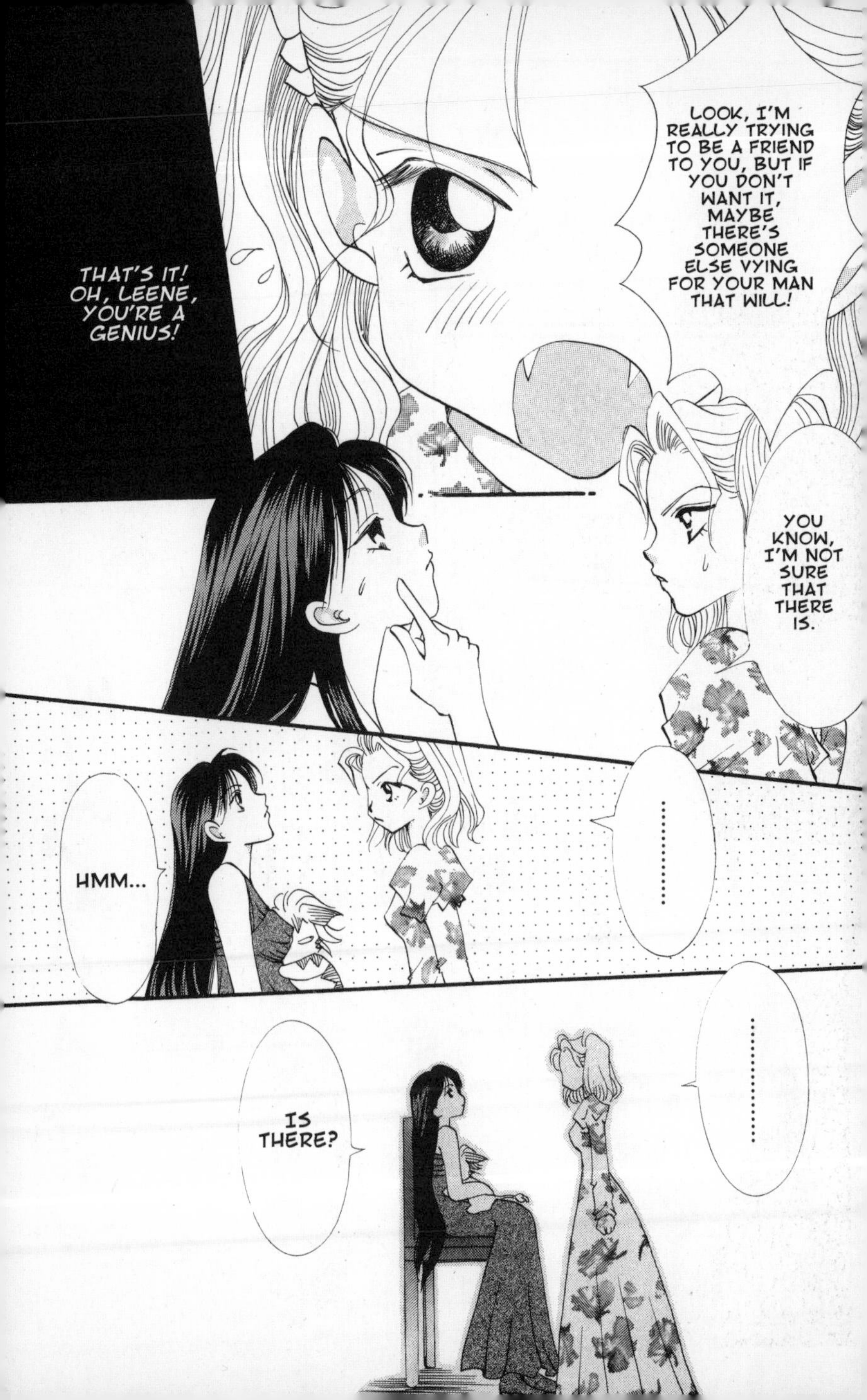
LOOK, I'M REALLY TRYING TO BE A FRIEND TO YOU, BUT IF YOU DON'T WANT IT, MAYBE THERE'S SOMEONE ELSE VYING FOR YOUR MAN THAT WILL!
THAT'S IT! OH, LEENE, YOU'RE A GENIUS!
YOU KNOW, I'M NOT SURE THAT THERE IS.
......
HMM...
......
IS THERE?

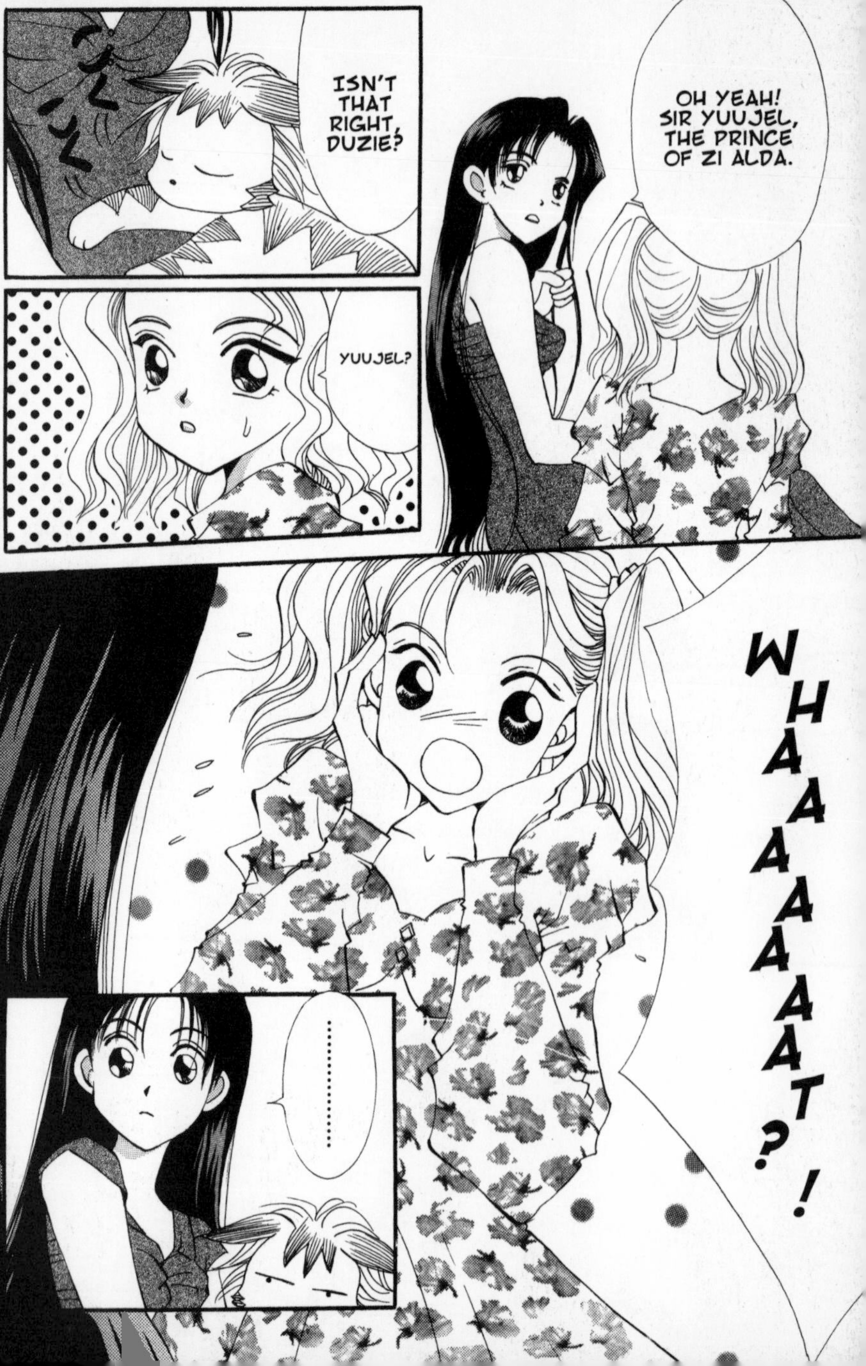
OH YEAH! SIR YUUJEL, THE PRINCE OF ZI ALDA.
ISN'T THAT RIGHT, DUZIE?
YUUJEL?
WHAAAAAAAT?!
......

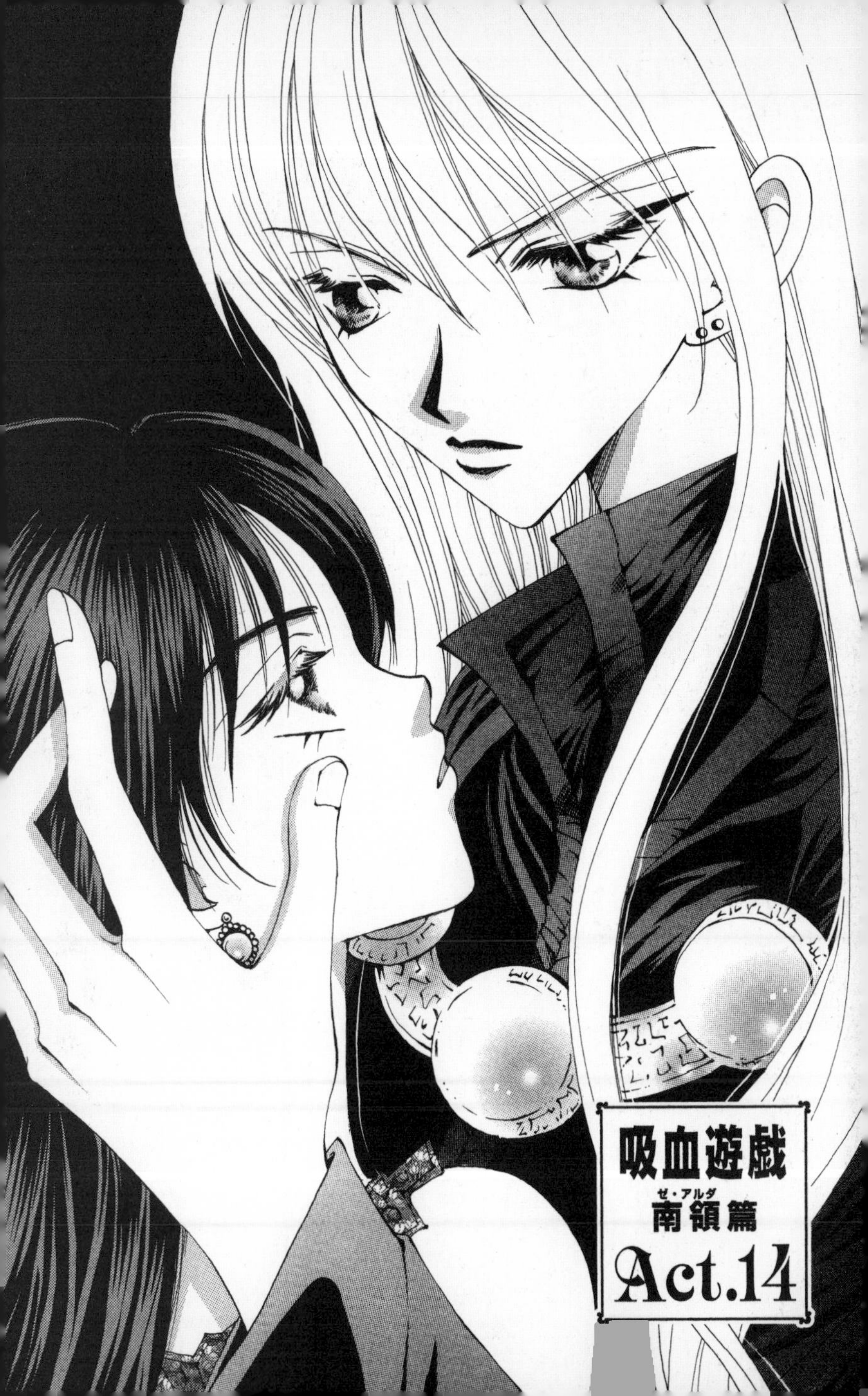

吸血遊戯
ゼ・アルダ
南領篇
Act.14

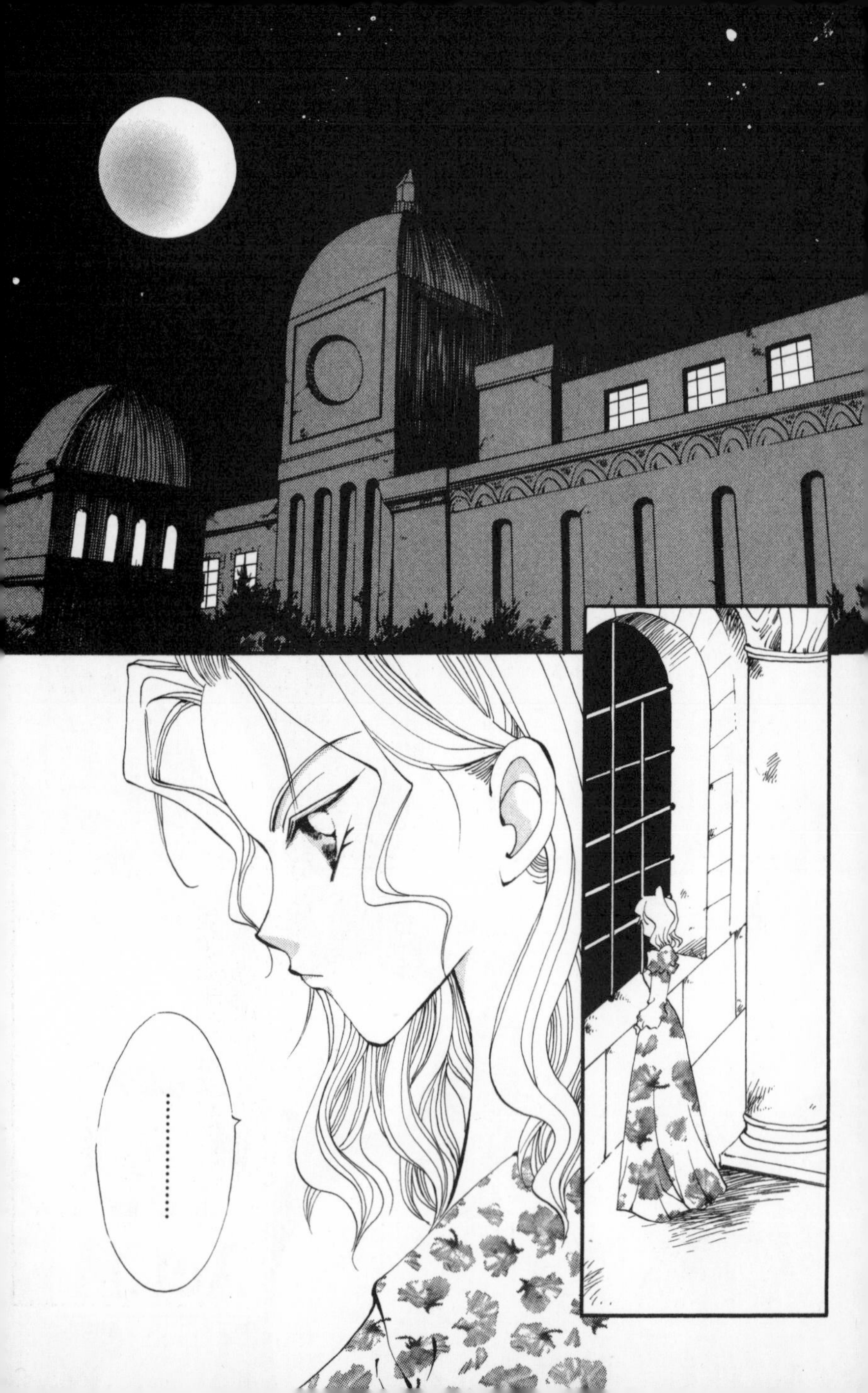

....

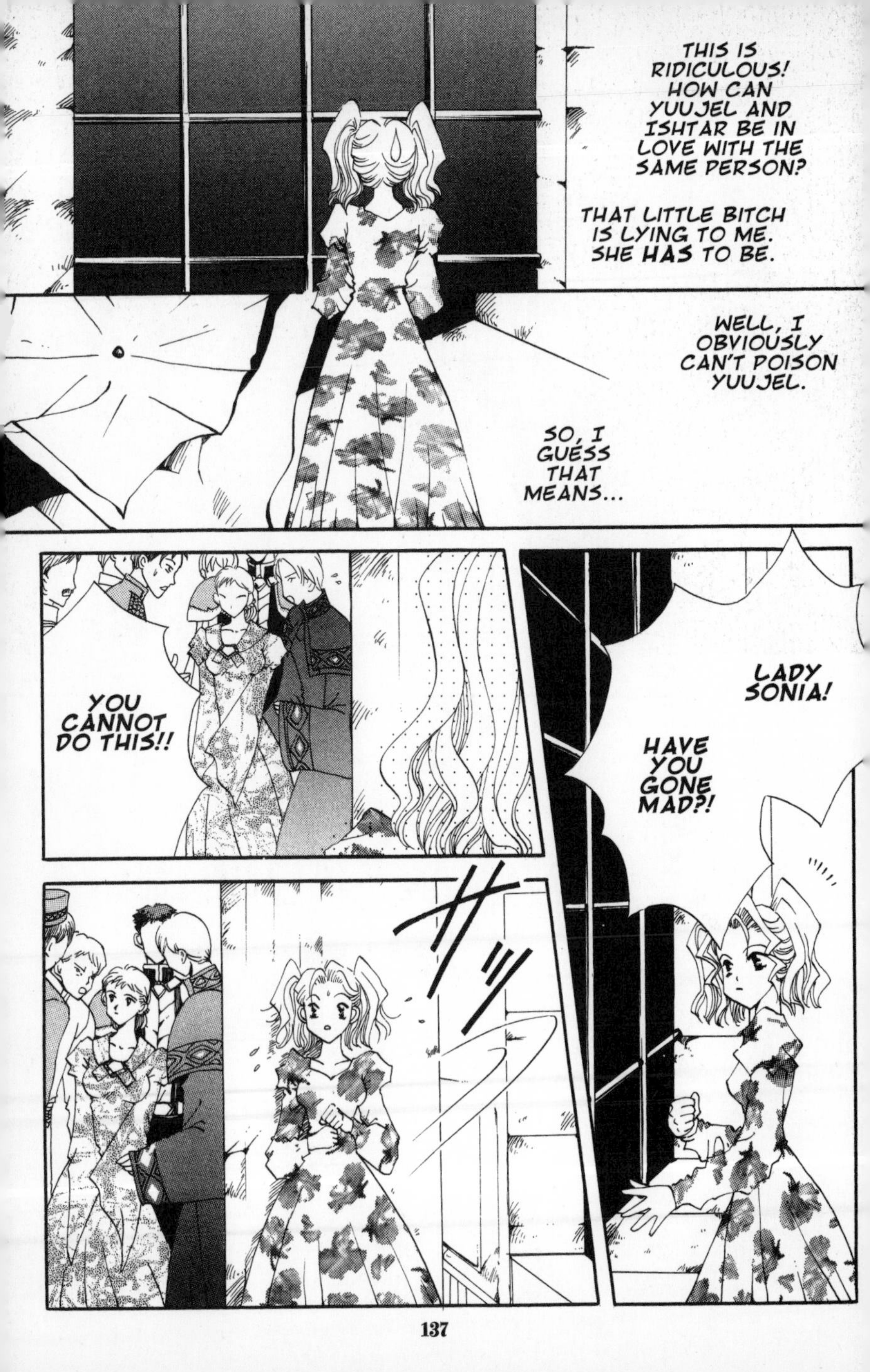
THIS IS RIDICULOUS! HOW CAN YUUJEL AND ISHTAR BE IN LOVE WITH THE SAME PERSON?
THAT LITTLE BITCH IS LYING TO ME. SHE **HAS** TO BE.
WELL, I OBVIOUSLY CAN'T POISON YUUJEL.
SO, I GUESS THAT MEANS...
LADY SONIA!
HAVE YOU GONE MAD?!
YOU CANNOT DO THIS!!
サッ

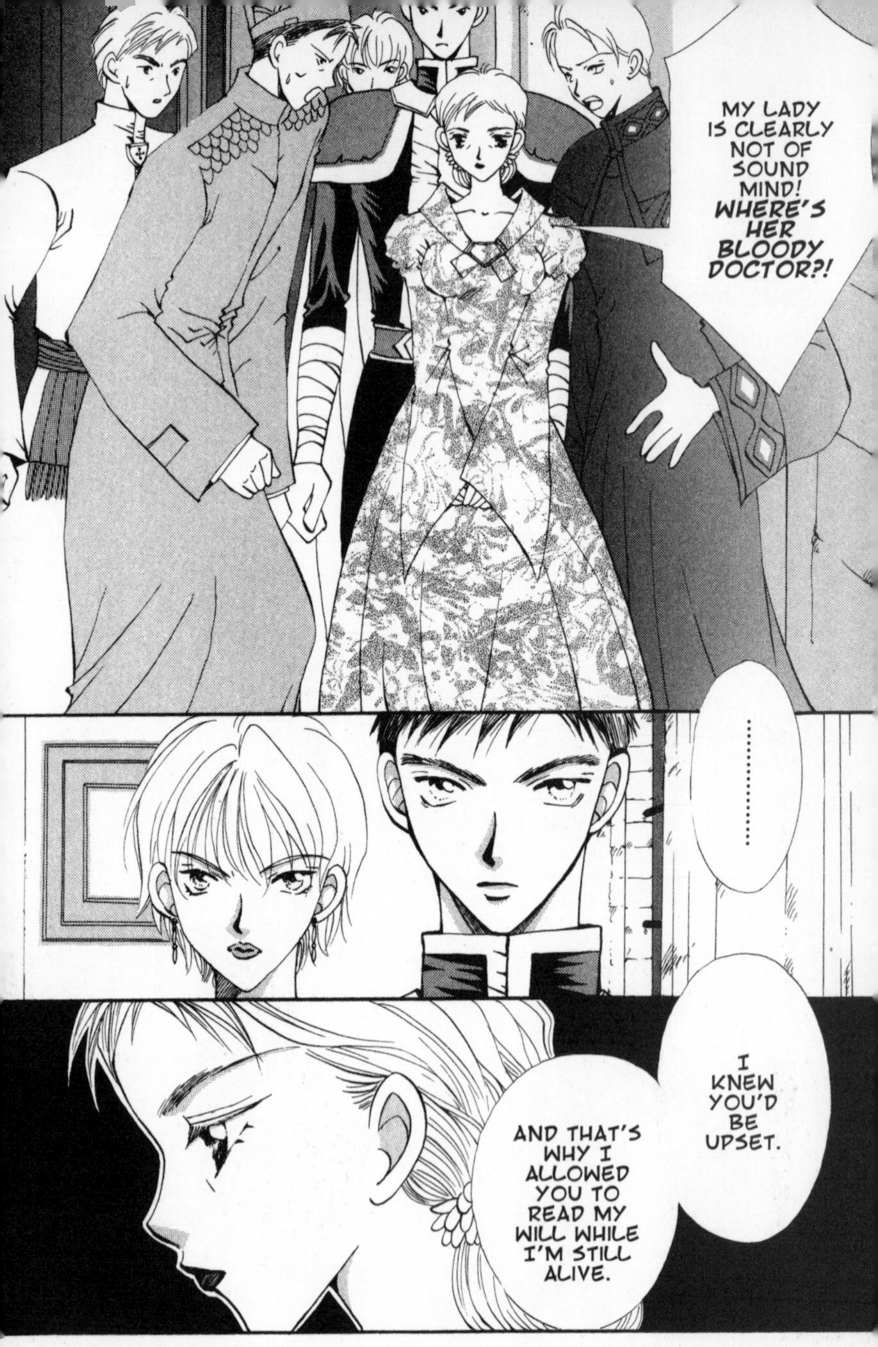
MY LADY IS CLEARLY NOT OF SOUND MIND! WHERE'S HER BLOODY DOCTOR?!
......
I KNEW YOU'D BE UPSET.
AND THAT'S WHY I ALLOWED YOU TO READ MY WILL WHILE I'M STILL ALIVE.

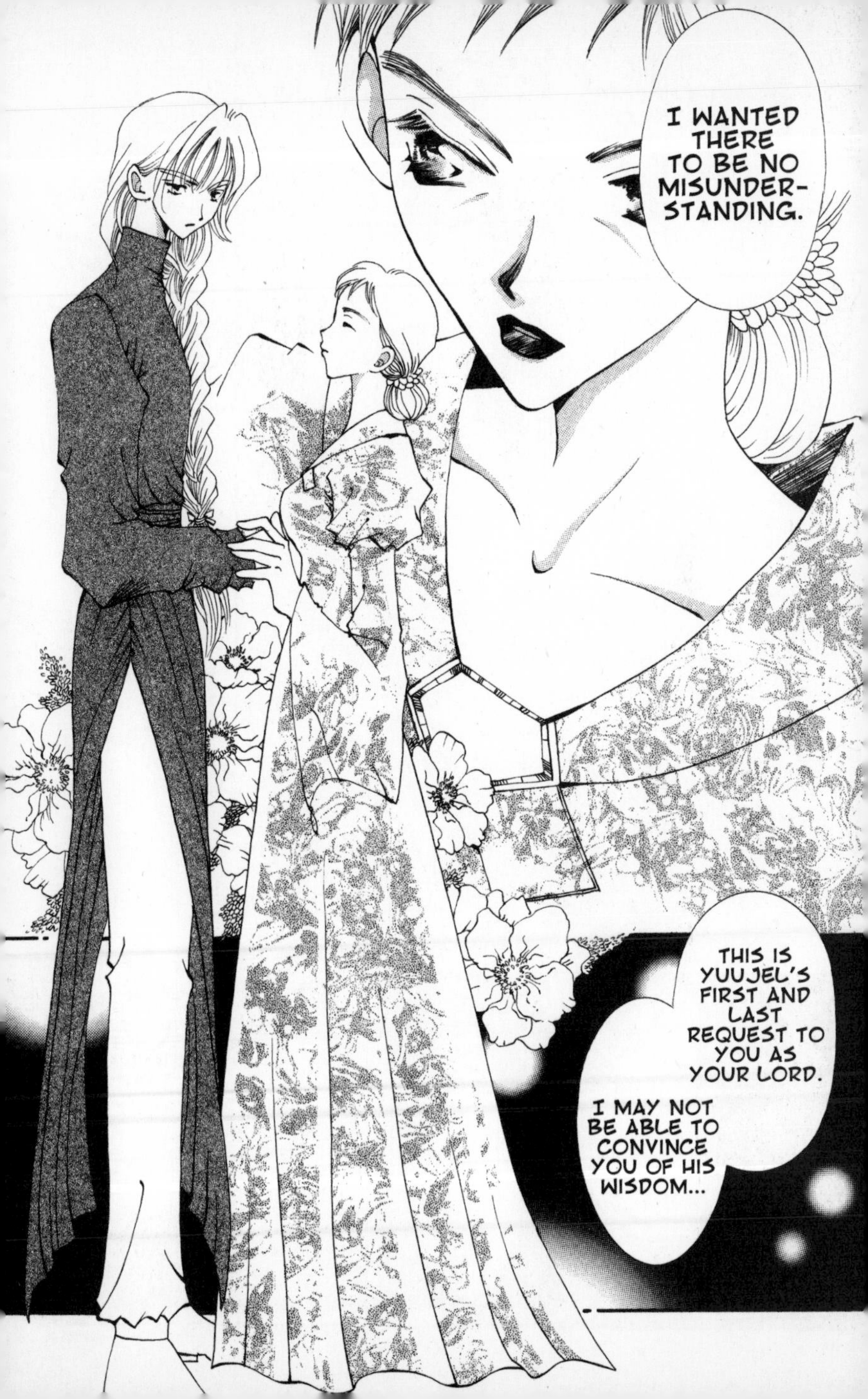
I WANTED THERE TO BE NO MISUNDER-STANDING.
THIS IS YUUJEL'S FIRST AND LAST REQUEST TO YOU AS YOUR LORD.
I MAY NOT BE ABLE TO CONVINCE YOU OF HIS WISDOM...

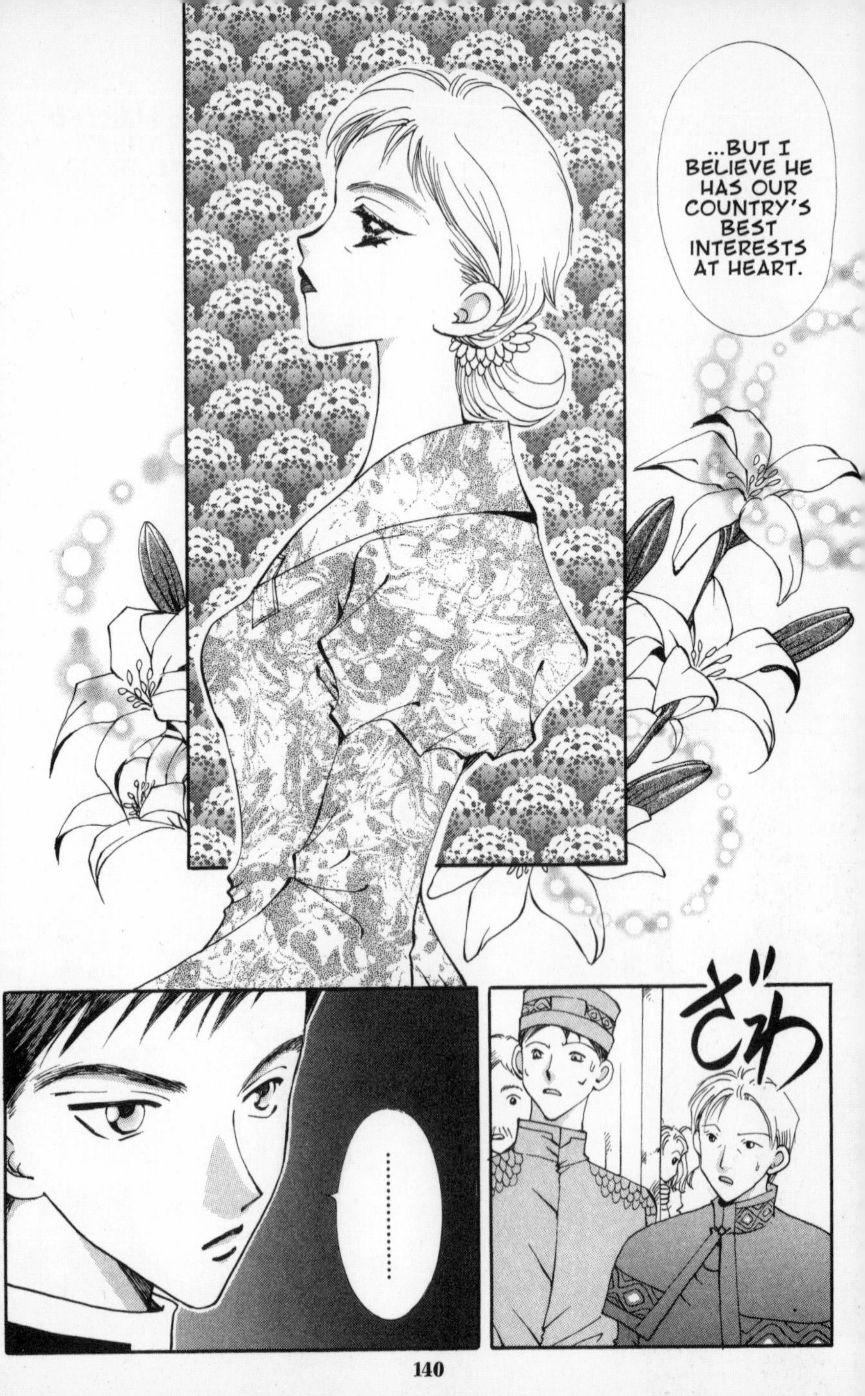
...BUT I BELIEVE HE HAS OUR COUNTRY'S BEST INTERESTS AT HEART.
さわ
......

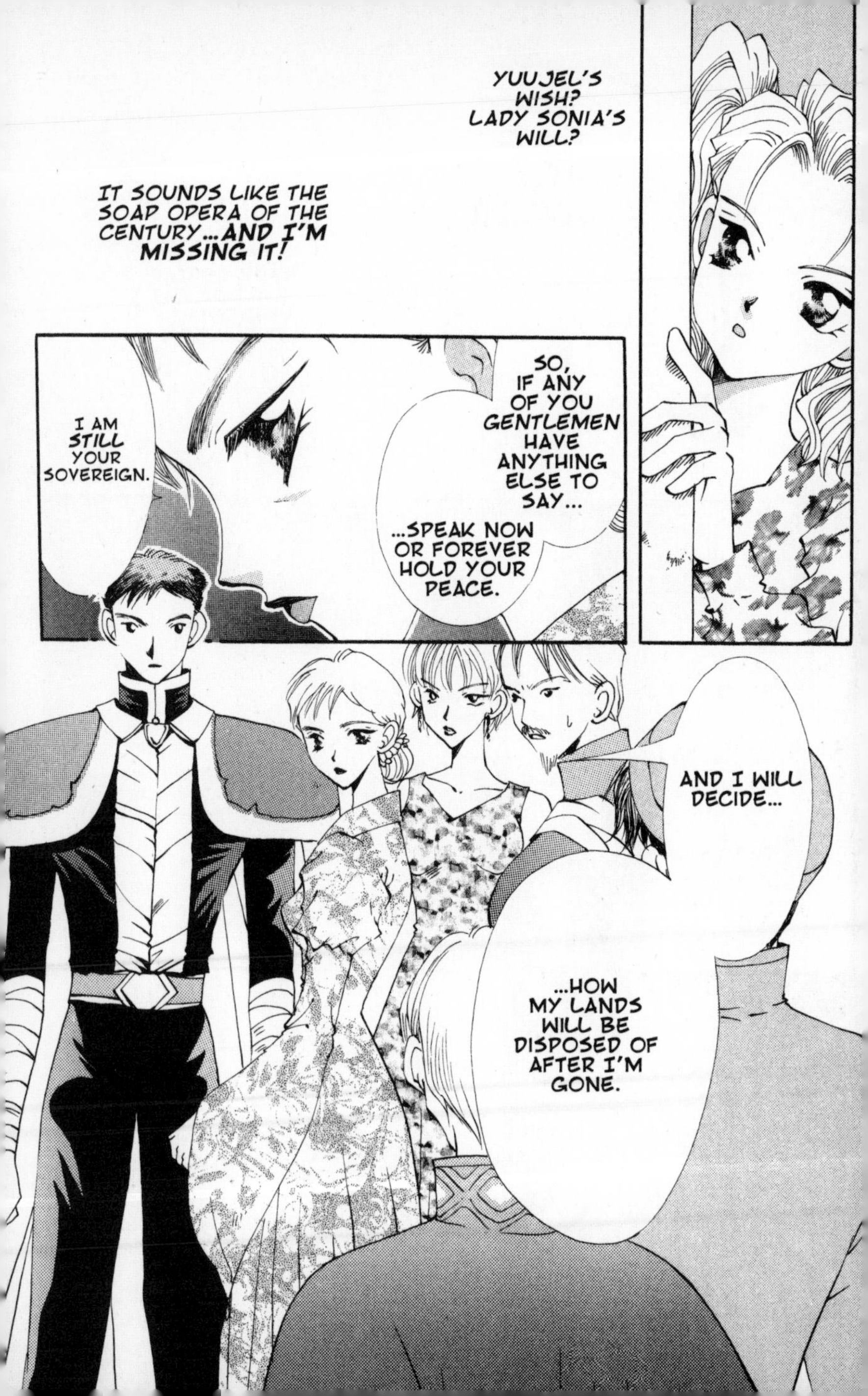
YUUJEL'S WISH? LADY SONIA'S WILL?
IT SOUNDS LIKE THE SOAP OPERA OF THE CENTURY...AND I'M MISSING IT!
SO, IF ANY OF YOU GENTLEMEN HAVE ANYTHING ELSE TO SAY...
...SPEAK NOW OR FOREVER HOLD YOUR PEACE.
I AM STILL YOUR SOVEREIGN.
AND I WILL DECIDE...
...HOW MY LANDS WILL BE DISPOSED OF AFTER I'M GONE.

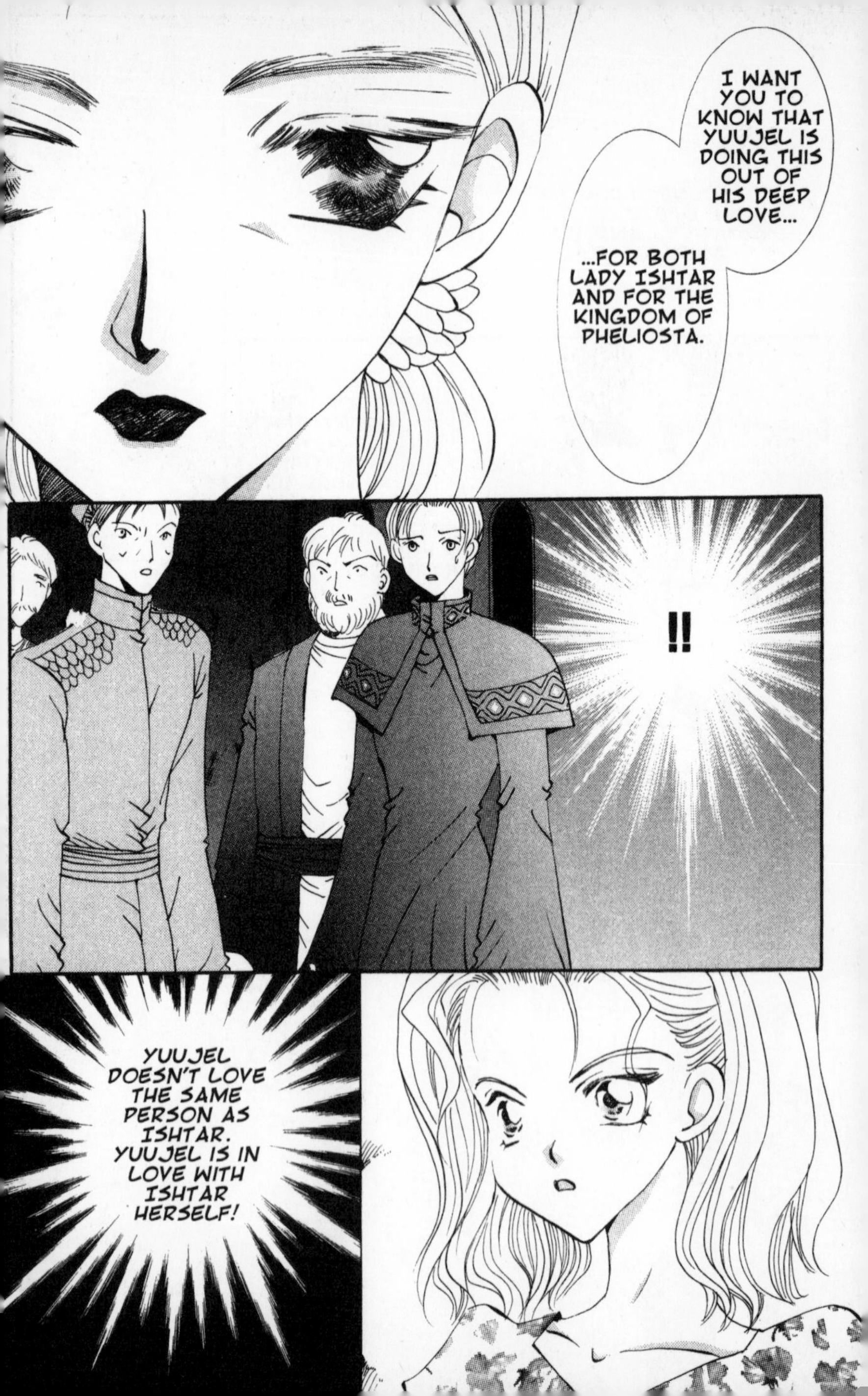
I WANT YOU TO KNOW THAT YUUJEL IS DOING THIS OUT OF HIS DEEP LOVE...
...FOR BOTH LADY ISHTAR AND FOR THE KINGDOM OF PHELIOSTA.
!!
YUUJEL DOESN'T LOVE THE SAME PERSON AS ISHTAR. YUUJEL IS IN LOVE WITH ISHTAR HERSELF!

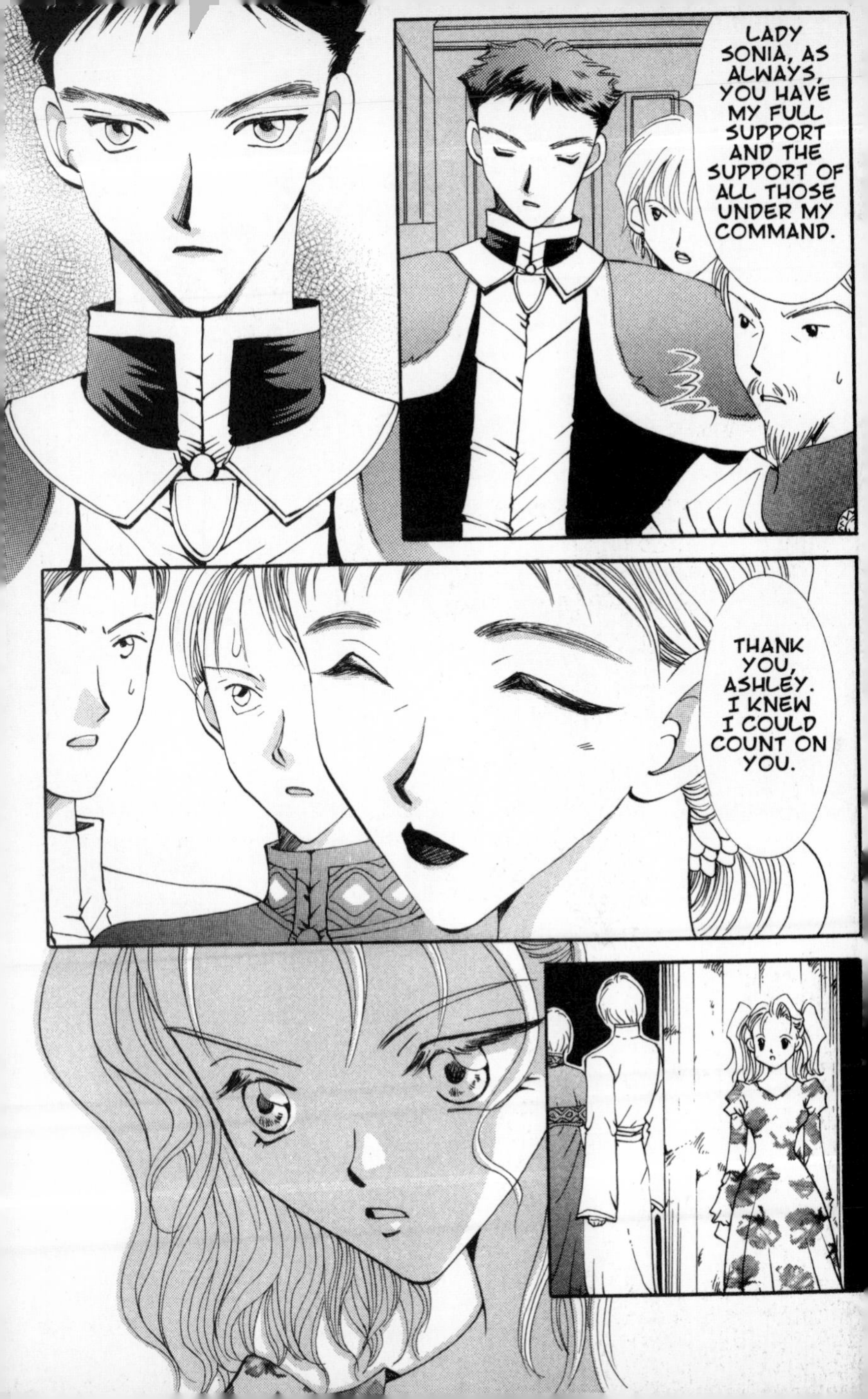
LADY SONIA, AS ALWAYS, YOU HAVE MY FULL SUPPORT AND THE SUPPORT OF ALL THOSE UNDER MY COMMAND.
THANK YOU, ASHLEY. I KNEW I COULD COUNT ON YOU.

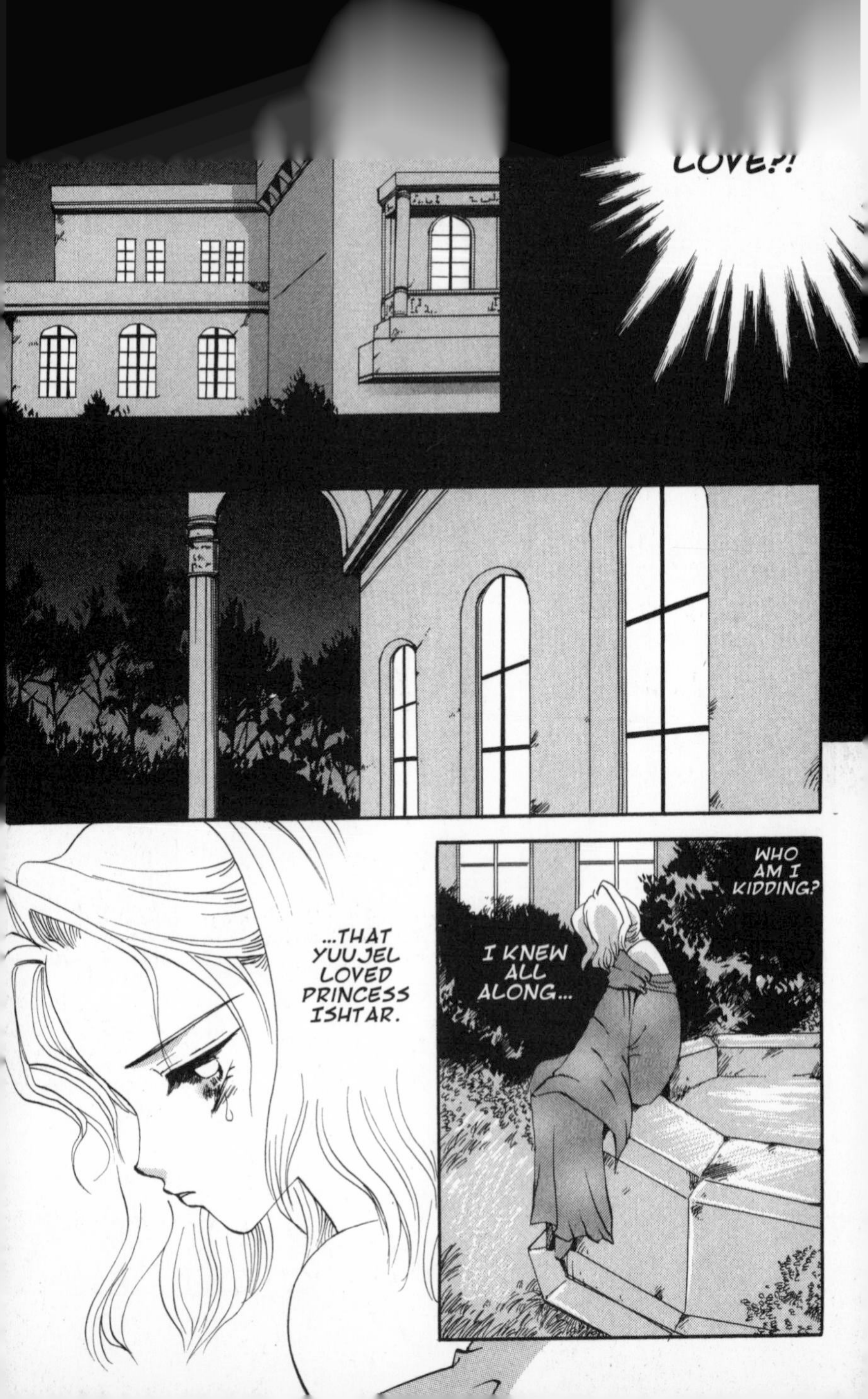
LOVE?!
WHO AM I KIDDING?
I KNEW ALL ALONG...
...THAT YUUJEL LOVED PRINCESS ISHTAR.

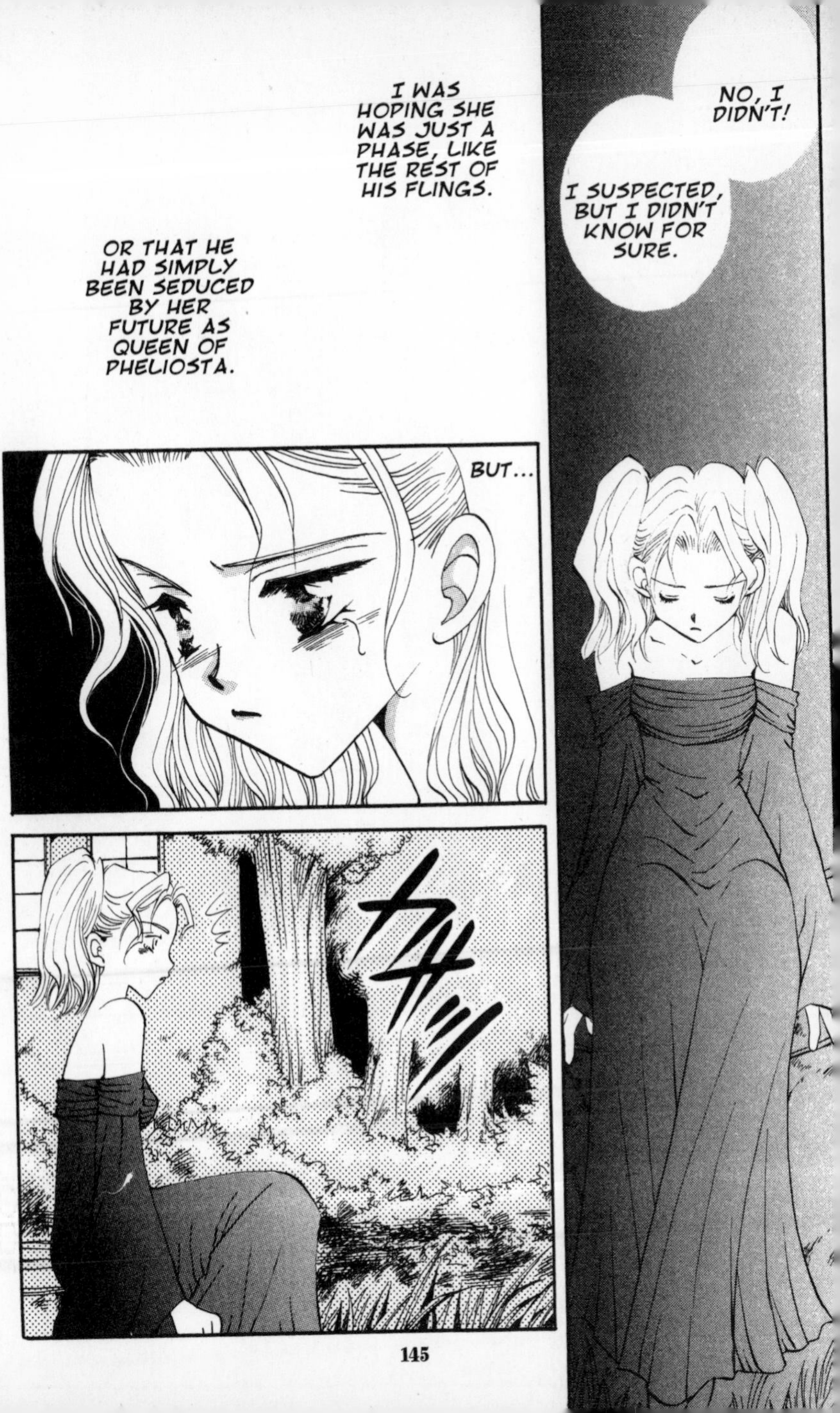
NO, I DIDN'T!
I SUSPECTED, BUT I DIDN'T KNOW FOR SURE.
I WAS HOPING SHE WAS JUST A PHASE, LIKE THE REST OF HIS FLINGS.
OR THAT HE HAD SIMPLY BEEN SEDUCED BY HER FUTURE AS QUEEN OF PHELIOSTA.
BUT...
カサッ

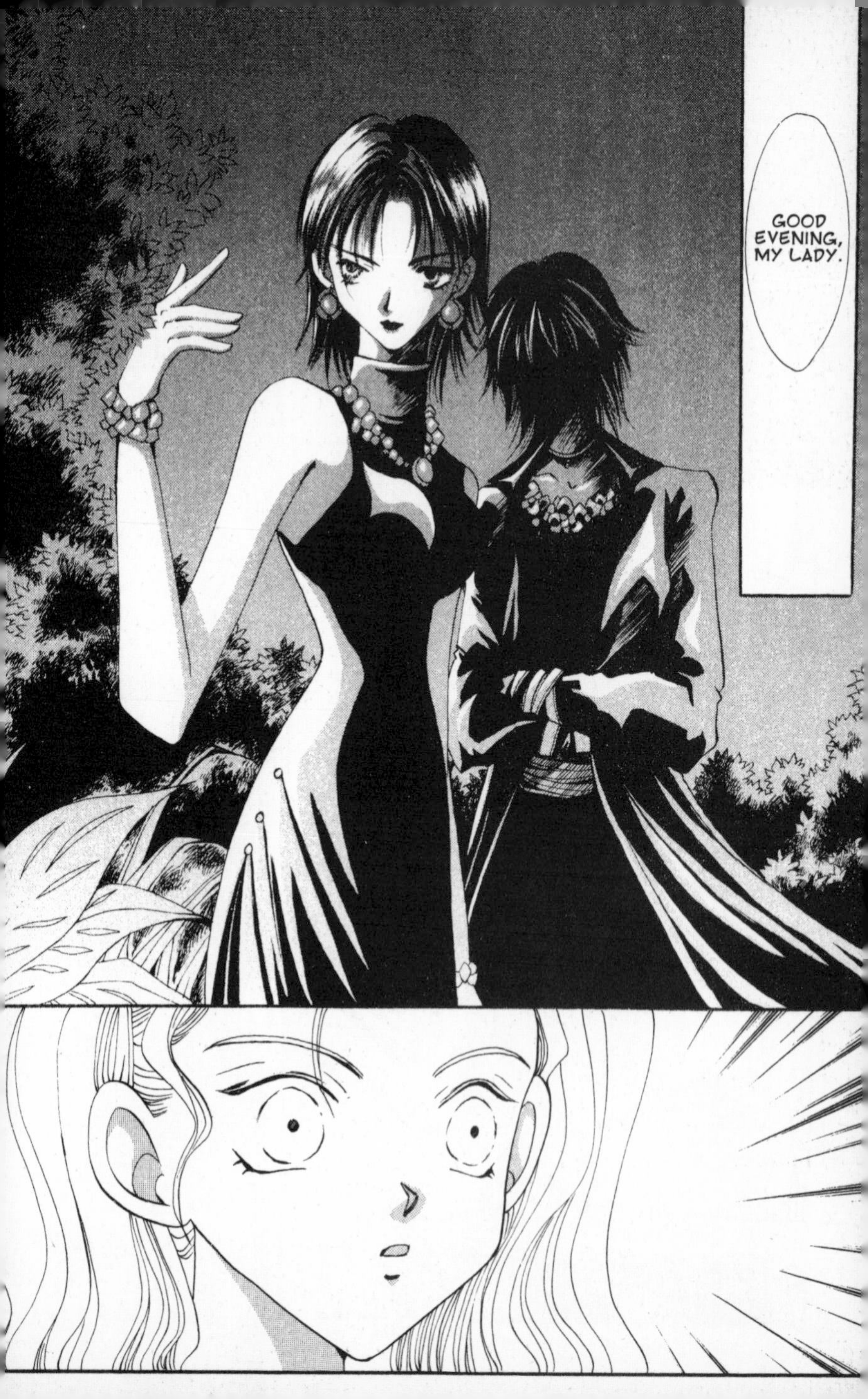
GOOD EVENING, MY LADY.

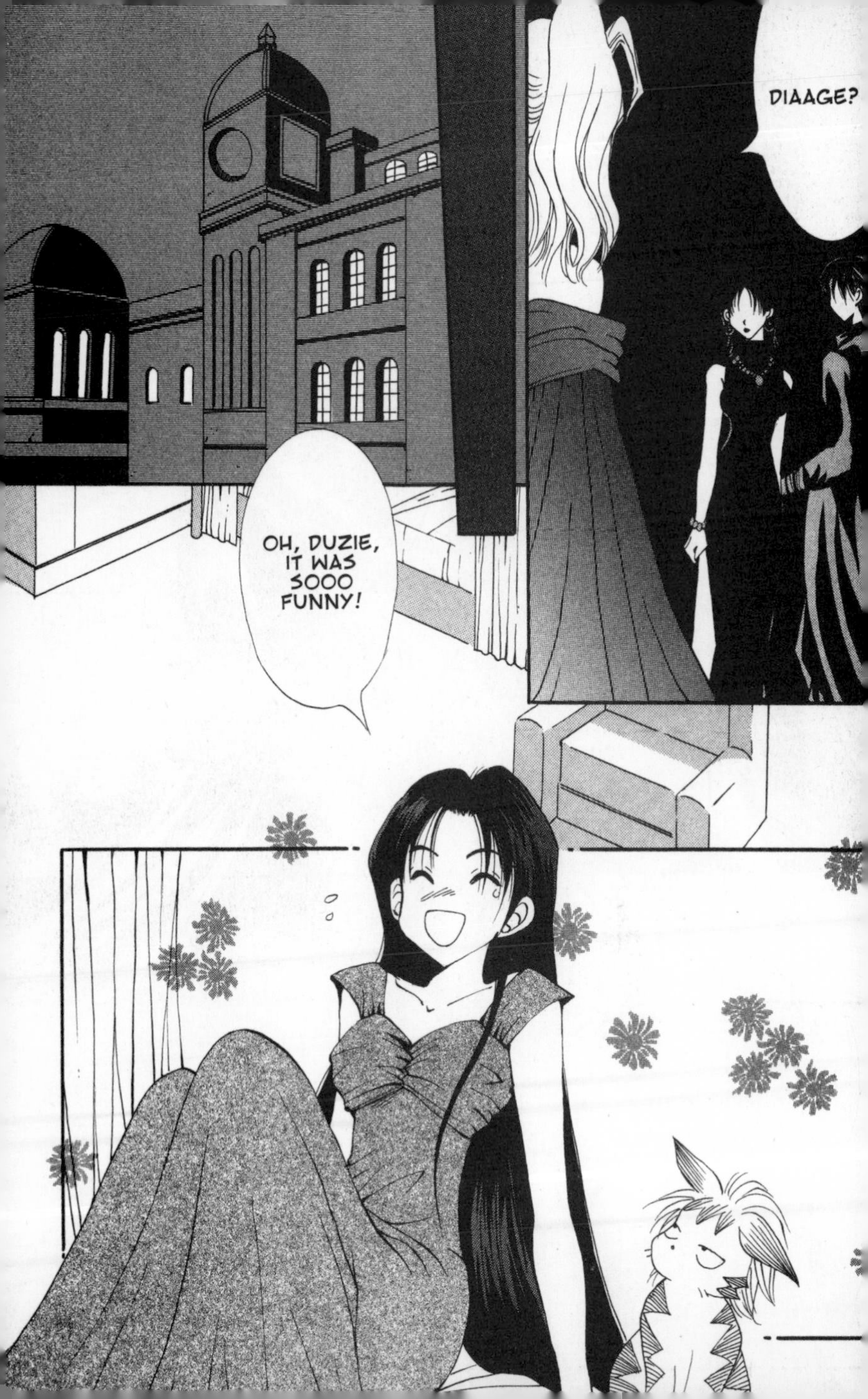
DIAAGE?
OH, DUZIE, IT WAS SOOO FUNNY!

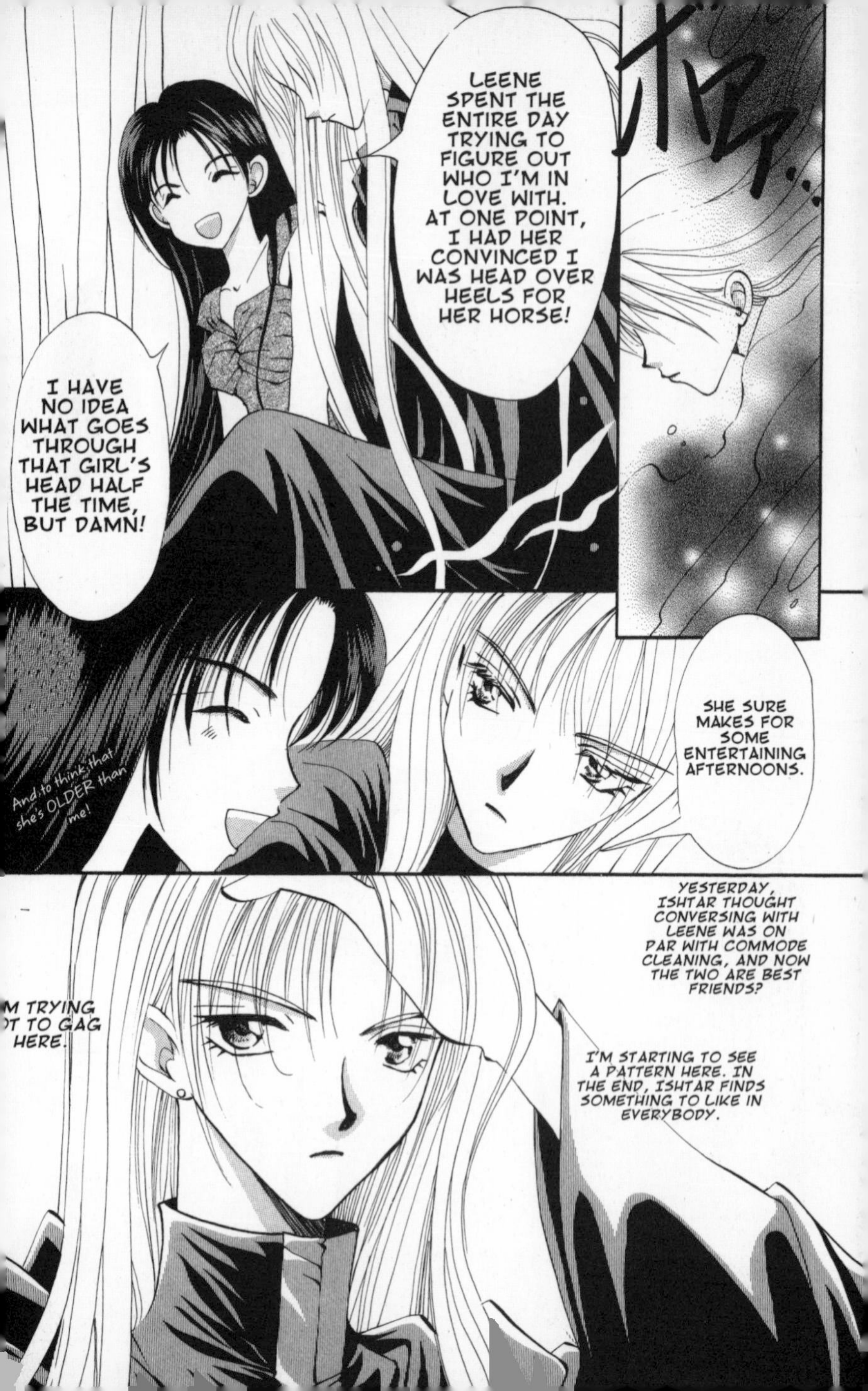
LEENE SPENT THE ENTIRE DAY TRYING TO FIGURE OUT WHO I'M IN LOVE WITH. AT ONE POINT, I HAD HER CONVINCED I WAS HEAD OVER HEELS FOR HER HORSE!
I HAVE NO IDEA WHAT GOES THROUGH THAT GIRL'S HEAD HALF THE TIME, BUT DAMN!
SHE SURE MAKES FOR SOME ENTERTAINING AFTERNOONS.
And to think that she's OLDER than me!
YESTERDAY, ISHTAR THOUGHT CONVERSING WITH LEENE WAS ON PAR WITH COMMODE CLEANING, AND NOW THE TWO ARE BEST FRIENDS?
I'M STARTING TO SEE A PATTERN HERE. IN THE END, ISHTAR FINDS SOMETHING TO LIKE IN EVERYBODY.
M TRYING OT TO GAG HERE.

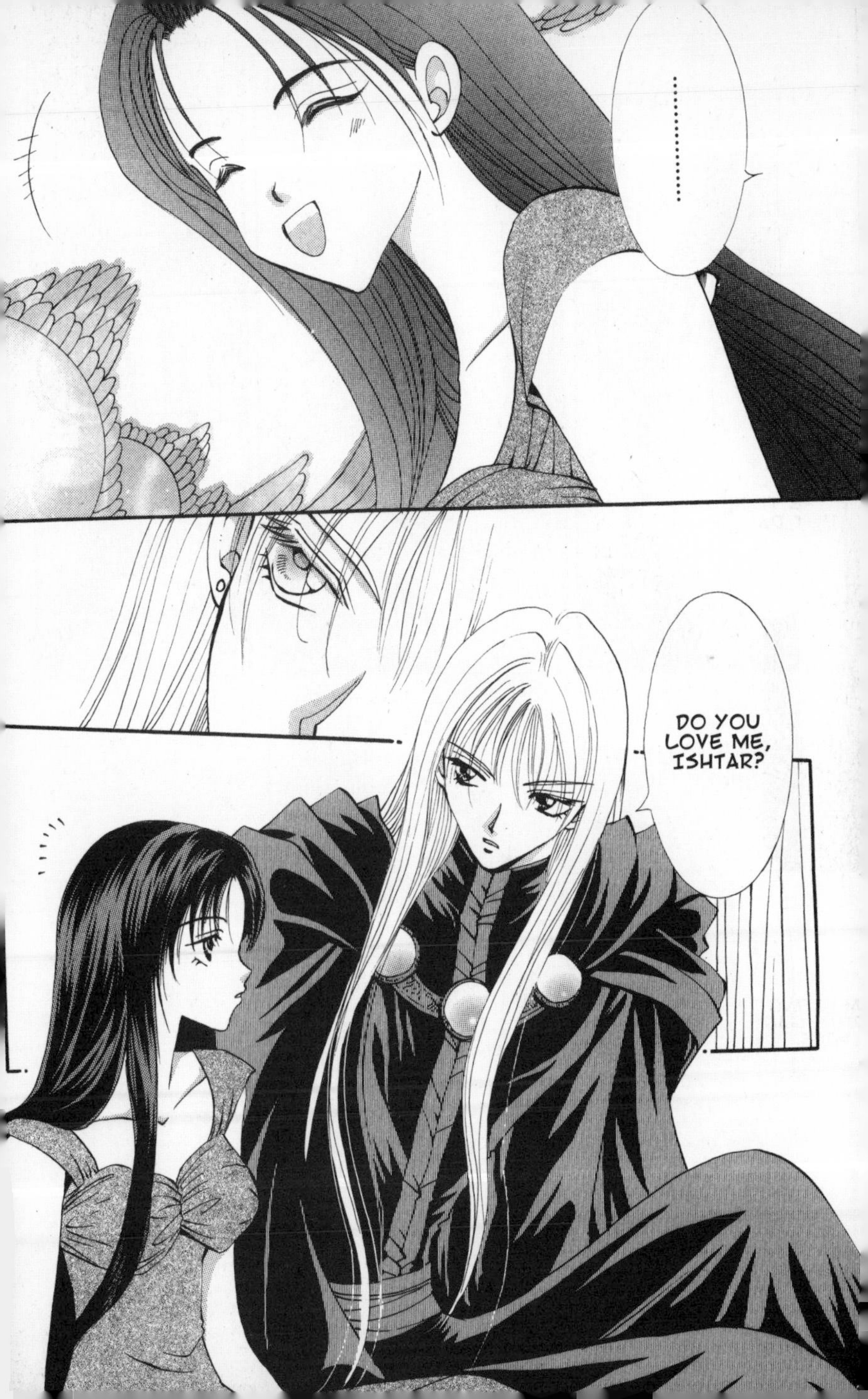
......
DO YOU LOVE ME, ISHTAR?

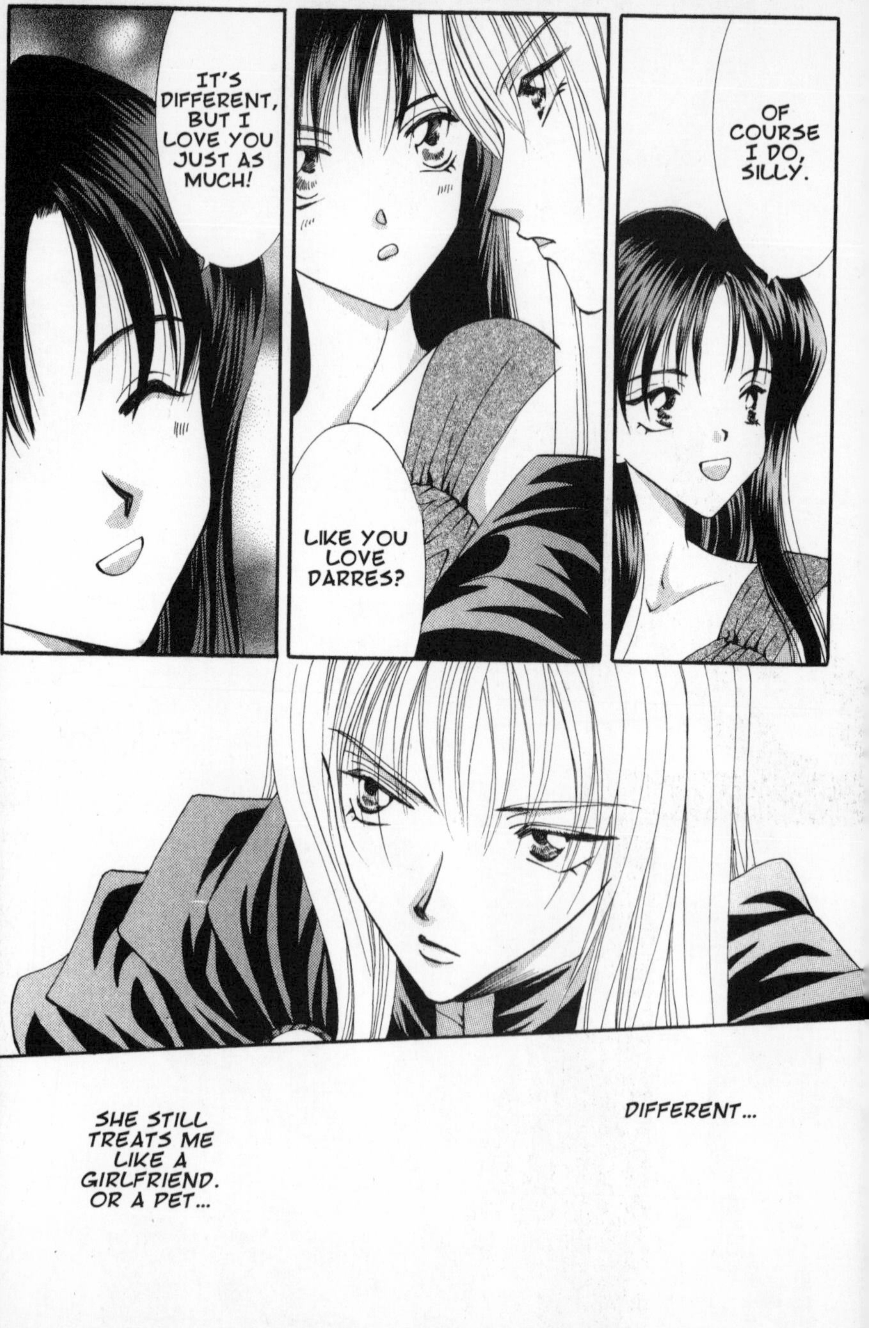
OF COURSE I DO, SILLY.
LIKE YOU LOVE DARRES?
IT'S DIFFERENT, BUT I LOVE YOU JUST AS MUCH!
DIFFERENT...
SHE STILL TREATS ME LIKE A GIRLFRIEND. OR A PET...

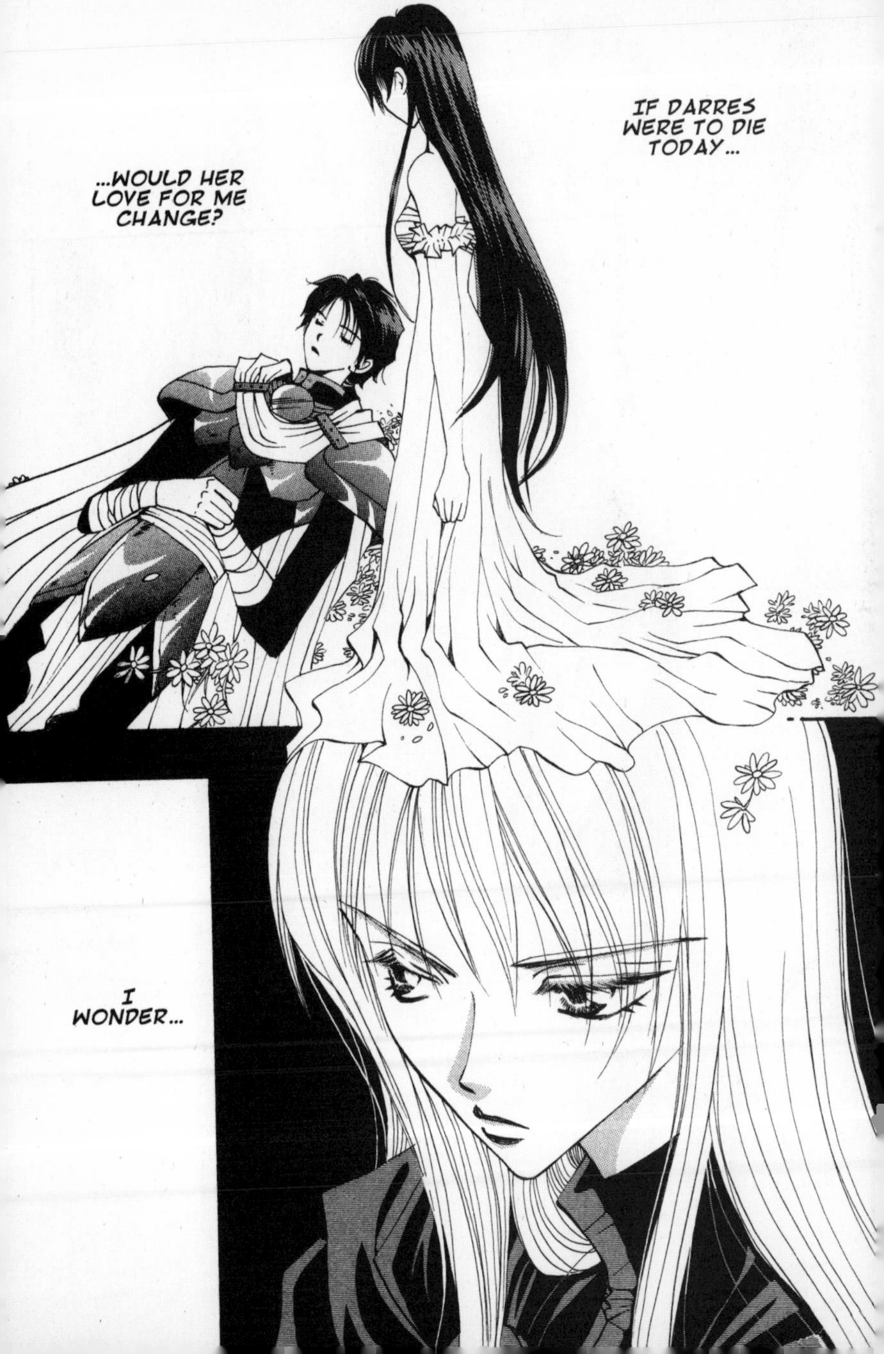
IF DARRES WERE TO DIE TODAY...
...WOULD HER LOVE FOR ME CHANGE?
I WONDER...

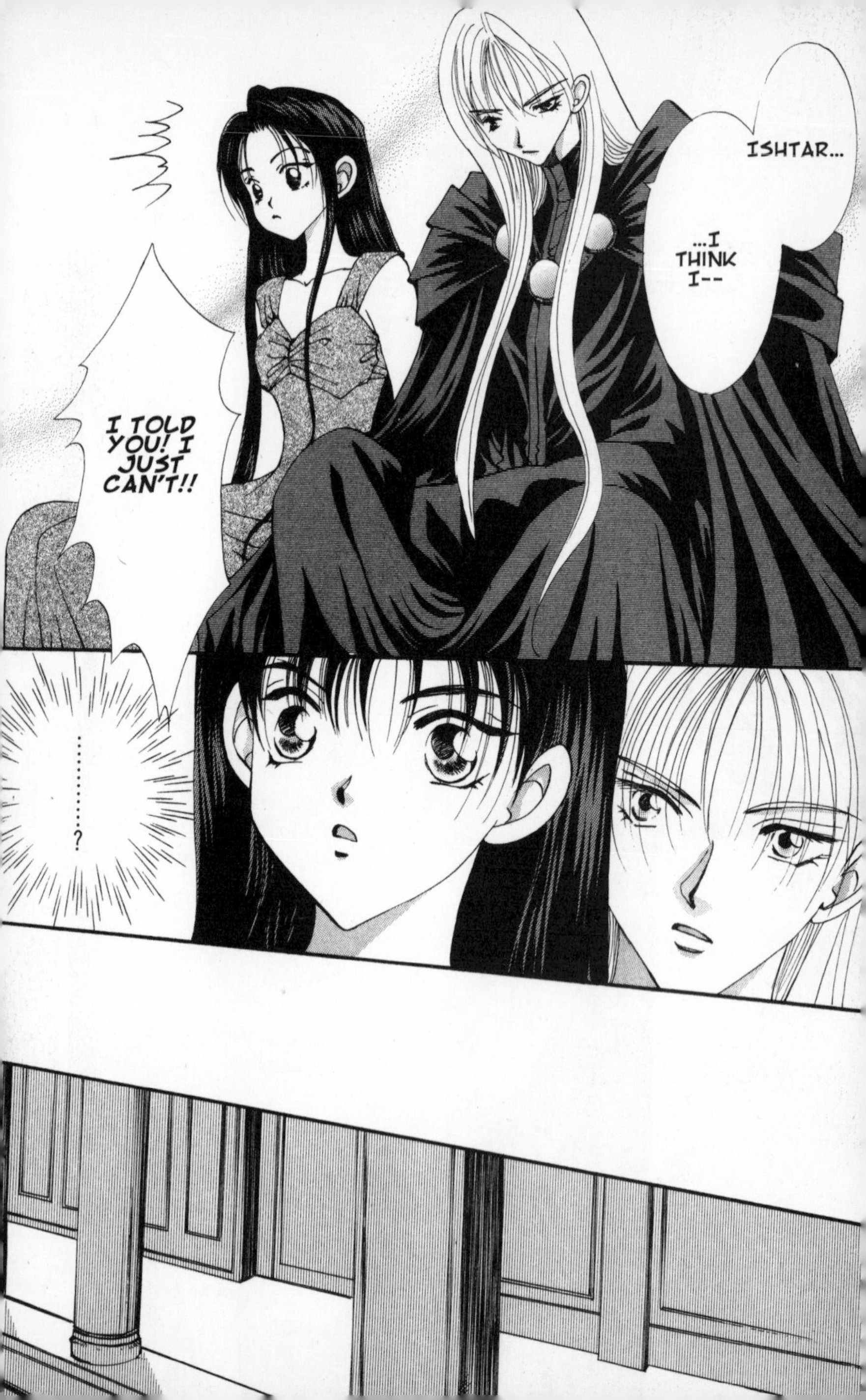
ISHTAR...
...I THINK I--
I TOLD YOU! I JUST CAN'T!!
......?

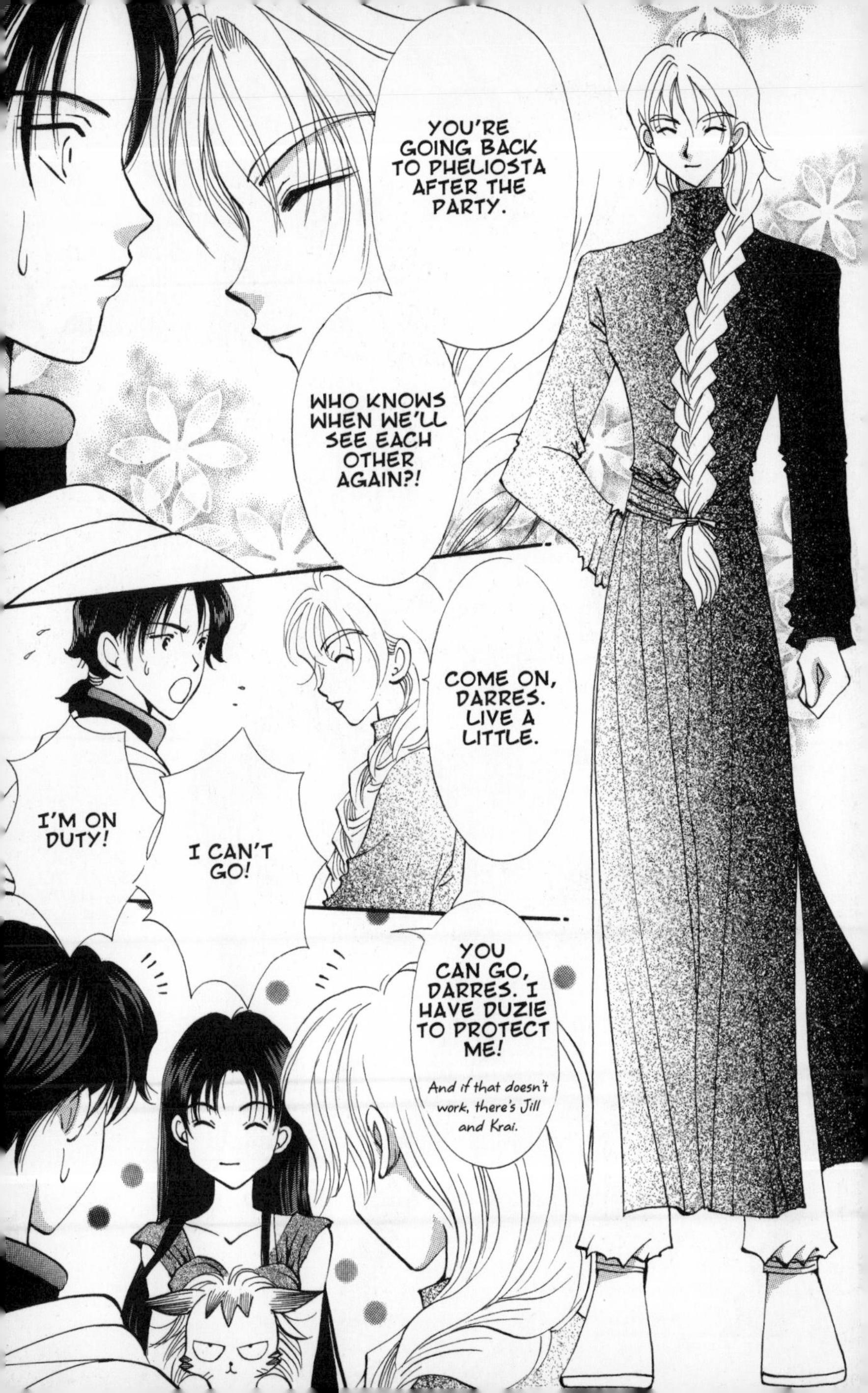
YOU'RE GOING BACK TO PHELIOSTA AFTER THE PARTY.
WHO KNOWS WHEN WE'LL SEE EACH OTHER AGAIN?!
COME ON, DARRES. LIVE A LITTLE.
I CAN'T GO!
I'M ON DUTY!
YOU CAN GO, DARRES. I HAVE DUZIE TO PROTECT ME!
And if that doesn't work, there's Jill and Krai.

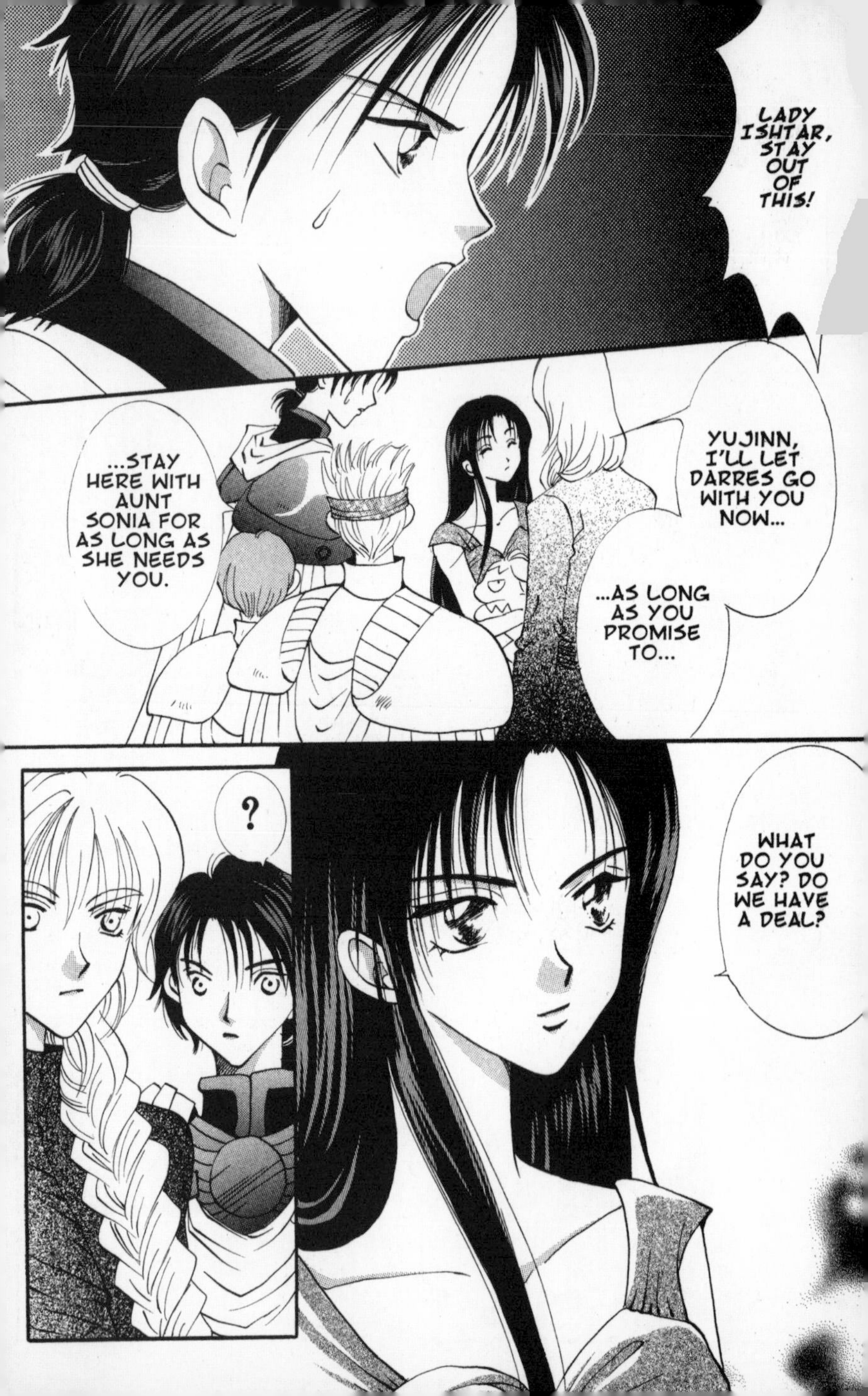
LADY ISHTAR, STAY OUT OF THIS!
YUJINN, I'LL LET DARRES GO WITH YOU NOW...
...AS LONG AS YOU PROMISE TO...
...STAY HERE WITH AUNT SONIA FOR AS LONG AS SHE NEEDS YOU.
WHAT DO YOU SAY? DO WE HAVE A DEAL?
?

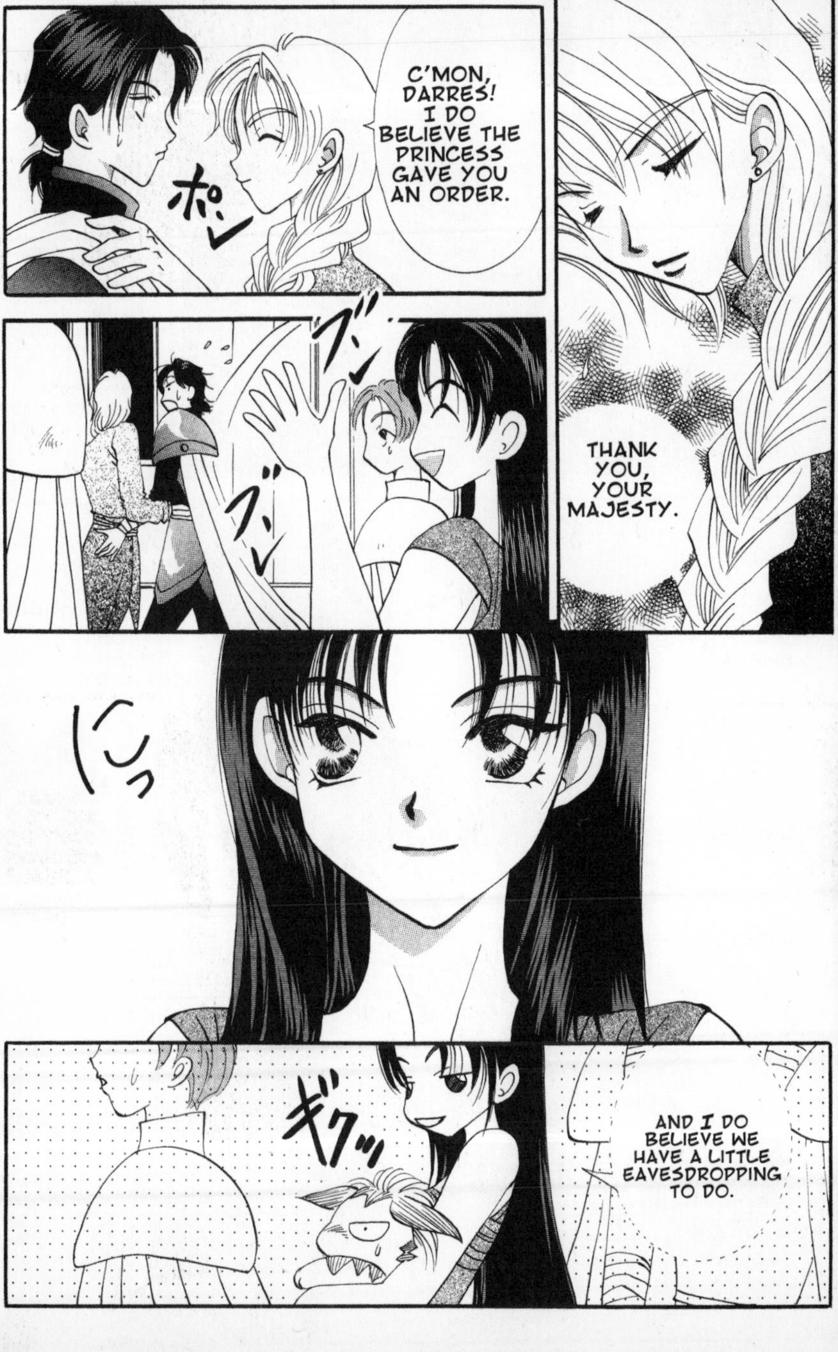
THANK YOU, YOUR MAJESTY.
C'MON, DARRES! I DO BELIEVE THE PRINCESS GAVE YOU AN ORDER.
ポン
ブン
ブン
にこっ
AND I DO BELIEVE WE HAVE A LITTLE EAVESDROPPING TO DO.
ギクッ

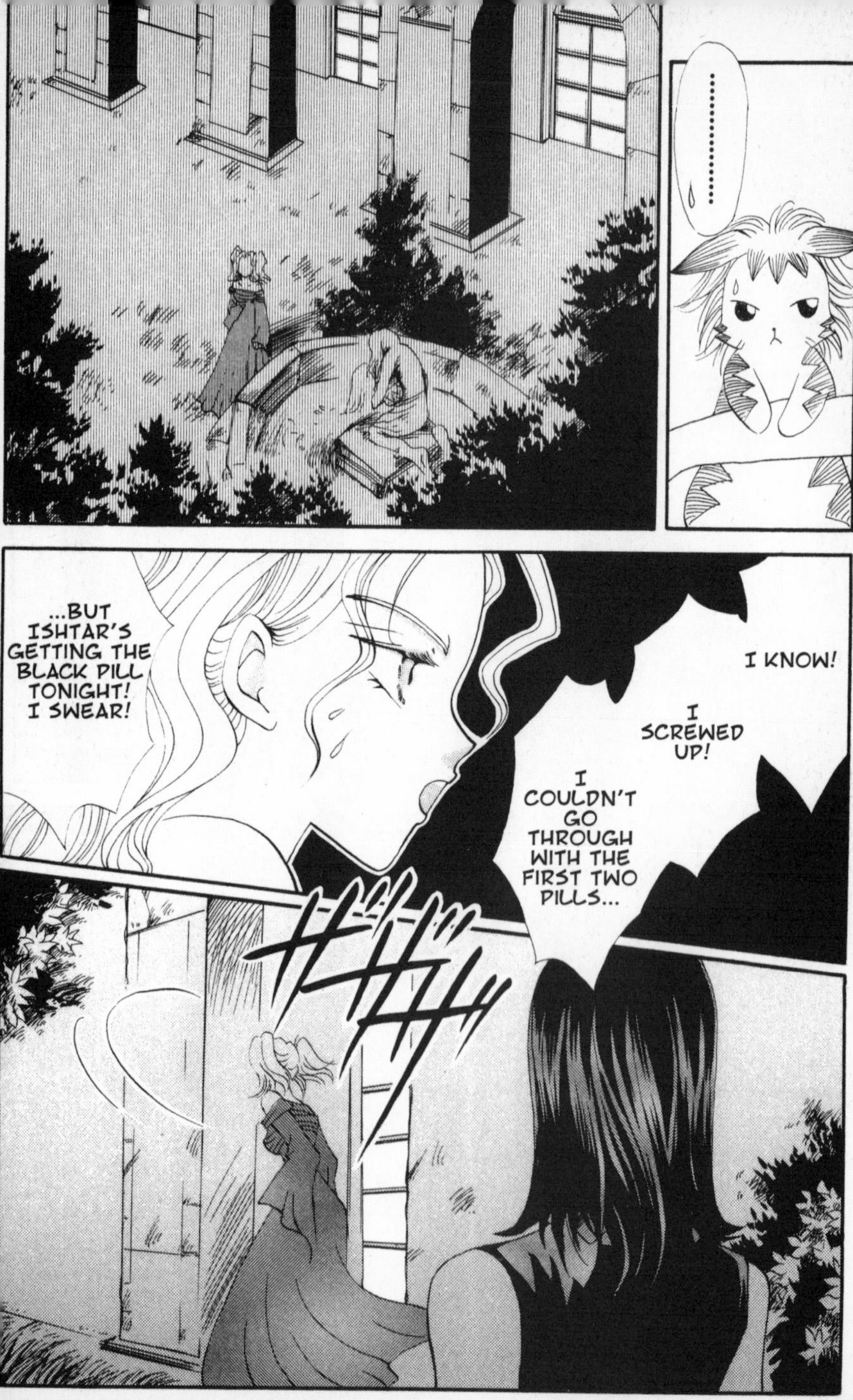
I KNOW!
I SCREWED UP!
I COULDN'T GO THROUGH WITH THE FIRST TWO PILLS...
...BUT ISHTAR'S GETTING THE BLACK PILL TONIGHT! I SWEAR!

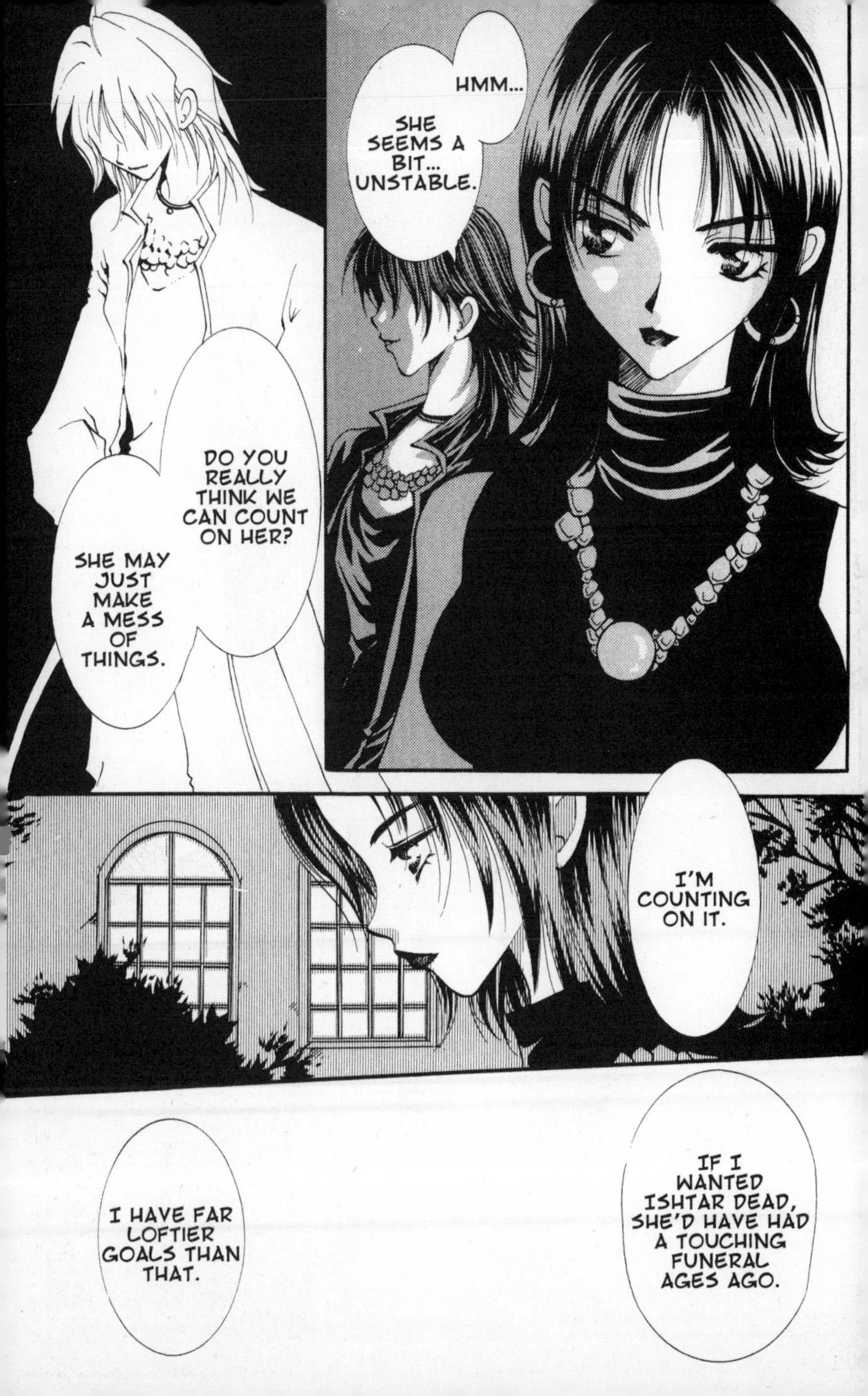
HMM...
SHE SEEMS A BIT... UNSTABLE.
DO YOU REALLY THINK WE CAN COUNT ON HER?
SHE MAY JUST MAKE A MESS OF THINGS.
I'M COUNTING ON IT.
IF I WANTED ISHTAR DEAD, SHE'D HAVE HAD A TOUCHING FUNERAL AGES AGO.
I HAVE FAR LOFTIER GOALS THAN THAT.

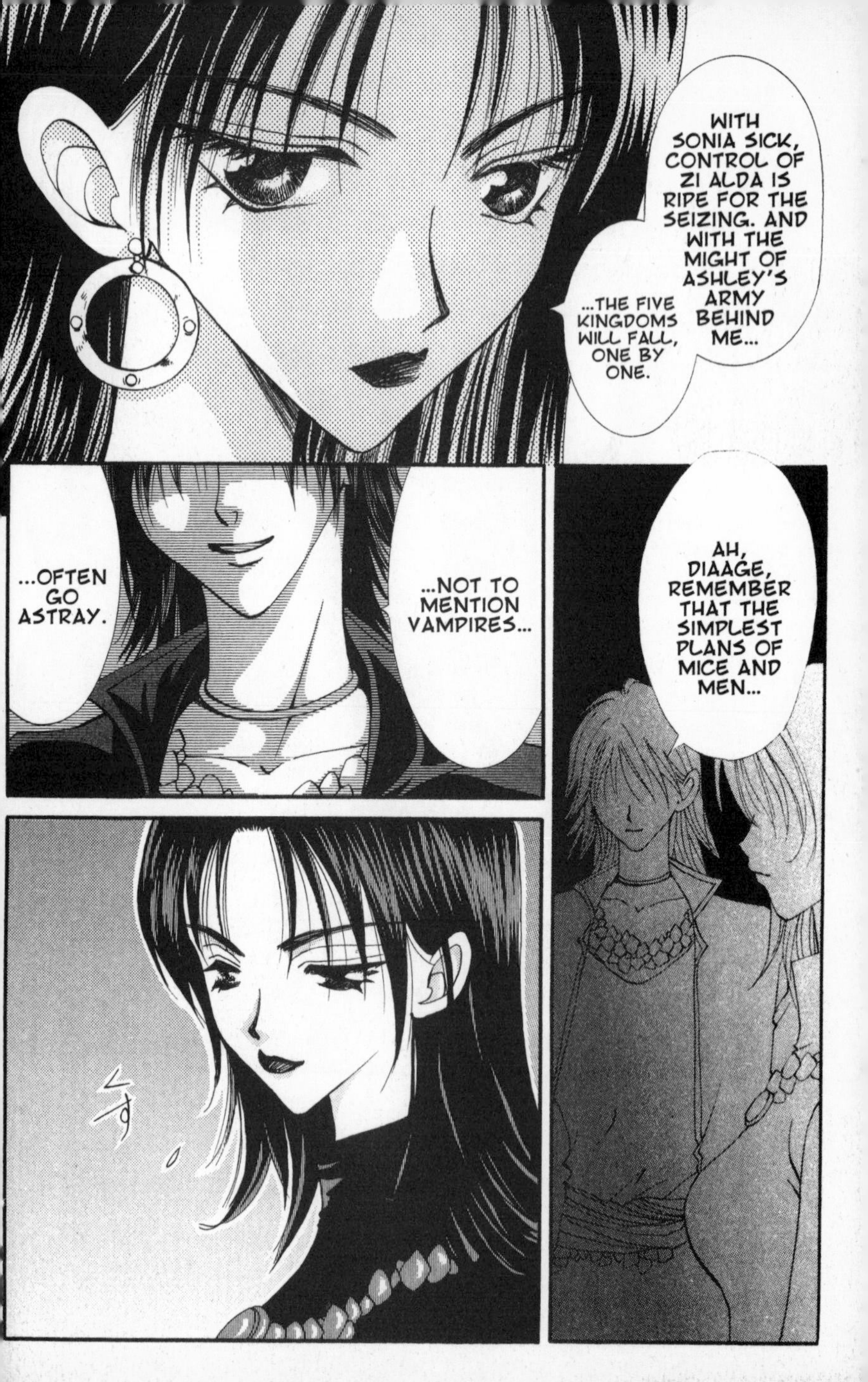
WITH SONIA SICK, CONTROL OF ZI ALDA IS RIPE FOR THE SEIZING. AND WITH THE MIGHT OF ASHLEY'S ARMY BEHIND ME...
...THE FIVE KINGDOMS WILL FALL, ONE BY ONE.
AH, DIAAGE, REMEMBER THAT THE SIMPLEST PLANS OF MICE AND MEN...
...NOT TO MENTION VAMPIRES...
...OFTEN GO ASTRAY.
くす

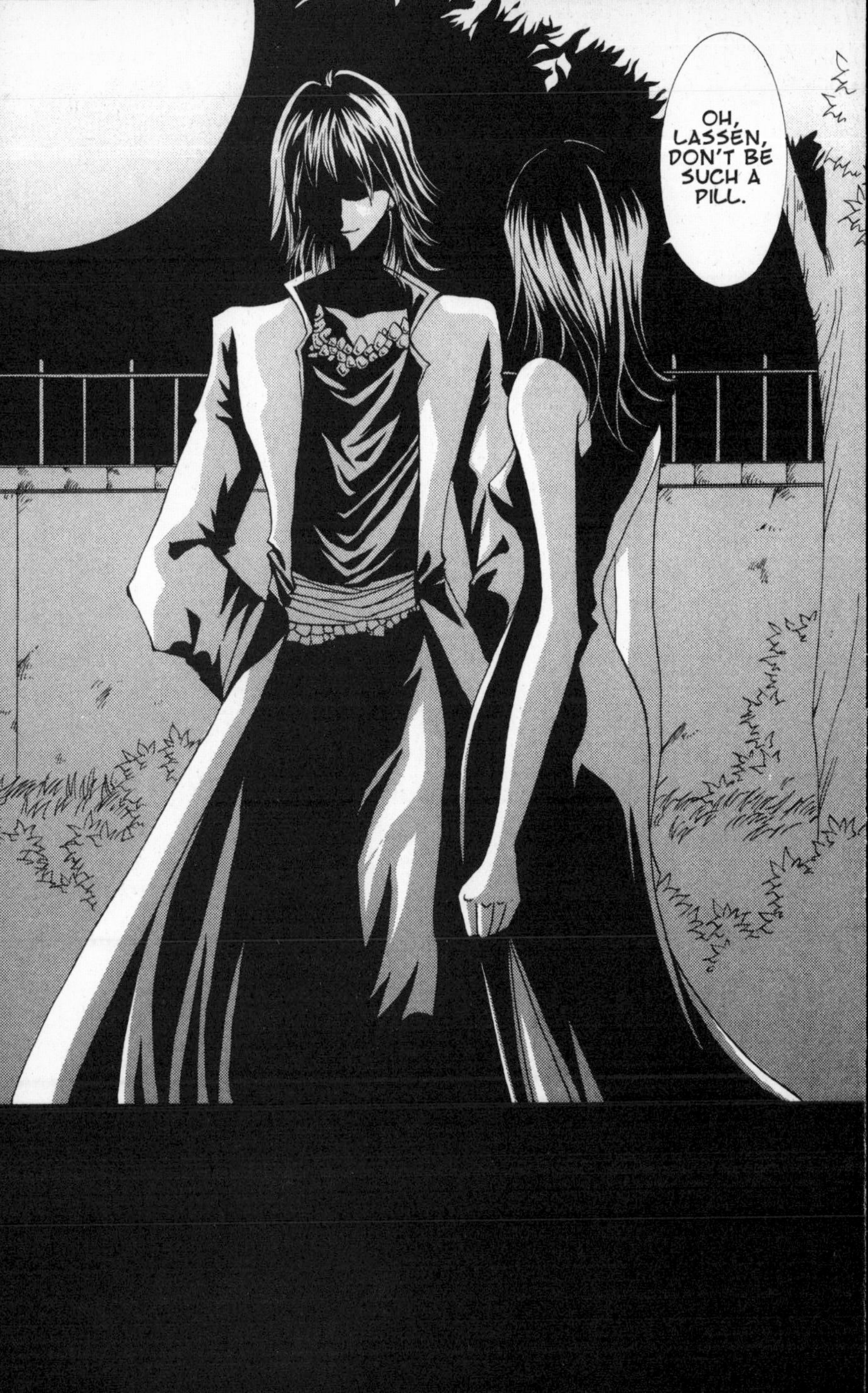
OH, LASSEN, DON'T BE SUCH A PILL.

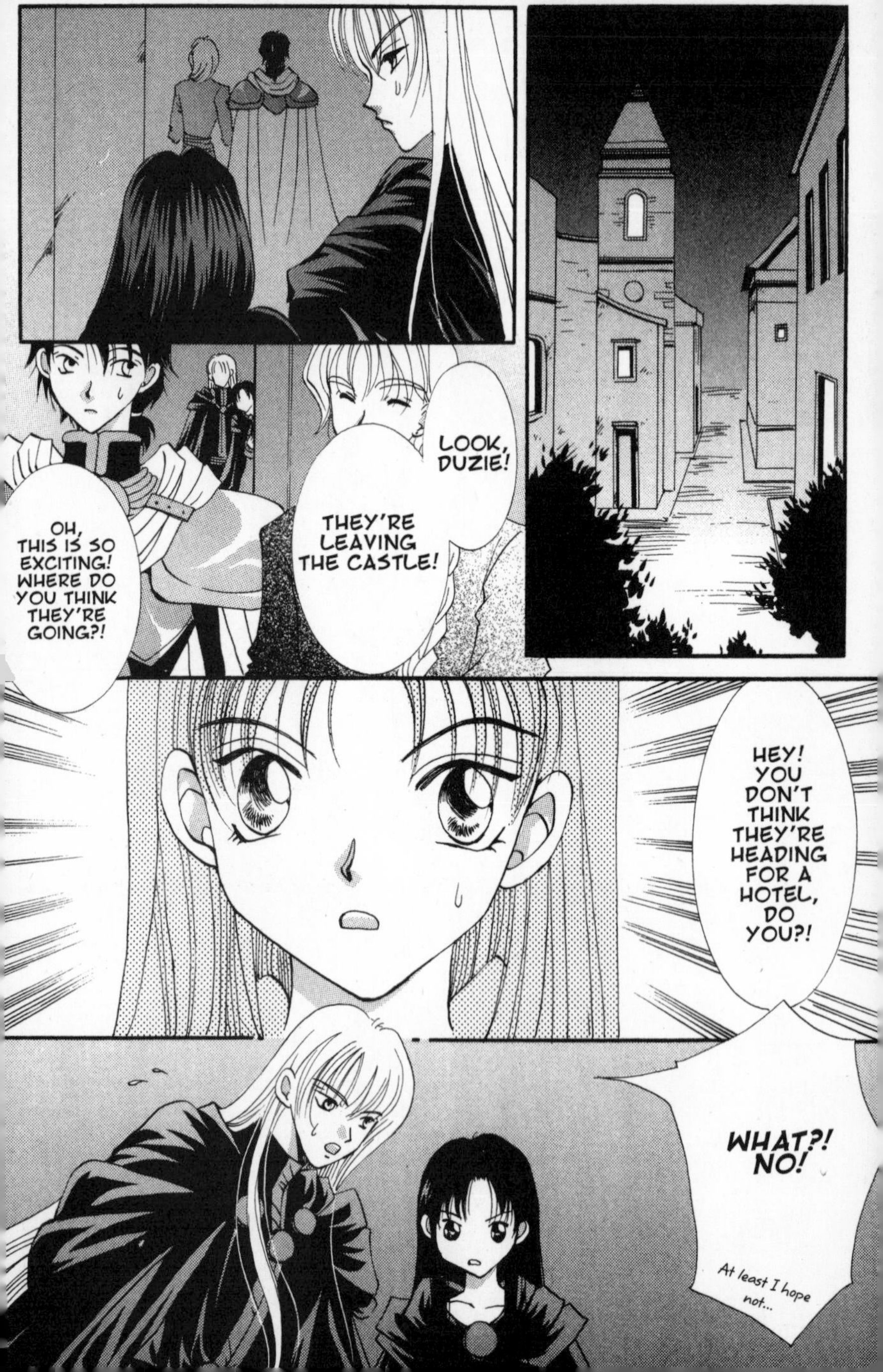
LOOK, DUZIE!
THEY'RE LEAVING THE CASTLE!
OH, THIS IS SO EXCITING! WHERE DO YOU THINK THEY'RE GOING?!
HEY! YOU DON'T THINK THEY'RE HEADING FOR A HOTEL, DO YOU?!
WHAT?! NO!
At least I hope not...

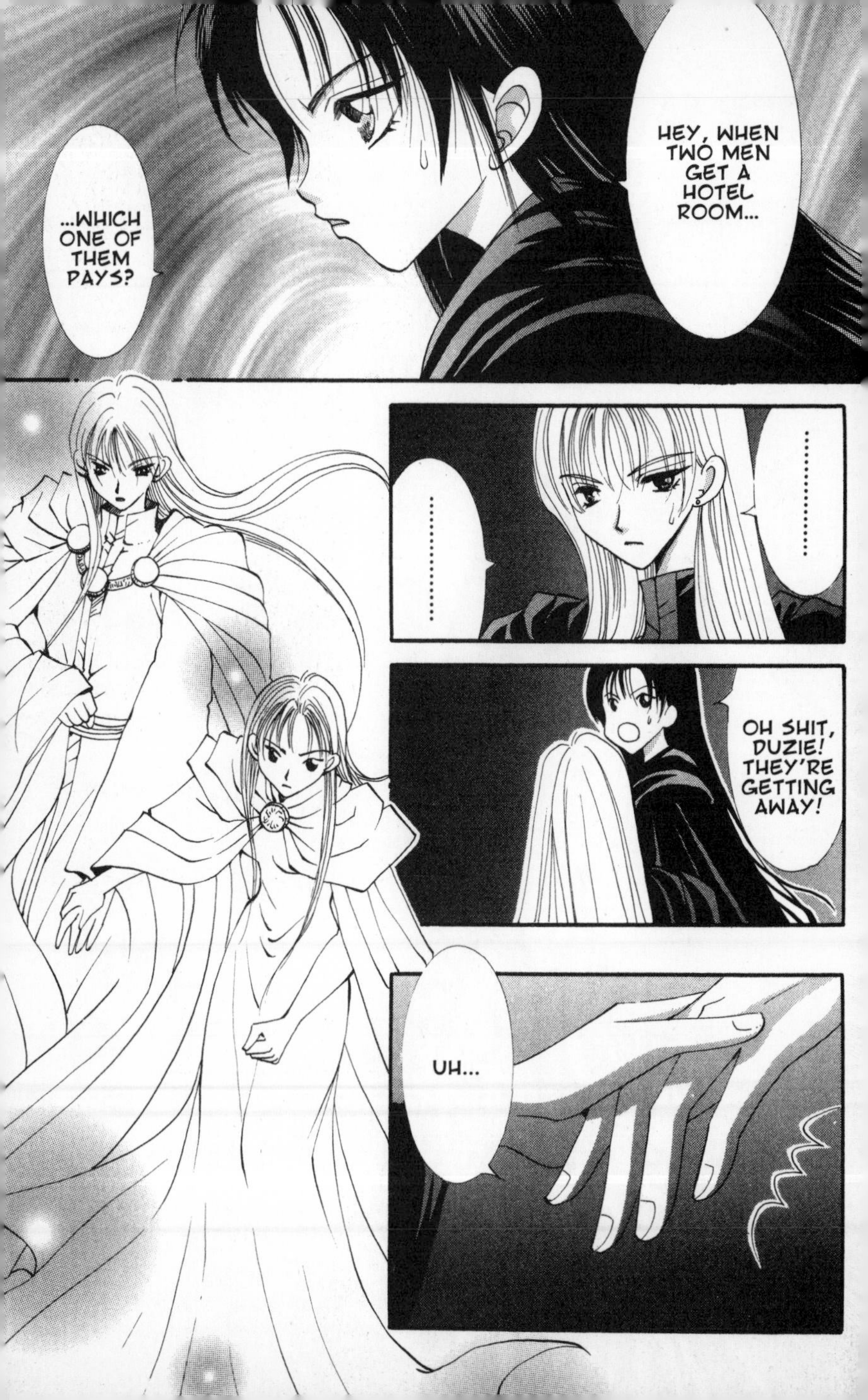
HEY, WHEN TWO MEN GET A HOTEL ROOM...
...WHICH ONE OF THEM PAYS?
......
......
OH SHIT, DUZIE! THEY'RE GETTING AWAY!
UH...

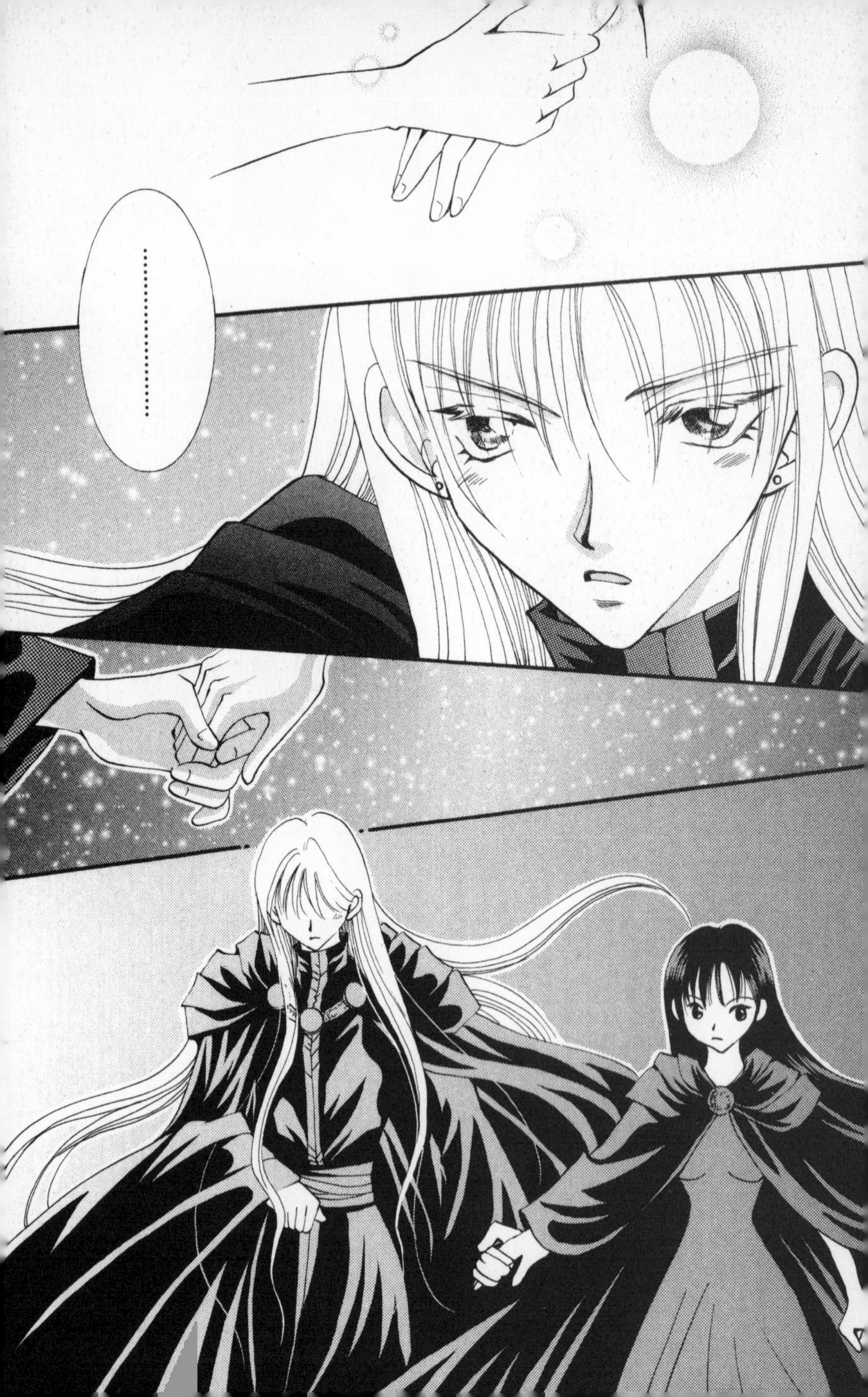
……

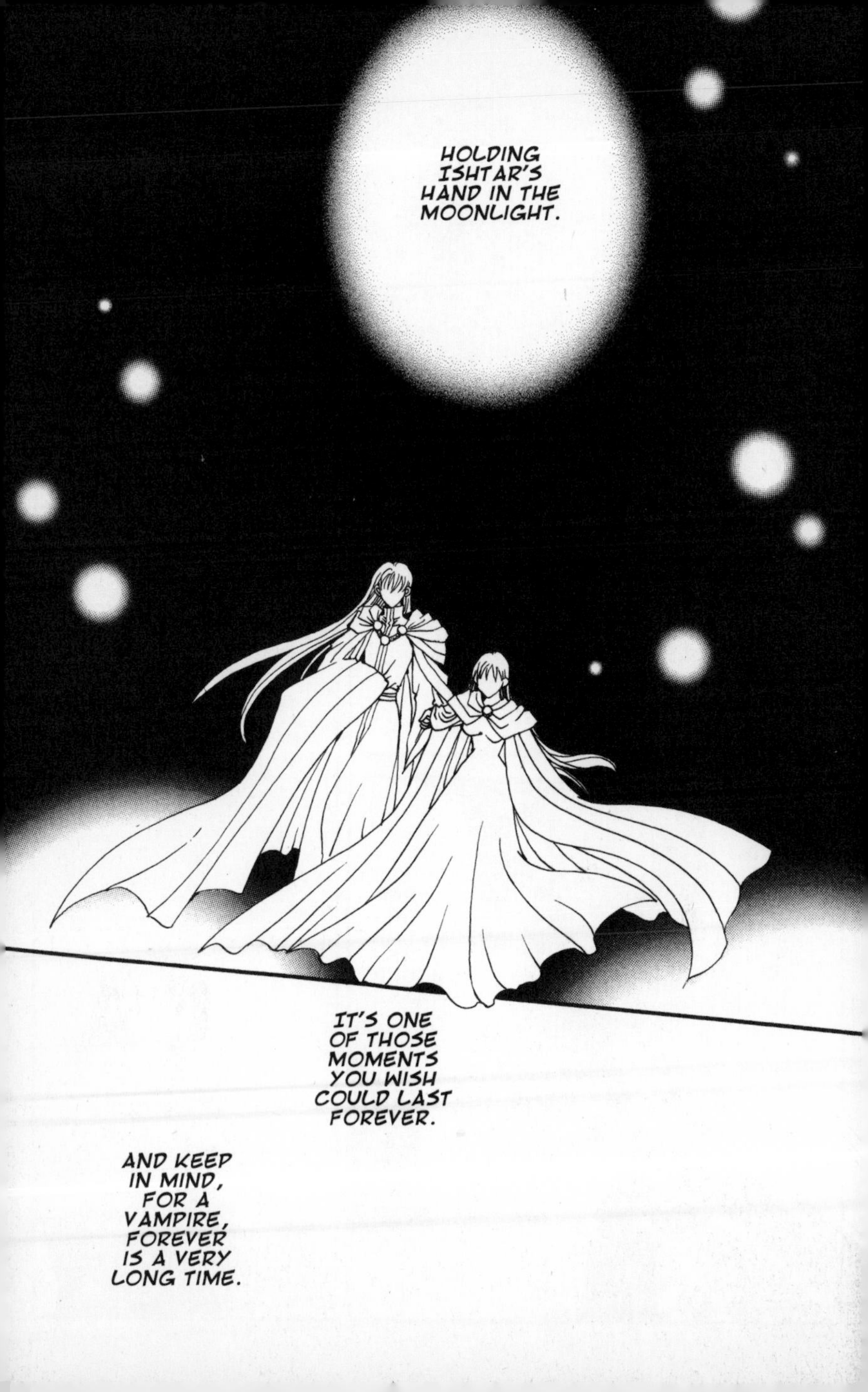
HOLDING ISHTAR'S HAND IN THE MOONLIGHT.
IT'S ONE OF THOSE MOMENTS YOU WISH COULD LAST FOREVER.
AND KEEP IN MIND, FOR A VAMPIRE, FOREVER IS A VERY LONG TIME.

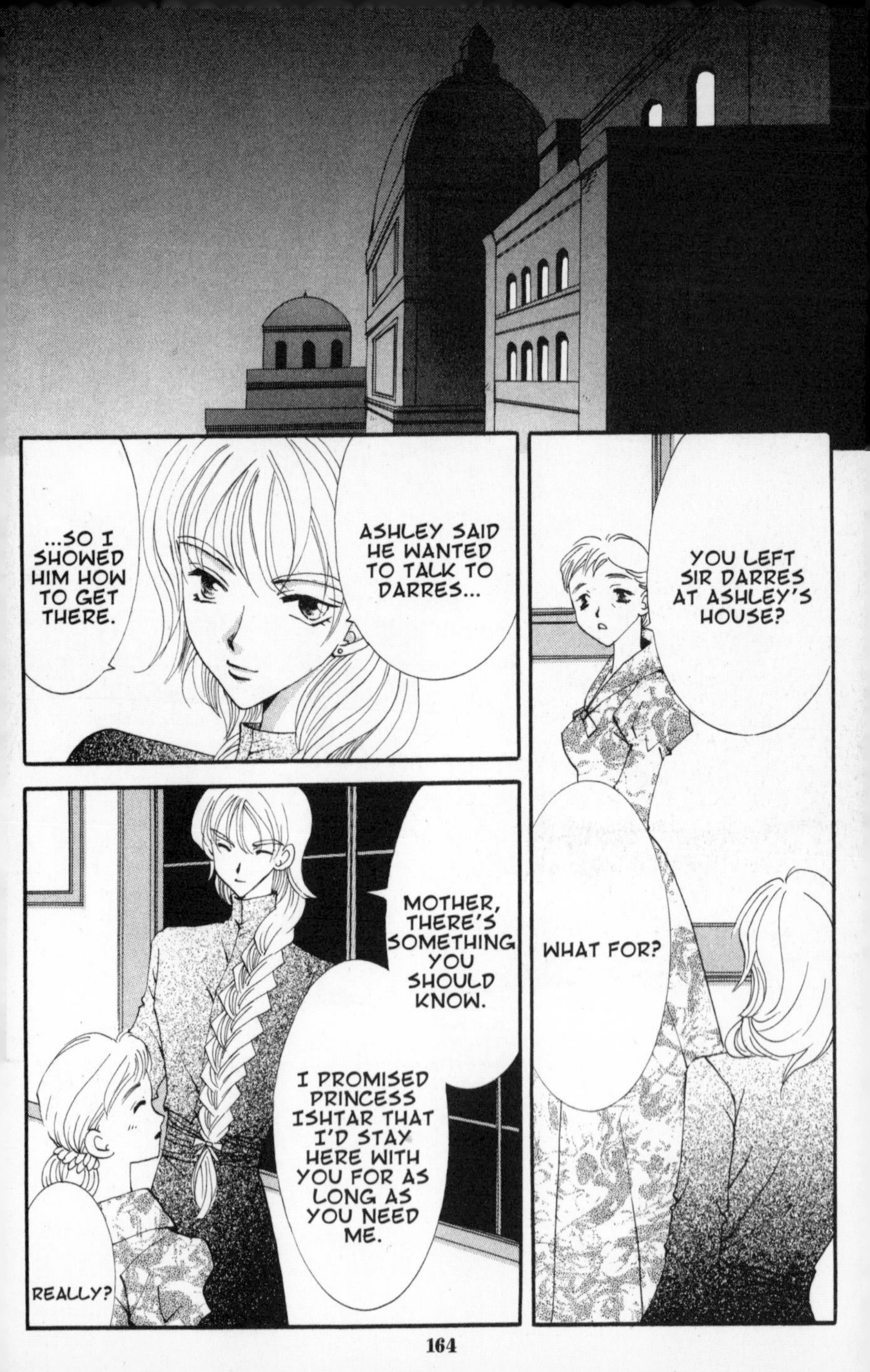
YOU LEFT SIR DARRES AT ASHLEY'S HOUSE?
WHAT FOR?
ASHLEY SAID HE WANTED TO TALK TO DARRES...
...SO I SHOWED HIM HOW TO GET THERE.
MOTHER, THERE'S SOMETHING YOU SHOULD KNOW.
I PROMISED PRINCESS ISHTAR THAT I'D STAY HERE WITH YOU FOR AS LONG AS YOU NEED ME.
REALLY?

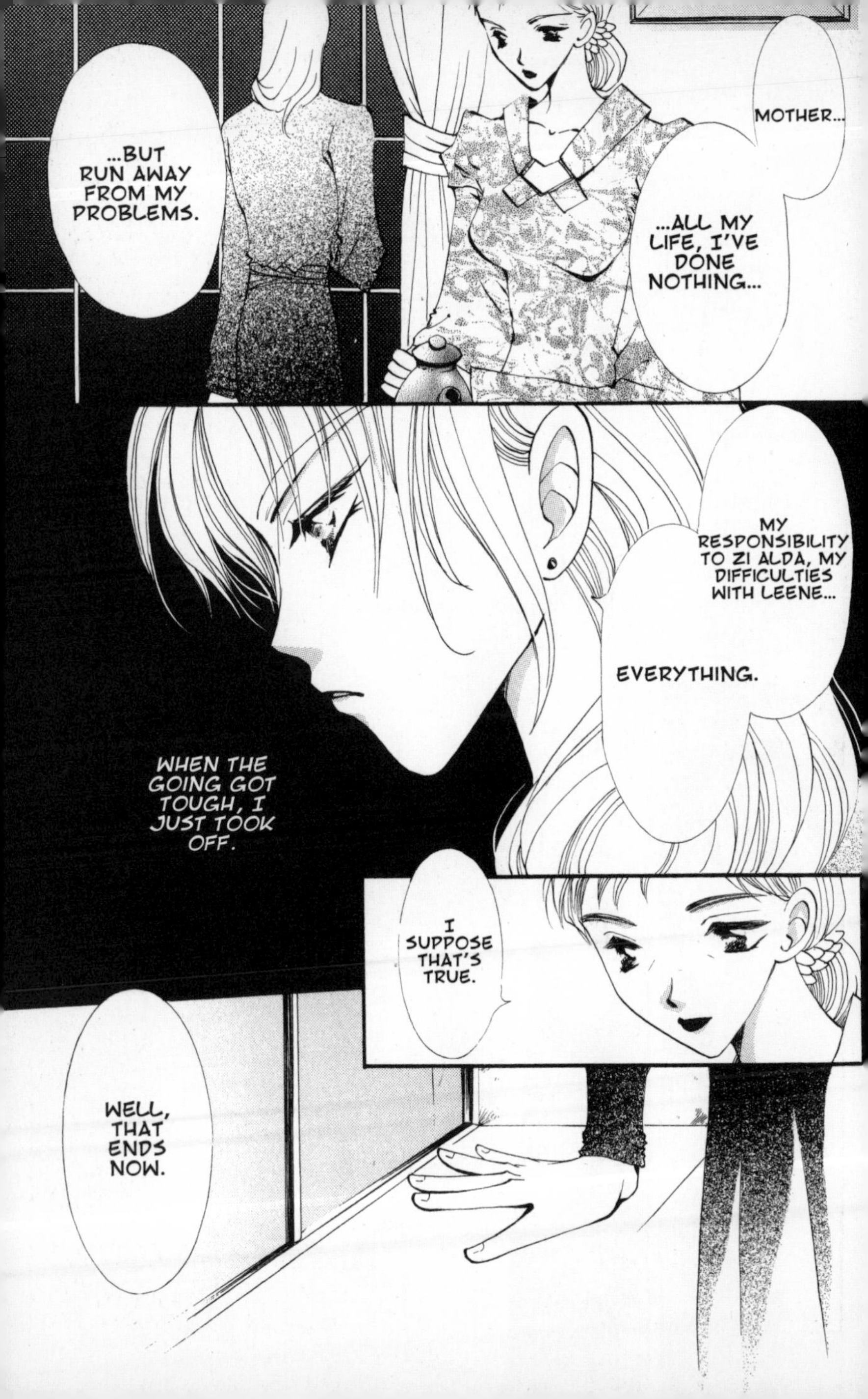
MOTHER...
...ALL MY LIFE, I'VE DONE NOTHING...
...BUT RUN AWAY FROM MY PROBLEMS.
MY RESPONSIBILITY TO ZI ALDA, MY DIFFICULTIES WITH LEENE...
EVERYTHING.
WHEN THE GOING GOT TOUGH, I JUST TOOK OFF.
I SUPPOSE THAT'S TRUE.
WELL, THAT ENDS NOW.

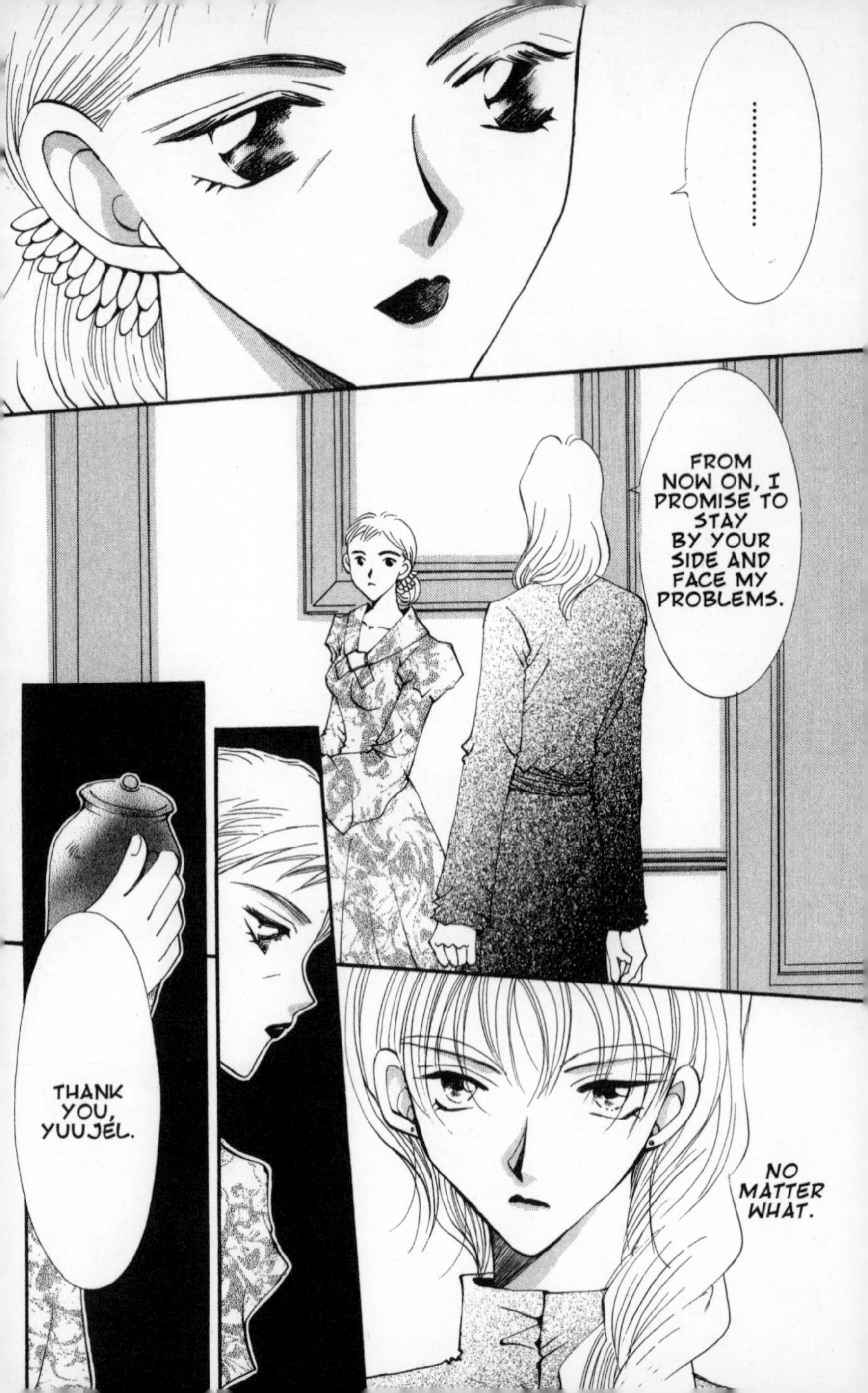
......
FROM NOW ON, I PROMISE TO STAY BY YOUR SIDE AND FACE MY PROBLEMS.
NO MATTER WHAT.
THANK YOU, YUUJÉL.

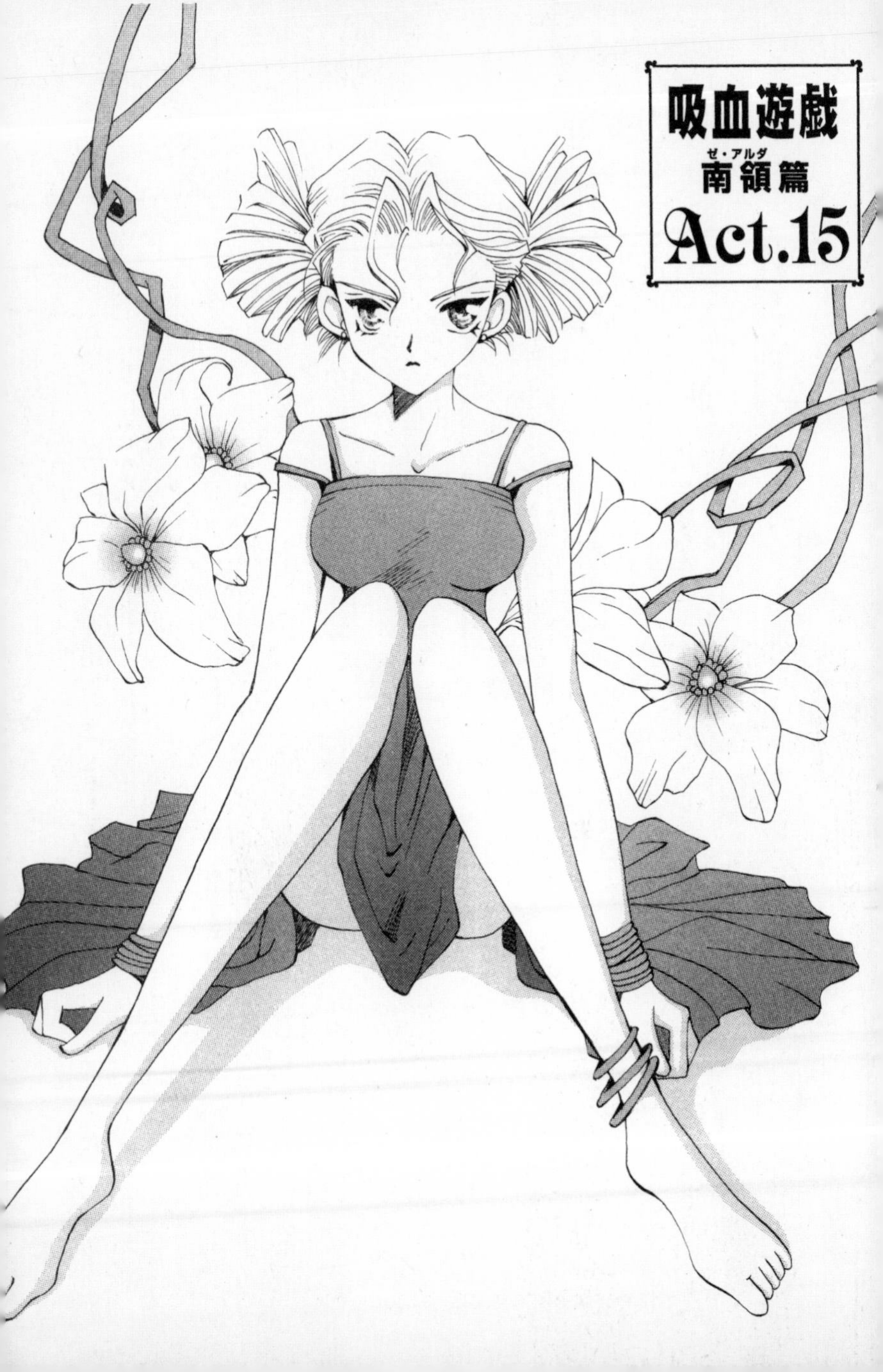
吸血遊戯
ゼ・アルダ
南領篇
Act.15

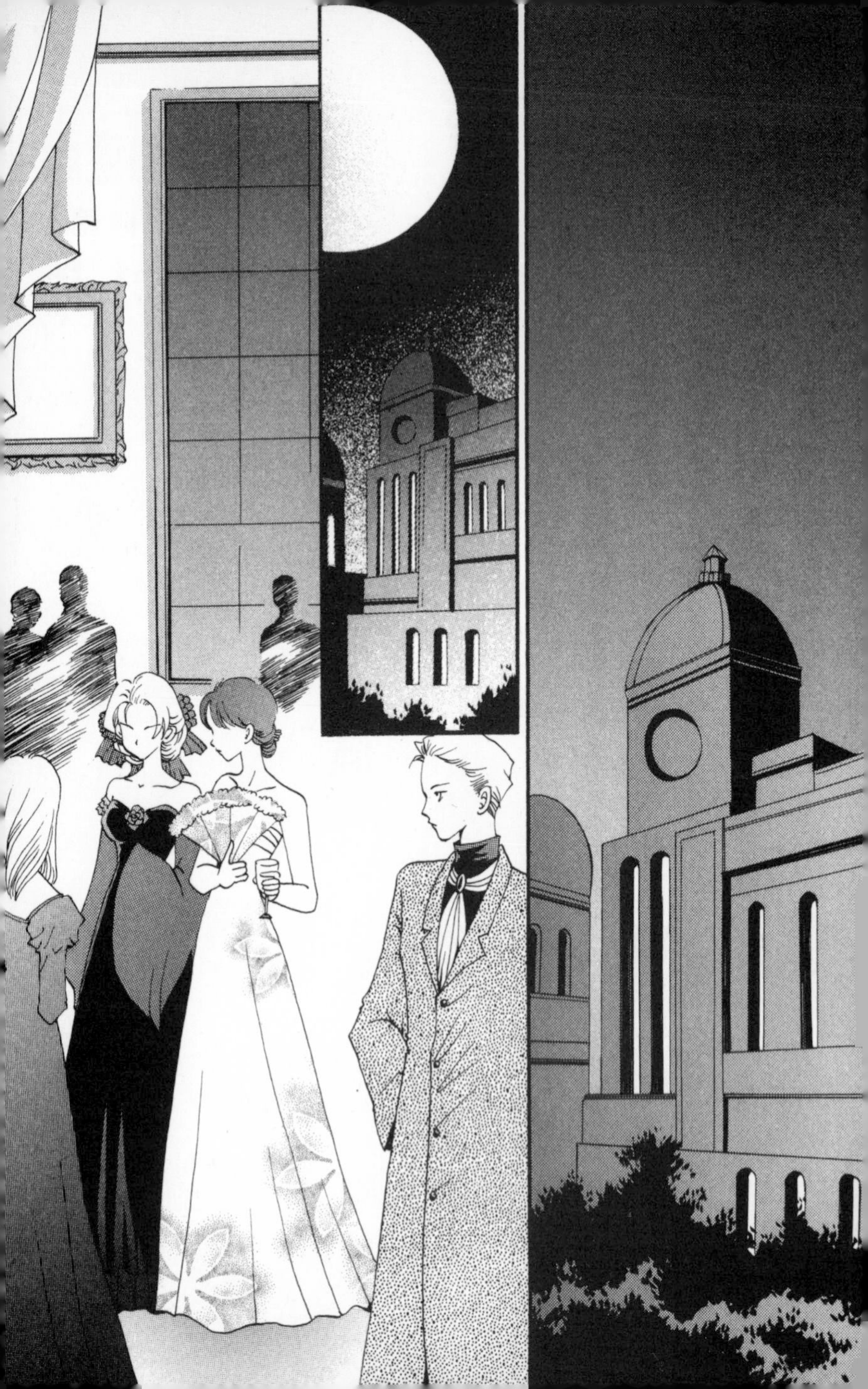

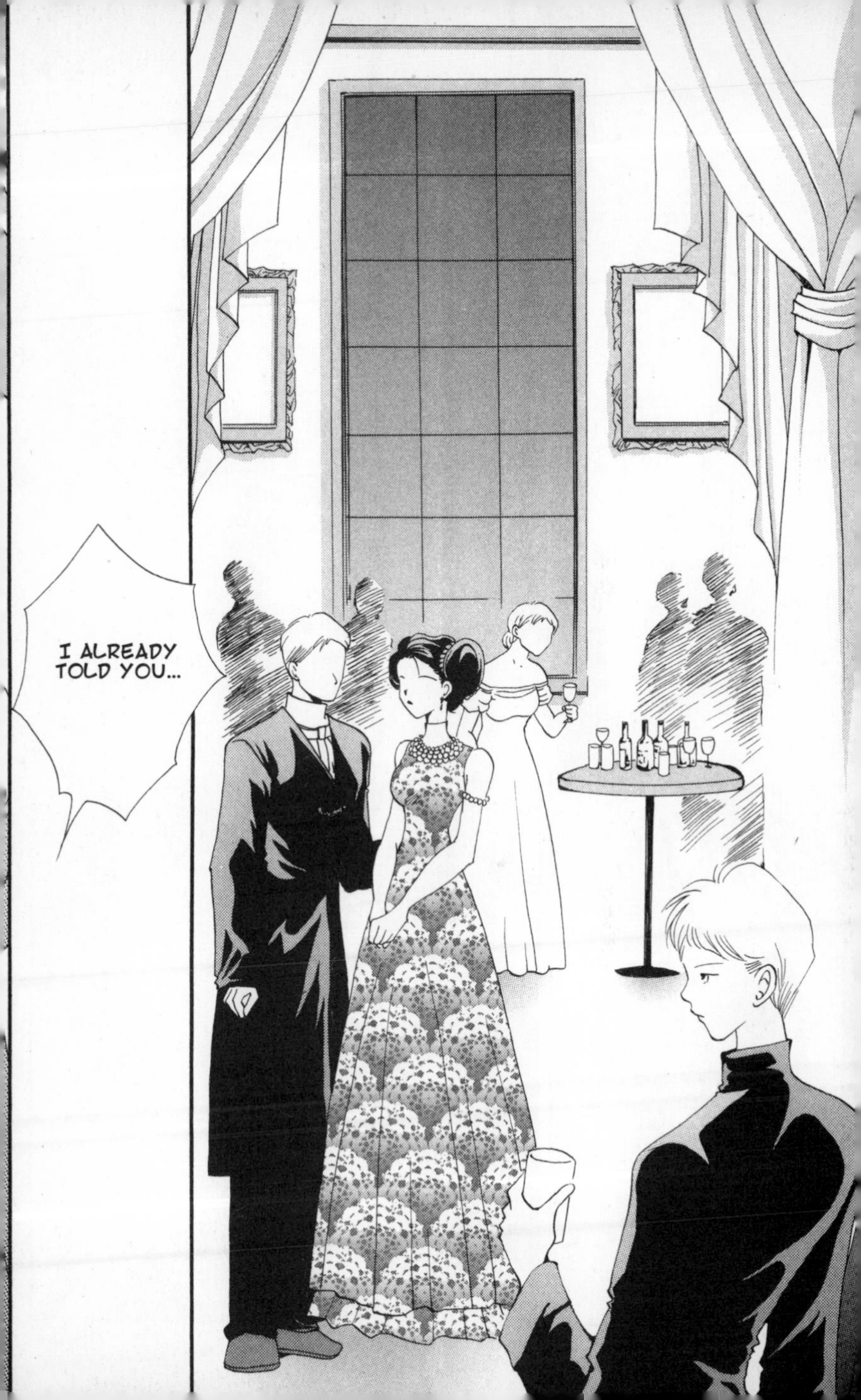
I ALREADY TOLD YOU...

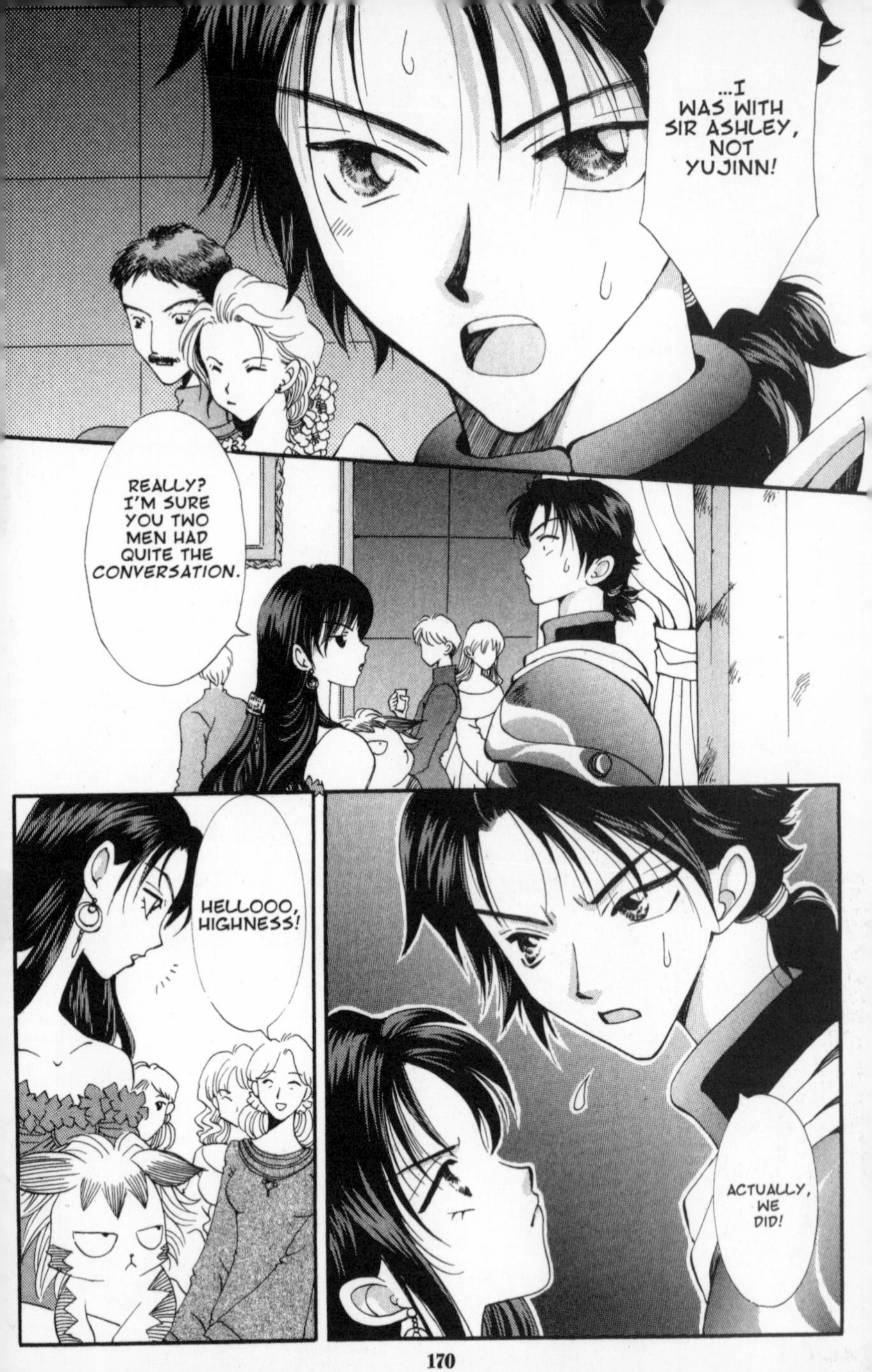
...I WAS WITH SIR ASHLEY, NOT YUJINN!
REALLY? I'M SURE YOU TWO MEN HAD QUITE THE CONVERSATION.
ACTUALLY, WE DID!
HELLOOO, HIGHNESS!

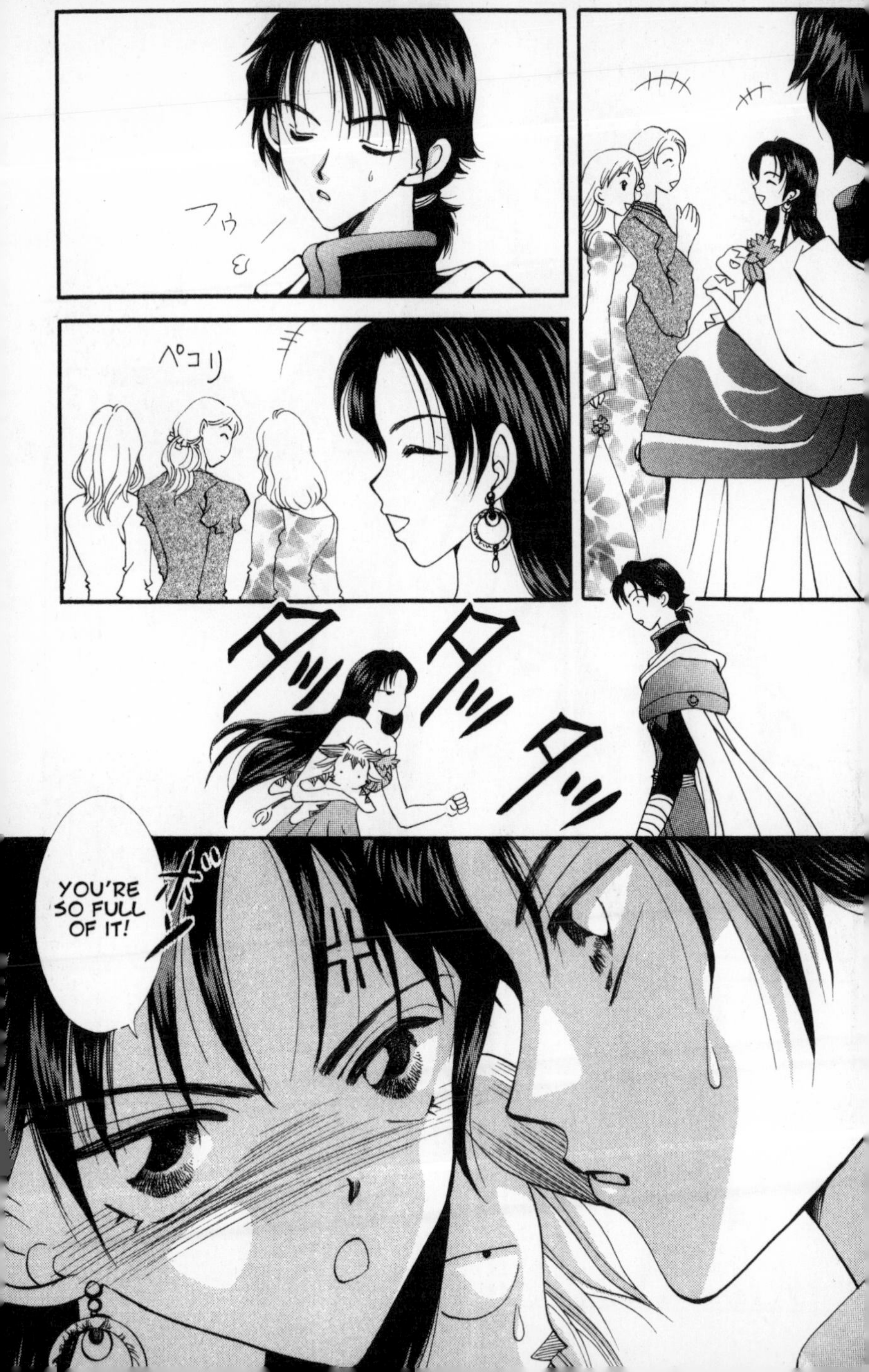
フゥ
ペコリ
タッ タッ タッ
YOU'RE SO FULL OF IT!

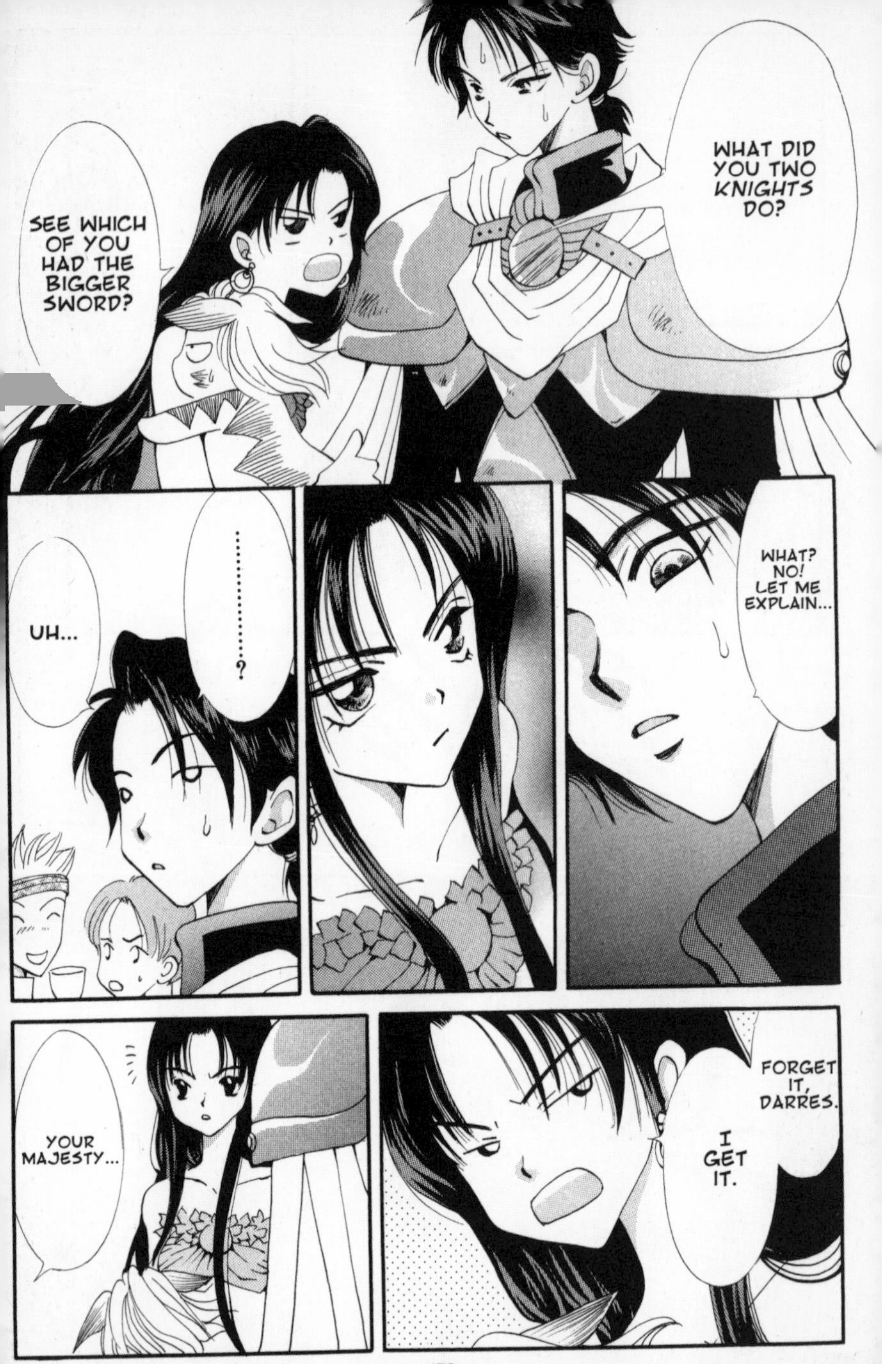
WHAT DID YOU TWO KNIGHTS DO?
SEE WHICH OF YOU HAD THE BIGGER SWORD?
WHAT? NO! LET ME EXPLAIN...
.........?
UH...
FORGET IT, DARRES.
I GET IT.
YOUR MAJESTY...

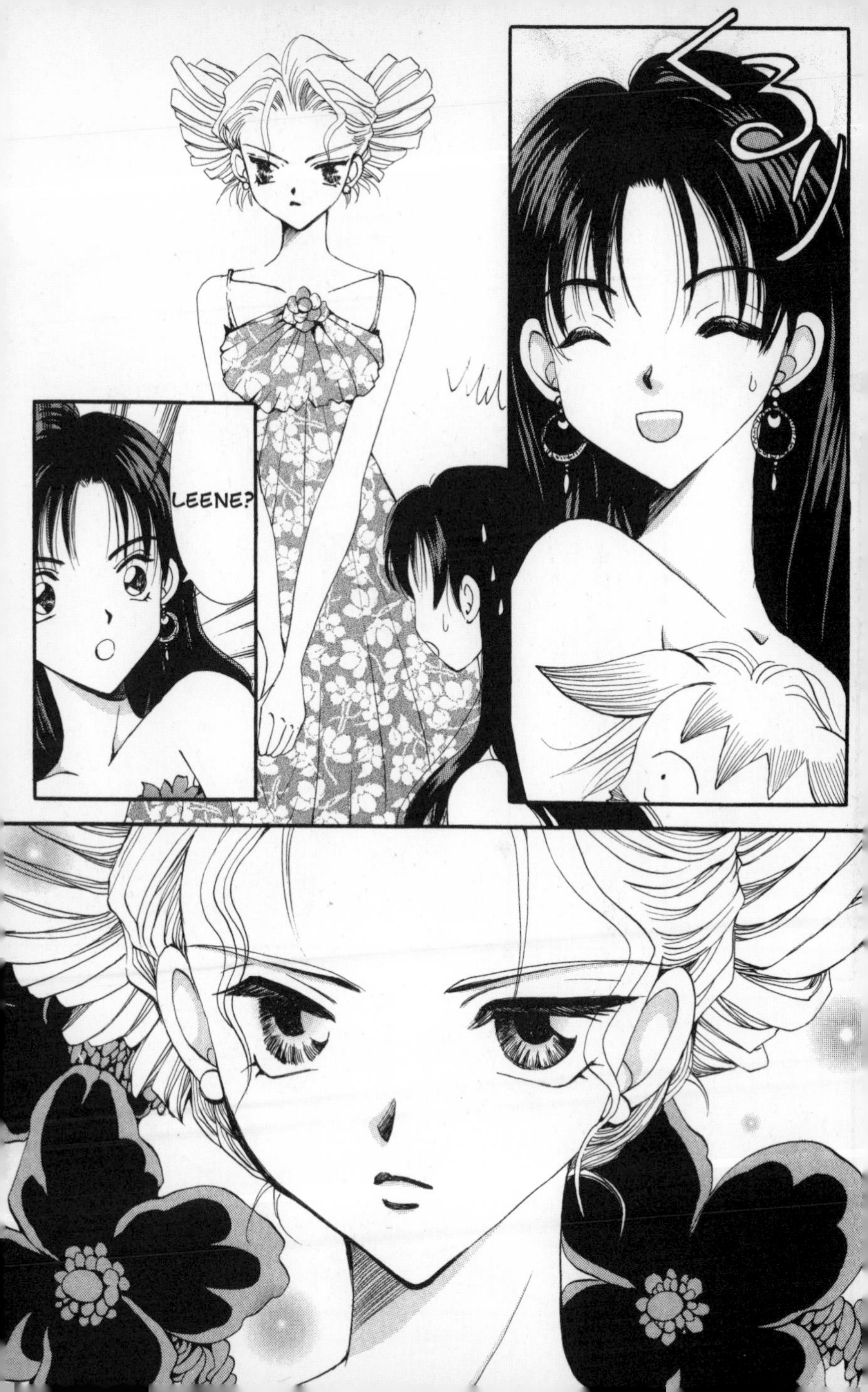
LEENE?

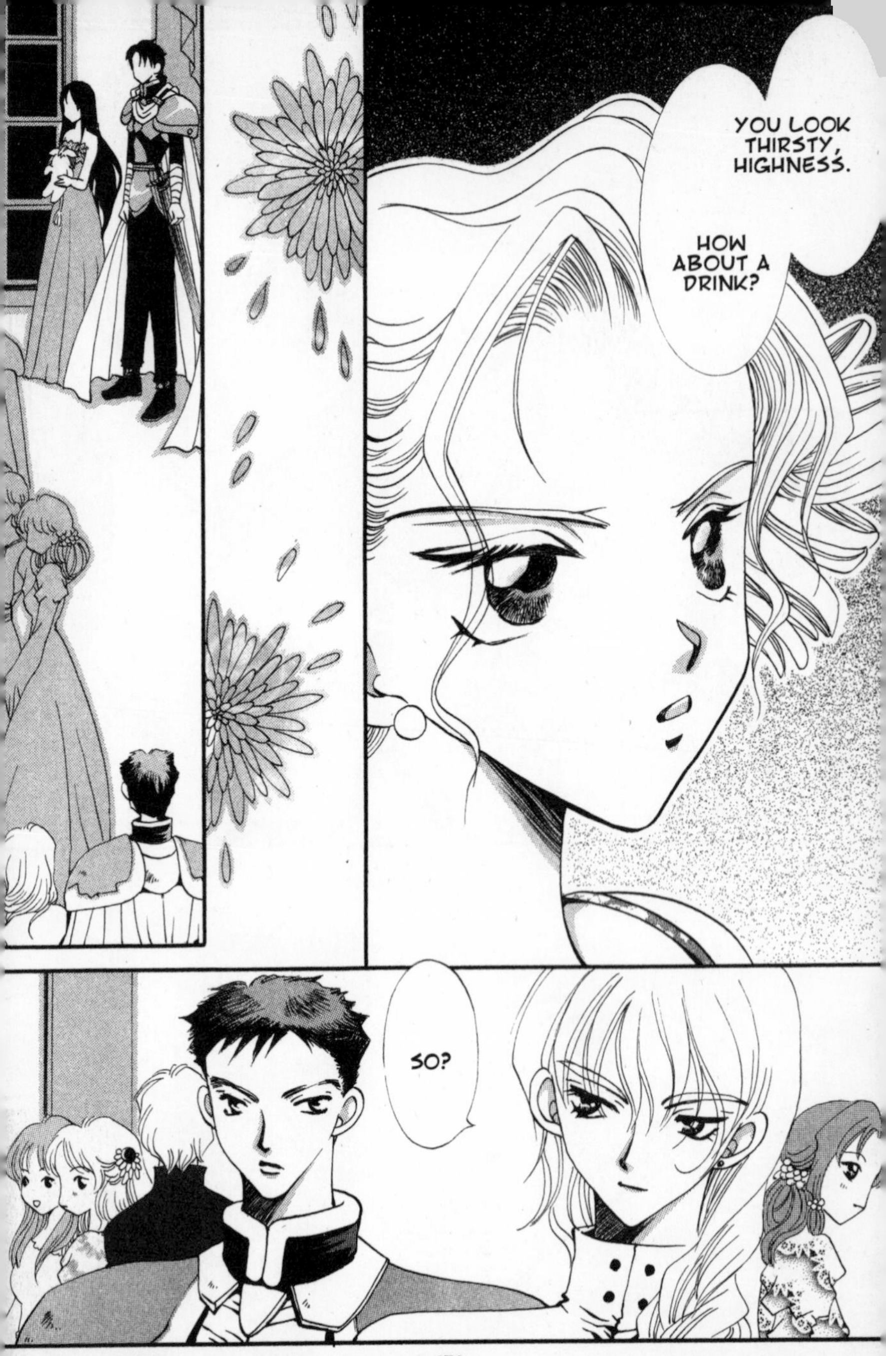
YOU LOOK THIRSTY, HIGHNESS.
HOW ABOUT A DRINK?
SO?

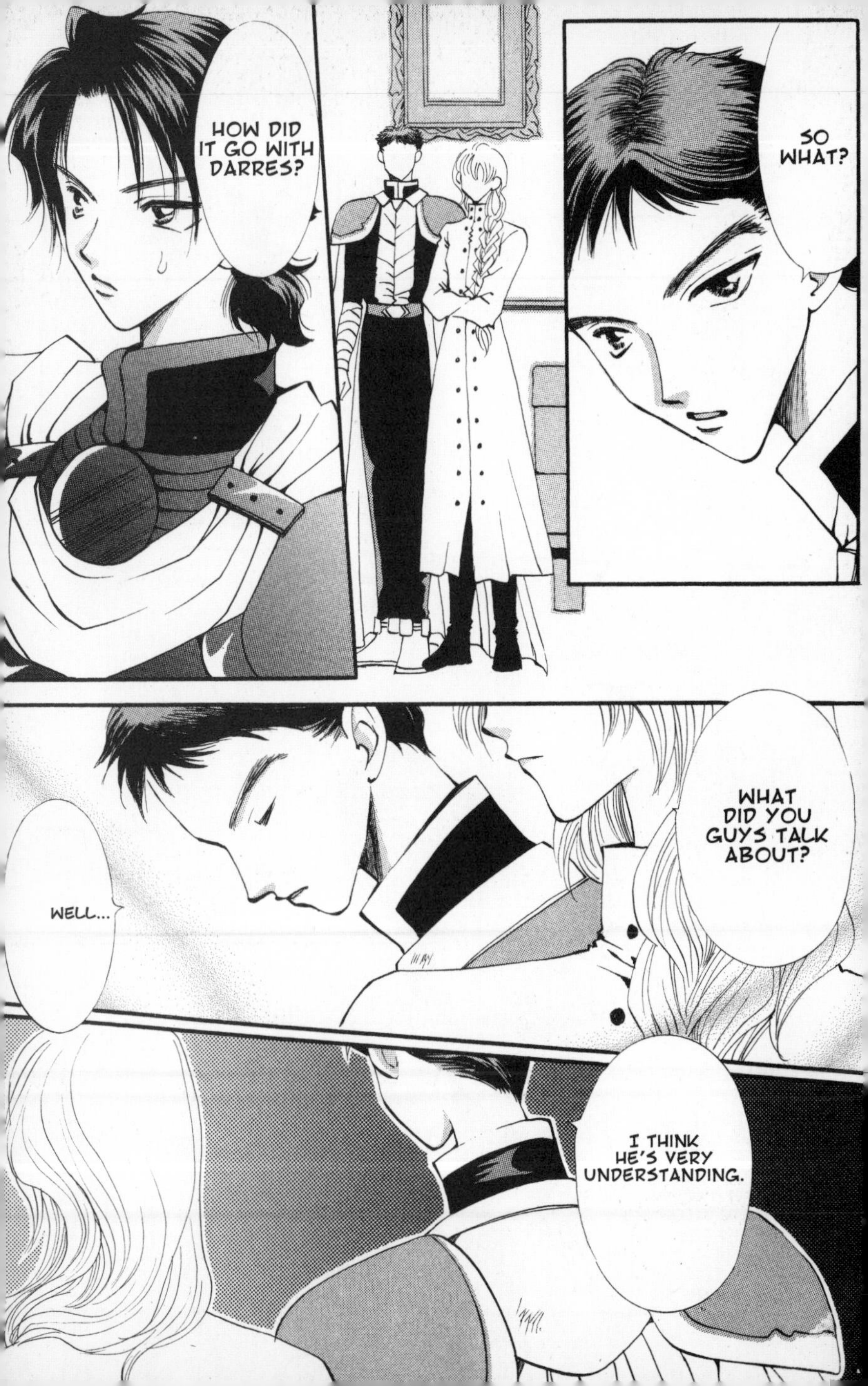
SO WHAT?
HOW DID IT GO WITH DARRES?
WHAT DID YOU GUYS TALK ABOUT?
WELL...
I THINK HE'S VERY UNDERSTANDING.

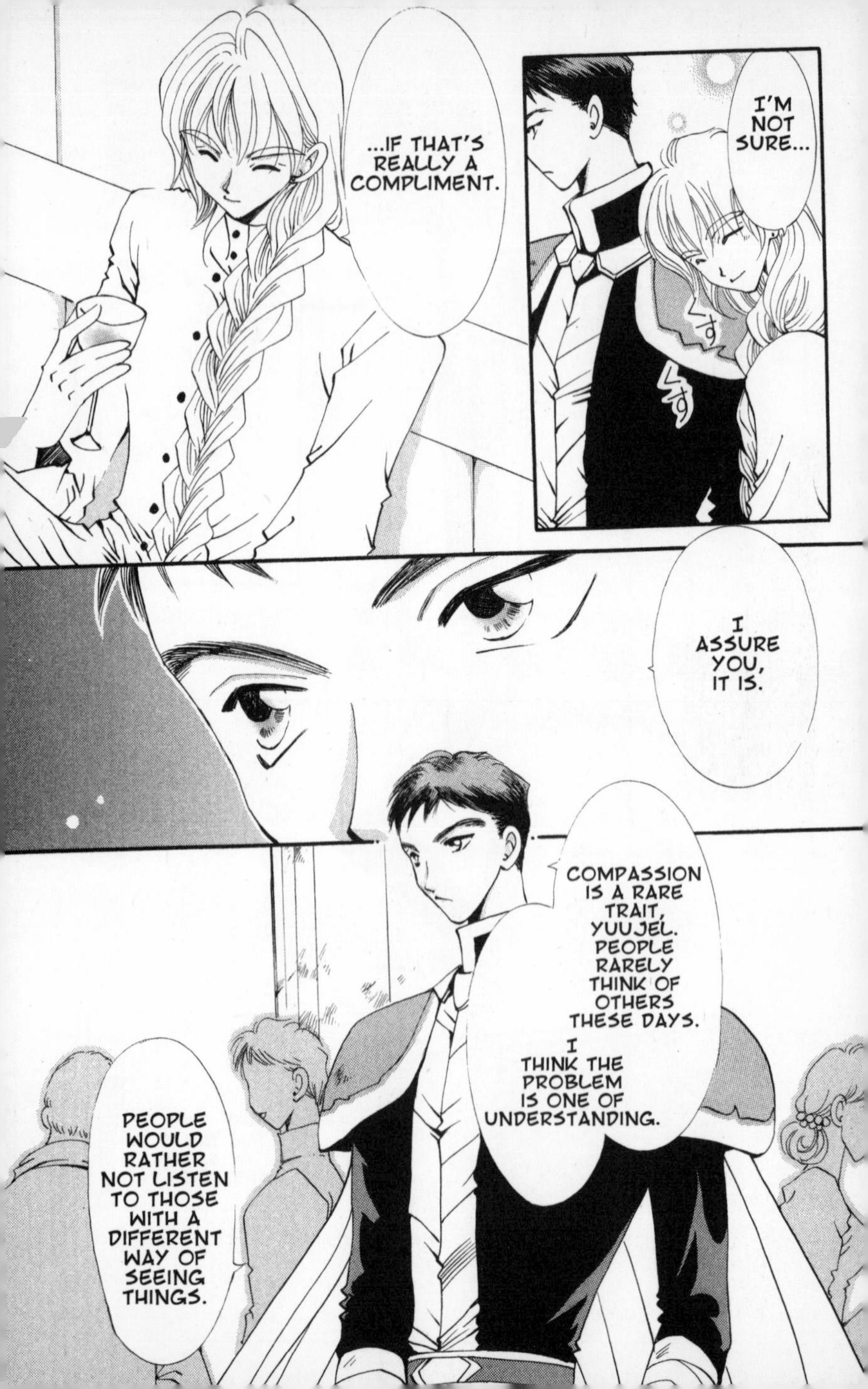
I'M NOT SURE...
くす
くす
...IF THAT'S REALLY A COMPLIMENT.
I ASSURE YOU, IT IS.
COMPASSION IS A RARE TRAIT, YUUJEL. PEOPLE RARELY THINK OF OTHERS THESE DAYS.
I THINK THE PROBLEM IS ONE OF UNDERSTANDING.
PEOPLE WOULD RATHER NOT LISTEN TO THOSE WITH A DIFFERENT WAY OF SEEING THINGS.

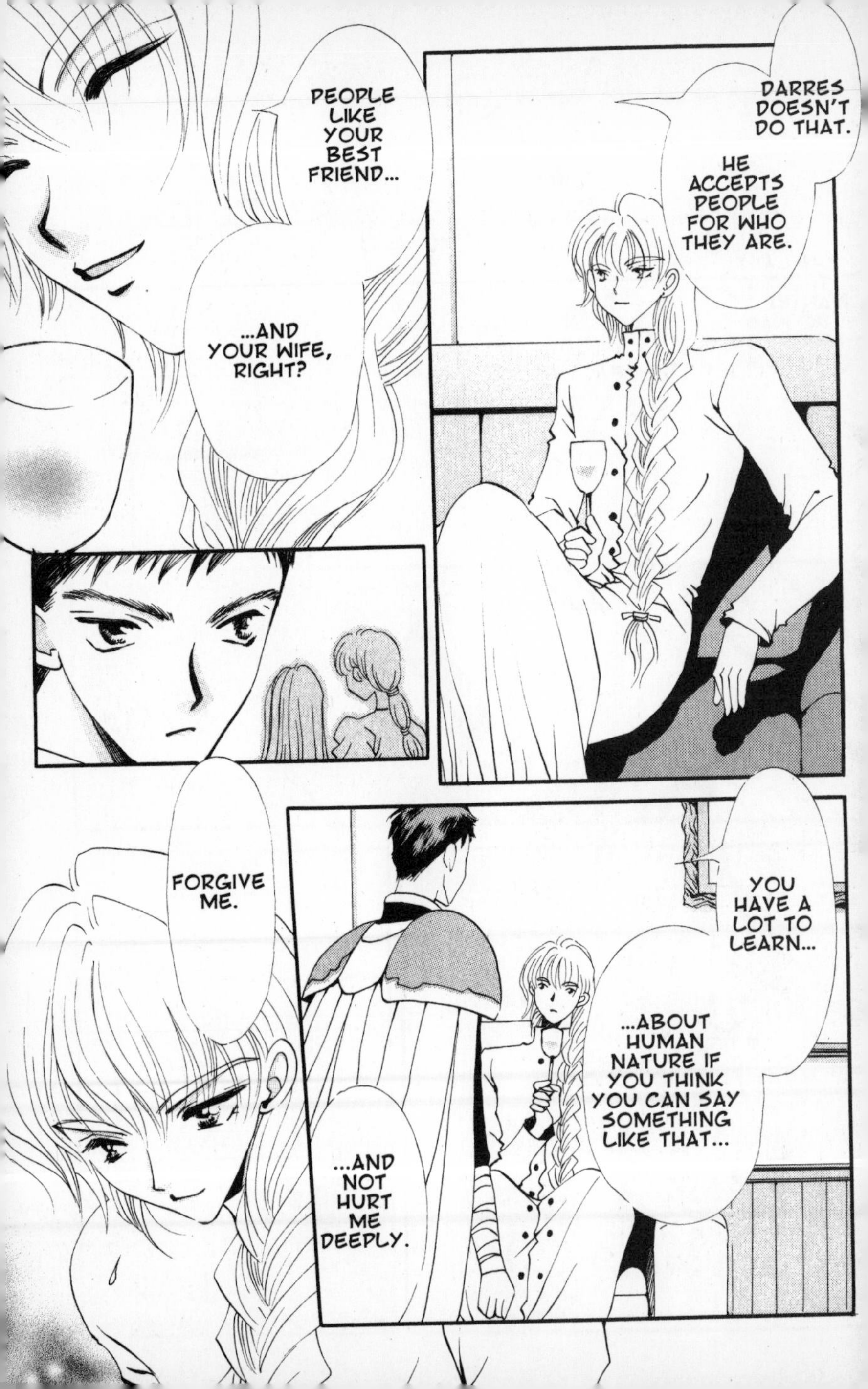
DARRES DOESN'T DO THAT.
HE ACCEPTS PEOPLE FOR WHO THEY ARE.
PEOPLE LIKE YOUR BEST FRIEND...
...AND YOUR WIFE, RIGHT?
YOU HAVE A LOT TO LEARN...
...ABOUT HUMAN NATURE IF YOU THINK YOU CAN SAY SOMETHING LIKE THAT...
...AND NOT HURT ME DEEPLY.
FORGIVE ME.

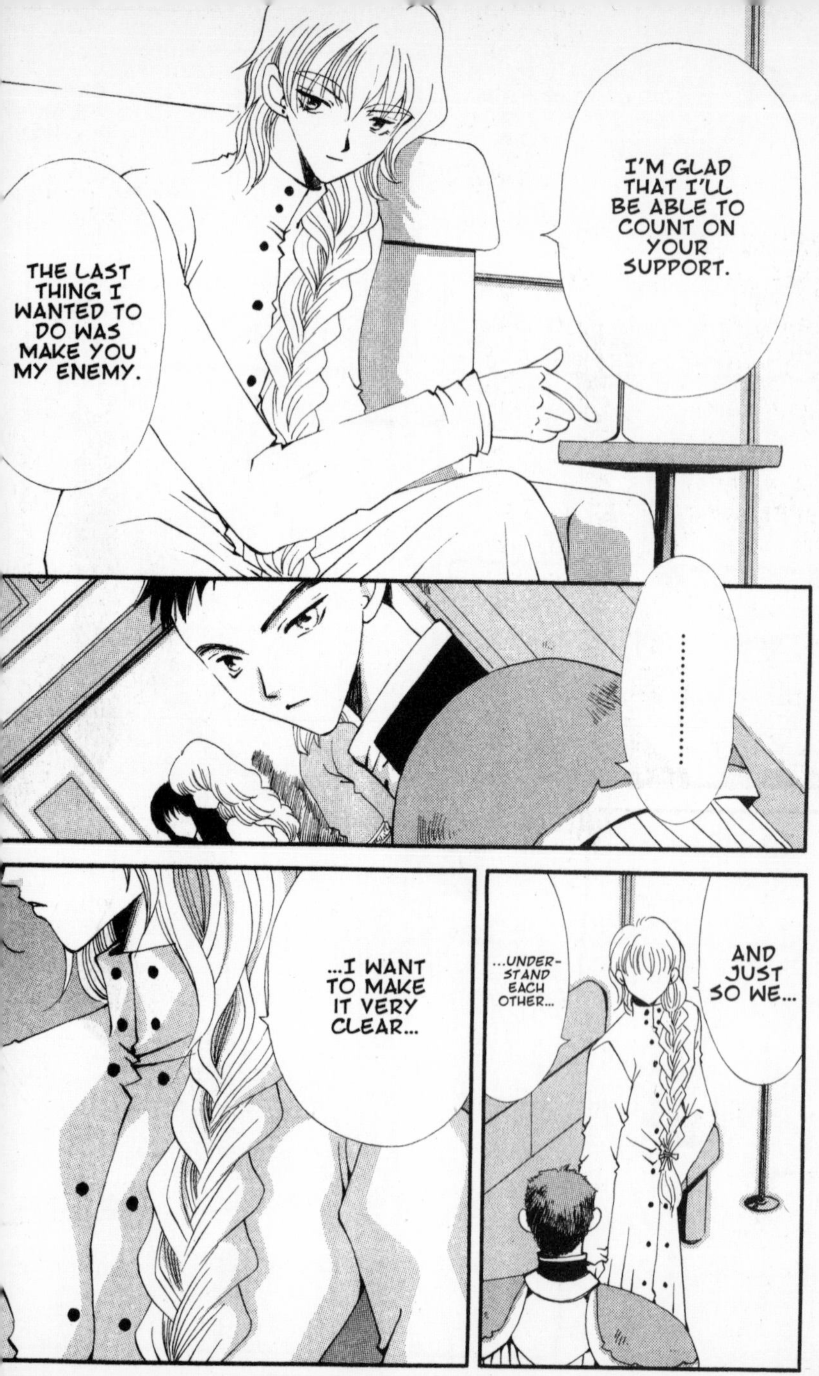
I'M GLAD THAT I'LL BE ABLE TO COUNT ON YOUR SUPPORT.
THE LAST THING I WANTED TO DO WAS MAKE YOU MY ENEMY.
....
AND JUST SO WE...
...UNDER-STAND EACH OTHER...
...I WANT TO MAKE IT VERY CLEAR...

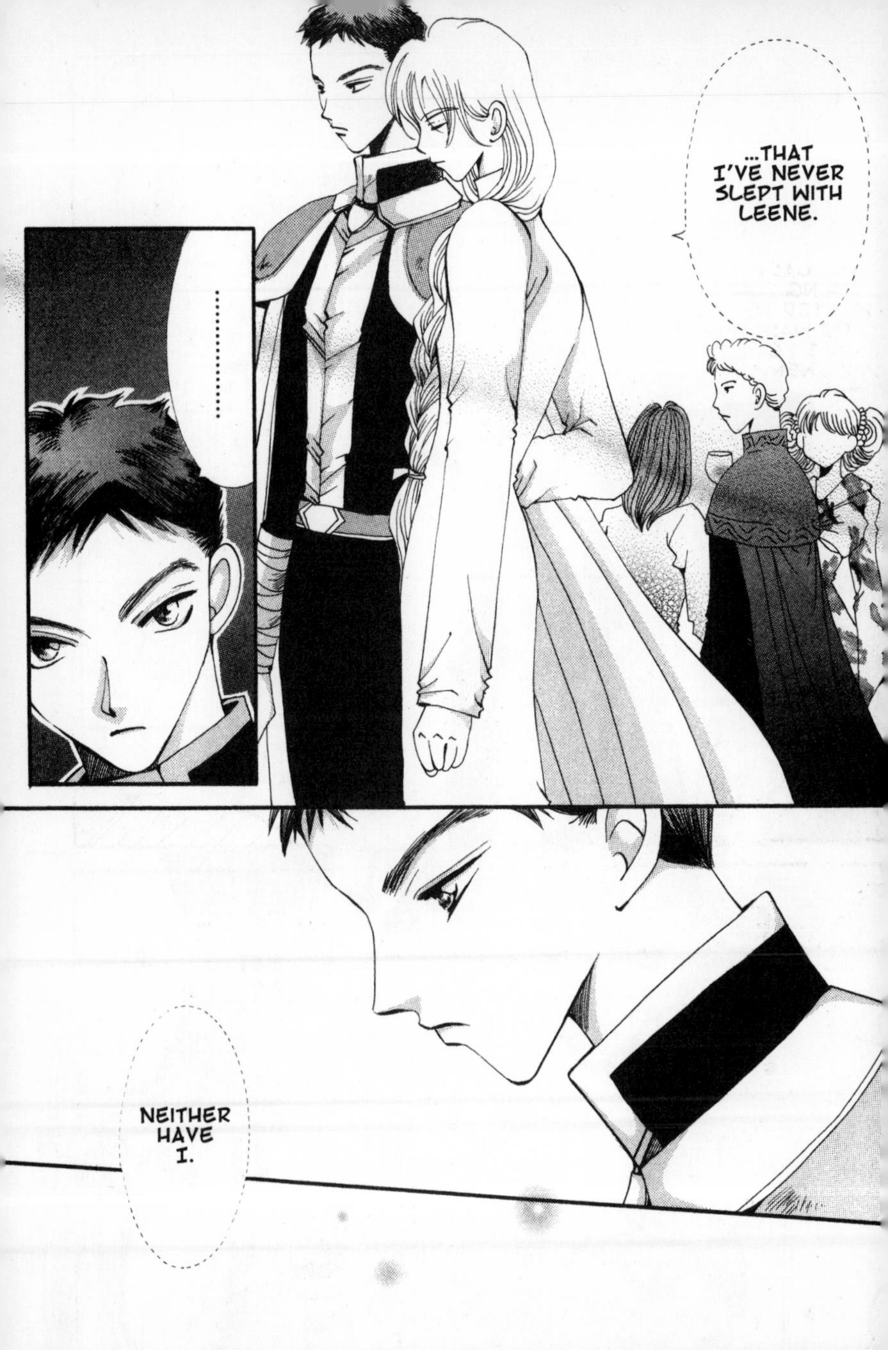
...THAT I'VE NEVER SLEPT WITH LEENE.
......
NEITHER HAVE I.

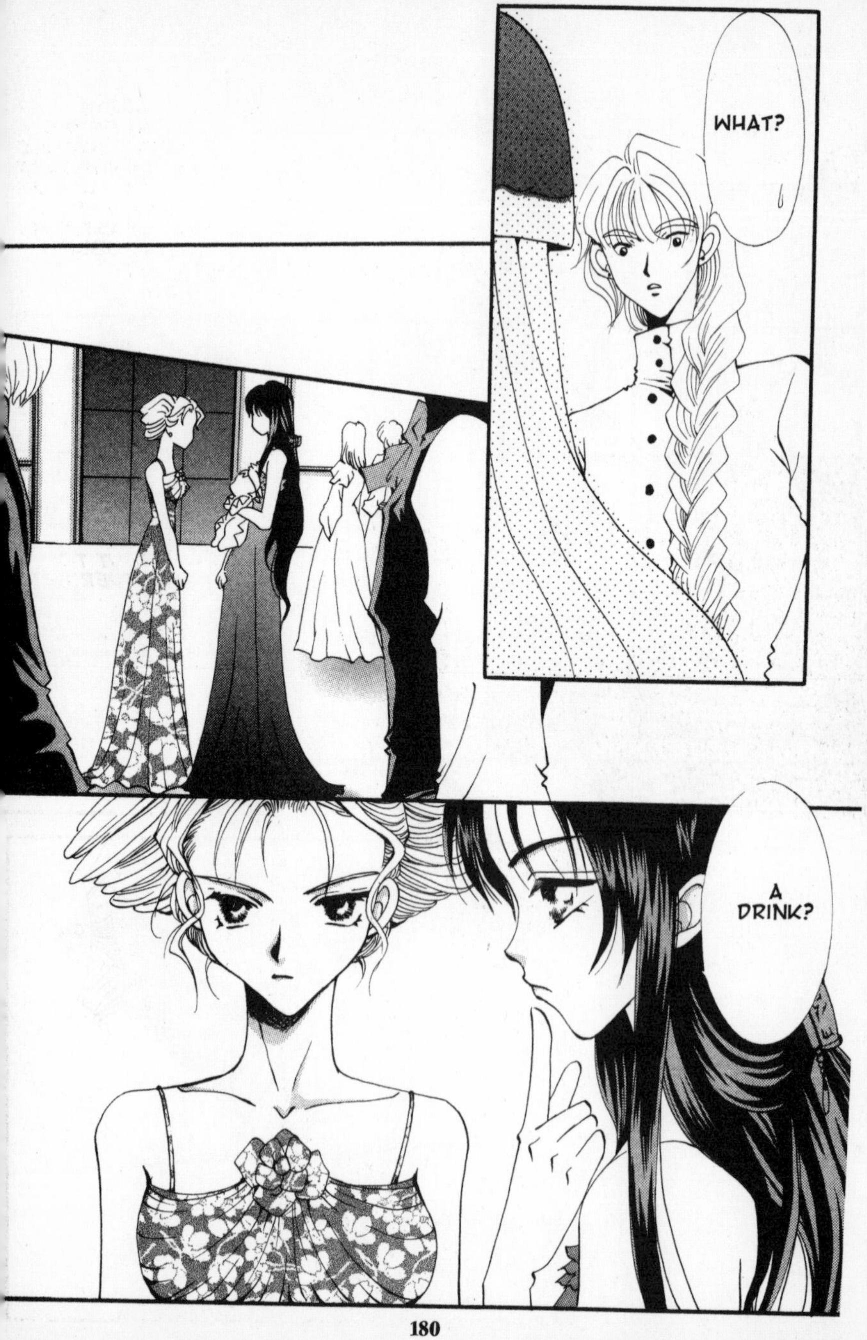
WHAT?
A DRINK?

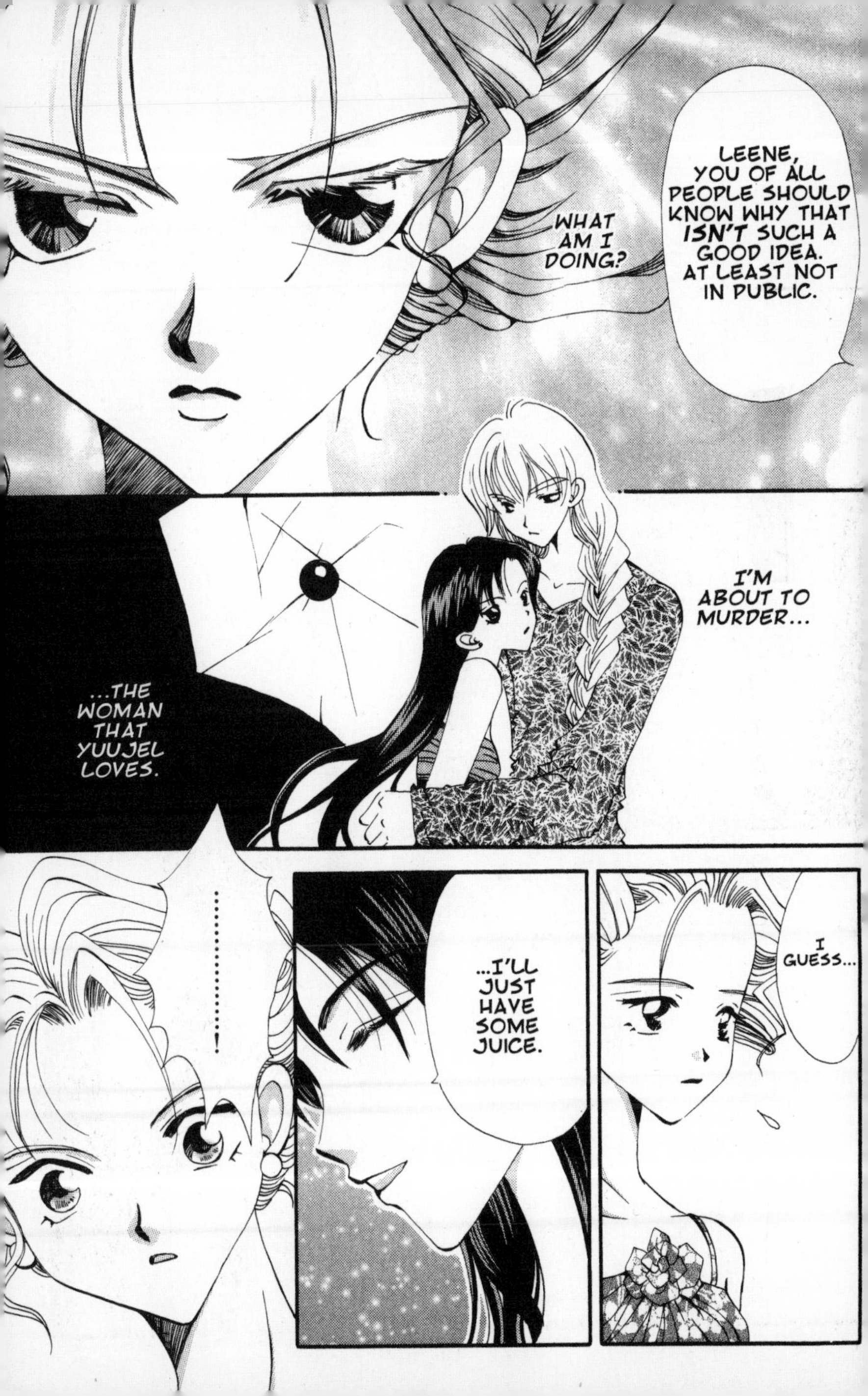
LEENE, YOU OF ALL PEOPLE SHOULD KNOW WHY THAT ISN'T SUCH A GOOD IDEA. AT LEAST NOT IN PUBLIC.
WHAT AM I DOING?
I'M ABOUT TO MURDER...
...THE WOMAN THAT YUUJEL LOVES.
I GUESS...
...I'LL JUST HAVE SOME JUICE.
......!

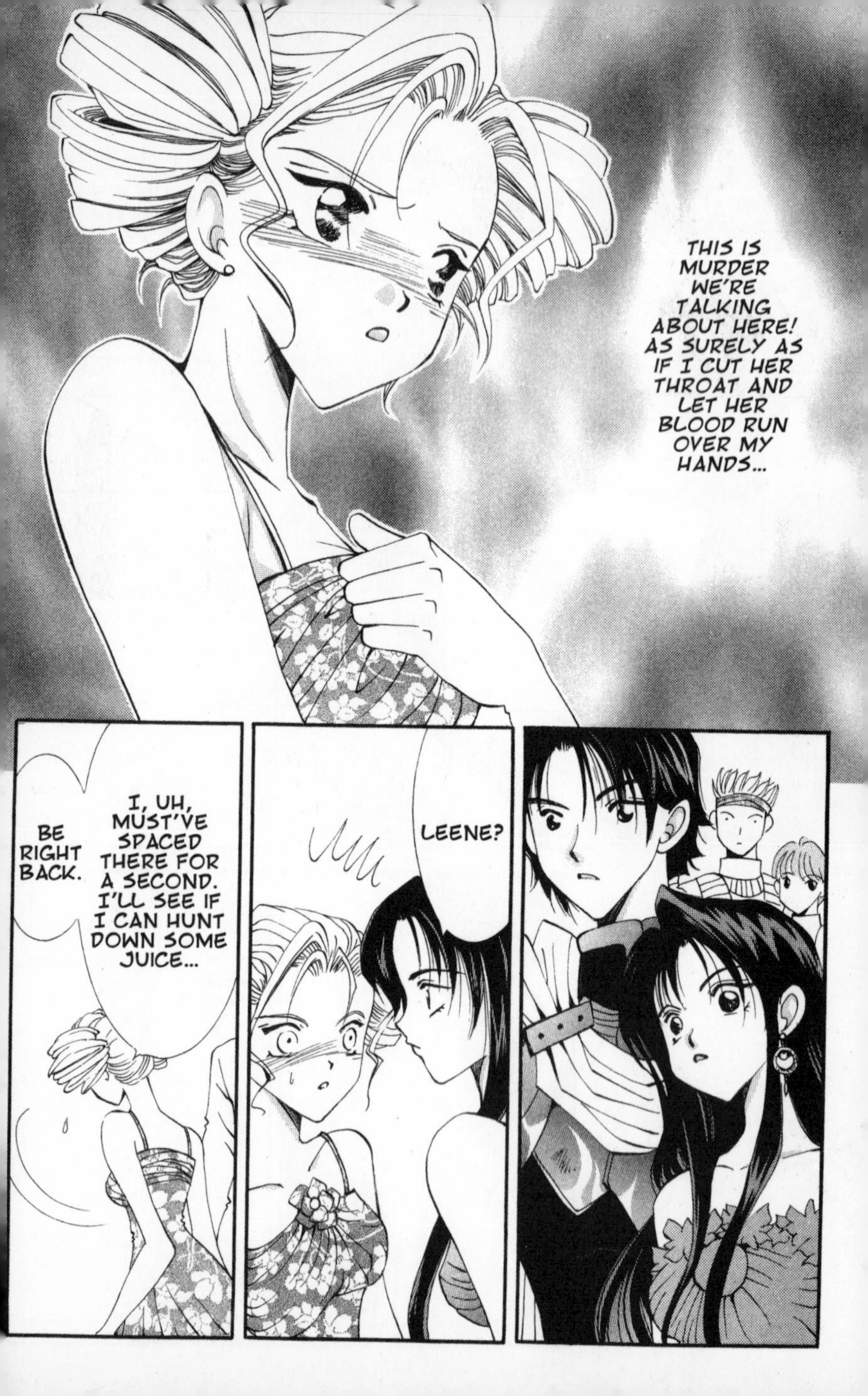
THIS IS MURDER WE'RE TALKING ABOUT HERE! AS SURELY AS IF I CUT HER THROAT AND LET HER BLOOD RUN OVER MY HANDS...
LEENE?
I, UH, MUST'VE SPACED THERE FOR A SECOND. I'LL SEE IF I CAN HUNT DOWN SOME JUICE...
BE RIGHT BACK.

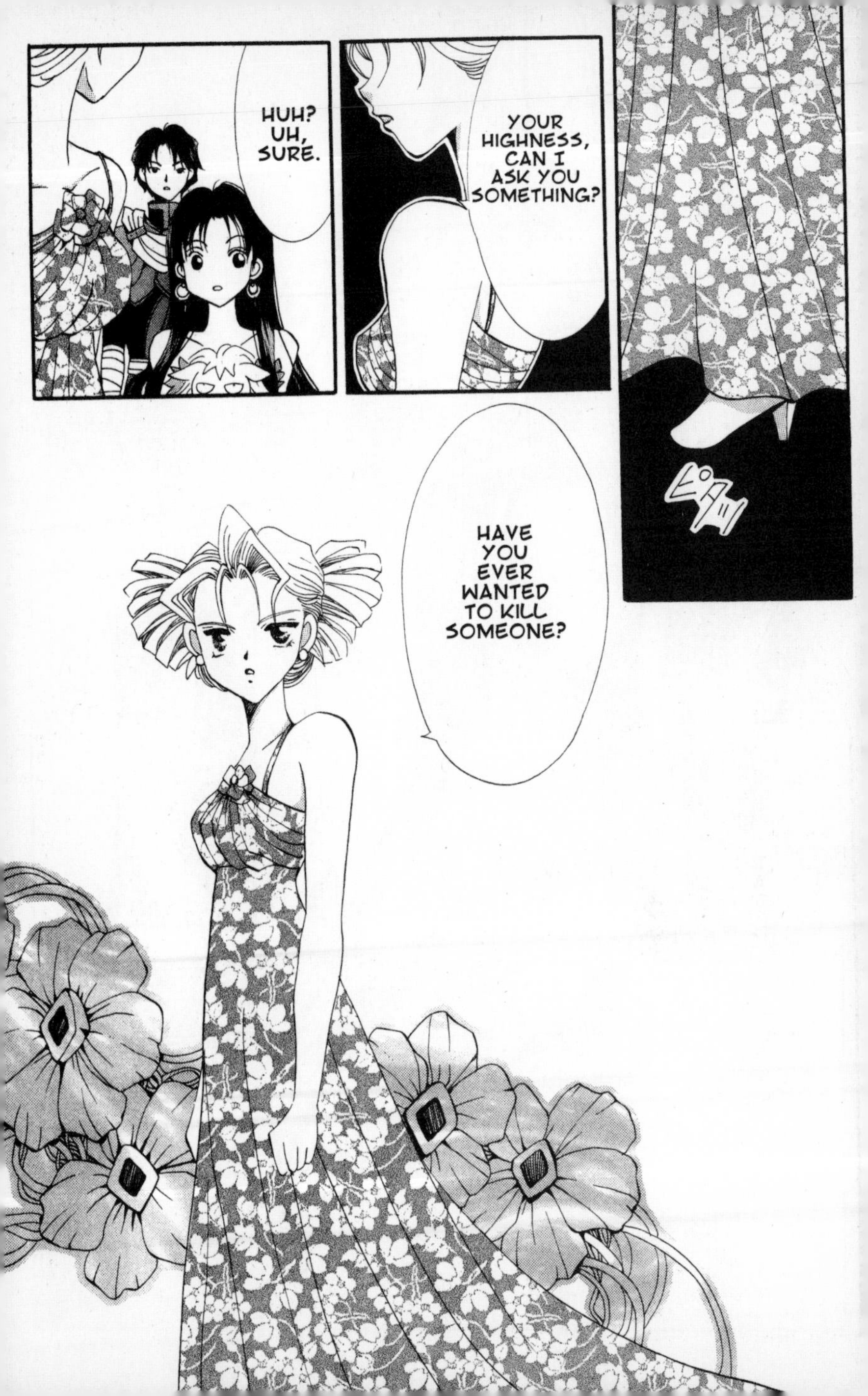
YOUR HIGHNESS, CAN I ASK YOU SOMETHING?
HUH? UH, SURE.
HAVE YOU EVER WANTED TO KILL SOMEONE?

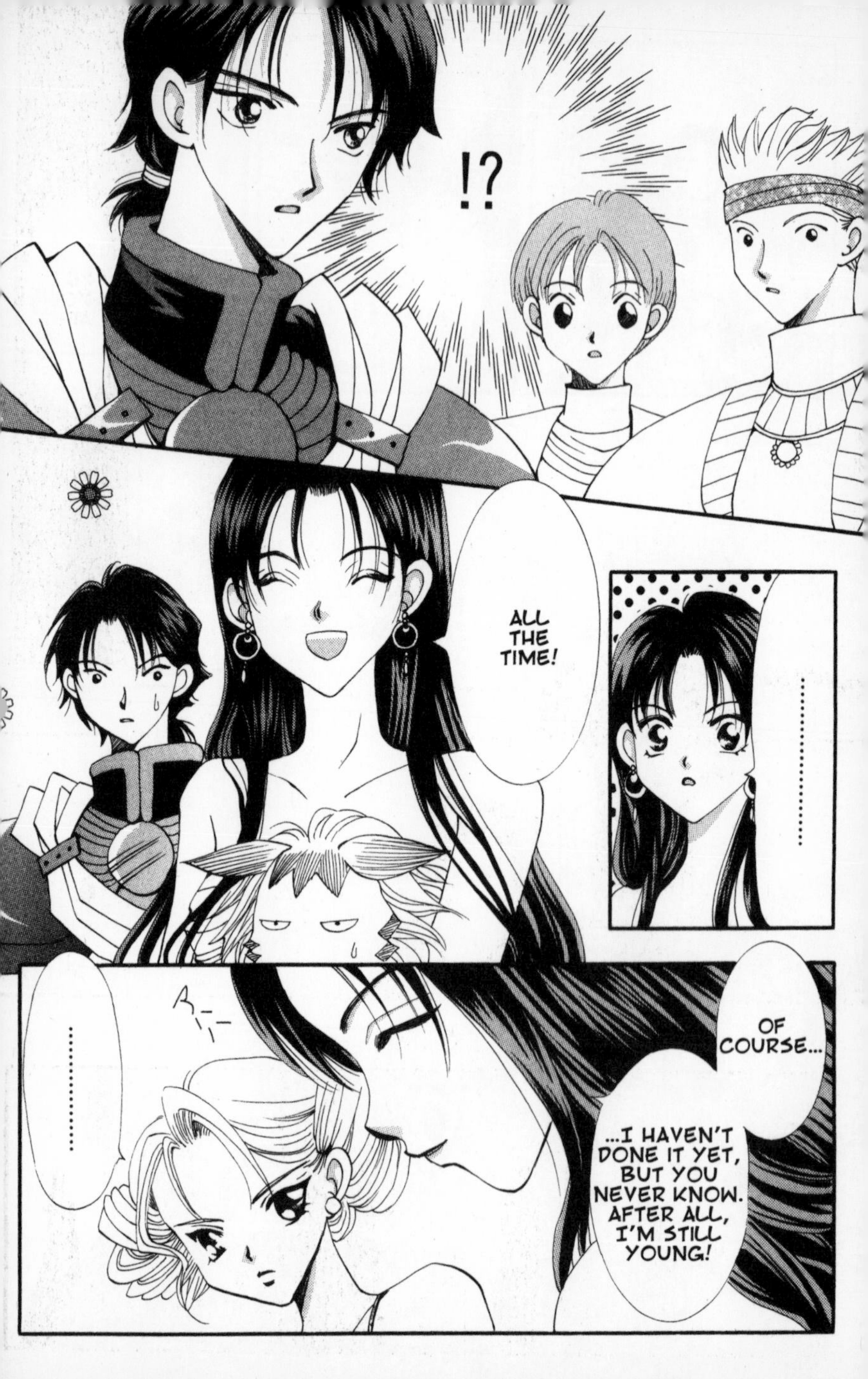
!?
......
ALL THE TIME!
OF COURSE...
...I HAVEN'T DONE IT YET, BUT YOU NEVER KNOW. AFTER ALL, I'M STILL YOUNG!
......

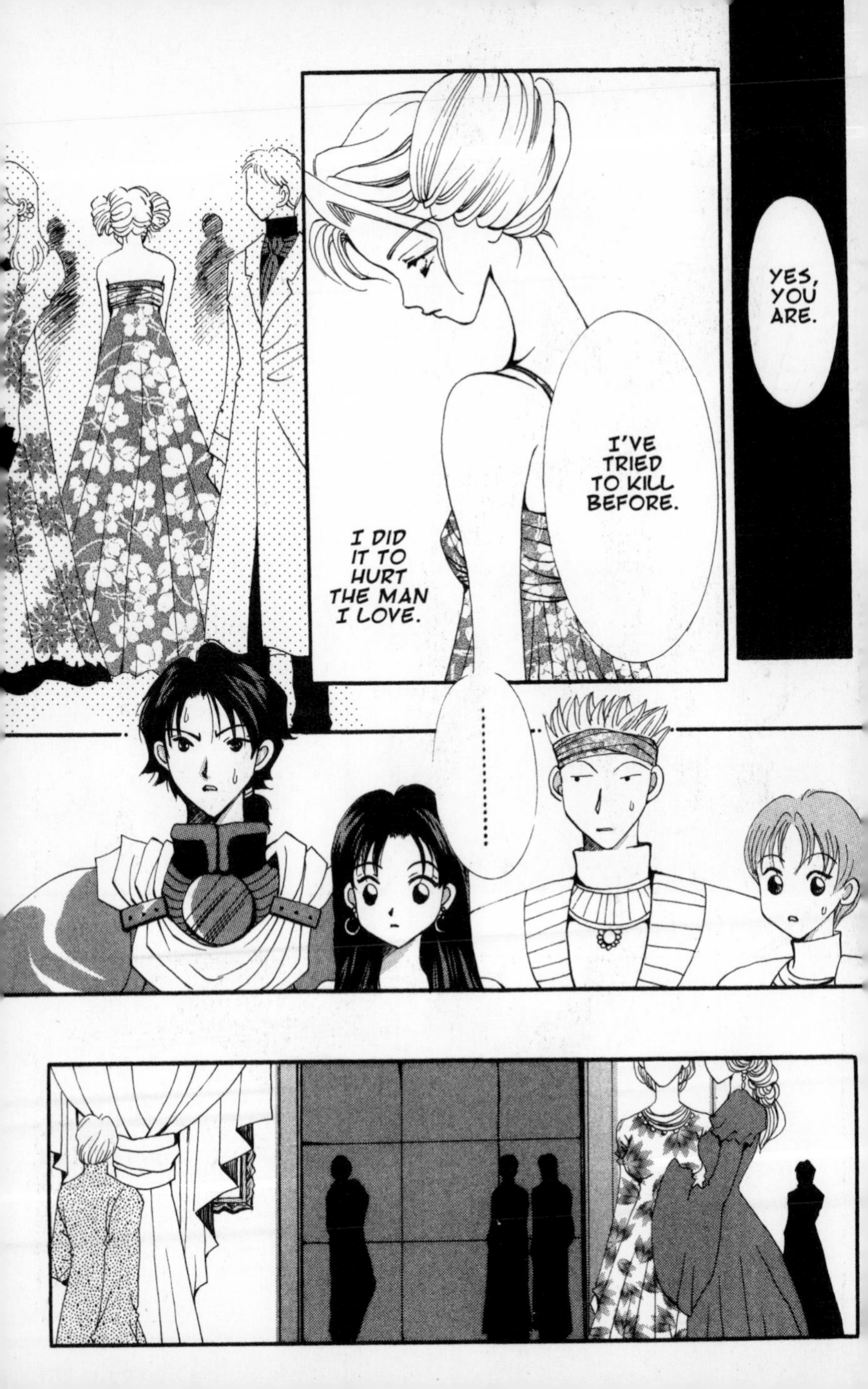
YES, YOU ARE.
I'VE TRIED TO KILL BEFORE.
I DID IT TO HURT THE MAN I LOVE.
......

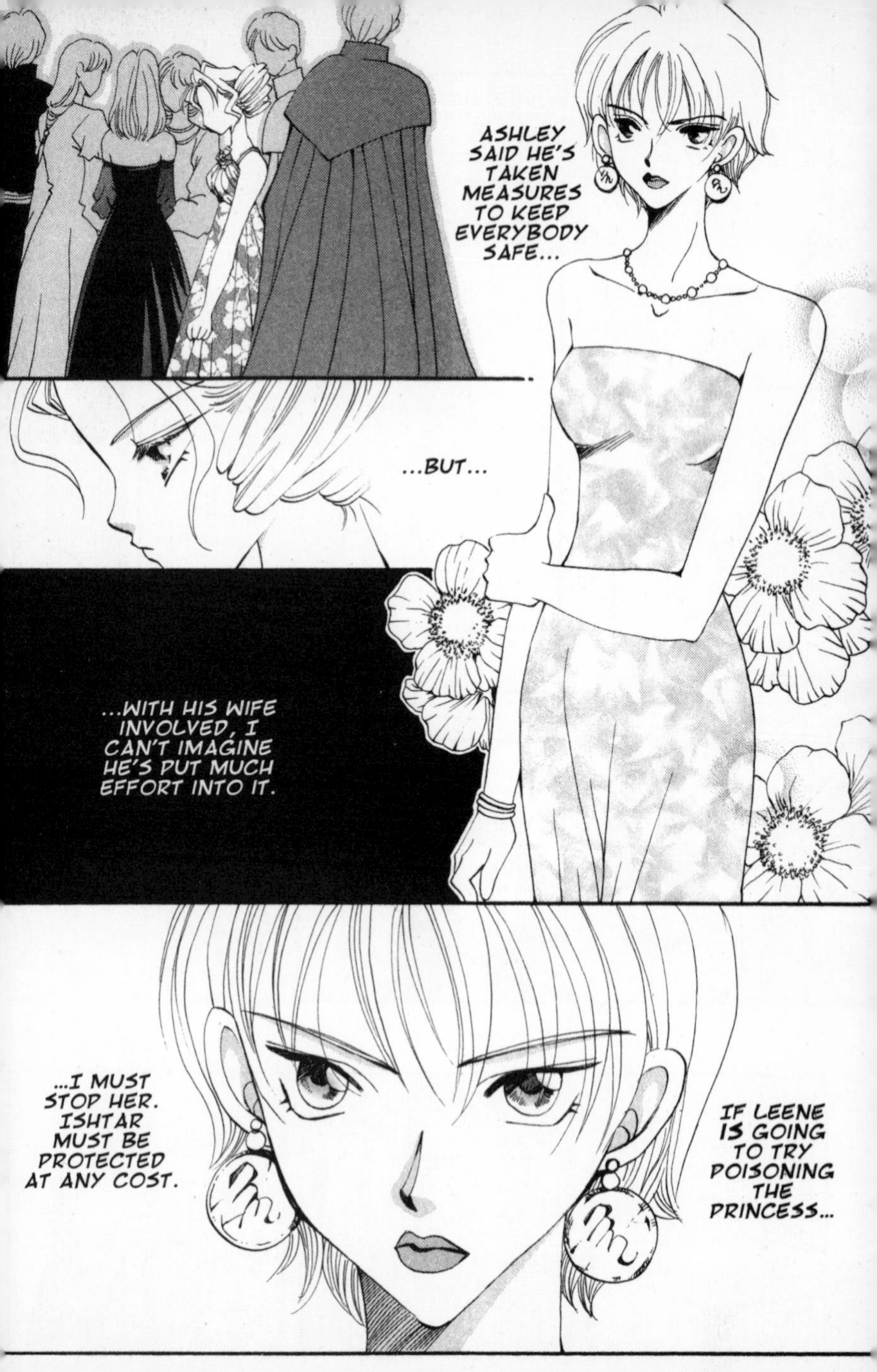

ASHLEY SAID HE'S TAKEN MEASURES TO KEEP EVERYBODY SAFE...
...BUT...
...WITH HIS WIFE INVOLVED, I CAN'T IMAGINE HE'S PUT MUCH EFFORT INTO IT.
IF LEENE IS GOING TO TRY POISONING THE PRINCESS...
...I MUST STOP HER. ISHTAR MUST BE PROTECTED AT ANY COST.

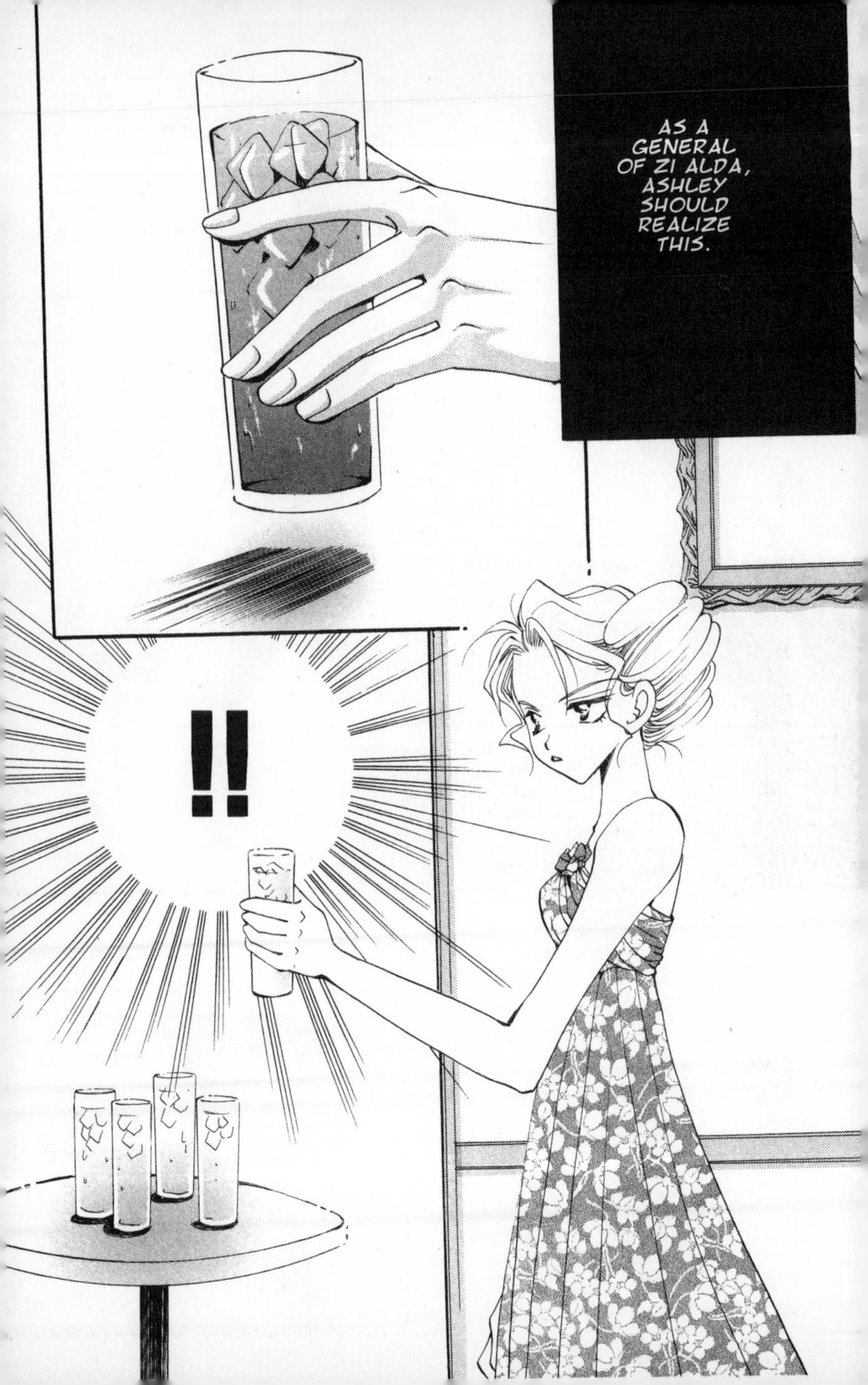
AS A GENERAL OF ZI ALDA, ASHLEY SHOULD REALIZE THIS.
!!

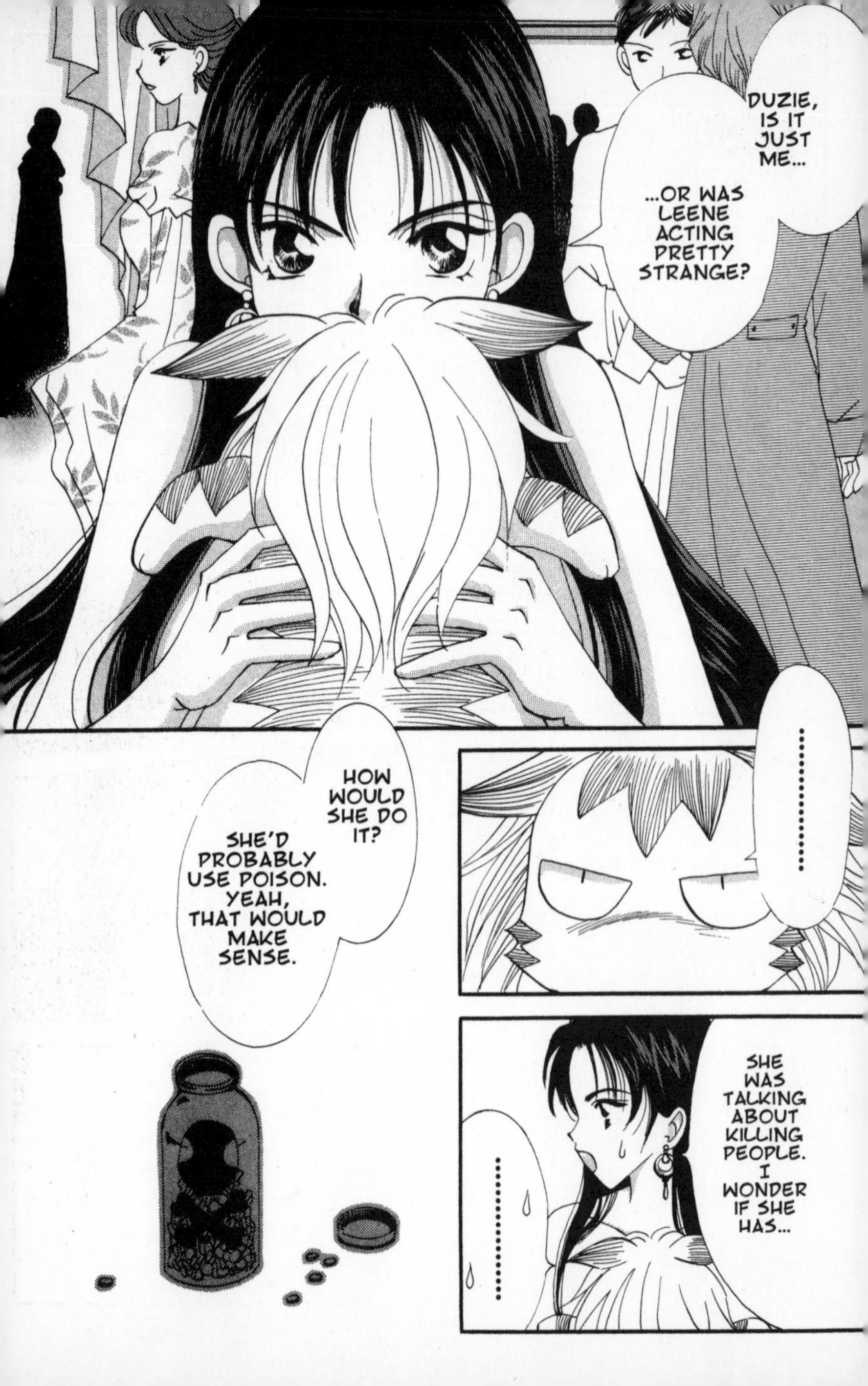
DUZIE, IS IT JUST ME...
...OR WAS LEENE ACTING PRETTY STRANGE?
......
SHE WAS TALKING ABOUT KILLING PEOPLE. I WONDER IF SHE HAS...
......
HOW WOULD SHE DO IT?
SHE'D PROBABLY USE POISON. YEAH, THAT WOULD MAKE SENSE.

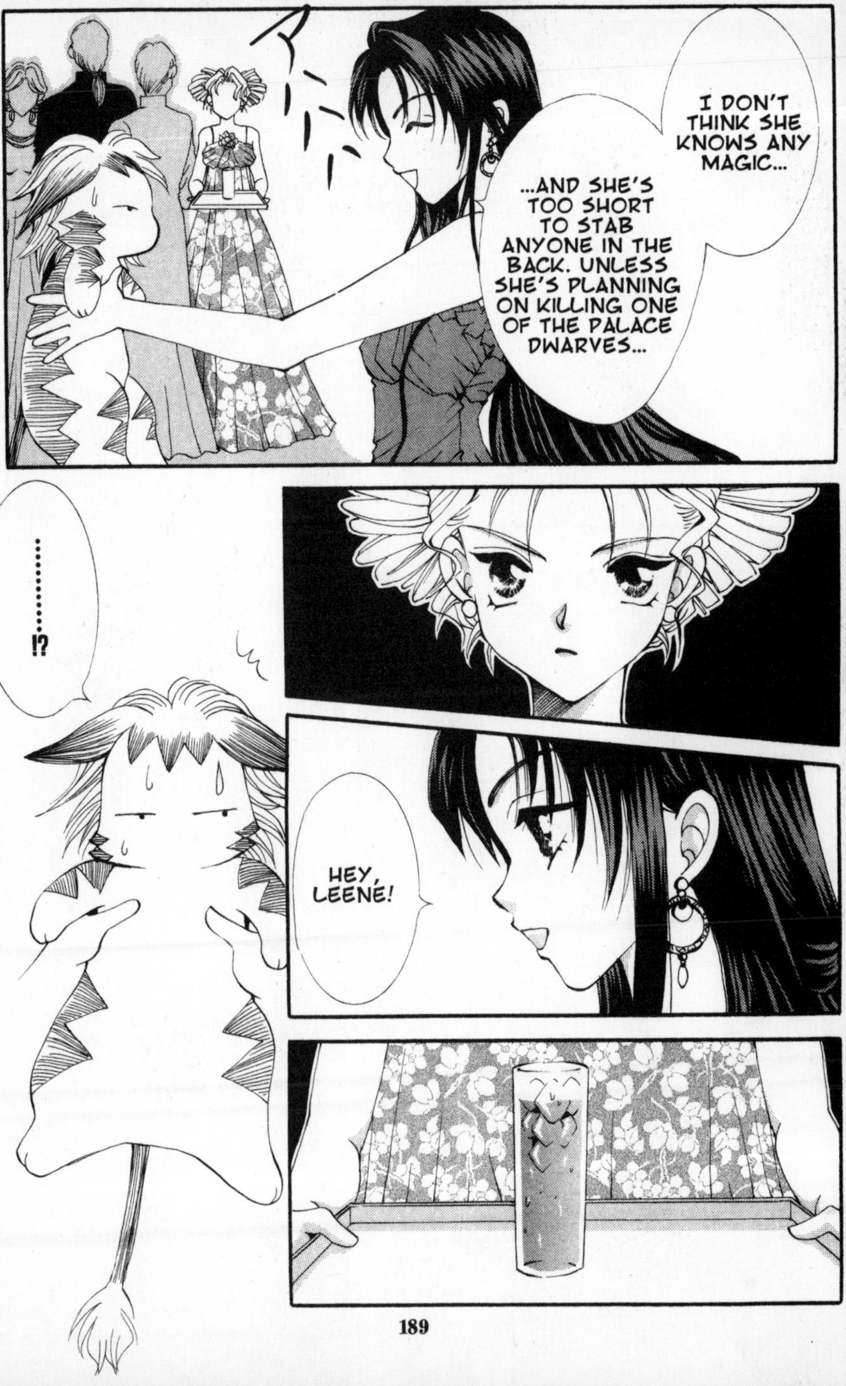
I DON'T THINK SHE KNOWS ANY MAGIC...
...AND SHE'S TOO SHORT TO STAB ANYONE IN THE BACK. UNLESS SHE'S PLANNING ON KILLING ONE OF THE PALACE DWARVES...
HEY, LEENÉ!
......!?

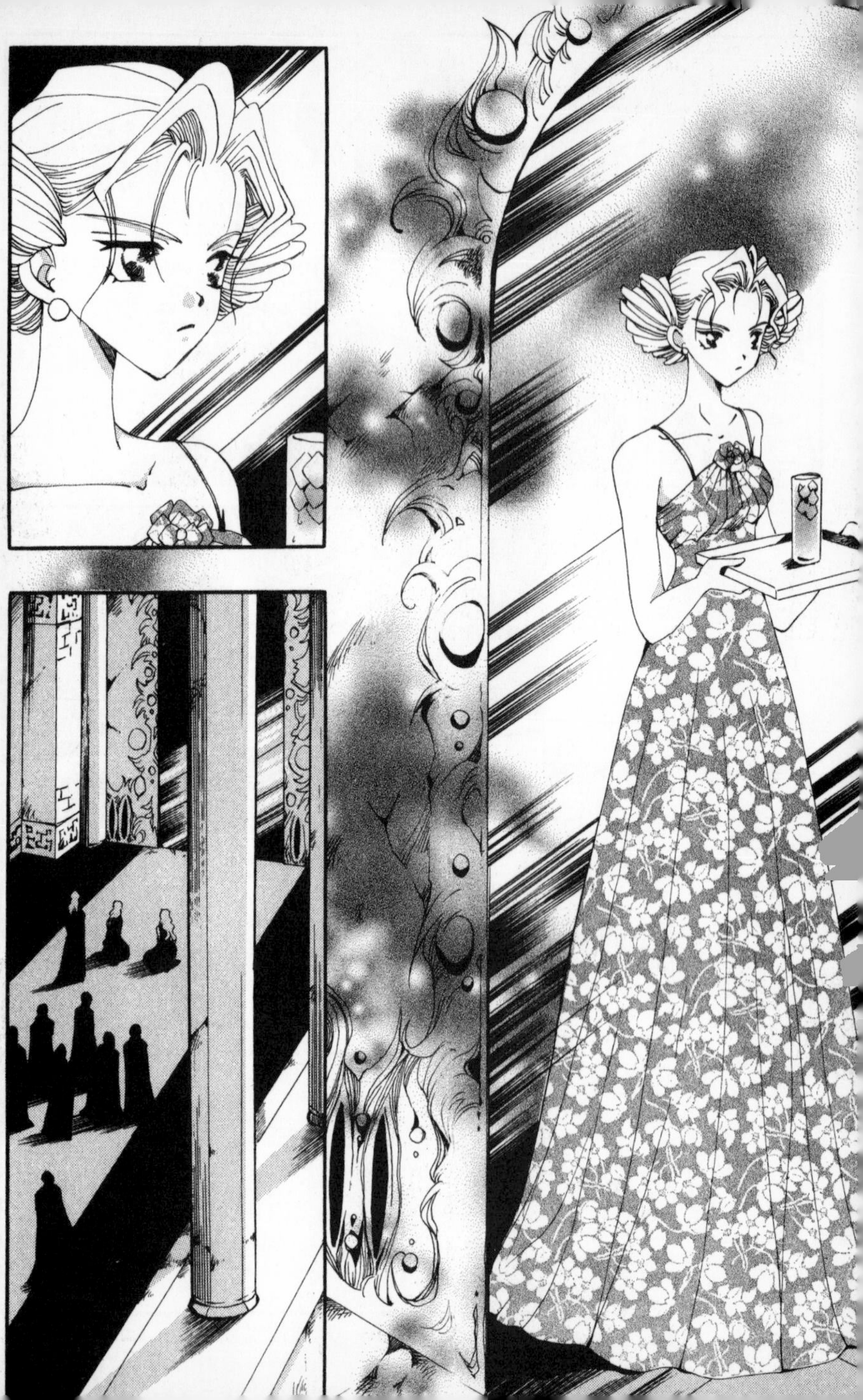

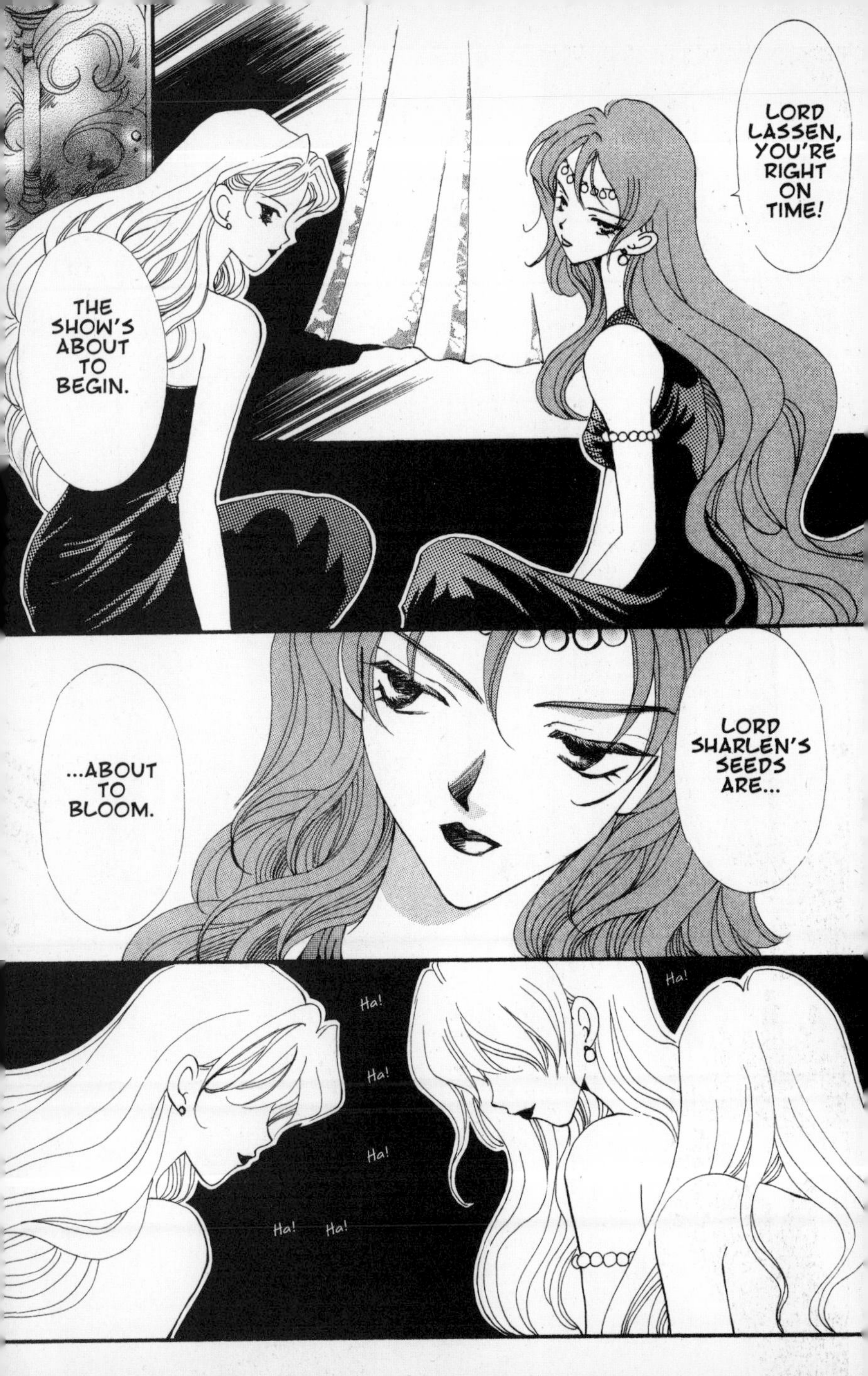
LORD LASSEN, YOU'RE RIGHT ON TIME!
THE SHOW'S ABOUT TO BEGIN.
LORD SHARLEN'S SEEDS ARE...
...ABOUT TO BLOOM.
Ha!
Ha!
Ha!
Ha!
Ha!
Ha!

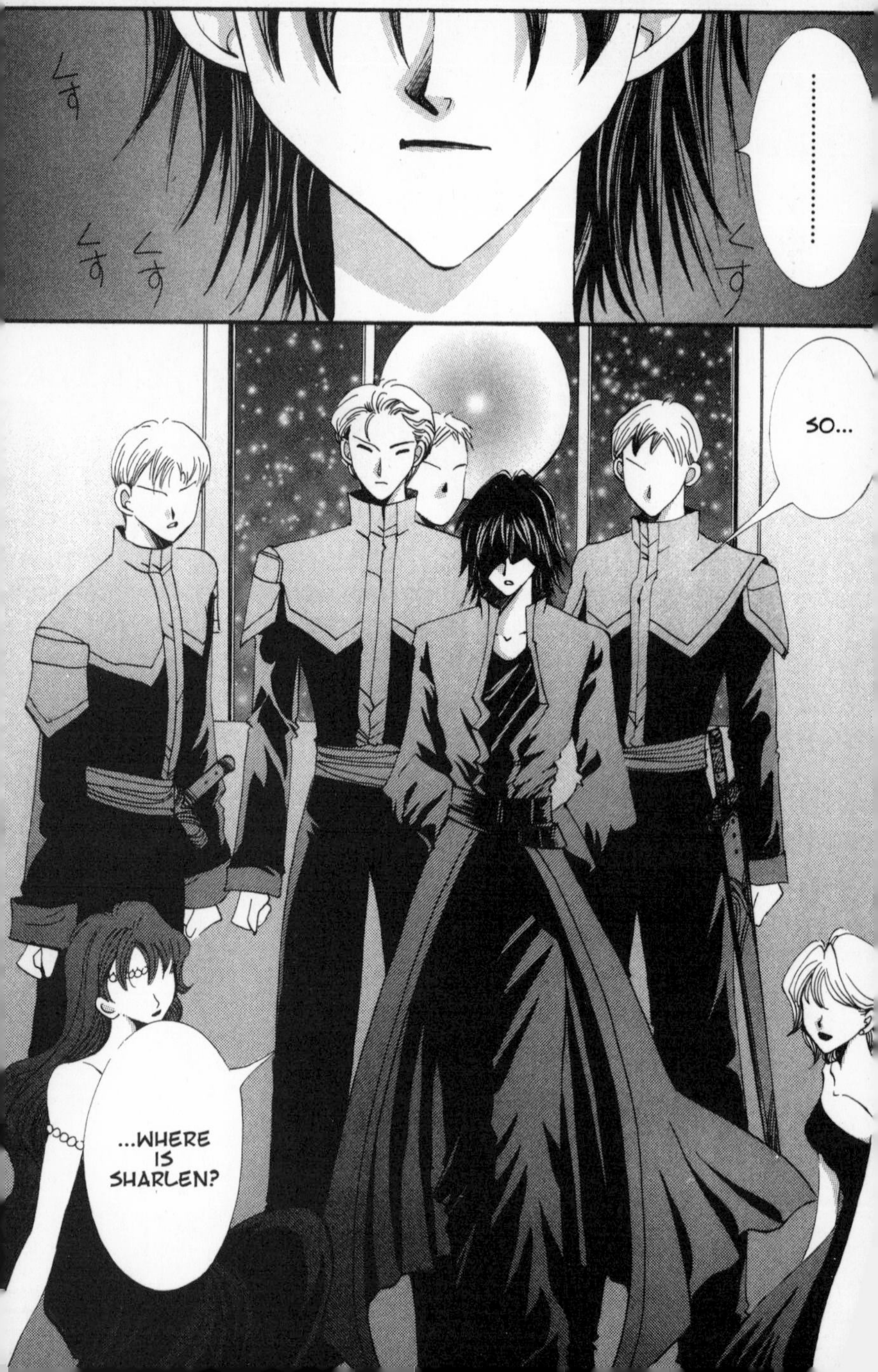

......
くす
くす
くす
くす
SO...
...WHERE IS SHARLEN?

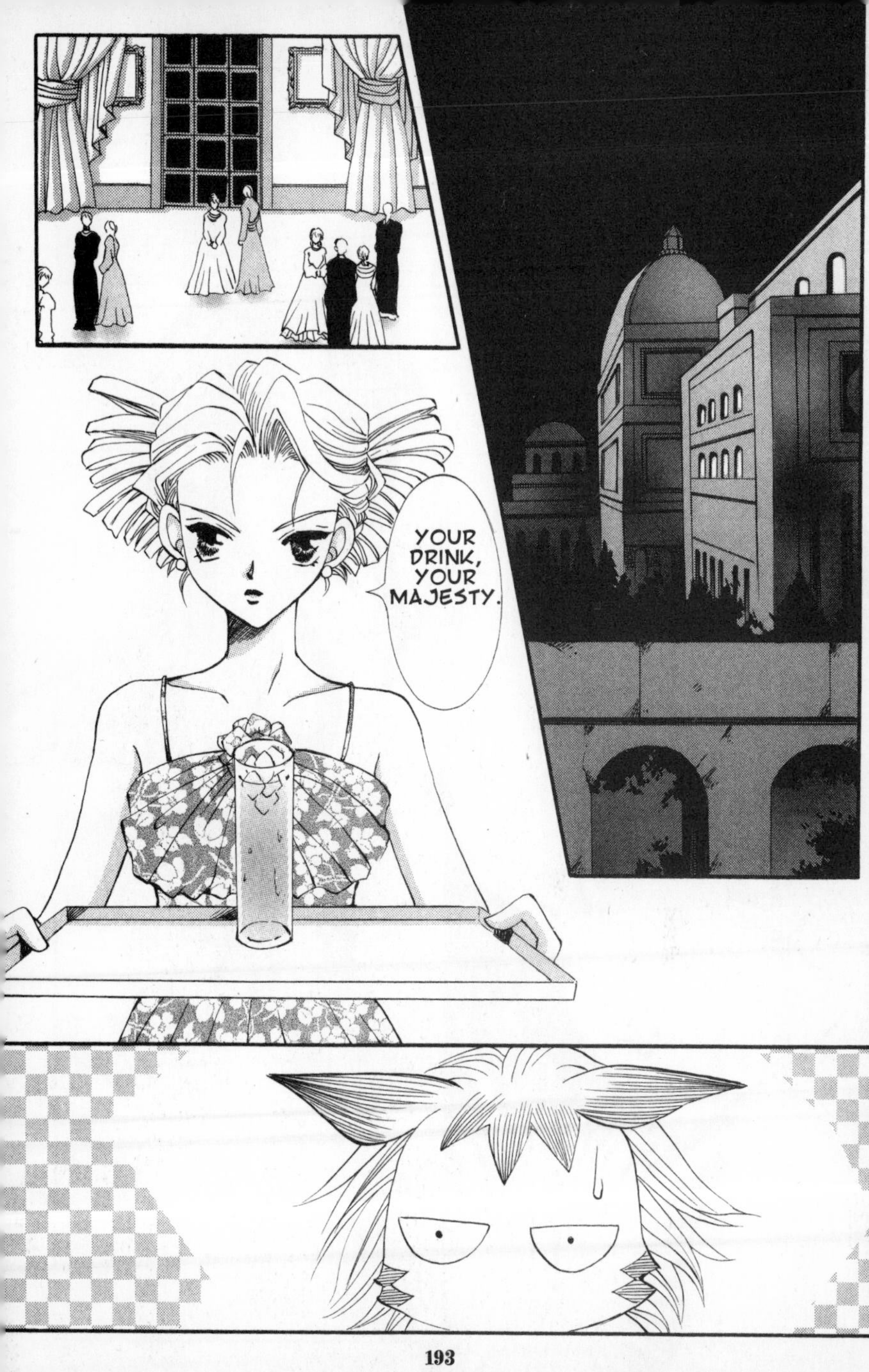
YOUR DRINK, YOUR MAJESTY.

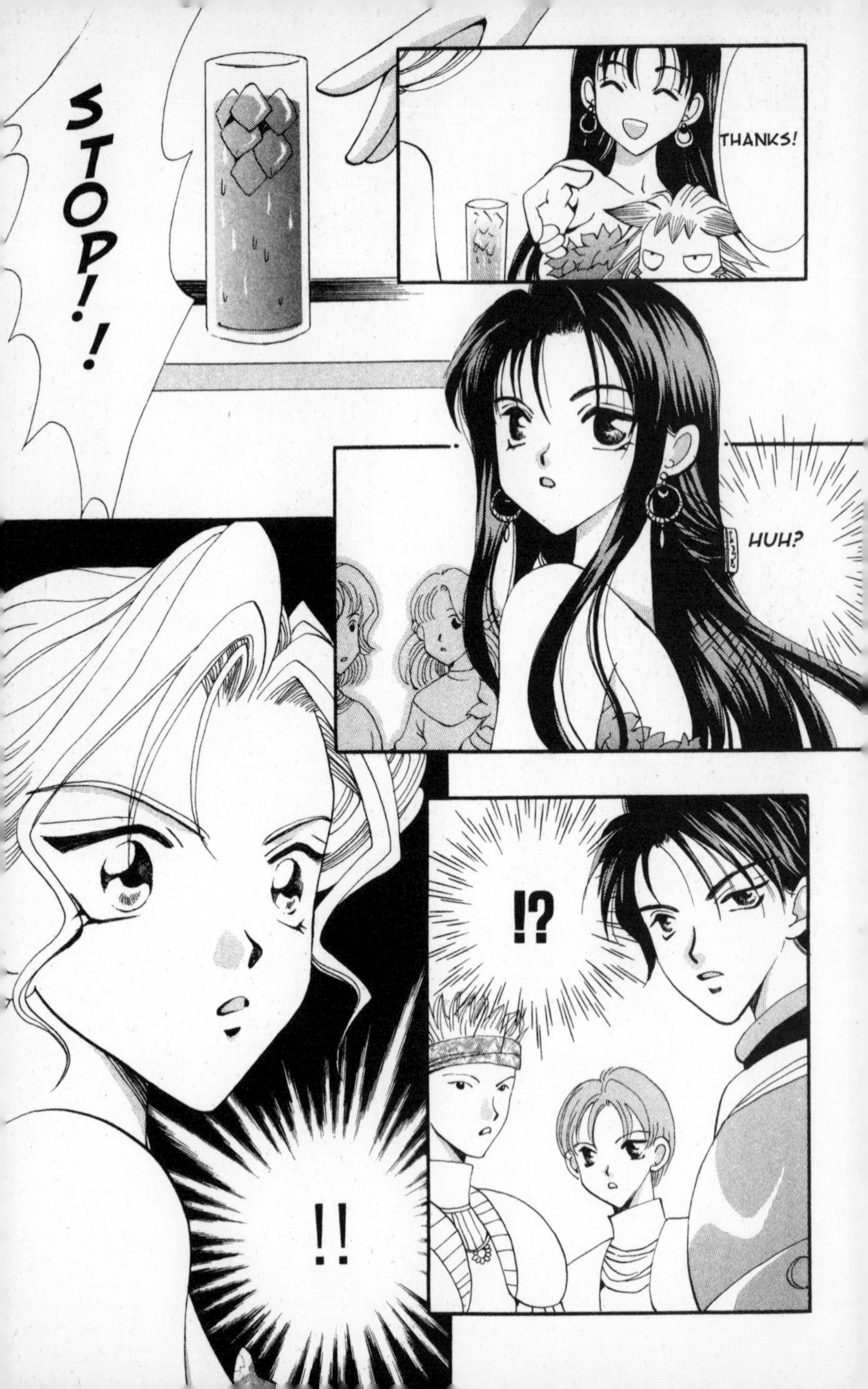
THANKS!
STOP!!
HUH?
!?
!!

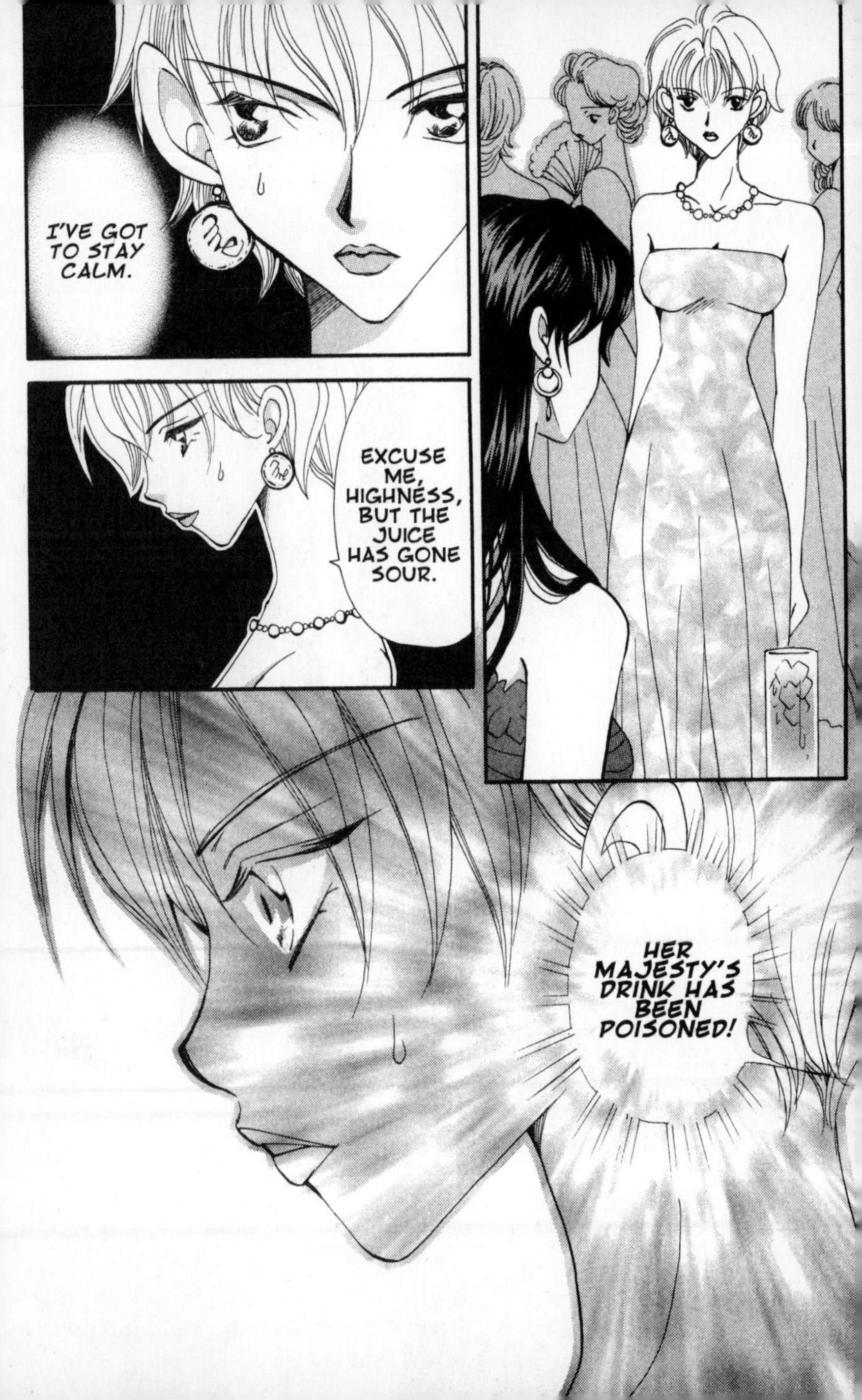
I'VE GOT TO STAY CALM.
EXCUSE ME, HIGHNESS, BUT THE JUICE HAS GONE SOUR.
HER MAJESTY'S DRINK HAS BEEN POISONED!

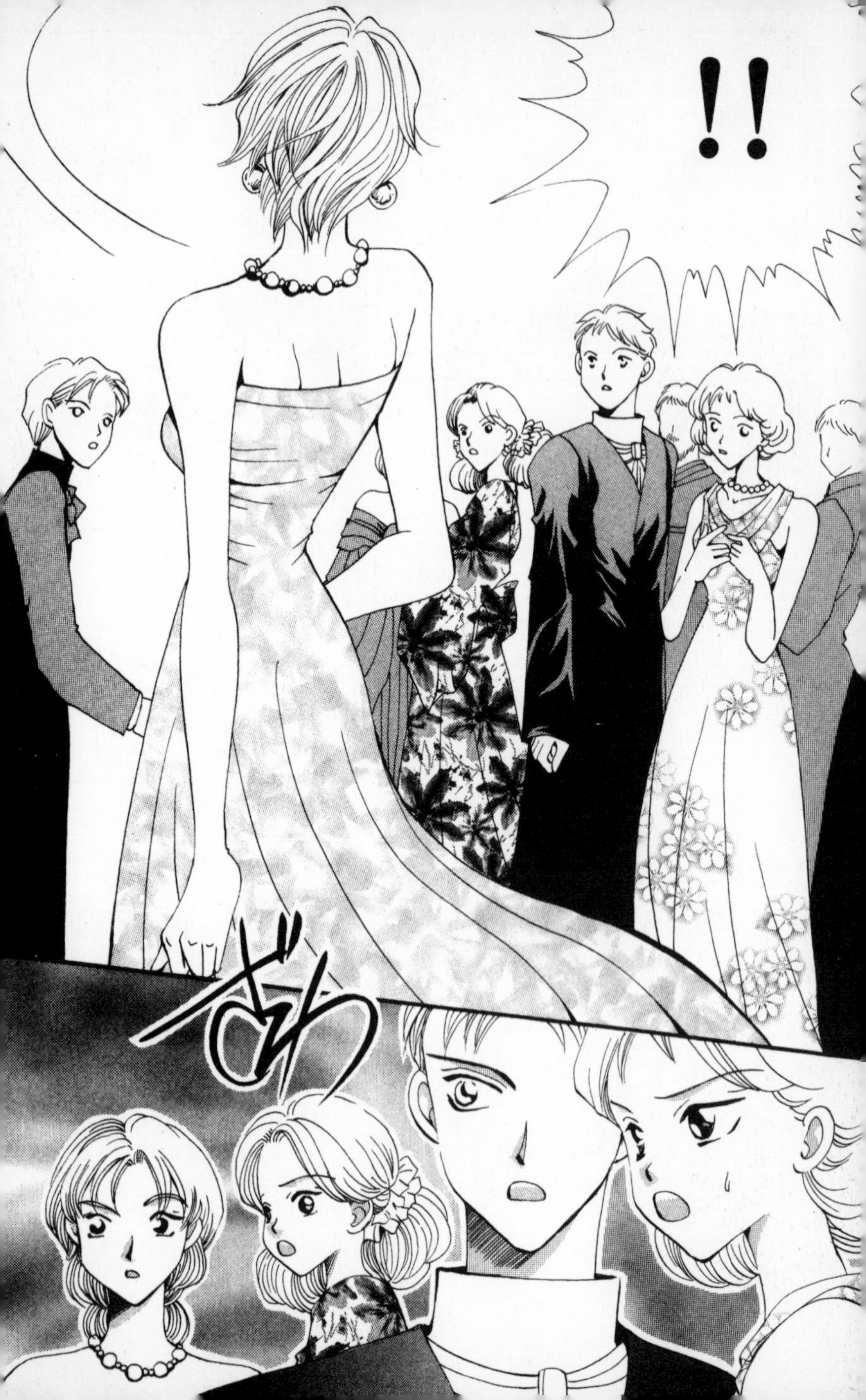
!!
ざわ

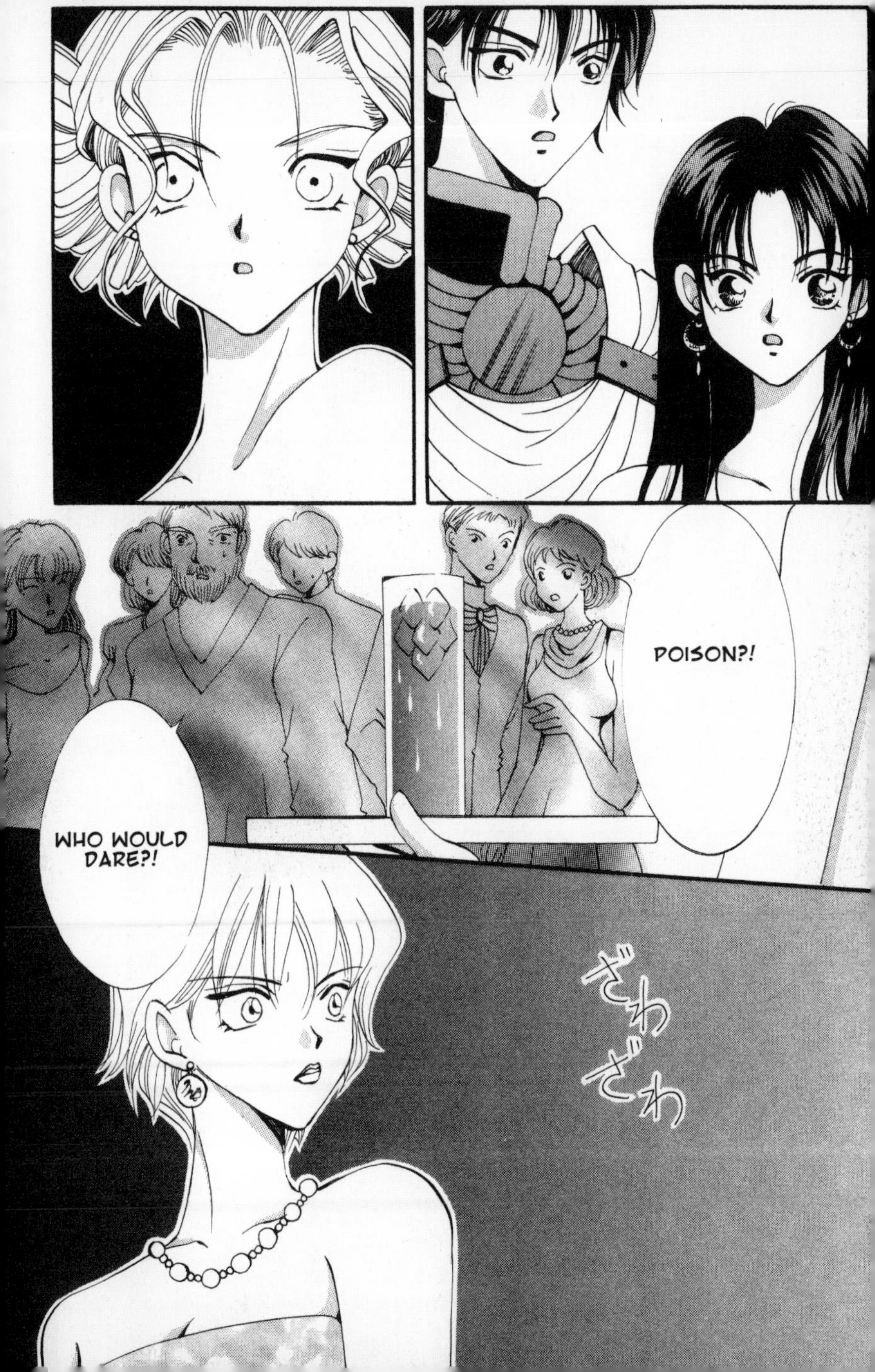
POISON?!
WHO WOULD DARE?!
ざわざわ

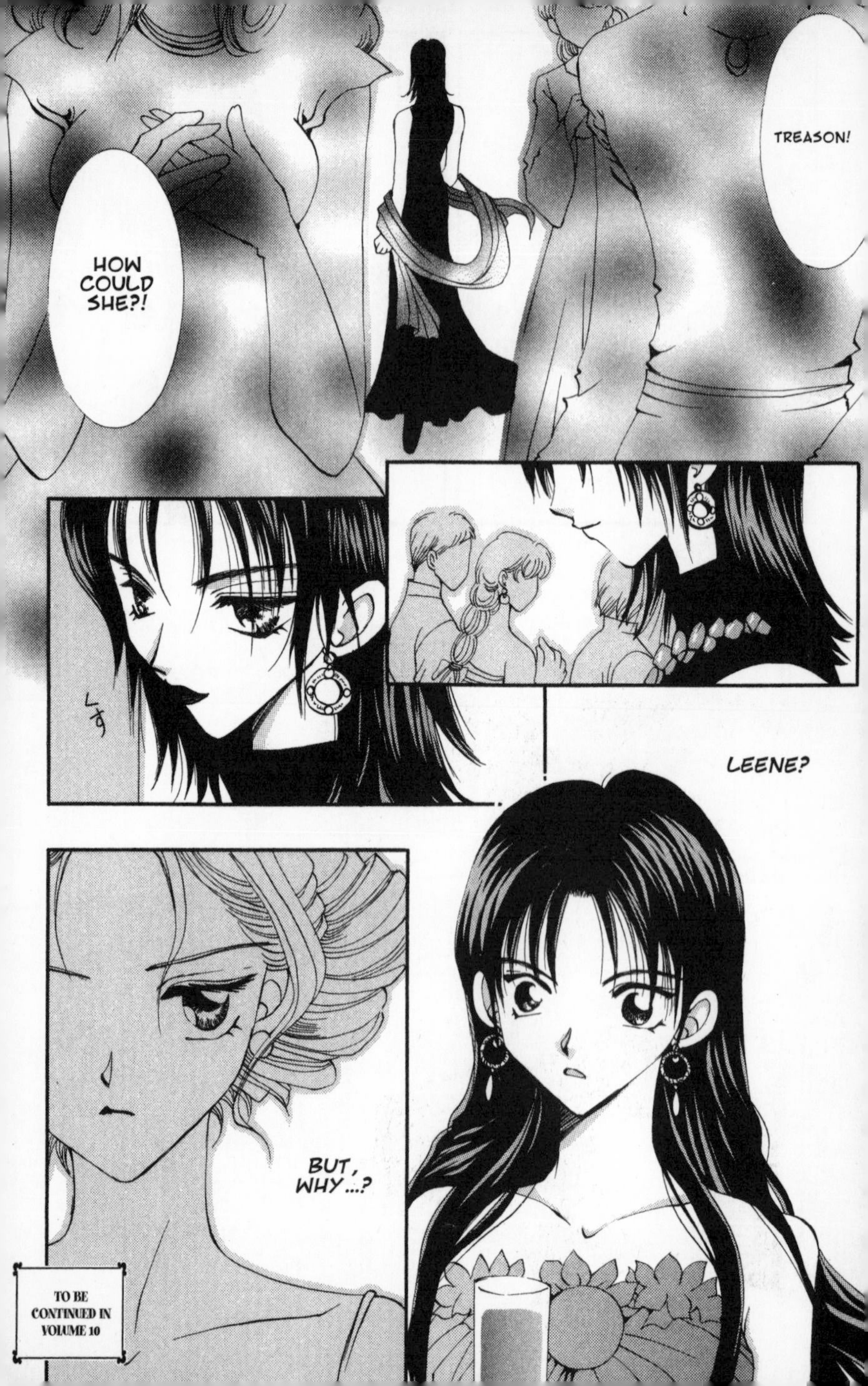
TREASON!
HOW COULD SHE?!
くす
LEENE?
BUT, WHY...?
TO BE CONTINUED IN VOLUME 10

Postscript

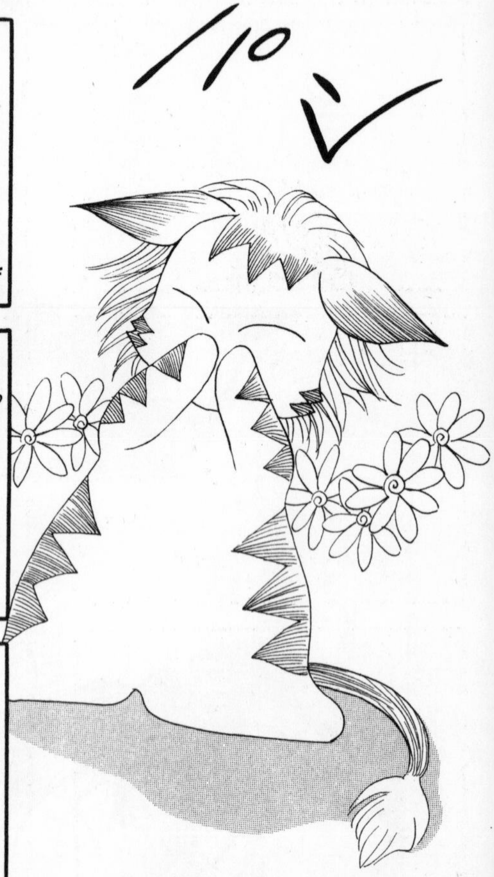

Hello!

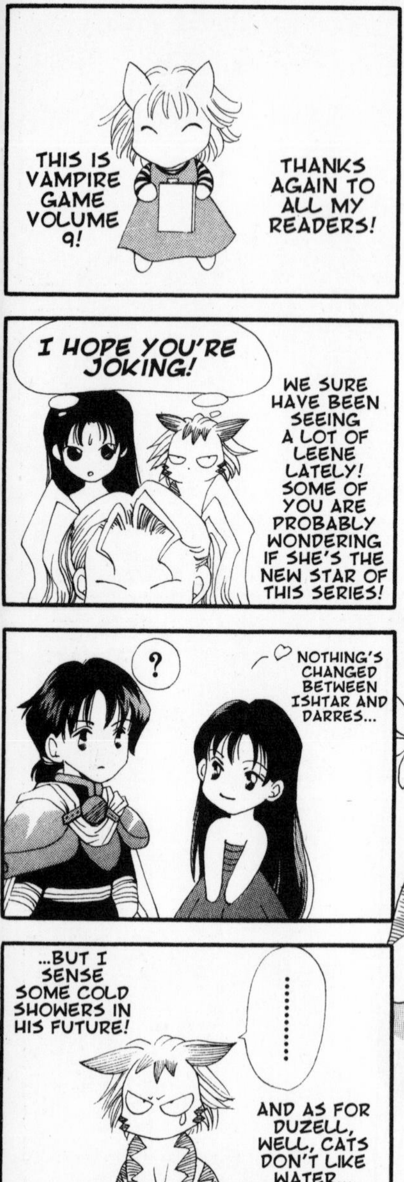
THANKS AGAIN TO ALL MY READERS!
THIS IS VAMPIRE GAME VOLUME 9!
WE SURE HAVE BEEN SEEING A LOT OF LEENE LATELY! SOME OF YOU ARE PROBABLY WONDERING IF SHE'S THE NEW STAR OF THIS SERIES!
I HOPE YOU'RE JOKING!
NOTHING'S CHANGED BETWEEN ISHTAR AND DARRES...
?
...BUT I SENSE SOME COLD SHOWERS IN HIS FUTURE!
....
AND AS FOR DUZELL, WELL, CATS DON'T LIKE WATER...

Ashley

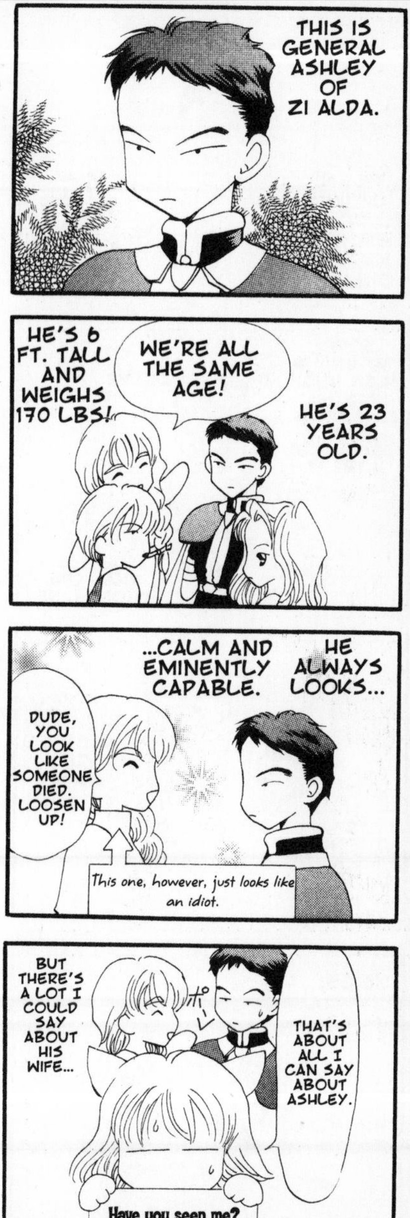
THIS IS GENERAL ASHLEY OF ZI ALDA.
HE'S 23 YEARS OLD.
WE'RE ALL THE SAME AGE!
HE'S 6 FT. TALL AND WEIGHS 170 LBS!
HE ALWAYS LOOKS...
...CALM AND EMINENTLY CAPABLE.
DUDE, YOU LOOK LIKE SOMEONE DIED. LOOSEN UP!
This one, however, just looks like an idiot.
THAT'S ABOUT ALL I CAN SAY ABOUT ASHLEY.
ポ
BUT THERE'S A LOT I COULD SAY ABOUT HIS WIFE...
Have you seen me?

Lucy

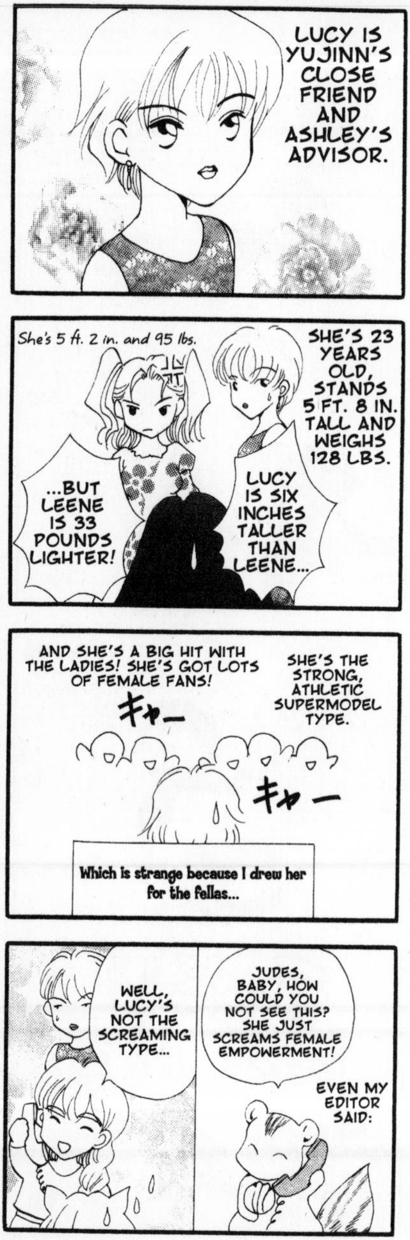
LUCY IS YUJINN'S CLOSE FRIEND AND ASHLEY'S ADVISOR.
SHE'S 23 YEARS OLD, STANDS 5 FT. 8 IN. TALL AND WEIGHS 128 LBS.
LUCY IS SIX INCHES TALLER THAN LEENE...
She's 5 ft. 2 in. and 95 lbs.
...BUT LEENE IS 33 POUNDS LIGHTER!
SHE'S THE STRONG, ATHLETIC SUPERMODEL TYPE.
AND SHE'S A BIG HIT WITH THE LADIES! SHE'S GOT LOTS OF FEMALE FANS!
キャー
キャー
Which is strange because I drew her for the fellas...
EVEN MY EDITOR SAID:
JUDES, BABY, HOW COULD YOU NOT SEE THIS? SHE JUST SCREAMS FEMALE EMPOWERMENT!
WELL, LUCY'S NOT THE SCREAMING TYPE...

Kuroron

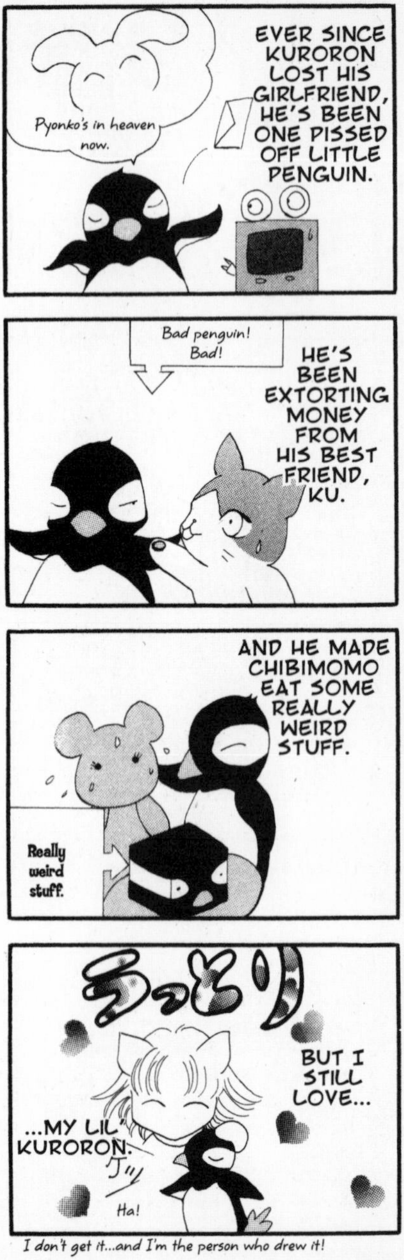
EVER SINCE KURORON LOST HIS GIRLFRIEND, HE'S BEEN ONE PISSED OFF LITTLE PENGUIN.
Pyonko's in heaven now.
HE'S BEEN EXTORTING MONEY FROM HIS BEST FRIEND, KU.
Bad penguin! Bad!
AND HE MADE CHIBIMOMO EAT SOME REALLY WEIRD STUFF.
Really weird stuff.
BUT I STILL LOVE...
...MY LIL' KURORON.
Ha!
I don't get it...and I'm the person who drew it!

Finally...

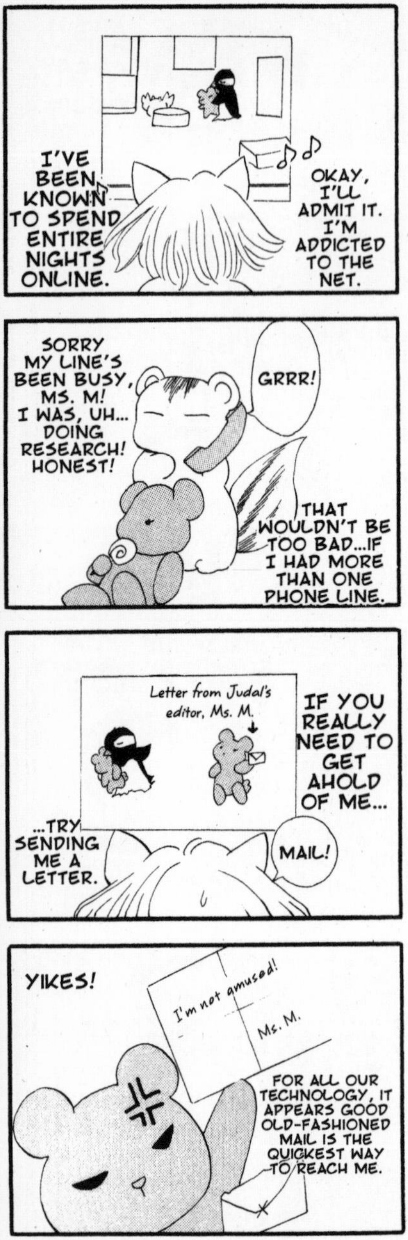
OKAY, I'LL ADMIT IT. I'M ADDICTED TO THE NET.
I'VE BEEN KNOWN TO SPEND ENTIRE NIGHTS ONLINE.
SORRY MY LINE'S BEEN BUSY, MS. M! I WAS, UH... DOING RESEARCH! HONEST!
GRRR!
THAT WOULDN'T BE TOO BAD...IF I HAD MORE THAN ONE PHONE LINE.
IF YOU REALLY NEED TO GET AHOLD OF ME...
Letter from Judal's editor, Ms. M.
...TRY SENDING ME A LETTER.
MAIL!
YIKES!
I'm not amused!
Ms. M.
FOR ALL OUR TECHNOLOGY, IT APPEARS GOOD OLD-FASHIONED MAIL IS THE QUICKEST WAY TO REACH ME.

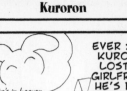

VAMPIRE GAME

Next issue...

TOKYOPOP
VAMPIRE GAME
JUDAL
10

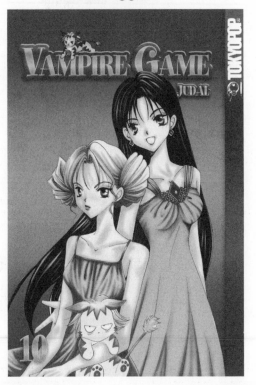

Lady Leene's thinking homicide. Darres and Ashley are thinking defense. Duzell is thinking life was so much simpler as a cat, and Ishtar just isn't thinking period in our next volume of Vampire Game. Leene's established a real love/hate relationship with Princess Ishtar. When she's not feeling sorry for the princess, she's plotting to kill her. And with the final poison pill, she has the ultimate murder weapon. Unaware that her life is in danger, Ishtar continues to enjoy her trip to Zi Alda, but with murder on everyone's mind, you know this little visit will turn violent. Will Ashley find the strength to stand against his wife? Will he be able to protect both the princess and Lady Sonia? Will he dump Lady Leene for a girl without issues? Castle corruption and thoughts of destruction all come to a head as the Zi Alda arc reaches its tragic, touching and more than a little warped conclusion!

ALSO AVAILABLE FROM  TOKYOPOP®

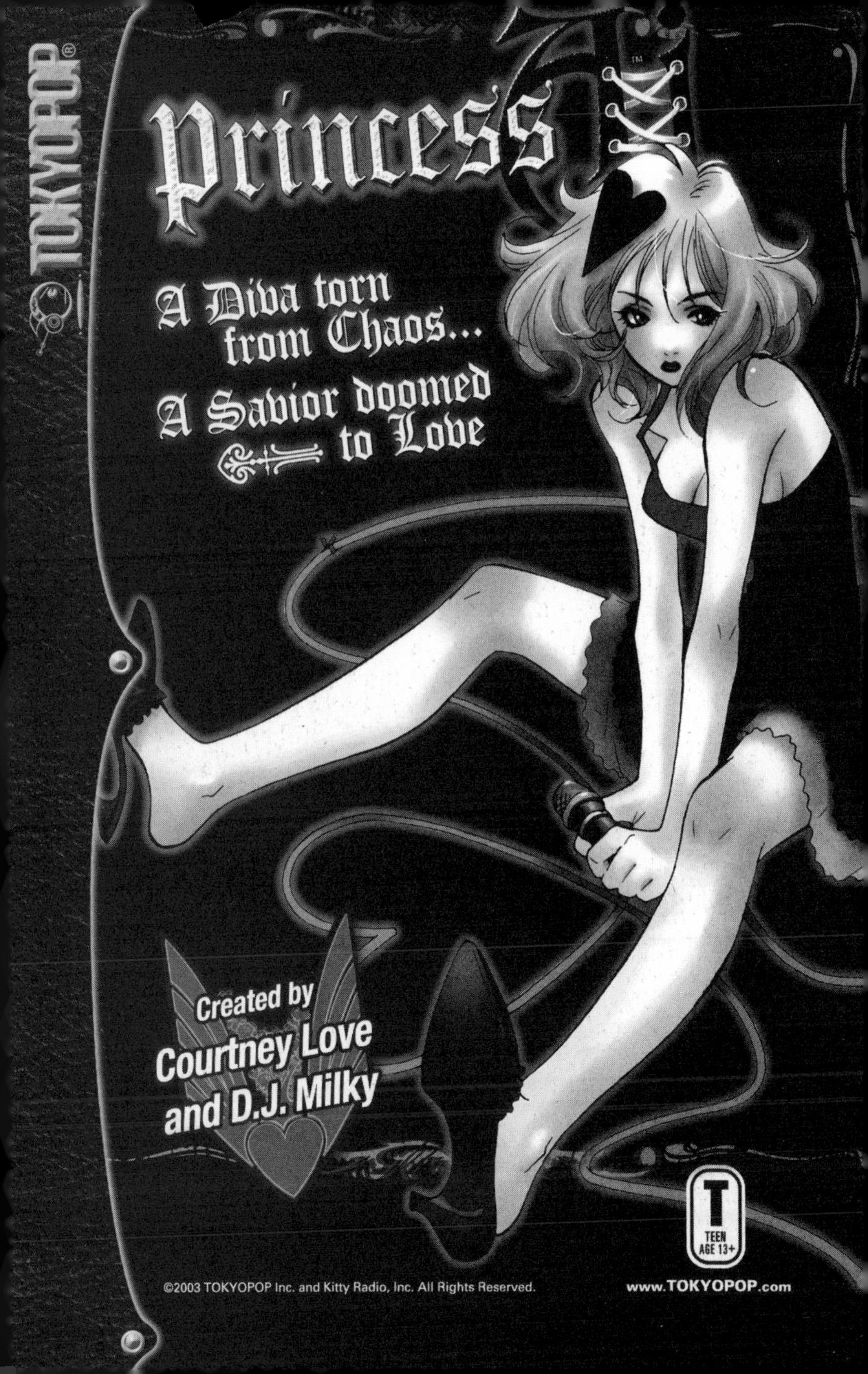
TOKYOPOP®
Princess
A Diva torn from Chaos...
A Savior doomed to Love
Created by
Courtney Love
and D.J. Milky
T
TEEN
AGE 13+
©2003 TOKYOPOP Inc. and Kitty Radio, Inc. All Rights Reserved.
www.TOKYOPOP.com

STOP!

This is the back of the book.
You wouldn't want to spoil a great ending!

This book is printed "manga-style," in the authentic Japanese right-to-left format. Since none of the artwork has been flipped or altered, readers get to experience the story just as the creator intended. You've been asking for it, so TOKYOPOP® delivered: authentic, hot-off-the-press, and far more fun!

DIRECTIONS

If this is your first time reading manga-style, here's a quick guide to help you understand how it works.

It's easy... just start in the top right panel and follow the numbers. Have fun, and look for more 100% authentic manga from TOKYOPOP®!